Willa Longworth

Willa was a woman with one chance at destiny and she wasn't going to let a man—or her longing for him—get in her way...or was she?

"Life's like the weather. You can never be sure of it. That's the miracle, don't you see?"

Luke McKade

He had done all the right things for the wrong reasons—until he met Willa. From that moment, his life would never be the same.

"You owe me a romp in the hay, Mrs. Longworth."

Little Red Longworth

This ailing heir wanted someone to care for him during his final days. He found an angel in Willa... and a wife.

"I went to kill me a lawyer and a bastard brother. I got a wife."

Hesper Longworth

The spiteful sister-in-law doesn't want Willa to get a single red cent.

"Your unfortunate past is hardly my concern, Willa dear. I'm here to buy you out."

Brandon Baines

A powerful lawyer with an ego the size of Texas and a dangerous need to keep things—and Willa—quiet!

"It's just me and you, sweetheart. We're all alone in the middle of nowhere. Now, where's the money?"

Also available from ANN MAJOR and MIRA Books
INSEPARABLE

ANN MAJOR

Wild Enough For Willa

MIRA

ISBN 1-55166-623-5

WILD ENOUGH FOR WILLA

Visit us at www.mirabooks.com

Printed in U.S.A.

DEDICATION

To my precious daughter, Kimberley Leta Cleaves,
who is quirky, funny, warm, witty, young.
And because she is all those things, she is a
challenge to me as a mother. When somebody asks
me, where do you get your ideas, I should tell
them from my daughter, who is my very own
adorable muse. Thank you for Willa, Kimberley.

ACKNOWLEDGMENT

I want to thank the following people:

To Tara Gavin and Dianne Moggy for more than I
 can say

To Karen Solem

To Patience Smith

To Ted, for realizing that dinners and a clean house
 don't matter nearly as much as writing

To Karen Olsson and Meg Guerra, who told me
 about Laredo

To Dorothy Deaver, who decorated Willa's house

To Steve Stainkamp and Geri Rice

To Chris Misner and Greg McKee for telling me
 about the computer business

To Patricia Patterson for streamlining my business
 affairs so I can write

POEM

If I were alone in a desert
And feeling afraid,
I would want a child to be with me.
For then my fear would disappear
And I would be made strong.
This is what life in itself can do
Because it is so noble, so full of pleasure
And so powerful.

But if I could not have a child with me
I would like to have at least a living animal
At my side to comfort me.

Therefore,
Let those who bring about wonderful things
In their big, dark books
Take an animal—perhaps a dog—
To help them.

The life within the animal
Will give them strength in turn.
For equality
Gives strength in all things
And at all times.
　　　　　　—Meister Eckhart (1260–1329)

(Author's note: As a cat lover, I change dog to cat.
When I go alone into my imagination to write,
Kanka, my cat, goes with me to help by sitting on
my manuscript.)

Book One

"What we call the ending is usually the beginning."

1

Marcie, his gentle, beautiful wife... Dead?

And it was all his fault.

Luke McKade sat alone in his vast penthouse office in southwest Austin. He willed the silence and the dark of his new gorgeous, empty building—the building that Marcie had helped design and decorate—to devour him.

Driven, he always worked later than his employees. Not that tonight was about work.

"Sa-a-ve the baby," Marcie had whispered in her pronounced Texas drawl with its elongated vowels. She'd gripped him fiercely when he'd knelt over her bed. Her final, hoarse cry was swallowed, strangled. Then she'd died in his arms.

His mind had raced. His heart had thundered. *What baby? What baby?*

"A son," the white-coated doctor had confirmed after the autopsy.

Luke wearily massaged the back of his neck. Restless by nature, always on the move, he rarely sat behind his desk this long—and never to reflect on his own shortcomings.

Murder. He'd done murder.

She'd been so beautiful. So gentle. So classy. How he had loved looking at her. She had known how to dress. Other men had envied him, which is why he'd married her.

He pushed his fingers through his untidy wavy black hair. On top of today's unread newspapers and his managers' reports from yesterday lay several mangled scraps of paper—his phone messages. Kate, his freckle-faced, madcap secretary with corkscrew red curls, scrawled numbers and names on whatever she had handy.

Among other problems, the Feds were suing him for restriction of trade, and he was trying to float a new IPO. Luke thumbed through the fast-food napkins, Post-it notes, and a couple of pages she'd torn from her calendar, his tension heightening. His lawyers had called. So had his ranch foreman. The name of the president of a rival company was highlighted by a smear of mustard. But what charged Luke was the name, Brandon Baines.

Brandon Baines had called three times.

Baines, big criminal lawyer in Laredo.

Laredo was a border town. As such, it was too far from Mexico City and too far from Washington, D.C. for either nation's laws to be taken too seriously. Men like Baines could prosper there.

Baines and he had gone to law school together. He'd been like most of their class—rich, handsome, lily-white, ultraconservative—a racist to the core, and worse things, too, underneath his politically correct exterior. Baines hadn't much cottoned to McKade's darker skin or rougher, cruder views about life—except where they concerned women.

Baines's tenacity and killer instincts had brought him fame and fortune in the free and easy Laredo. He had a rare talent for getting down and dirty in the courtroom. No lawyer in Texas had gotten more criminals acquitted than he. With the rise in crime, especially in drug dealing, his talents were in demand. He never gave up on a case. Never. Even when all seemed lost for the guiltiest of his drug-dealer clients, his mantra was, "This is good."

Luke had forgotten all about Little Red's imminent release.

I'm gonna shoot myself a lawyer and a bastard.

Luke didn't like Baines or Laredo even though the two men shared a common enemy.

Little Red Longworth. What was he now—twenty-three?

The Longworths would be happy to have their precious son and brother home in New Mexico again.

Luke swallowed, trying to rid himself of the sudden bad taste in his mouth.

He wadded Kate's scribblings and pitched them in the trash.

Later. Tomorrow.

Tonight was for Marcie, for his guilt.

Maybe everybody else in the whole damned world thought Marcie had slammed head-on into that limestone cliff all by herself, but Luke McKade knew differently. He'd killed her, and their unborn baby boy, as surely as if his hand had been on her black leather steering wheel.

Somehow it was easier to sit in the solitary gloom of his office with his own regrets than to endure the well-meant comfort of friends, colleagues and employees. He even preferred the fury of his hot-tempered, impossible mother-in-law to their consolation.

Sheila blamed him for the separation...for the accident...for her only daughter's death.

Luke felt the muscles of his jaw tighten. World-famous in computer circles, he was tall, well built, black-haired. He stayed in shape. During the week he jogged or went to a gym. On weekends he did manual labor on his immense south Texas ranch. Indeed, he was well disciplined in all areas.

Ruthless, his competitors called him. Competent and innovative were the labels his friends attached.

Luke had sea-gray eyes. "And when you smile," Marcie used to say, "you have the most devastatingly gorgeous face. Your eyes sparkle like dancing waves on a stormy day. I married you for that smile that gives your face so much energy. Now the only time I ever see it is when you perform for the press."

Marcie had been right. His virile good looks, especially the practiced smile, were a facade. The man behind the mask was cold...dead...and wanted to stay that way.

He hated how he felt tonight—alive, raw, in pain, about to explode. He had to find a way to recap the volcano.

Luke McKade believed in order, in control. He lived by rules—his own. He never drank alcohol in front of his employees, and he wouldn't be drinking tonight if he hadn't closed LMK for the funeral.

Luke sat behind a mammoth mahogany desk. Nursing his second whiskey, he clenched Marcie's framed photograph and stared unseeingly at the brilliant Austin skyline glittering against the black hills.

The world thought he was a hero. He'd had more fun when he'd been poor and fighting to make it. The higher he climbed, the more alienated and lonely he felt...the more powerless....

Marcie? His brown hand touched the pale cheek behind cold glass. He had more money than Midas. But he couldn't bring her back. He couldn't tell her he was sorry.

He began to shake. Such white skin, such warm, soft skin she'd had...compared to his. Her golden hair had felt like the richest silk while his had been black and coarse like his mother's. She'd been so high-class compared to him. His claim to fame was wealth. And power in the hottest business on the planet. They said he was a modern-day pirate, that he'd gotten where he was by greed and underhanded tactics.

Whatever. He was rich, unimaginably rich, now. CEO of a dozen computer companies, he was a giant in a world he'd helped shape. Known for his razor-sharp intelligence, tough negotiation tactics, and ruthless business instincts, he owned several highly competitive software and Internet businesses.

He'd known that the only reason an impoverished socialite like the exquisite Marcie Wilde had married a driven computer nerd like himself was for his money. He'd thrown that up at her the day she'd asked for a divorce.

"Your money used to be attractive...once," she'd

admitted. "But I always wanted you. I used to think that maybe someday you'd feel that way about me."

"What the hell did I tell you before we got married—"

"I was in love. I thought I could change you. I thought I could settle till you fell for me, too. I thought I had enough love for both of us. You're good-looking. Good in bed…at least at first I thought so. Then I realized you weren't there. It was always your money and always going to be your money. I was like some object you'd bought to show off…a trophy. Nothing more. And I want more, to be more. I deserve more. You're a dead man, Luke, at least with me."

"I gave you everything."

"And it's killing me. I—I can't go on like this…. This house we built together is not a home. It's a monument like the pyramids or the Taj Mahal, tombs built for the dead to impress the living. You're not rich…not really. You don't have money. Your money has you."

You're killing me.

He'd remembered how eagerly she'd run to the door every night when he'd come home in the beginning of their marriage. Until he'd made it clear he didn't like such exuberant displays of affection—in bed or out of it. But divorce?

He'd said, "So, how much are you going to take me for?"

"I don't want a dime of your precious money."

"One day some slick lawyer will call me and show us both what a liar you are."

She'd stuck to her noble sentiment, taken a low-paying job. She'd rented a one-bedroom apartment. He'd hired a guy to keep tabs.

Even before she'd called three days ago, he hadn't been able to get her out of his mind. Still, he'd been surprised and pleased; but furious, too, that he was so happy to hear from her.

She'd said she'd changed her mind about the divorce; she'd had something important to tell him, something too important and too thrilling to discuss over the phone.

"You want more money, don't you—"

She'd begun to sob. "I wish...I wish I'd never met you."

He'd been about to apologize.

"You are a bastard."

Bastard. Her tearful insult had pushed him over some wild edge. He'd been vicious, gotten her completely distraught. She'd slammed the phone down. He'd had a premonition that had taken him to a cold, dark place in his heart and terrified him. Desperately he'd tried to call her back. Six times he'd dialed that number he'd known by heart.

She'd raced out and jumped in her car.

He'd jumped in his.

He'd been the first at the scene.

Marcie couldn't handle stress or fighting. She hadn't been the best driver under normal circumstances.

Luke imagined her racing up that narrow road that wound through limestone cliffs out to the lake and to the house in the hills they'd built together as newlyweds.

His house now.

In her fury, she'd taken the turn too fast. There'd

been an oncoming car in her lane. She'd swerved and lost control. He saw her slim body hurtling into unforgiving rock.

Too late, he'd realized she'd been coming to tell him about their baby.

"She was a damn fool about you to the end," Sheila had said. "She truly believed the baby—my grandbaby—might work the miracle she couldn't. That's why she was so pathetically eager to attempt a reconciliation. She'd thought that if the two of you adored the same child... Why couldn't she see what a cold-blooded bastard you are? This divorce thing was your fault! You killed her! She loved you—poor fool. Not that you can understand that. You murdered my daughter! And my grandson!"

Marcie had loved him.

Which was the last thing he'd wanted her to do.

She'd been several months along. Why hadn't she told him she was pregnant sooner?

Words from the mourners came back to him.

"—terrible accident! Not your fault—"

"—leaving him, you know—"

"—do you blame her—"

"—going to take him to the cleaners—"

"—nothing you could have done—"

Never as long as Luke lived would he forget holding her, watching Marcie's eyes glaze, feeling her slim body go slack in his arms. When she'd told him about the baby he'd realized she'd loved him...not his money.

If only.

Luke McKade didn't believe in second chances.

"Nothing he could have done—"

Luke opened a drawer and slammed Marcie's picture inside facedown. He wanted to forget her.

He flexed the fingers of his right hand. "Nothing? Like hell!"

He closed his eyes and saw Marcie's beautiful face, so still and untouched by death as she'd lain in her coffin. The image was etched like a brand in his brain. He'd taught her to lie still when they'd had sex.

Not your fault.

Wrong.

He'd married a vulnerable young woman for her class—to improve his image, to add glamour to the lie that was his life. Everything about Luke McKade was a lie, including his official bio. There was no Luke McKade. The press's Man of the Year was a myth. Every word in every article, in every magazine and newspaper that had ever been written about him were fantastic fabrications that a poor, ambitious boy with a head full of dreams had invented so that nobody would ever know what he really was—a Pueblo Indian woman's bastard born in shame and despair to a man...

"Cut!"

Even in his wild, dark mood, Luke wasn't about to think of his rich, powerful father...or the rest of that blue-blooded bunch he wanted to have nothing to do with in New Mexico.

He yanked Marcie's picture out of the drawer and set it on his desk. He would keep it there until the sight of her beautiful face no longer made his gut clench. Only then would he put it away.

But he couldn't look at it. Not tonight.

When he sprang to his feet and headed toward the door, the phone rang.

Curious, he stopped to read his Caller ID.

Brandon Baines.

Baines wasn't calling about Marcie. Lawyers, who defended Mexican drug lords like Spook Rodriguez and Texas big shots' kids gone wrong, didn't call old law school classmates just to be nice.

Five years ago, Luke had sent Baines a client, a very special client.

Baines had screwed up so royally, they hadn't spoken since.

The client had gotten five years in the federal pen with no chance of an early parole. At the sentencing, the eighteen-year-old client had screamed at Luke, "You deliberately set me up."

"This is good," Baines had said without missing a beat. "We'll appeal."

"You think this is good—'cause you charge by the hour. I'll tell you what's good, you slick, lying jerk. When I get out, I'm gonna shoot myself a lawyer—" the boy had turned on Luke "—and a *bastard*."

Luke had lunged at him.

"This is good," Baines had said, grabbing Luke, holding him back as three deputies stepped protectively in front of the prisoner.

"I'll show you who the bastard is, you no-good, spoiled, son of a bitch," Luke had snarled.

"Easy. Little Red's your half brother, McKade," said Baines.

"The hell he is. Nobody can know that. Understand? Nobody!"

Luke McKade's official bio didn't mention a pampered little brother gone wrong, didn't mention Big Red Longworth, the famous ex-governor of New Mexico who was their biological father. Luke had deleted those folders from his database. They didn't exist. He'd deleted them from his heart—an organ that didn't exist, either.

Killer instincts. Baines didn't give up easy. When the phone wouldn't stop ringing, Luke slammed out of his office.

Little Red was due for parole any day.

I'm gonna shoot myself a lawyer...and a bastard.

Maybe the kid was already out. Maybe he was in Austin.... Maybe Baines was calling to warn him.

Luke was on his way home.

If the kid was here or on his way, Luke decided he'd leave the doors unlocked tonight. That way he'd be easy to find.

It was time he and the kid had it out. Way past time. *This is good.*

2

The temperature was still ninety degrees when Luke's Porsche leapt the last cedar-clad hill. Wheels spinning, the Porsche took the drive on two wheels, skidding to a halt. As the garage door lifted, he saw the empty space on the right side of the garage.

Marcie.

She was never coming back.

He parked on her side and got out. She was everywhere, almost a living presence tonight. If their sprawling one-story showplace with its tall chimneys, numerous balconies, and the impressive copper roof had been built with his money, it reflected Marcie's taste and exquisite beauty. Adjoining the house were guest cottages. Beneath the mansion were the maid, Lucinda's quarters. Marcie, who had loved to entertain, had thought of every comfort, caring even about Lucinda's.

Marcie had loved stunning views and had chosen this lot to build their modern dream palace a thousand feet above shimmering Lake Travis. Windows that lacked lake views looked out upon lush gardens with fountains, reflecting pools and bird feeders.

These barren limestone hills covered with cedar and live oak on the outskirts of Austin with their vistas of the jewel-blue lake were fast becoming Texas's answer to the Mediterranean. Or at least they had been Luke McKade's answer—until Marcie had walked, taking her furniture and that hideous cat of hers, Mr. Tom. Without her and that spoiled beast she'd been so devoted to, the place felt as cold as a tomb.

Not that there weren't any number of computer jackals with money to burn who'd made offers on the house the minute Marcie split. Lake Travis was *the* place to live among his set. Every day more trees were cleared, more castle sites started, each castle having to be bigger and more impressive than the one before.

He wasn't about to sell. The house was image. He'd live here, in desolate splendor even if it reminded him of *her*—if it killed him. He'd buy a second car or maybe a new boat first thing Monday, so he could quit staring at that empty spot in his garage.

When Luke pushed open the immense brass-studded, teak front doors, he heard his phone. He raced for it. Brandon Baines was on his Caller ID.

Baines was persistent as hell. He took what he wanted or kept pushing until he got it. He wouldn't let go of anything or anyone he considered his. He was especially ruthless with women. When they'd been in school he'd gotten a law student, a friend of Luke's, pregnant. Even after her powerful daddy had made a stink, Baines had considered the girl his property to do with as he pleased.

When Baines had offered her money for an abortion, she'd refused. Her father had thrown her out then. In the end, Luke had let her move in with him for a couple of months until she could get on her feet, a fact that had infuriated the possessive Baines, who'd wanted to run things. When the baby was born, Baines had come to the hospital and tried to force the woman to give up her little girl and come back to him.

When she'd taken her daughter and vanished, Baines had blamed Luke. "Because of you, I've got a little bastard out there. The bitch could turn up with her brat at an awkward time...."

"Because of me, your kid's alive."

"You would be partial to bastards—"

Luke's fist had slammed into that golden jawline before he could finish his sentence. They hadn't spoken for a year. After that run-in they'd graduated, gotten jobs and been on opposite sides of a case.

The phone started up once more.

Again, Luke avoided it. He went to the window and watched a boat speeding across that brilliant expanse of blue. He picked up his binoculars. A man held a woman with golden hair in his arms as they raced across the lake.

Marcie and he had gone boating most evenings. He hadn't used the boat once since. Luke watched the white speedboat until it vanished behind an island. When it didn't reappear on the far side of the island, he knew they'd thrown an anchor out, probably gone below to enjoy each other.

High on his hill, Luke felt alone, cut off from every living being on earth. Suddenly, he felt restless in the big, empty house. He needed to talk to somebody. The phone rang again. Luke went to the kitchen, grabbed a beer out of the fridge and then the receiver.

"Where the hell have you been?" Baines demanded.

"Funeral." Luke took a long pull from the bottle.

Baines's quick, inappropriate laugh was a little hollow. "This is good—yours or mine?"

"My wife's."

"Sorry. Hey—I heard she left you."

"We'd decided to get back together." Not that Baines cared.

"Your brother's here."

Alert suddenly, Luke felt his hair spike on the back of his neck. Carefully he kept his voice casual. "Give him my regards."

"He's got a gun."

"So does every other macho Texan."

"You know what I mean. He threatened—"

"If you're scared, call the cops. He's violated parole. They'll send him back to prison."

"He's sick. Cancer."

Luke sucked in a breath. He was glad Baines couldn't see him, couldn't detect... Luke felt cold, so cold. And it was a hot night.

Baines was still talking. "But do you think the crazy little bastard went home to his old man or checked himself into a hospital?"

Old man...

"Didn't he?"

"Hell, no. Says he's dying. The cocky little shit says he's gonna kill himself a lawyer first. You know who...yours truly." Baines paused. "He's after

Spook, too. And then…after he does us, guess who's next, old buddy—"

Luke stood unmoving, his hand frozen on his icy bottle. Cancer? Little Red…?

"You really want me to call the cops? That'll mean publicity. I thought you said you didn't want anybody to know you had a piece of scum like him for a brother."

Scum? Once Baines and his rich white law school buddies had called Luke scum.

Cancer? The kid was barely twenty-three. Five years in prison…and now a diagnosis like that. Would he die young like Marcie?

A quietness stole over Luke. His computerlike mind raced. What the hell kind of cancer? Could something be done? Options? Doctors? Experimental treatments? M.D. Anderson Cancer Center?

He thought of the stacks of sealed manila envelopes in that locked safe in his bedroom closet. Reports in those envelopes told all about the kid whose existence Luke publicly denied, whom Luke had denied to himself—until the day the *old man* had barged into his office and said, "I need a lawyer."

"I would have thought a man with your connections would have any number of lawyers of his own."

"I need a dope dealer's lawyer. I hear you're friends with that piece of slime in the valley—Brandon Baines."

"Friends? Call Baines yourself. I'm busy. Kate, show this…er…this *gentleman* out."

"You can't throw me out like I'm nobody."

"What exactly are we to each other? Are you my father?"

Big Red had glared at him. Then he'd looked away. Finally the old man had broken the silence.

"Baines says he's too busy to see me."

"That's too bad."

Luke knew, as he'd known that day, a whole lot more about *the kid* than he had ever let on. Oh, yes he knew a lot. He'd been keeping tabs for years. Even then he'd had a secret filing cabinet bulging with information about the kid.

Not that Luke had personally set foot in New Mexico to get that information. He hated that state, the people and the culture—what they'd done to him; what they'd done to his mother. Most of all what the old man had done to her.

Still, Luke knew the exact day, the exact minute, the exact place Little Red had been born. He had every school picture stapled to a single sheet of typing paper. He knew every basketball game the kid had ever won, knew every grade he'd ever made, knew the kid could add like a computer the same as he could. The kid was lousy in English the same as he was, too. Knew the kid had had a complex in high school because he'd been skinny and unattractive to girls.

Luke even knew the name of the first girl Little Red had screwed in college, knew they'd gotten high on pot and done it in the back seat of the brand-new, red Chevy the old man had given Little Red so he could make a splash in college.

Luke hadn't had a car in college or law school. He'd had jobs. He hadn't gotten to screw girls. At least not as often as he'd wanted. He'd had to work too damn hard.

Every time Luke had read a report he had visualized

the boy and his charmed life, trying to get into his head the experiences he'd only dreamed about. He had wanted to know what it was like to be beloved and legitimate—to be the pure-white son.

Luke knew the brand of the first cigarette the kid had smoked. Just as he knew when the kid had taken the first false step, made the first bad friend that had led toward his dealing dope for Spook. Luke could have called the old man, could have warned him long before the kid went bad. Big Red had cut the free-spending kid off when he'd flunked out. The kid had been desperate. Instead of getting a real job, he'd started selling dope to friends.

He'd been a natural salesman. Girls had been easy to get after that. His life and travels had made fascinating reading. And the ritzy Longworths had been fooled by the lies the kid told them, believing he was a whiz in the computer business and had a real job.

Will Sanders, a private detective in Albuquerque, still made his monthly visits to Austin to update Luke's files. Sanders had even had contacts in prison, so Luke knew everything that had happened to Little Red during the past five years, too. He knew about that night seven guys had held the kid down in his cell and nearly killed him.

Luke had taken steps then, used connections to get the kid moved. Gradually, Luke had begun to feel pride about how stoically Little Red had endured prison. A lot of pampered rich kids couldn't have stood up to the abuse Little Red had suffered.

The kid was out. Free.

But cancer?

The kid needed doctors—fast.

"McKade, have you heard a damn thing I've said? *He's got a gun*," Baines repeated.

"And he knows how to use it. Stay out of his sight. I'll be there as quick as I can."

"Look, I've got another big problem that can't wait. A woman..."

"Hold tight."

"What are you going to do?"

"Give the kid a target he can't resist—me."

"This is good."

Luke slammed the phone down, his gut churning. He waited a minute, grabbed his cell phone to call his pilot.

No! He'd drive.

He didn't bother to pack. He was out the door, running.

The smell of raw sewage hung in the air, no doubt, vapors from the Rio Grande. Heat glued Luke's white collar to his neck. His long-sleeved, cotton shirt felt heavy and wet against his armpits. He wore jeans, boots, and a black Stetson. Three blocks shy of the posh, tourist zone of Nuevo Laredo with fancy restaurants like his favorite, El Rancho, and glitzy silver and leather shops, Luke stomped through paper cups, papaya peels, plastic bags, broken bottles, not to mention the human debris—beggars and pimps.

Familiar territory to a man with his past.

Nuevo Laredo, Mexico was an old city with a crumbling infrastructure. Like all poor places it was noisy, hot and dirty. It was in-your-face, gutsy, colorful and alive.

A shiny, low-riding American sedan cruised up to

Luke, its radio blaring. A skinny, Mexican punk with a silver crucifix dangling from his glistening brown neck got out. The boy rushed him from the darkness, flipping pictures of naked girls.

Gleaming white smiles in pretty brown faces. Iridescent straight black hair. Breasts. Thighs.

Girls who didn't look a day over fifteen. Girls willing to do whatever perversion a man could pay for. There were illustrations of those perversions.

Unsure of Luke's nationality, the boy switched back and forth from English to Spanish.

"Meester...pretty girls.... *Putas*.... *Muy baratas*.... Cheap! They do anything."

Luke shook his head, waving him off, only to have a dozen more swarm him.

"*¡Vayate!*" Luke growled, knowing but not caring that he probably botched the grammar.

"*Chinga...*"

The boys made vile hand gestures, such gestures having a rich obscene vocabulary all their own in Mexico. Aloud, they cursed him with a virulent stream of Mexican profanity. Then on the next breath, they sauntered jauntily across the street to cajole a fat-stomached tourist in Bermuda shorts who was smoking a cigar. Rap music pulsed from the low-slung sedan as the gringo leered at their pictures and then pulled out a fat wallet.

"*Putas*. Very pretty."

Fun and games? In Mexico? Tonight?

They do anything.

It had been a while since Luke had had a woman. Sucker that he was, he'd been true to Marcie. It struck him he'd been waiting for her call and not her lawyers. His pride, his stupid pride had killed her.

I'm sorry. Why had that been so hard to say?

Sweat dripped from Luke's brow. The heat. The damned desert heat. In July, even at night, Nuevo Laredo was like a furnace, baking him from above and below.

Why the hell hadn't Baines done what Luke had told him? Why couldn't he have stayed put in the good old U.S. of A.? But, no. Baines, like a lot of lawyers, had a penchant for drama. He was up ahead, leading this caravan of fools through the dense NAFTA traffic.

Little Red was not far behind.

Baines had gotten a green light when he'd crossed the border. His companions were a gorilla in a jogging suit, a small, skinny guy with greasy, black hair and a goatee, and a yellow-haired whore in red polka dots who was so pretty she made Luke's stomach knot.

The Americans had stopped Little Red. But the paunchy-gutted idiots in their tight uniforms had let him go. When Luke got across the traffic-clogged border, which was bumper to bumper with eighteen-wheelers, he found Baines's and Little Red's cars two blocks from the main drag, their doors open in a dirt lot as if the occupants had scrambled out of them and taken off running. The radios had been ripped out. In another hour, the tires would be gone, too.

Beside Baines's car, Luke had found his brother's wallet, all the money gone and a high-heeled, red pump. Was the shoe the whore's?

So where were they? He'd asked questions. Paid people. So far, he'd come up with zip.

Suddenly something that looked like bright red hair

shimmered under blue neon a few blocks ahead. When Luke sprinted, a beggar with a mouthful of black teeth grabbed his ankle. Stumbling, he threw a fistful of pesos at the woman. Pushing himself free of her, he raced toward blue neon.

The redhead had vanished. Luke ran until he was thoroughly out of breath and thoroughly lost. When he stopped, he was on some dusty, rutted lane that wound in an indefinite course through a warren of shabby, graffiti-splashed buildings. Breathing hard, Luke rocked back on his heels.

Buildings? The houses were crude shacks made of sticks, adobe and cinder block. They leaned against one another like a row of dominoes ready to fall.

Hell on earth had to be junked cars lining a road like this. Hell was dirty, mean-looking, starving cats and dogs, half-naked kids with big brown eyes and ragged clothes. For an instant Luke was back at the pueblo. Then he stopped himself, not letting himself go there.

A lone rooster wandered in circles in the middle of the road. What was the use? Little Red could be anywhere. Luke might as well find a bar, have a tequila, the good kind, and pray for a break. But as he was scanning the houses for a familiar landmark so he could retrace his steps, a woman screamed.

Harsh slaps quieted her.

Then a gun popped, and she screamed again.

"Get off her, so I can kill myself a lawyer!"

Luke knew that voice.

The kid!

Another low-throated cry. This time Luke placed it

as coming from the cinder block shack two houses down.

The silence that followed unnerved him. A brown bottle in the gutter caught Luke's eye. He needed a weapon. Crouching, he swiped his sweaty hands on his jeans and then grabbed it by its long neck.

When the girl screamed again, he knocked the bottom off against a wall. Pulse pounding in his temple, Luke pressed himself into the warm shadows and inched nearer the house.

When he was close enough, he yelled from the street. "Damn you, Little Red...you're crazy to carry a gun into Mexico. Cops down here will lock you away. You'll never get out."

"This is good," mocked his brother drunkenly. "Not before I kill me a lawyer and...and...a bastard.... You're next—Indian."

The door banged. Bloody fingers against his golden face, Baines staggered outside. As always he was dressed impeccably in a dark custom-made suit. His two goons, the giant in the jogging suit and the runt with the slicked-back hair, stumbled outside behind him, grabbing Baines before he fell.

"Run, you sons of bitches," Little Red whooped, rushing after them. "Vengeance is mine."

The three men took off running. Luke sidestepped into a black pocket between two houses. Something he'd read in one of Sanders's reports came back to him. Little Red had starred in a dozen plays in high school.

"Corny. Prison damn sure didn't dim your flair for cheap drama, did it, kid?" he shouted.

"Where the hell are you?" Elbowing his way into

the shadows, Little Red waved his gun. "Step out where I can see you."

"This isn't a high school play—*kid*. And you ain't Rambo. And I ain't stupid."

The gun swung wildly.

Luke shrank against the wall.

"Luke! You...you...coward! You *bastard!*"

Silence.

Then a roach scurried out of the dark past the rooster. Scrawny wings spread.

When Little Red fired, the confused rooster flapped straight at Little Red.

"Sonofabitch!" Swatting wildly at the bird, the kid dropped the gun.

Racing footsteps at the other end of the alley.

Mr. This-is-good and his goons hadn't gotten far after all.

Little Red roared in rage, then gleefully scooped up his gun and lurched after them.

Silently, swiftly, Luke pursued them.

He got ten feet before she yelled. Then she moaned.

When nobody answered, a final hoarse cry was swallowed, strangled, broken off.

She was scared. The bastards had left her all alone in that shack.

Luke remembered the gunshots and stopped running. With acute frustration he watched Little Red's bright red head vanish into darkness.

She could be hit. Dying.

Marcie.

3

"Help..." This girl's Texas drawl was as pronounced as Marcie's. Thus, the *e* was elongated.

Luke stared at the black door as if it were the gate to hell.

"Please..." Again her prominent vowels seemed endless. "P-le-e-ease..."

"Marcie?" he whispered.

No. But this girl's faint cries held raw urgency. He drew in a savage breath and then pushed against warped wood that creaked heavily on ancient hinges.

"Help..."

He cursed the dark and Mexico and the heat that had him dripping with sweat. Most of all he cursed the whore and her soft, alluring drawl that compelled him into this black and forbidding shack.

A bar of moonlight backlit his tall, muscular body and the broken bottle he held raised above his black head. More of that same silver light slipped through the cracks in the mortar left by shoddy workmanship and glistened against dirty, broken windowpanes.

The room was squalid, hot and hellish; its ceiling

so low he had to stoop slightly. Plywood had been nailed against a hole in the wall. Corrugated tin was both ceiling and roof. The dirt floor was carpeted with cigarette butts and loose boards. Then he saw a Mexican bullwhip coiled like a black snake around a brand new, red high-heeled pump on the dirt floor, this shoe an exact match to the one he'd found earlier.

He picked the shoe up, turning it in his palm, and whistled. "Cinder-eff-ing-rella!"

"Who are you—Prince Charming?" drawled a small wavery voice, in an attempt at bravery. "What gives? A prince in blue jeans and cowboy hat?"

He liked her spunk.

The yellow-haired girl was tied by her wrists and ankles with remnants of her own nylons to a metal bed in the middle of the room. She lifted her drugged gaze to his.

A board groaned under his weight.

Her eyes bulged when she saw the bottle. Trying to free herself, she squirmed on the bare mattress. Moonlight rippled over her long shapely legs that were spread widely apart.

The room seemed to shrink, and the confines of it were suddenly more stifling. He drew a sharp breath.

Masses of reckless, yellow hair framed her exquisite oval face.

Sexy. Sexy as hell.

He thought, *Wow.*

He muttered, "Damn."

It was only natural to want to keep his reaction to himself and to be repelled by it. He averted his eyes from the girl's face and her awesome legs. But he felt like he'd fallen into a sensual barrel of forbidden delights. A girl with looks like hers made a man think of only one thing.

Images of those endless legs, a short polka-dot dress pushed above shapely thighs, black lace bikini panties and a garter belt had burned themselves into his testosterone-charged brain. Her breasts bulged against a low neckline. And that face...with those slanting eyes that caught the moonlight. Those full red lips...

Ah, such a face would give a saint wet dreams. Not that McKade was a candidate for sainthood. For as surely as there was a devil in hell keeping tabs, McKade's name would be scrawled in roaring flames at the top of that fiend's list of sinners.

"Are you going to he-e-e-l-p me...or..."

"Shhh..."

Why did she sound so much like Marcie? Why did she have to be blond?

Don't look at those legs, or at that face. Don't notice that her skin is pale and luminous, her shapely lips so moist and bright with paint they make your mouth go dry.

Her makeup, her costume, the mere fact Baines and his goons had brought her here and tied her to this bed to play kinky games told Luke what she was—a whore. As a kid, he'd had fun with her kind.

Was this hellhole her room? Or Baines's?

Glazed, startlingly blue eyes, lined in heavy black, stared up at him. "It's our honeymoon. Love me. Love me... P-please...just love me."

Love?

What Luke felt had a lot more in common with what she would do for a dollar than with love. He wanted sex; she sold sex.

She moistened her lip with her tongue. Then she seemed to suffer a moment's shortness of breath beneath his direct gaze.

His stomach lurched. She represented sex and the forbidden, all the vices he'd learned young and tried to rise above when he'd crawled out of the gutter. She had designed herself to bring out the beast in him.

She did.

"Shhh…"

With a muted whimper, followed by more slurred endearments, she strained toward him. Black stockings jerked, and she collapsed against the bed.

She was drunk or very high on something. Yet not so high that she wasn't conscious of him. Nor did she act ashamed to be lying there with her breasts and legs so exposed. Instead, she twisted her hips deliberately to entice him, begging, "Love me…."

At that honey-soft plea, his breath stalled. His body hardened. Her cheap beauty and suggestive posture paralyzed him. For a second or two, he even forgot about the heat.

He hadn't changed. His fine suits, his fine house, the fine wife he'd buried only this afternoon… The fine schools he'd attended but hadn't fit into… His whole damn life was a lie.

This girl was real. Too damn real. And she made him real.

"Don't play your whore tricks on me," he snarled even as he sank down on the bed beside her.

On a whimper, she shrank from him. Her wide eyes fixed on the broken bottle in his hand. Strips of black nylon held fast and put her at his mercy.

He saw a brown boy, facedown, in a vacant lot and

the bullies standing over him, kicking dirt and rocks at him.

"Be still. I won't hurt you. I'm going to cut you loose."

She watched him. He fought not to look at her. Still, sitting on her bed, their hips touching, he felt joined to her in ways he didn't understand.

He caught the scent of her perfume. Gardenias. Sweet, sweet gardenias. The fragile scent took him back to a summer day, to a cool, shady garden, to a haughty white woman who'd frowned at him with fury when he'd picked that single perfect blossom. He remembered her children in the same garden and the bouquets they'd held.

No.

The heat of the whore against his hip was a wholesome pleasure compared to his bitter memories. Perspiration beaded his brow. Better her. Better this hellish shack than his own shameful past.

The girl stared at his face unblinkingly. "Hawaii? Love…"

He waved the razor edges of the brown glass under her chin. Then he deliberately sliced a brown fingertip across the glass that was like a blade. Blood bubbled, oozed. A single drop splashed her cheek.

She started, whimpered.

"Hold still. Understand? So I don't cut you."

Her expression was grave, but she didn't move when he began sawing with the bottle.

After a few swipes, the nylon gave, and her limp arm fell across her breast. Trouble was, he had to lean across her to reach her other wrist.

The second he felt her female flesh molding his, something hot and dangerous consumed him.

His heart slowed to painful thuds. Male nerve cells registered body heat, registered gardenias, woman smell. Registered *her*. She fit him like a glove.

She was available. *She would do anything.*

Wildfire.

Her breasts pressing into his chest made him dizzy. His hand began to shake so badly he had to stop so he wouldn't cut her.

She held her breath.

So did he.

Get a grip. Don't let her know. Work fast.

Again, jagged brown glass sheered the flimsy nylon. *But she knew.* The instant she was free, her hands were all over him.

"I love you. Love me. I love you. Love me," she pleaded in Marcie's drawl.

Her hands. Her body.

Marcie's voice.

Love me. That constant refrain pounded through him like a drumbeat. Eagerly her hands moved over his torso.

He had to get away. It had been a mistake to lean over her. Her skillful, expert hands, her whore's hands knew exactly what to do to arouse a man like him.

Lightly, ever so lightly, she stroked. Sliding across his chest, her heated fingertips had his damp shirt out of his pants in no time, his belt unbuckled. Then like heat-seeking missiles, her hands were inside his jeans, circling him with her fist.

Low moans rose from her throat, her excitement matching his when she found him already hard.

Marcie used to moan like that. Until he'd forbidden her to make that sound in bed. *You're not a whore. You're my wife.*

He'd liked what Marcie had done too much. He'd known she'd win him through sex. It was a way to that deeper part of him he'd sealed and locked, so he'd be safe. With a whore, he could let go in bed. Because there were other lines he wouldn't cross with a whore.

The girl writhed. To hold her still, he threw a leg over her thighs. She wiggled, snugged herself closer. He slashed her ankle bindings loose with the broken bottle. Their hips joined.

Meltdown.

Wrapping herself around him, she clung.

For years he'd been alone—his whole damn life. This woman, the soft warmth of her, erased all that. He gulped in air as her fist caressed him.

"Love me...."

"You're a whore."

He saw tearing pain in her gaze. She froze, and he was moved beyond words by the sheen of tears misting her black-lashed blue eyes, by the way she drew back with proud dignity. "I love you...B-B..."

But whatever drug she was on got the best of her. Before Luke could register the name she called him, she wiggled closer, bringing her lips up to his. She caught her lower lip with her teeth. When she released it with a soft kiss, the swollen softness was pink, wet and shiny. And so damned kissable.

She kissed him, and her adoration, sweetness and innocence amazed him. Her *seeming* innocence, he amended.

He held his breath, his heart beating hard and fast. *Don't. Don't.*

But she kept at it, this spontaneous nibbling of his lips. She had a marvelous mouth. And not just to look at. She tasted, oh, God, she tasted delicious and so damned innocent...and so utterly utterly sweet.

Her tongue teased his, traced along the upper edges of his teeth. Nobody kissed like that but an expert.

Almost at once, he was shaking. Hardly knowing what he did, his mouth opened. He wanted more.

Gently, marveling at the softness of her skin, he let his knuckle touch her face. She didn't recoil. For a long moment he just held her. He felt her breasts rising and falling beneath his chest.

Ravenous, he began to kiss her. "You are beautiful," he breathed, his lips moving from her mouth, to her cheek, to her throat. Suddenly, he could contain himself no longer. Peeling her panties lower, he pushed her down into the mattress and straddled her. He tore at his jeans, unzipped his fly and shoved his jeans down. Somehow he had the presence of mind to fumble in his wallet for a condom. He tore it out of its package, put it on.

"How many others...besides me? How many, damn you? Brand Baines? Those jerks with Baines, too? What games did you play with them?"

"Only you, Brand..." She raised soulful eyes to him.

She didn't even know who he was, didn't care.

Then she saw him. Really saw him.

"You're not—Brand!"

"How many—"

"Where am…" She moaned, shut her eyes, thrashed her golden head back and forth. "Oh, dear!"

"You're in a shack. You were playing bondage games with three men."

Another voice, bright and sassy, not Marcie's. "Don't you dare say things like that to me, mister." But she was very pale. "Why, who are you anyway?"

In the next breath she saw the nylon around her wrist and moaned. "Bondage? You—you monster!"

"Me? This little game was all your idea!"

Panicking, wild to escape him now, she pounded on his chest, kicked at his legs. "No… No… No…"

He hated teases. "Whores don't say no."

"Don't you dare tell me what I can or cannot do. I can too say no if I want to. No… No…"

"No?" He laughed harshly, covering her sputtering lips with his hand. "I can have you. Anybody can. You can't say no. Not now."

"*No,*" she mumbled and most defiantly against his thick fingers. Then she bit him, rather ferociously.

"Ouch!" His hat fell off.

Furious, he jammed a knee between the girl's legs, positioned himself to lunge. She was too slim, too small to stop him.

"You want me to tie you up again. You'd like that, wouldn't you?"

She countered with a piteous, mewing sound. Terrified eyes locked on his for a long, shocked moment. Then she slumped lifelessly.

Blood pumped. *Take the sexy, sassy witch.*

Rigid, she lay beneath him, blue eyes wide-open.

They were isolated. She was helpless. He could do whatever the hell he wanted.

So, do it. Nobody would know. Not even her.

He was swollen, on fire. The room was an oven. His black hair dripped perspiration onto the bed, onto her pale skin that gleamed with sweat, too. The need to take and ravage was so powerful, it almost robbed him of his humanity.

I can say no if I want to. No… No…

Sassy. Even when her face had been bloodless and she'd been so scared.

"Oh, God…" Had it come to this?

Panting hard, he drew back and moved a hand in front of her face. She didn't blink, didn't even see the five splayed fingers. He ran his hands through his soaking hair, smoothed it back, inhaled a ragged breath.

Something really was wrong with her. He fingered her wrist, found a pulse.

Wild with relief that at least she was alive, he pushed himself off her. He sat in the hot, stifling dark, cursing himself and her blasphemously. Through gritted teeth, he sucked in more deep breaths as he fought to regain normalcy…sanity…decency.

When she just lay there, her glassy eyes fixed on the ceiling, he got scared, too. Lifting her, he began to shake her.

"Wake up."

She frowned, struggling to focus on his scowling face. "Sleepy… You are being most unpleasant…."

Near panic, he dressed quickly, pulled her panties up those incredibly long legs, smoothed her dress. Touching, redressing her stirred him almost more than he could bear.

"Stand up."

"Can't... Dizzy..."

"Keep talking." He slapped her. Not hard. But hard enough to leave a red mark on her pale cheek. He instantly regretted having done so.

"You're mean."

He grabbed her shoe and his Stetson. When he jammed her bare foot into the high-heeled red pump, she couldn't balance and swayed into him.

"Oops."

He grabbed her. "What kind of pills are you on?"

"You really are most disagreeable.... I'm a good girl. I don't do drugs."

"Liquor then? How much?"

"Brand... Drink... Not liquor, though."

Luke didn't know much about drugs.

"Whatever it was, you're higher than a kite."

Bottom line. He had to get her out of here. "Put your arms around my neck."

"Are we going on our honeymoon?" Then she realized who she was really with. "I think you'd make the most dreadful bridegroom."

Jostling her into his arms seemed to waken her. She was lighter than he expected. Effortlessly, he carried her outside into the close, hot, humid dark, which reeked of diesel fumes, charcoal smoke and other fouler pollutants.

"Are we in Maui yet?" she asked, a tinge of desperation in her dazed, curious voice.

They were standing on a crumbling sidewalk in front of a shack smeared with graffiti. He'd nearly raped her. She'd called him a monster.

She thought they were on their honeymoon.

He played along. "Can't you hear the surf and see the hula dancers?"

"Maui. Darling. Just like you promised."

Her wistful eyes and impish smile of sheer joy both dazzled him and terrified him.

Darling. The word, the way she said it wrapped itself around her soul. And his.

And her smile. That incandescent smile.

He wanted that irresistible smile to be for him. For him alone.

She took off his hat, turned it over and then plopped it on her own golden head. It swallowed her. She looked like a little girl playing cowgirl.

His gut clenched. So did his heart.

He could feel nothing for her. Nothing.

4

"Oops." The yellow-haired whore shot him an irreverent grin.

His heart paused for a beat or two.

Cute. Childlike. Sassy.

All woman.

Those were Luke's first thoughts when she tiptoed out of the hotel bathroom in a blue terry cloth robe, nearly tripping on the hem of the voluminous thick folds that swallowed her.

"I'm sorry. Do you need to go—" She blushed slyly at this mention of bathroom activities, and scooted against the wall. She ran her fingers through golden, damp curls. "How long was I?"

Not that she looked like she cared in the least.

"An hour. More than an hour," he grumbled, not because he was angry, but because he'd been too aware of her in there and she was too damn pretty with all that honey-gold, flyaway hair cascading in rippling spirals all over her slim shoulders.

"Sorry," she whispered without the least bit of sincerity. Fingertips fluttered quickly to her lips.

She didn't look like a whore anymore. Then she stared at him suspiciously, and he almost wished she did. He had the strangest feeling he didn't have her figured at all. But that was absurd.

She was tall, five eight if she was an inch. Yet she seemed smaller. She was too thin for his usual taste, but her delicately boned frame and her natural grace made her easy on his eye. And those soft, ample breasts and long, shapely legs made him forget how skinny she was in other places. Not that he could see much of her lush curves with so much blue terry cloth swaddling them, hem puddling at the slim ankles, thick, long sleeves dangling over her nervous fingertips.

Without her makeup, with her cheeks flushed from the long bath, without the tight polka-dot dress to cheapen her beauty, she looked sweet and young—as delectably innocent as a high school virgin, as classy as the priciest cover model, but a bit bratty, too.

The deep blue intensified the brilliant color of her eyes. It was those eyes, the way they sparkled with such mischief, that made her look... What? Sort of spontaneous and unpredictable.

She was so alive, incandescent, mesmerizing, sexier than hell. She drew him. Indeed, she had some gut-clenching power over him no woman had ever had. Or maybe, it was just that he felt so damned lonely and vulnerable after Marcie.

The girl's golden hair shone, and he wanted to slide his fingers through its lustrous thickness. Who was he kidding? He wanted to do way more than that. Sex appeal—she had it in spades. At least for him. Which put him on dangerous ground.

With looks like hers, she could make a fortune. She was wasting herself on the border.

Maybe he should hire this lively girl on a permanent basis—to service him. Him alone. He wouldn't share.

He could hire somebody to teach her how to talk and act at his parties. In the right clothes, she'd prance about palaces like a thoroughbred. *Just like he did.* Nobody would ever know they were a pair of fakes from the gutter.

She'd be more suited to him than the highbred socialites he dated. She knew what women were really for. He wouldn't let her near those self-help books and women's magazines that had made Marcie so dissatisfied. No expensive shrink like Marcie's for this girl.

This girl turned him on. He needed a simple, basic relationship with a woman. Sex. A woman like her wouldn't demand what he wasn't capable of giving.

"Long bath," he said, attempting to consider her as coldly as he would any commodity he was interested in buying.

But she wouldn't have it. She glared back at him with an impish ferocity that stunned him.

No. Don't even think about it. This girl spelled trouble. Besides, a woman of any sort was the last thing he needed as a permanent fixture. Especially when he was still so raw from Marcie...

"I always take long baths," the girl retorted. "Not that my habits are any of your business, mind you." She softened this bit of rudeness with the most enchanting blush; she squirmed, too, toes curling into the carpet. Sensing danger, but not about to run from him, her long-lashed, blue eyes flashed. Her mixture of

boldness, reticence and obvious discomfiture around
him caused a tightness in his chest.

He remembered their fight. Maybe, just maybe, it
wasn't totally unreasonable of her to distrust him.
He'd forced her to walk and drink coffee until she'd
collapsed in angry tears and called him a bully. When
her mind had cleared, she'd thrown everything he'd
told her about Mexico right back at him.

"Why, you raped—"

"I saved your cute little ass," he'd thundered.
"You were tied to bedposts…half-naked…alone…
like some damsel in distress in a porn comic book."

"And what do men in those comic books do to such
women?"

"The point is I got you out of Mexico."

"You're determined to paint yourself as a hero and
me as a—" She'd blushed then. "You don't know
anything."

He'd learned quickly she blushed at nearly everything. Then she'd looked stricken and profoundly
ashamed. Naturally, she'd launched an attack. "You
almost raped me—"

"*Almost* being the operative word. You teased me,
kissed me. You wouldn't even know about it if I
hadn't told you."

"Ha! I'm surprised you did," she'd huffed. "I'm
sure the only reason you did was to put me down. You
just love telling me how low and awful you think I
am. You called me a—"

Whore? He'd restrained himself and hadn't said the
word out loud again. "Your *career* of choice was all
too obvious."

She'd blushed again, bitten her lips. "Ha! And are you always right about everything?"

He'd laughed. "Don't act so coy. You came on to me like a pro. You put your hands on me, remember? You unzipped me, fondled me, begged me for it."

"Because I—" She went stock-still. Her blush was no longer becoming. Her face had deepened to angry purple.

Were those tears glistening behind her eyelids, too? Tears of outrage? She had a misplaced temper, this girl.

"*If* I did those things..." Her lip quivered. "Not that I'm at all sure I should believe you...I—I must have thought you were somebody else...somebody decent...although how I could have thought such a thing about you—even drugged—I'm sure I can't imagine."

The indignation and despair in her soft voice jarred him. Still, he defended himself with a burst of temper equal to hers.

"That same decent somebody who drugged you and tied you to those bedposts and left you there for anybody to find?" he shouted. *He never shouted.* Not at underlings. "Lucky for you I came along and not somebody else."

"Lucky? You're judging me...when you don't know anything about me. You said yourself you nearly raped me...."

"Don't be inane," he said in a low, controlled voice. "I stopped when you said no."

"Then why did you feel guilty enough to confess?" Her voice was equally controlled. But she stuck her pretty little nose in the air and faced him with a startling amount of belligerent spirit. "You say I fainted.

You say you're my hero. How do I know what you really did?"

"I stopped." He ground his words like meat through a grinder.

"You don't look like a man who would stop once he got started."

Her perverse compliment maddened him. The gall of this girl!

"I got you the hell out of Mexico. It cost me five hundred dollars cash to bribe the border guard."

"You bribed a border guard?" Her eyes widened. "I wish they'd thrown you in jail. I would have liked seeing you behind bars—caged."

"Well, they didn't, because like everybody else in this world, especially you, they're for sale, sweetheart."

"You must have a limited and unlikable bunch of acquaintances."

"Carrying unconscious young females across international borders is a highly suspicious activity. I had to pay them. They were strangers, not acquaintances."

"I don't much like you—even if you are as handsome as Mr. Darcy."

Handsome? She thought him handsome. "Who the hell is Mr. Darcy? A client?"

"Do you read? Never mind. An almost rape?" She eyed him skeptically. "Bribing a government official? You are a man who's capable of highly suspicious activities."

"Then we're a matched pair."

"No, we aren't."

Huffiness. Morality. From the likes of her?

"I found you tied to bedposts," he thundered.

"You keep saying that! If that's so, you've made the most of it ever since!"

"You were drugged."

She glared at him. "I don't take drugs and I don't like being insulted."

"Do you like being alive and in one piece on this side of the border?"

"I do," she admitted. "Thank you. But I don't much like sharing a…a cage with a beast like you."

"I'm not a beast."

Her lack of gratitude, her refusal to admit her own shortcomings, her ability to see the worst in him—everything about her maddened him. But what really set him on edge was her standing there in the bathroom doorway in that robe, looking sexy as hell as she stared daggers through him.

"Come out for God's sakes. I won't bite."

Shyly, she took a trembling step. "I have to go home."

"Not till I'm sure you're okay…safe."

"You don't care about my safety," she said in that soft, knowing tone. "I know why you won't let me go. What sort of games do you play, Mr. McKade, with your women?"

His pulse accelerated. "I worked my ass off to sober you up. I fed you supper…breakfast…."

"You made me eat eggs. I don't like eggs."

"How was I supposed to know that?"

"I told you."

"For God's sakes, I'm not running a short-order grill. I ordered eggs. I ate them myself."

"But you like eggs."

"You have the most illogical mind."

"Don't say that."

As if she were remembering the other battles they'd fought, she stared past him, to the closet, to the skeleton key in the closet door. "You deliberately scared me."

"Relax. Forget that," he growled, ashamed of that little episode.

"You threatened to lock me in there."

"You ran out."

"Because you're a big bully."

"Only sometimes...when pushed."

"All the time, I bet."

"I couldn't let you run off drugged—"

"Quit saying I was drugged."

"When you quit calling me a bully." His heart darkened with a bitter memory. There was ice and yet pain, too, in his deep voice. "Where I come from...it was bully...or be bullied." Why had he said that? Why had he betrayed himself to the likes of her?

She lifted her chin, studied him. "I bet you were the biggest, baddest bully of all."

He glared. She chewed on her bottom lip, considering him with one of those intense glances that unsettled him and made him wonder what she might do next.

They were in Little Red's hotel suite. The room key had been in his brother's wallet. Luke had brought her here on the thin chance his brother would show up...alive...and he could, thus, kill two birds with one stone.

His brother's suite had seemed as good a place as any to sober her up. Once, after pouring countless cupfuls of coffee down her, when he'd been forcing her to pace the room with him, she'd panicked and broken out of the suite. He'd caught her in the hall, shoved her back inside, and pushed her into the closet. She'd pounded wildly on the door. He'd opened it and told her to be quiet, threatening to tie her up the way Baines had or gag her and lock her in the closet if she didn't behave.

She stared at the skeleton key in the lock of the closet door and went still.

"My aunt used to lock me up...in the dark," she said. "And tonight..." Her eyes filled with terror.

"Difficult aunt."

"Oh, she was. She was a lot like you. She believed all people were for sale, too, especially women. She even saw marriage in that light. She was always saying, 'It's just as easy to marry a rich man as a poor man.'"

"Every woman I know thinks like that."

"Not me. I believe in love, in chemistry, in magic— in excitement." She snapped her fingers. "Or I used to. Till Brand." Her voice dropped. "Till you." Again her eyes held fear although she strove to talk about something else. "My aunt and I drove each other to distraction. But she taught me to read and to appreciate the fine arts. On the whole, she was a lot nicer than you." She tried to smile. "And at least she was very well educated and way more honest about what she was up to than you are—McKade."

"Call me Luke."

"I'm not sure yet if I want to know you that well."

"You're rude."

"Me, rude? That's rich."

"Ungrateful too," he accused.

She seemed to make an effort to concentrate on what he was saying instead of on what she was so afraid of.

"My aunt used to say I was a brat. And maybe I was…sometimes. I used to follow her when she didn't know it. I was too curious about what went on…. There were the most fascinating rumors about her, you see. And I was way too lively just to accept what she said as gospel." She was silent. "As if anything she could say would be gospel." Her voice changed. "I am a brat by day…and brave…but by night…I'm afraid of the dark."

"You chose an odd line of work, considering that fear."

"Ha! You don't listen any better than—"

"And you're afraid of me."

She shook her head. "Not of you…"

She didn't fool him. If she wasn't afraid, why did she keep glancing from him to the bed? Why was she pressing herself against the wall?

He advanced upon her, to prove his point. "Feel better after your bath?" he asked silkily.

But she didn't back away as he'd expected. "My brain still feels…weird…. Like the thoughts are drifting…not connecting."

"Why don't you get some sleep then," he suggested.

"What will you do?"

"Watch over you."

"Just watch?"

"Disappointed?" he inquired softly.

She blushed. "Do you ever stop with the sex talk?"

"That might be hard…with you around. I can't

seem to forget I found you higher than a kite tied to a bed.'' He picked up the red polka-dotted dress. "This little number was shrink-wrapped to your body." He wadded it up and threw it at her. "What kind of girl wears black mesh hose and a dress like this two sizes too small?"

Unfolding the suggestive garment, her eyes rounded. She jiggled the dress and made the flounces bounce. "Oh, my!"

"Not much dress. Lots of girl," he said.

"It isn't mine!" She threw it at him and stalked toward the bed away from him.

"You were quite...fetching in it," he taunted darkly.

Another blush. She sank into a chair.

"You want me to be some idiot you can fool with your fake blushes and little-girl smiles and sly glances."

"I know about you, too. You brought me here...because you thought I *was* that kind of girl. That's why you won't let me go. I wonder... If I did what you wanted, would you let me go then?"

He stared at her, scared to the quick and yet darkly thrilled, too, by her tantalizing suggestion.

She shut her eyes. "It's all so extraordinary...like a bad dream." Her hollow, fearful tone floated to him. "Brand said he'd marry me. At least I think he did. But..."

She rubbed her forehead, her eyelids and strained to think. "Only...only...maybe he did ask me to put that awful rag on. I thought he took me to Mexico to get married."

"Some wedding dress."

She stared about the room as if seeing ghosts, seeming to hear and see him only vaguely. "He gave me... Oh, dear... No... He couldn't have drugged..." Frowning, she stared at the dress he'd dropped on the floor.

"What?"

"Was I really wearing that?"

He nodded.

"Brand loved me."

A low moan rose in her throat. Her hand went to her belly. Then her face changed as if she'd come to a decision. Big blue eyes widening on his strong face, she looked up at Luke. There was something so proud, so desperate and so responsible in her gaze. He felt a fierce, insane need to protect her.

"What's wrong?" he demanded, feeling ridiculous.

"If Brand did that..." She rubbed her temples. "He wouldn't listen. He wouldn't even listen. He won't stop now, either.... He's very determined. He's rich, powerful...."

"So am I."

She stared at him. Her eyes lit up, as he'd known they would at the mention of his fortune.

"You have to help me. I have to get out of Laredo away from Brand—tonight."

"No way."

"I can't let him find me." For an instant she looked on the verge of panic.

He remembered his old friend, the pregnant law student who'd felt she had to run away from Baines.

As this girl studied him, she seemed to regain a bit of control. After a while, she even forced a slow, sexy smile. "What if...if I was the kind of woman you think I am...and you want me to be...the girl of your most lurid comic book dreams?''

He sucked in a breath. *Here we go.*

"We're alone. In your hotel room." Her gaze drifted suggestively to the bed. "What if I'd do anything? Absolutely anything? Would you help me?"

Anything. Pictures of women playing in provocative love games flipped in his mind. The pictures changed. Every face, every lewd position was of her.

Heat spiraled inside him. "One minute you play a whore, the next a virgin. Don't tempt me unless you mean it."

"Or the big tough, rich guy will grab me?" She trembled, hugging herself. Her blue eyes grew even more enormous. Then she licked her mouth with her tongue. "Anything," she purred.

The imaginary pictures of her flipped again. He had a fleeting sensation of shame. She was in some sort of trouble. What kind of heel took advantage of a desperate woman, even a whore, who needed his help?

A man who came from the gutter. A man who used every opportunity for his own gain. A saint would have been tempted by her, and he was no saint.

She was so damn pretty she made every male sense knife sharp. His bones melted. His weaker nature won. Down in hell his name on that list blazed brighter. "Anything?"

She nodded.

"What do I have to do?"

"Money. And I need a ride north."

"How much money?"

Her eyes locked on his. "A lot."

"Undress."

"Cash…before I—I begin—"

"Strip first."

Meekly lowering her lashes, she gulped in a deep breath. For courage, he thought. Then she slanted her eyes at him as her fingers fumbled with the sash of his robe.

"Take your time," he said with a touch of irony.

Untying the rope of blue cloth, she coiled the sash between her fingers.

He appraised what he could see of her body, watched her fingers stroke blue cloth. "So, I was right about you?"

Her wounded eyes stung him. She flung the sash full-force at his face.

That temper of hers turned him on. He caught the sash, recoiled it and plunged it inside his pocket. "Take it all off."

She paled.

He grinned. "Act like you're having fun."

She brought a hand to her throat protectively. "You better hope I'm never in the position to exact revenge."

"You said anything."

"A gentleman would help a lady for nothing."

"Gentlemen are an extinct breed."

She gave him the once-over. "How right you are."

"Nor does the term *lady* apply to any female in this room."

"Ha! Someday I'll make you regret this."

"You blame me…for your idea!"

"It's always the man's fault."

"Right," he said.

With a little shrug, she flashed him an infectiously

warm smile, covering it with fluttery fingertips. Then she squared her shoulders and blew him a kiss. The next thing he knew she winked and began to hum a ribald burlesque tune.

While he watched, she mimicked a stripper's high-stepping strut, moving fast as was her custom, peeling the terry cloth back and giving her full, shapely breasts a little jiggle for him.

Lust arced through him. He began to burn.

His response paralyzed her. Her quick steps faltered; her humming paused in midnote. Her outstretched leg hung suspended in the air. She stared at it in openmouthed astonishment as if she were terrified to find it there.

Long seconds passed in which each was too aware of the other. Then she recovered, threw her head back, cupped her breasts as if to offer them to him.

She looked so damn cute, so eager, holding her breasts like that.

Available. She was like a fantasy in a dream. Only she was real.

She let the robe slide from her slim, rounded shoulders, down the length of her voluptuous body. His heart thundered.

His sea-gray gaze flicked over full, soft breasts, her narrow waist, and the fullness of her hips...and those incredible legs that went forever.

She blushed, as if stunned by what she was doing, and then quickly averted her gaze to the blue pool of terry cloth at her feet. Her modesty only enhanced her charm and beauty. He wanted to grab her, take her.

"You won't say no again...just when things get interesting?" he rasped, taking a step toward her. When her smile froze, her fingers falling from those voluptuous lips, and she shrank back an inch or two instinctively, he softened his tone. "You didn't answer me."

She bowed her head, her cheeks crimson in shame. "I won't say no...if you make me go through with this...."

His eyes narrowed. He moved in for the kill, took her chin in his callused hand before she could escape. "How much?"

"W-what?"

He studied her slender neck, her swollen mouth. "How much do you charge...for this little dance...for all the rest?"

He loathed himself when she looked from him to the bed and began to shake. Then he saw the tears glistening in her eyes. "A thousand dollars," she snapped. "But you have to take me with you... tonight." Her strangled voice was so low and hot with that temper of hers he could barely hear her. "Like I said, I need a ride."

"You're gonna get the ride of your life."

Hot color crept up her throat, warming the skin beneath his fingertips.

"You like thinking of me as an object, a toy you can play with, don't you? But if you give me the money...and help me..." She shut her eyes. "I—I'll try not to let myself care what you think."

She was so soft. His blood pumped at an alarming rate. His breathing was so shallow and quick, he couldn't get enough air.

"I want my thousand dollars now."

"A thousand dollars. You'd better be good. You'd better do—anything."

"Oh, dear." Then she said, "You got it!"

He pulled out his wallet, counted ten bills and laid them across her open palm. She took her time, folding them. In slow motion, she set them down one by one on the table.

That done, she lifted her gaze from the ten green bills. Squaring her shoulders, she faced him, wild emotion flaring in her pale face. "Go ahead," she whispered, fighting to keep her voice steady. Her body went stiff.

Instead of seizing her as a girl in her business, no doubt, expected, he knelt at her feet as if in worship, his fingertips starting at her toes. Tracing the arch of her narrow foot, he noted how she quivered, gooseflesh springing beneath his lightest touch. When his hand reached the top of her thigh, he forced her legs open.

"My, my...a natural blonde."

His gaze climbed, fixed on her face. "I have a thing for blondes."

Her eyes were closed. Was she pretending he was someone else? Brand maybe? Or imagining this wasn't happening? What was she thinking? He had to know. She had to know she was with him. For some inane reason that was vital. More vital than sex itself.

"Open your eyes," he commanded.

Her cheeks flamed. Her black lashes fluttered reluctantly.

"Are you sure about this?" he demanded.

Her eyes clung to his in mute desperation, but she nodded.

"Smile, then."

Her bottom lip wobbled, but she tried. Dear God,

she tried. Despite her smile, a tear trickled down her flushed face.

He jerked his hand away. The fact that she didn't want to look at him, that when she forced that tremulous smile, she wept, angered him. Had she wept in that shack with those goons?

"A girl of your…er…talents ought to be able to act like she wants it…as bad as her client."

More tears welled. "I'm trying. It's just that with you…" Her smile died. Her control slipped. She lifted her nose in outrage, stared down its length. Her wet, dilated eyes cut him like daggers. "With you, it's difficult."

"More difficult than with other men?" he growled.

"I imagine so."

"You did say…anything," he reminded her, trying not to show the dark jealous emotion that had begun to gnaw at him. "And I have a lifetime of fantasies. The girls in my dreams never cry."

"Would I be the girl of your dreams…if I didn't cry?"

"No way."

A blink brought more of the same liquid pooling in those beautiful eyes. "Then turn off the light if you can't handle a real girl's tears."

"Can't handle—"

She stabbed at the switch behind her. Darkness enveloped them. Then she reached for him. "Dream on," she whispered.

He felt her shaking, felt her reluctance, knew she was still crying. When he kissed her, she shuddered.

She didn't want to do this. And, damn it, he wanted her to.

Why the hell did that matter? *He would handle it.*

She'd sold herself. This was business. He could use her any way he liked.

"What's your name?" he demanded even as his hand blindly touched her wet cheek to comfort her.

After a breathless pause, she said quaveringly, "Willa."

More than sex, he wanted to hold her close, to make her feel safe—which was ludicrous.

"I've never paid a woman for sex before."

"You're the first for me, too."

Guilt crept over him. If she was telling the truth, if she wasn't a whore, some desperate need he knew nothing about was driving her to this.

She was a whore. Of course, she was a whore.

He'd bought companies, ruined men of far more worth than she.

His gut knotted.

"Get into bed," he growled.

As her bare feet scampered in the dark, pictures of a naked golden girl in a dozen way-out fantasies flipped in his imagination.

Sheets rustled. He heard her reluctant sigh.

He was as hard and hot as a brick just out of the kiln.

He couldn't wait.

She didn't want him.

Why the hell did that matter?

5

Willa de Mello was afraid of the dark, afraid of going to sleep, afraid of bad dreams. Especially when there was a big bad wolf lounging in the stuffed armchair right beside her.

So, she lay in the dark and wondered how in the world she would get away from Luke McKade. Not that she was really worried. For all his macho bravado, the big, oversexed lug was a pussycat...at least compared to Brand.

She'd known he wouldn't force her to do *it*. Not if she didn't want to. A man like him lived for challenges. He was so conceited he truly believed it would be child's play to win her, before he bedded her.

Willa was a cat lover. Thus, she understood predators. Cats liked to stalk and wait, to play a bit with their prey. They savored the chase, anticipating the treat. In his mind the treat was a yellow-haired party girl. A lot of men had been fooled by her hair color and sexy looks.

Ha! This was one lady who wasn't about to serve herself on a silver platter to another oversexed rogue, even if he had paid a thousand dollars for the meal. Under different circumstances, he might have been fun. Not tonight. But Brand, what he'd nearly done, had changed Willa forever. Willa's secret agenda was a matter of life and death.

Not that McKade wasn't attractive, if a girl went for tall dark and disturbingly handsome and rich and powerful, which did have a certain appeal to a fan of Jane Austen and the Brontë sisters' novels. But Willa was way too disillusioned and in way too much trouble to take on a new man, especially another know-it-all bully who thought the worst of her. All her life she'd been misunderstood. If her appearance didn't get her into trouble, then her wacky responses to life and literature did.

What she'd been looking for was someone who believed in her, who accepted her—who respected her, who saw past her sexpot, dumb-blond good looks. She'd known she had to have a man who didn't mind a woman who was a little different. A man who didn't expect her to be a deb or a Martha. Here in Laredo, the highest class debs were known as Marthas and Marthas were the equivalents of New Orleans Mardis Gras queens. And Willa had thought, until tonight's rude awakening, she'd found such a man in Brand.

Desperate moments. Wild impulses. Reckless deeds.

She was used to this sort of thing. Like a cat, she would land on her feet.

It isn't just you anymore though. You can't keep flying by the seat of your pants, Willa dear.

Her conscience always had Mrs. Connor's voice. Dear, soft-spoken Mrs. Connor had been her favorite art teacher at Trinity Elementary. Mrs. Connor hadn't minded if she hadn't colored in between the lines, if she'd drawn her own pictures instead. When all the other kids had been coloring red apples on apple trees in their workbooks, Willa had drawn an upside down orange tree floating on a cloud because there had been an orange grove right in her backyard. And sometimes, when she'd lain under her favorite orange tree and stared up at the branches, she'd seen clouds floating above her tree.

If it hadn't been for Mrs. Connor, Willa wouldn't have majored in art in college. She wouldn't have become the biggest success in her class by going on to the grand career of painting T-shirts for a living. Of course, real artists despised her. Or, at least, Willa imagined they did. But she did make a good living. Which was more than a lot of real artists could say.

If things were half as bad as McKade described, you were in a heap of trouble tonight, girl.

Willa always talked back to Mrs. Connor.

Tied to a bed in that vulgar, uncomfortable costume? Who me? McKade probably ripped it off some other woman and then embellished what happened to exaggerate his own importance and humiliate me.

As if he read her rebellious thoughts and saw through her denial, McKade grumbled and shifted his large body in that chair that was much too small for him. Poor boy. He probably wanted to attract her attention, so she'd feel sorry for him and invite him to bed.

Ha!

Not that she wasn't grateful. If it hadn't been for him, there was no telling what might have happened to her. But Willa didn't have the sort of mind to dwell on such things. She believed life was an adventure. She believed in destiny, that everything that happened was supposed to happen—and all for the best. One didn't have to understand. One had to accept and go on.

But tonight... Brand...

If half of what McKade said was true, and deep down she knew it was, tonight things had gone way too far. Well, she was safe now, or she would be when she got out of town and escaped McKade.

Soon.

Willa was warmhearted and irrational. High drama was her forte. From birth she had been a handful, getting herself into more mischief than ten curious little girls.

Was it any wonder? After all, she'd barely been five before she was the tragic heroine of a grand adventure. Her adoring parents, both every bit as whimsical and reckless as she, had been swept off their yacht in a stormy sea only seconds after they'd lashed poor Willa to the mast.

Willa had survived two days and two nights in that storm while the boat broke up beneath her. Like the ancient mariner in her favorite poem, she'd gone mad with grief and fear, but she'd found her courage, too. That was why, or so her imminently practical if ever-so-scandalous aunt, Mrs. Brown, said, ''Willa's exasperating because she can't take life, or at least what normal girls consider life, seriously. She can't plan for the future. She's too busy living.'' Not that the tyrannical Mrs. Brown was always so philosophical about Willa's shortcomings.

To Willa, the moment was all. Nobody had more

fun than Willa. Nobody got into more trouble. As a
little girl, she hadn't cared a fig about making good
grades.

"She even fails subjects she's a whiz in," her teach-
ers complained. "She could be so brilliant in math.
And she's fast when she takes a notion to be."

But math had bored Willa. Why should a little girl
waste precious life working problem after problem she
already knew how to do? Especially when one preferred staring at mysterious creatures such as butter-
flies or pill bugs and wondering what the world was
like to them? Did pill bugs have schools that were
dreadfully boring with dull books and endless, repet-
itive exercises?

She never painted the same design twice on her
T-shirts. She never cooked a recipe the same way, either.

Willa, the woman, had a fatal weakness for the
wrong kind of man, the bossy, judgmental McKade
running true to her type. He wanted to tie her down
but blamed her for his own desire.

But surely, surely he wasn't as horrible as Brand.

Ditch McKade. The sooner the better, said Mrs.
Connor.

But he's so cute. And he thinks I'm cute.

A girl does love to have fans.

I'd think you'd have learned your lesson.

He's fun to tease.

With McKade on her mind, Willa drifted off to
sleep and was instantly enveloped in nightmarish vi-
sions from hell.

Ever since her parents' accident, she'd had bad

dreams. Tonight, the monster was Brand. As always he was dressed elegantly. A wolf in sheep's clothing.

Unaware that she clawed the sheets, unaware of Luke McKade growing alert in his dark chair, she moaned aloud.

Dreams move more quickly than reality and make connections and reveal secrets that terrify. At first, Brand was sweet and loverly—her very own Prince Charming. Then he was holding a plastic bag over her face and she was gasping, clawing holes in it to get air.

The bag shredded. Brand laughed and said he'd been trying to pull it off.

Then she told him about the baby.

"A baby?" He was smiling; that meant he wasn't listening. "This is good, princess."

"Oh, Brand, I'm so in love."

He was laughing, but there was something dark about his eyes. "In love? With me? This is good. I love you, too."

"What about our baby?"

"Willa, my princess, you're so young."

"You said you loved me."

"And I do. But are you ready for a baby?"

"I'm pregnant. We have to marry."

"Of course we do."

She could tell he wasn't listening.

"You'll tell your parents?"

"The sooner the better. They'll love you. We'll have a huge wedding. We'll go to Hawaii for our honeymoon. We have a house in Maui, you know. This is good."

"We'll be so happy…as happy as I was when I was a little girl and my parents were alive."

She thought of all the sexy, shameful things Brand had forced her to do even when she'd told him she hadn't wanted to. Oh, she'd tried so hard to please him. So hard, she often hated herself after they'd finished making love.

Irrational fear consumed her. Suddenly, she was running from something dark and monstrous that had a fiery green tongue.

Brand was so beautiful and golden, so rich and powerful. She had loved him ever since she'd been a little girl. He'd been so much older, he'd never noticed her back then.

If Brand was smiling, why was she terrified?

Not going to be a baby. Not going to be a baby.

Who had said that?

"Let's get married tonight. In Mexico." How Brand's green eyes had sparkled.

"What about your parents? Our big wedding?"

"We'll tell them later, my love. We'll have a second wedding." He'd made her drink…to toast the baby. She'd choked on the bitter stuff and then gotten woozy.

"Not good for the baby…"

"There's not going to be a baby."

That's when he'd said it. Brand had said it. In Mexico. In the shack. Before he'd told her what he was really going to do.

Two men held her. She was weak, drunk or drugged, not herself in any case. Brand was ripping off her nylons, not caring that those awful men with those lust-filled eyes were watching them. She didn't care much, either, not when she knew what he was up to. He was tying her hands and her ankles to the bed.

The baby. Don't hurt the baby.

Brand leaned over her with a syringe. She felt a sharp prick in her left arm. His face whitened in a blinding blaze that looked a lot like a halo.

"There's not going to be a baby. Everything will be okay. You love me, and I love you. And we'll go on as before."

Before her eyes a green horn sprouted from Brand's thatch of golden curls, and his halo fell and dangled there. Brand winked at her, his green eyes sparking fire.

She screamed and screamed. Somebody else was there—a wiry, sickly looking fellow with haunted eyes and greasy, spiked red hair. Moonlight glinted off something black in his hand.

Brand dove behind her, using her as a shield.

She was staring up into stormy gray eyes. "Don't shoot my baby!"

Gunshots. Little bits of concrete falling onto her face.

They were all gone. Except McKade looming over her, his contemptuous, piercing gaze more lustful than Brand's or his men's. When she struggled, McKade brandished a broken beer bottle near her face, slicing his own finger with those razor-sharp edges. A drop of his blood fell onto her cheek. Who could have illusions about such a man?

She wanted Brand, who was elegant and golden, Brand whose family was rich and famous and respectable.

By comparison, McKade was big-boned and rough, his appetites blatantly carnal.

Brand was her Prince Charming…not…

Not going to be a baby.

A tongue of green fire shot out of McKade's mouth.

Then Brand, toppled halo and all, returned. The vision caught fire and turned the most livid shade of green.

She began to scream.

It was deliciously disconcerting to awake in McKade's arms, her lips pleasantly smothered against the villain's warm, wide furry chest, the very same villain who'd caused her nightmare. Brand had made her do awful things in bed. McKade, who had rescued her, had not forced her to earn that money.

Then McKade, his voice tense with the strain, said, "Not going to be a baby. What did you mean? Whose baby?"

"Nobody's," she lied, nestling closer because his warmth was so lovely. The last thing she would tell him about was the baby.

She was pregnant.

The powerful father of her baby, for all his surface charm, didn't want her or their child. He would have killed her. McKade had saved her from Brand and other worse dangers in Mexico. He'd saved her baby. But McKade didn't respect her. A man of his obvious limitations never would. And he certainly wasn't the fatherly type.

Not going to be a baby. Oh, yes, yes. She was going to have her baby.

I saved your cute little ass.

McKade wanted that cute little ass. He'd paid a thousand dollars for it.

And he would get it, pregnant or not, if she didn't get out of town—fast. She couldn't go home. No telling who Brand had at her aunt's house waiting for her to return. Too bad for McKade that her purse, her car and her money were at her aunt's because that meant she needed *his*. If he was as rich as he said he was, he could get more.

McKade's large hand stroked her hair, her back. "It's over. You're safe."

Safe? When the Baineses controlled Laredo? When Brand had said he'd never let her go? When the rogue who'd found her tied up in Mexico, and bought her because he thought her cheap and awful, held her in his arms? When the brain beneath her mussed curls was spinning worriedly with ideas about how to best him?

Safe? With him? If he thought that, then he was even more clueless than she'd thought.

The impossible devil laughed, the pleasant rumble deepening the grooves that bracketed that beautiful, ever so sensual, male mouth.

Safe? She hardly knew him, but the chemistry or whatever it was that was between them was so volatile they'd almost had sex twice. She felt as if she were a delectable mouse waiting for some big cat to pounce. After Brand, she was afraid of sex.

She stared up at McKade, and was aware of harshly carved features, of his animal white smile, of that unruly lock of midnight-black hair that tumbled over his brow. A sensible woman would be terrified to bump into a man like him in a dark alley.

Sensible? Nobody had ever accused Willa of that failing.

Safe? The sooner she outwitted this beguiling devil and got out of his clutches, the better.

"Thirsty," she whispered, shuddering against his chest so he'd go, so she could think, if that's what her churning mental processes could be called.

He left her, splashed water into a glass in the bathroom, but returned too soon, the mattress dipping beneath his weight once more.

He lifted her into a sitting position again, holding her against his heated length while she sipped from the glass. When she'd gulped it all down, he set the glass aside and continued to hold her.

Leave. Leave.

Of course, he didn't. His head was too thick-boned and dense for telepathy to work. Slowly, shyly, she became aware of that heavily muscled, big-boned body against hers, aware of his heat seeping inside her, aware of her nipples hardening against his massive chest. Meltingly pleasant sensations rippled through her.

She sighed blissfully. Then she caught herself.

Aware of her response, he tensed.

It was just the terror of her nightmare that made her so vulnerable. That made him feel so good...so natural. So right. She'd been shy about sex...even with Brand, only letting him because she'd loved him so much. Only playing the games he'd wanted later because she'd wanted to win his love.

Letting a man hold her like this wasn't sex. Still, it was exciting. Her feelings were like those of a seventeen-year-old girl with a first crush. How, after all she'd been through, all he'd put her through, could she feel... It was too soon after Brand.

He saved you.

McKade.

The clever rascal was using that to his own advantage.

"I'm okay," she said, so he would leave.

"Good." His voice was gruff. He almost pushed her away as he shoved himself up from the bed. "No more bad dreams, promise?"

The minute he stood up, his wide muscular shoulders were silhouetted against the light from the window. Suddenly, irrationally, she ached to have him back. "What do you want from me?"

"Sex. A thousand dollars' worth."

"And that's all?"

"Of course."

"Then why didn't you take—"

"All in good time. When you feel better."

"I'm surprised you have any qualms."

"I want to get my money's worth."

"You're vile."

"And you're such an excellent judge of character."

She drew a sharp, little breath. She was stung, but she liked sparring with him. It distracted her from her more serious problems.

"If you're disappointed we didn't..." His suggestive voice was low and hoarse. "If you're feeling lusty...just say the word. I'll be happy to oblige."

"Go back to your chair."

He laughed but obeyed. She clutched her sheets and was secretly bereft and disappointed.

As soon as he was safely ensconced, she said,

"McKade, if you were the last man on earth, I wouldn't want you."

"Then, pretend, the way you pretended when you danced. If you're half as good at sex as you were at stripping, we'll be dynamite together."

"Good night, McKade."

"Good night, Willa."

He snapped out the light and fell silent. Suddenly, the darkness and the walls seemed to close in on her. She was a little girl tied to the mast again. She was a woman tied to that bed in that fetid shack.

He'd come, saved her.

Saved her baby.

No matter how she tried, she couldn't seem to get over that.

"McKade?"

"Change your mind about sex?"

"Is that all you think of?"

"When I've got a thousand bucks of my money on the line and a girl like you in my bed—"

"I'm beginning to think your bark's worse than your bite."

"I've got a helluva bite. I promise you'll love it." His voice was a soft, sensual rumble. "Just say the word and I'll nibble you all over."

"Would you quit!"

When he fell silent, the shadows in the room seemed to darken. When she'd been a little girl, her aunt had told her the witches lived in the closet and they'd get her if she got out of bed.

Willa had thought the witches had yellow eyes and long black fingernails. On a shudder, she closed her eyes. Terrifying darkness enveloped her. Instead of witches she saw Brand. Her eyes snapped open.

Willa got out of bed and scrambled across the floor to McKade's chair. Her hands climbed his jeans, fingernails clawing the denim. Huddling at his feet, she seized his long fingers and held on tightly. His long, brown fingers closed over hers.

He drew a breath. So did she.

"I'm scared of the dark."

"You've been through a lot."

"You don't know the half of it."

"Why don't you tell me?"

So, she told him about her parents, about the accident, about the two days and nights before she was saved.

"I was dehydrated and sunburned, but most of all, ever since, I've been terrified of the dark. Tonight when I was alone in that shack, it was like that storm. I had lost everything...all my illusions. The shack was so dark. I—I could hear things crawling. I—I couldn't have stayed there two days...and two nights...wondering what would happen to me.... I would have gone really mad, died of fear. I know I would have. You came. You saved me."

He stood up. Slowly, he pulled her up with him. He said nothing, he just held her, and never had rougher hands felt more gentle. After a long time, he lifted her into his arms and carried her back to the bed where he tucked her under the crisp sheets.

When he rose to go, she blindly circled his neck with her arms and held on. "Move your chair closer."

His fingers tightened on hers. "Be careful what you ask for." His eyes blazed.

She let him go.

When he'd scooted the wooden legs across the floor and sat down, she fell asleep almost instantly. This time, because she knew he was there to keep her demons and her aunt's witches at bay, her dreams were pleasant.

6

"I'm going to kill me a bastard."

Willa's eyes slitted open. Blearily, she fought to focus on the blaze of pink splashed on the far wall. Through the screen of her dense lashes, she saw that the fake leather chair beside the bed was empty.

McKade. He was gone. He'd left her. But her fuzzy thoughts were brain chatter, delivering no emotional punch. Then she heard more chatter. No, raised voices from the next room!

"You can't tell me what to do, you bastard. You're nothing to me. Nothing."

"Ditto, you histrionic, self-destructive...*punk.*"

"You'd give anything to be me, to be *his* real son...."

"You're wrong." But McKade's voice was soft, and strangely hoarse.

"You don't like being our bastard, do you?"

"If you shot him, you sorry sonofabitch, and talked to the press about me, my name might get in the papers."

"Your precious name? What a laugh."

For an instant, Willa was back in the shack. The redheaded man, no boy, the redheaded boy with the scary eyes was waving his gun and acting crazy. He was here, threatening McKade of all people.

No. She was dreaming.

"You're going home, Little Red," McKade said in that firm, irritating, grimly condescending tone she resented every bit as much as this kid did—at least when Mr. Macho directed it at her. "Home to New Mexico." McKade paused. "You're going to behave and keep your filthy mouth shut."

"Save your high-and-mighty act for someone who doesn't know about your mother—"

You tell him, kid, Willa thought.

McKade must have launched his big body at the brat. Willa heard the rumble of heavy furniture, the crack of bone and sinew and then what sounded like both men rolling and fighting on the floor.

The kid had a gun.

Don't shoot the big lug. Please, don't shoot him.

Was that her or Mrs. Connor, pleading for McKade's life?

"Hold your tongue, you sonofabitch!"

Despite the life-and-death drama in the next room as well as the squabble in her own heart, Willa awoke slowly, the way she liked to, drifting through pink clouds.

"Don't shoot me." The kid's voice this time.

Oh, goody, McKade had the gun. He wasn't going to get all shot to pieces this nice pink morning. Not that she cared.

Then a lamp crashed.

Oh, please don't do murder.

Muffled male curses and scuffling sounds broke through her muzzy consciousness, and she began to fret about McKade again. Oh, dear. Why couldn't they just cool it? Men were so difficult, such attention-getters. And they were making a horrendous mess that some poor woman would have to clean up.

"Bastard."

"You crazy, sonofa…"

She knew that tone. McKade was getting mad. Really mad. A fearsome, yet thrilling vision of a huge powerful street warrior, holding a broken beer bottle, towering over her, ready to do battle for her, rose in her mind's eye.

"What the hell did you think you were doing? A gun? In Mexico?"

Shrill hysterical laughter. The boy's. Then his whining voice. "What do I have to lose?" He sounded desperate.

There was a great clump. They must've hurled each other to the floor again. Bodies rolled. She heard grunts, fists slugging flesh again.

And then silence.

McKade? Was he hurt?

More likely, the boy was dead.

They'd put McKade behind bars.

Curiosity, not concern for McKade, got the best of her. She pulled sheets and blankets around her and rushed into the living room. McKade was sprawled on top of the skinny redhead. The two men's entwined bodies lay beside a toppled chair, a fallen lamp and shards of glittering glass. Not that either of them were cut. McKade, his silver eyes wild with the lust of battle, was stretching a hand toward the gun that lay six inches beyond his reach.

No man in such a mood could be trusted with a gun. Certainly not McKade. Quick as a flash, she stepped on his wrist and reached down and snatched the weapon away.

He yowled. "Give me that!"

She jumped to safety. "Get off him, you big bully." Then she scooted backward toward the bedroom. Not that she stopped her bossy scolding. "You're twice his size! You'll kill him!"

"Give me the gun and get back in the bedroom where you belong."

"And let you blow that poor child's brains out?"

"For the last time! Mind your own business, Willa!"

"You saved me last night from my own stupidity. I'm returning the favor."

McKade lunged. She raced for the bedroom and locked the door behind her. The gun dangled from her fingers and she opened a narrow glass door that led out onto the balcony.

Where to hide this awful instrument of death?

Where? There were four stories down to bushes, dirt and cactus, where it could be buried.

Where? Nowhere!

Besides, if she dropped the gun, it might explode or something. Like men, loaded guns were not to be trusted.

Leaving the glass door open, she ran back inside and nearly tripped over the red dress. McKade had a key in the lock of the adjoining door. Grabbing the horrid heap of silk flounces, she dashed into the bathroom, slammed the door and locked it.

She eyed the gun, scanned the dull, sterile, white-tiled cubicle. Where? Where?

Nowhere.

Somewhere a door slammed open. "Willa!" thundered that most irritating of bullying voices.

She knew that yowl. Knew that fist pounding her bathroom door. The door rattled alarmingly.

"Just a minute, *dear,*" she cooed with wifely, saccharine sweetness.

"Willa!" he muttered. "Quit acting like a fool!"

She stared at the black gun.

Where?

Absolutely nowhere. Still, she had to put the gun somewhere. So in desperation, she opened the toilet tank and dropped it into the water.

Plop. Gurgle. Lots of satisfying bubbles.

Did bullets rust? She scooted the lid back in place, seized the postage-stamp bit of silk and wriggled into it as best she could. As she adjusted the flounces that barely covered her derriere, McKade kept up his furious pounding. When she was dressed, or rather squeezed into the awful playsuit, frilly skirt and all, she stared at herself in the mirror.

Oh, dear, dear, dear, said Mrs. Connor.

Breasts. Legs. All those wild curls. That drowsy look in her hot, sexy eyes. And that telltale blush that betrayed an alarming amount of excitement. Terrible as last night had been, there was nothing like danger and drama to give life a keen edge, or to make a girl who'd been blinded by love see clearly.

Brand had been the biggest mistake of her life. He

hadn't respected her, hadn't seen past her sexy, good looks.

She studied her reflection. *Cheap. Tarty. Come on, honey.*

But cute.

No wonder a man of McKade's low sexual instincts had formed the same opinion Brand had had, that she was a party girl who would put out.

Do not concede a moral inch.

Thank you, Mrs. Connor. McKade had no right to judge her on her appearance. It was most unreasonable. But she would use it. Maybe if she could get his mind on sex, she could outthink him.

Don't get all conceited because you turn him on.

"Thank you, Mrs. Connor," she whispered to the tart in the mirror.

Willa, of course, prided herself on being unreasonable. Most unreasonable. After all, it was a woman's prerogative. If McKade was such a fool not to see the intelligent, vital woman inside the tarty, bimbo getup; if he was such a cad he'd take advantage of a desperate woman he deserved whatever he got.

Her wanton reflection jumped—due to McKade's bellowing and male bluster on the other side of the door. She watched the door rattle, almost relishing his thunder.

How long could the big lug keep that up? Such fierce male energy—it was rather exciting having all that bluster and determination directed at her. She decided to wait and see how long he could rant.

For no reason at all, she wondered what he'd be like in bed. All that energy. Would he attack? Or be gentle? He certainly had a lot of bad-boy passion. She turned him on, too.

Only when McKade stopped slamming his fist against the door, and all got quiet outside, did her curiosity get the better of her.

She fluffed her hair, threw back her head, opened the door, and went into the bedroom in the tight red dress. McKade's eyes blazed, so she wiggled her hips like a burlesque queen, strutting almost…just to get his goat…and to unhook the wires to his brain, too. McKade liked it when she strutted her stuff.

One minute, the men had been glowering at each other by the glass door. Then she sashayed out like a stripper about to start her act and tension charged the three of them like a jolt of blue-hot electricity. Her wanton wiggle was like a match, arcing into a pool of gasoline.

McKade's gaze grew fiercer. A slow smile broke across his disreputable captive's thin face. When the boy ogled her, McKade got so mad he looked like he was about to blow a gasket. Which, oddly enough, greatly pleased Willa.

"Don't even think about her," said McKade. "She's mine."

The kid's smile thinned sardonically. "Really? She doesn't look to me like she belongs to anybody."

The kid, Little Red, with the crazily spiked orange-red hair, was growing on her fast.

"Where's the gun?" McKade demanded.

She notched her nose up defiantly. "I said, you don't have to shout. The last thing you two need is a gun."

"I like her sass," Little Red said.

"Shut up." McKade scowled at Willa. "Is it out here?"

"Do you ever listen?" she demanded.

"No, he does not," said Little Red. "What's a nice girl like you doing shacked up with a rude jerk like him?"

"We're not shacked up," said Willa huffily.

"Good for you," said Little Red.

"Not yet," growled McKade.

"You didn't shoot Brand, did you?" she asked, batting her lashes at the kid, mainly because it had such a powerful effect on McKade. His face had gone as dark as a prune.

Little Red looked sullen...until he caught on she was flirting with him to bedevil McKade.

"I bet you're a good shot," she said to the boy.

McKade swore in an undertone. "He missed, didn't he?"

"The asshole stole my rented car," explained Little Red.

Which meant Brand could and would come after her. Which meant that she had to get out of here fast.

"Sorry to break up this little party," said McKade. "But I'm taking you back to New Mexico, kid."

"Can I come, too?" Willa asked.

The men were too wrapped up in their own war to answer her.

"Nobody, especially not you, is gonna tell me what to do—you—you bastard," the kid whispered.

McKade grabbed the boy by the collar, shook him and then shoved him roughly out the door.

Bastard. Willa made a mental note. That particular word really got to McKade.

They slammed the door in her face. She opened it and rushed outside into the hall after them. "Don't you two dare leave without me."

McKade shot her an insulting grin over his wide shoulder. "So, get that cute polka-dotted fanny of yours in gear, girl. You've yet to earn your keep."

Her keep! The nerve! But she rushed back into the room, grabbed the thousand dollars off the table, came outside, and stuck it between her breasts, while both men watched her little maneuver so appreciatively that the elevator door closed and the elevator went down without them.

"You're really paying her? You're really that hard up?" asked Little Red with lewd interest. He lowered his voice. "How much?"

Willa pulled out the bills and flapped them saucily. "A thousand dollars."

"Would you choose me...if I gave you more?"

"Butt out," growled McKade.

"Sure. I'll go to auction. Go ahead. Make me an offer," Willa snapped sassily, not because she was serious, but because this game might have possibilities, because she felt afraid and chose to mask her fear with an air of bravado. McKade's scowl had gone as black as a prune again. As always, the dramatic held appeal.

The madder McKade got, the slower he would think. And why couldn't she amuse herself? Why shouldn't she distract herself from the very real terrors of last night? After all, she knew she had no intention of sleeping with either of them. So, why not play their silly little male game and pretend she was a slave, up for grabs on an auction block?

"Money, lots of it. And me," said McKade.

"Marriage," said Little Red without missing a beat.

Marriage. One little word. Willa felt breathless. Marriage.

Suddenly, the stakes had changed.

7

"*Marriage,*" *Little Red had said.*

McKade studied her, his gaze alert. "Don't even think about it." His low tone was suddenly brusque, strange. "Marriage? A girl like you..." He laughed, but uneasily.

He can't compete with that offer. He's a little scared she thought, pleased. Too pleased...because he cared.

Because Brand had not cared.

But still...

Marriage. The word reverberated in that tender, dark corner of Willa's heart, that hopeless, unfurnished corner where she'd longed to hang curtains, that forlorn corner she'd been afraid to visit ever since Brand had set her straight about how he intended to handle her accidental pregnancy.

Marriage.

To an unwed mother-to-be, a terrified mother-to-be, the word and all it implied—respectability, a nest to raise her precious child...and it, not it, a human being, her child, he or she, would be so precious.... Ah, respectability...in New Mexico...far, far from Laredo…far, far from Brandon Baines, who had designed a sordid role for her in his life…a role she did not want to play. With a new name, she might be safe in New Mexico.

She saw a darling house. Yellow. Yes. A yellow cottage with white shutters and a picket fence. Vivid bright, *her* yellow. And on that picket fence she would grow sweet peas. She could see those delicate, pastel blossoms aflutter in a cool evening breeze, while she rocked her baby. No. New Mexico was all red rock. Desert and dirt. Like Laredo.

Not like Laredo. Not so hot, hopefully. Far away from Laredo. Far from her aunt, Mrs. Brown, whose scandalous reputation would sully the baby's name… as it had hers. Not that she was ungrateful to her aunt, who'd given her a home, if you could call it that. But Willa wanted to give her darling baby the kind of childhood she'd had before that desperate stormy night that had left her an orphan.

Never would her baby stand on a porch with a shabby suitcase and a door open and a scarlet-haired woman stare at him in wonder and say, "A child? What on earth will a woman like me do with a child?"

Her parents had been reckless. As a result, she'd grown up in an inappropriate environment. Willa was determined to settle down, to provide a loving, respectable home for her baby.

Marriage. Her baby needed a father.

"Tell me more," said Willa, her voice soft now and a little too eager as she considered the thin young man and his outrageous offer.

"This conversation has gone entirely too far," cautioned the know-it-all, ever bossy McKade.

"For you, maybe," Willa said.

Willa was aware of a speculative gleam in the boy's eyes as he watched her now, savoring McKade's growing ire. She said no more, for she deemed it smarter not to.

Willa would wait, see where this bizarre rivalry between this quarrelsome pair went.

Yes, she would learn more about this boy who wasn't really a boy. He was older than she. Was he serious? And if he was, what sort of marriage did he have in mind?

Prison? Could an ex-con who'd come after his lawyer with a gun his first day out possibly make a good father? The fact that Brandon Baines was deserving of punishment swayed her just a tad in favor of the boy.

But a husband? And not just anybody's. *Hers.* Would he expect her to sleep with him? His rangy, birdlike body held no appeal. She could not imagine herself in bed with him while it was all too easy to do so with the well-built, insolent McKade.

Still, marriage wasn't just about sex which was all McKade seemed to want from her. Perhaps...

Willa pondered the puzzle. You could never tell. Life turned by chance, whim and bizarre circumstance. Tragedy had taught her that. Life went along, followed a certain order, seemed not to change and then suddenly all was different—people, place and circumstance.

This offer of marriage was off-the-wall, if an offer it was. If there was anything Willa was really good at, it was change and off-the-wall. Not that she liked changes that worsened her life as last night had, but a

woman with a mind as creative as hers was more open
to chaos and adventure than her more logical sisters.

After all, last night was the second time she'd lost
everything.

She saw her parents floating away on tall black
waves, felt the salt burning her sunburned lips; heard
that final great rending of fiberglass. Then the mast
broke off and was pulling her under.

She heard Brand's voice. *Not going to be a baby.*

There *was* going to be a baby.

She had not lost everything.

No.

There was the baby, and the baby had to come first.

Way to go, Willa, said Mrs. Connor.

Thus, as if the men sensed Willa's profound inner
dilemma, tension mounted between Willa and her two
unlikely suitors as they stepped into the elevator. The
door shut, and she was squeezed too tightly against
McKade as they rode that awful little box to the
ground floor.

"He wasn't serious," grumbled McKade into her
ear, his breath too warm in her hair.

Little Red eyed her squarely, giving her that look
that said he was.

"You're a fool," snorted McKade cynically.

"Are women who prefer marriage to one-night
stands fools?" she retorted. "And what are you? Only
a conceited fool would think such insults would win
a woman. Little Red...that is his name, isn't it? Well,
he had a point when he said you must be hard up to
have to buy a woman. You are. I think...I think...it's
because you're hard and cruel."

She was aware of smoldering depths in those sea-gray eyes...of some terrible emotion just beneath the surface. Strangely, that made her want to push him, want to find out... What? To find out whatever it was he was so determined to keep his own. She wanted to know him.

No, all she wanted was to hurt him as he seemed determined to wound her, to hurt him in his most vulnerable secret place where the real man hid. "I bet you haven't had much luck with women, McKade? With real love? With marriage?"

His eyes narrowed. Even though he looked fierce and angry, she sensed some volatile emotion inside him that was every bit as deep as the heartbreak Brand had caused her.

But she didn't stop. "Who could love a man like you? Sex. No wonder that's all you want. That's all you know. All you understand. All you can ever understand. There's more between men and women than mere sex."

He seized her by the arm, yanked her closer. Together they blocked Little Red's exit from the elevator. "What would you know about it?"

"Nothing. Why, my life's been a picnic." She remembered her parents...Brand's betrayal. What he'd almost done to her. Suddenly the pain in her heart was as profound as the pain in McKade's eyes. And she was as lost and terrified as he was.

"I hate you," she whispered.

"Then be quiet," he roared.

Willa blinked hard. "Who made you my boss?"

But she said nothing more during that tight, confining ride. There was something too dark and terrible about McKade now.

Cruel, she'd called him. Had she not been equally cruel? Like her, there was a bruised, aching place inside him. A place he was determined to keep others, especially someone like her, from seeing. Oh, why had she deliberately gone for his Achilles' heel?

Not that she would ever apologize. She wasn't the least bit sorry. She wasn't. She was glad, very glad she'd hurt him.

Yes, they remained silent. Far too much had been said. Felt.

No. She felt nothing. He was cruel. Unlikable.

I saved your cute ass.

Nor did anybody speak as they trooped out single file to McKade's shiny blue Porsche.

Little Red's proposal charged the air as did her unkind words, charged the blistering morning, and most of all, charged Willa's conflicted heart. Why couldn't she forget McKade's tortured eyes?

McKade's Porsche was an old model, but in mint condition. She told herself McKade probably loved the thing more than he loved people. Which was another strike against him.

To Willa, cars were just cars. They got you places. The back seat of this little status symbol was a narrow bench with no headroom. Such a bench would be most uncomfortable for a tall woman. Not a car for three people.

And look where he'd parked! For a smart dude, McKade could be dumb. Willa couldn't believe he'd carefully parked this prized jewel of his in a secluded place near an alley and a pile of debris. He'd probably done that so nobody would park by him and ding it.

Women who were afraid of the dark had a sixth

sense about the dangers of such spots. Even though
the morning was bright and sunny, the spot still felt
desolate and abandoned, dangerous. Even before she
saw the unshaven creeps in rumpled clothes near their
dusty bedrolls and motorcycles, even before she knew
the three of them were targets, she shivered.

One minute they were in the shadows and McKade
was unlocking his gleaming dark sports car. The next,
Little Red taunted the creeps about their motorcycles.

"What's this? A little gang? Somebody steal your
motel money?"

Bright feral eyes lit up four dark faces. They were
a pack. Like wolves, they attacked.

"Nice car," a guy in black leather who seemed to
smolder said.

"I want the girl," said another who wore a dirty
T-shirt that said Fang.

McKade turned. Little Red sprang into a crouch.
The first man he kicked was McKade. Little Red's foot
thumped like a rabbit's. Once, twice. In McKade's
groin.

"Bull's-eye!" Little Red yelled when McKade bent
double.

"You sonofa—" McKade's voice was strangled.
He had crumpled like a rag doll to the ground as he
grabbed his crotch.

Little Red landed a blow that looked like a karate
chop into Fang's throat and a fist to the back of the
neck of another gang member. They fell to the ground
and lay there in a heap. The other guys in black leather
watched from a cautious distance.

"I learned a dirty trick or two in prison," Little Red
bragged to Willa. Thrashing about helplessly on the

ground, McKade emitted truly horrifying curses of pure agony.

Feeling sorry for him, Willa knelt over him. The sun baked her back. Heat rose up from the black asphalt. She touched McKade's perspiring brow, smoothed back his hair. He continued to writhe on the tarry tarmac. Then she saw Little Red lunge for the keys that had fallen from McKade's open palm.

Whim was Willa's genius. Without thinking, she snatched the keys and McKade's Stetson from under both men's noses. If Little Red was fast, she was faster. Or probably, he was just exhausted from the labors of battle. Then Willa jumped free of them both as lightly as a dancer.

"Sorry," she whispered, when the helpless McKade scowled at her as if she were Judas reincarnated.

"I'm not a whore," she said. "I'm not sorry for what I said in the elevator, either. Not one bit sorry."

When Little Red squatted to jump her, she socked him in the neck. If he thought she was going to let him get the best of her, he was wrong, too. Her baby came first. In a maternal fury, she shoved him on top of McKade. They both yowled as they began to fight each other.

Then she ran and sprang inside the Porsche. She locked the doors and got the big engine roaring. She gunned it. Clouds of black smoke showered the men.

Too bad panic made her forget what little she knew about shifting. She hit all the wrong gears. They made a dreadful grinding noise. There was a bad, oily smell too. McKade was bellowing as his powerful car lurched forward into the pyramid of trash.

Branches and smelly garbage bags rained onto the

hood. More nasty gnashing of gears. More nasty cuss words spewing from McKade.

What a vocabulary he had!

Reverse. Thank God. She'd found it.

The car jerked backward just as Little Red flung himself against the passenger side and banged his fist against the window.

"Take me with you."

How thin and pathetic and scared he looked. Pity welled up in her. Little Red had said something about cancer in the shack. And there was his marriage offer. Did he really have cancer? She understood suffering, dying and being afraid of dying.

McKade was struggling to his feet, shouting more colorful curses, groaning. Stumbling toward them, his foul language grew even more creative. That muscle-bound brute would make hamburger meat of this frail young man.

She threw Little Red's door open.

No sooner had Little Red hopped in and slammed the door than McKade burst at them like a cannonball.

"Back over the bastard."

"I won't commit murder."

Little Red grabbed the wheel. Willa slammed her foot on the brake. The Porsche screeched to a stop.

"Karate won't help you now. If you don't let go of my steering wheel and allow me to drive, I'll wreck this car—deliberately."

Willa spoke softly and very slowly as she did when she was teaching one of her beginning apprentices how to paint shirts. And the twangy slowness of her Texas drawl added a great deal to the tension of the moment.

''I'll let McKade catch us. He's kinda cute...if you go for dark, rugged, and dangerous...which in certain moods I do. Now I know all he wants from me is sex.... But he doesn't have such a tender interest in you. He won't treat you nearly so sweetly as he will a woman as pretty as me, now will he?'' She smiled her most dazzling smile.

''Okay!''

With the fury of a dervish, McKade threw himself at the car, grabbed the roof and held on tight.

''Let go!'' Willa screamed. Of course, he didn't. So, she hit the gas, slammed on the brakes and hit the gas again.

Pedal to the metal. Pedal off the metal. *Voilà.* McKade tumbled backwards.

Tires spun gravel into that darkly handsome face. Too bad. The last she saw of him, he was a haggard, lone figure, his broad shoulders heaving as he coughed in whorls of desert dust. Guiltily she watched him grow smaller until he became a tiny speck. Indeed, she watched the skunk until he disappeared altogether.

Pedal to the metal. The Porsche gathered speed. Ahead, she saw headlights, streetlights and traffic. Lots and lots of NAFTA traffic.

''Pull over,'' said Little Red.

She pressed her foot down harder. The car sped up. To avoid the eighteen wheelers, she careened down a side street she knew. ''You want to get out of Laredo, am I right?''

She waited for him to answer.

He didn't.

''Well, I do. Without me, you're going nowhere fast. Like I told you, all I have to do is smash this car.

Then we're both stuck. We can make bets on which snake finds us first—McKade or Baines. Get my drift?''

His eyes flashed with new respect. ''I'm beginning to like you.''

''I like a reasonable, agreeable man. You're a switch after McKade.''

''We do have a common enemy—him.''

''Them.''

Little Red smiled, studying her. His gaze fell to her bosom. ''That money—''

''McKade's?''

''Do you still have it?''

She patted her bosom, felt the wadded bills. With a smile, she nodded.

''How come you stole his hat?''

''It was a whim. To tick him off, I guess.''

''I like you better and better.''

''That's nice.'' She stared straight ahead. ''After all, you did ask me to marry you.''

Little Red put McKade's black hat on and studied her. ''Good move on my part.''

She pushed down on the accelerator and wondered if he was going to be another of her mistakes, but she smiled anyway, giving him and their situation the benefit of the doubt. If he was a bad idea, she'd figure it out soon enough—and bail.

''You drive fast.''

''Very,'' she agreed. ''I do everything fast. I have lots and lots of bad habits.''

''Such as?''

''I hate housework. So, I'm messy and disorganized. I lose things.''

"You call that bad? I could tell you a thing or two about bad habits."

But he didn't.

They sped north into the desert in silence.

She had McKade's car and his thousand dollars. Not to mention his Stetson.

Not good.

What if he turned her in to the law?

He wouldn't dare. Somehow she knew that.

The big lug would come after her himself.

She smiled, almost thrilling at the thought. Which was ridiculous. She never wanted to see that loathsome individual again. To prove it, she turned the full force of her charm on her passenger.

"Why did you ask me to marry you?" She batted her eyelashes. "Did you mean it?"

"Not now. Look at the fuel gauge. We're running on fumes."

"Uh-oh."

8

Little Red knew an out-of-the-way bed-and-breakfast in San Antonio, a limestone mansion shaded by tall pecan trees. The mansion was in a hilly historic section of the city and had a tin roof and many porches. The landlady had garages for the guests' cars. Perfect—for guests' hot cars.

Inside their sparsely decorated bedroom, Little Red sat on the edge of the red velvet couch and Willa in a Bentwood rocking chair. He'd bought her new clothes, jeans and blouses, a pair of sneakers.

Most women, or the older generation, and definitely Mrs. Brown would have said he had good taste and an eye. The new jeans fit her like a second skin. But Willa preferred loose clothes. She usually shopped in secondhand stores, choosing wild mixes of styles, fabrics, colors and time periods. She would never have chosen white sneakers.

After she'd dressed and screwed her curls back into a messy knot at the nape of her neck, they talked, at first awkwardly and then intimately, becoming closer in half an hour than some people do in years. For weren't they like two strangers thrown together by horrific circumstances? Weren't they like plane crash victims, getting to know one another, revealing their innermost secrets and most heartfelt desires in the aftermath of shared trauma? Didn't such people always exchange confidences that would have taken them years to reveal under more normal circumstances?

She told him of her love of literature and art and adventure, of the way she thought fast when she found herself in trouble.

"Like now...leaving Laredo...leaving my aunt without even telling her.... See, I broke up with this guy because he refused to listen to me. I only came home when I found out about—" She stopped. "Now, well...after tonight...I—I can't stay. I'll call my aunt later. She's used to me making fast decisions and changing my mind on the spur of the moment when I suddenly decide I have to. Not that she approves... But then, most people don't approve of me. I'm too different, you see."

"You're wild," he said, following her outside to the rockers on the porch.

"Look who's talking. You've been to prison. I think we have a lot in common."

Beneath them, sparrows were fighting over a bird feeder. Texas was suffering a drought. Thus, the sprinkling system was on.

"I was framed. Then my daddy hired the worst damned attorney in Texas to defend me. Or the most corrupt."

"Don't tell me—Brand?"

"I don't want to talk about him. "

"That makes two of us."

Little Red's eyes shone. "You! You were something! A girl of action! And high drama! You bent down and acted like you were sorry for McKade. You should've seen that look on his face when you did that. The bastard's soft on you. Then, as fast as lightning, you took his keys!" He paused thoughtfully. "Why did you stop for me?"

She was rocking back and forth. She liked rocking. It made her feel maternal. "I'm not real sure. Partly, because I was scared, too scared to be alone. Partly, because I felt sorry for you. Partly because you asked me to marry you. Mostly, I just did it. Then there's…there's… I'm kind of lazy when it comes to driving. I need you for that, too."

"I don't lose stuff, either. Maybe we could make a pretty good team."

They laughed. Then they discussed every detail of their shared adventures again. And again, for they both thrived on high drama. Finally, they fell silent.

"Marriage." She stopped rocking and breathed the word aloud.

"I had no right to ask you that." But then he added, "You see, I'm dying."

"I couldn't possibly accept such a proposal. That would be taking advantage of you." It was her turn to pause and study him. She blushed, started rocking, faster than before. "I'm pregnant. On the run."

"An unwed mother on the run?" He grinned. "No-the-hell kidding?" He stared at her stomach. "This gets better and better."

"Only you would see it that way."

He put a hand on her chair, stilled it. "Baines knock you up?"

She grimaced, her blush deepening, as she remembered Brand had been equally crude. More than that, she felt afraid. "He's why I can't stay in Laredo. But like I said, I don't want to talk about him."

"If he is the one, you're not the first."

Willa didn't much like being reminded of that. She stared at the sunlight on the sparkling spray of water beneath them. "He told me about the others," she snapped, "told me I was a fool, that *girls like me* are supposed to know how to prevent pregnancies. He wanted us to go on together...as if nothing had happened."

She stopped, remembering the hurt. "*Girls like me.* I—I was a virgin." For some reason she felt compelled to make excuses. "When I was growing up, he was this big football star in high school. I was in the sixth grade when I got a crush on him. I was at the tennis court. He came up to me, touched his nose to mine."

"What? Why?"

"I don't know. I guess he thought I was a cute kid." He said, 'You're Mrs. Brown's niece. You'll be something when you grow up. I can't wait."

"That bastard."

"I thought it was so romantic, him saying he'd wait. I didn't realize he saw me only as a—a sex toy. I fell head over heels. Stayed that way, too. My aunt sent me away to boarding school, to college. I thought he was—was the most handsome boy in the whole world. All that golden hair, that big smile. I wrote him sometimes."

"Once he sent me a postcard. I—I framed it. My aunt was against him from the first. She knows things about all sorts of people.'' She stopped. ''But I was impressed. His family was powerful, respected.''

''So is mine.''

That got her attention.

''Families like that aren't what they're cracked up to be,'' he said almost gently. ''They have secrets. Think of an aristocratic family with pretensions as an iceberg. All pretty and shiny on the surface...with dark, huge ugly secrets trailing underneath them.''

''Well, Brand was my secret hero. When he finally noticed me again last fall, when I came home because my aunt was sick, he said, 'Well, well, Willa. You're all grown-up. I was right. You were worth the wait.' I—I was so thrilled he remembered. I thought it meant something. I let him make love to me the first night.''

''Well, your Adonis is a real asshole.''

''I know,'' she said. Oh, dear, did she know.

''With women. In court, too. You're lucky all he did to you was knock you up and break your heart. He botched my case. Nicest thing I can say is I served five years 'cause of his inept defense. The worst is somebody paid him to shaft me. Maybe, good old Señor Emilio Rodriguez—known in Mexico as *El Fantasma*. Up here, we call him Spook.''

''Spook, huh?''

''I got five years federal time with trash who did things to me in that dirty, rotten cell I can't tell anybody about. Probably what they did is what made me sick.''

''What did they do?''

His eyes, McKade's eyes, in that thin, wasted face, were bleak and dark with some unspeakable shame.

But the look of sympathy she gave him made him concede, ''Maybe some day, I'll tell you.''

She took his hand, squeezed it.

''My rich daddy paid Baines over two-hundred thousand to defend me. For some reason, the brilliant jerk didn't do his homework. He didn't even read the briefs his associates prepared. I don't know if he was paid off by Spook, but I swore that the minute I got loose, I'd kill me a lawyer.''

''Why McKade?''

''He's my bastard brother. Not that we claim him. He sold me down the river to Baines. I halfway think he paid Baines to destroy me.''

''But you're not sure?''

''He's jealous. Poisonous jealous like a snake.''

''I never thought of snakes as being so passionate,'' said Willa, who was afraid of snakes and had thought a good deal about them.

''McKade's a snake, and he hates me. Just like I hate him.''

''Your hatred eats you, not him. I think you should try to be happy just to be a free man—''

''Maybe I would…but I'm dying. That sort of gave me a grudge against the pair I hold responsible.''

''You're not dead yet. But if you are dying, you of all people shouldn't be thinking of murder. You should be trying to save your soul.''

''My soul? You believe in hell then?''

''Of course, just as I believe in heaven. You want to go to heaven, don't you?''

''Heaven? I don't know about heaven, but hell's right here, and I've served my time.''

''You could be wrong, but even if you aren't, you

shouldn't serve another day in hell on this earth. Every single day you have left to be alive is a gift. If you hold grudges and hate people, your grudge will eat at you. You can't give up on life... Not ever.''

He raised his chin in the air. Clearly, he didn't believe her, but that only inspired her all the more. ''Life's like the weather,'' she rushed on passionately. ''You can never be sure of it. That's the miracle, don't you see? It's why, no matter how bad things look, you can't just give up.''

''What do you know about it?'' he demanded grumpily, getting up out of his rocker.

She stood up too, moving swiftly as she always did. ''You'd be surprised what a woman like me knows.''

Then she told him about the accident, about being tied to the mast all night long, about her parents' boat breaking up right before the fisherman found the mast sinking and her drowning in the waves. ''I thought I was going to die when I breathed in all that salt water. My whole life flashed before my eyes. I was unconscious when they pulled me onboard. But you see, I didn't die. Or maybe I did. I am a completely new person since that night.''

''In what way?''

''I don't take things for granted. I don't believe in the future, in worrying about it. Because you can't know what to do till a thing happens.''

In the deepening shade of those tall pecan trees, he was silent for a long time. The water sprinkler shut off.

''We aren't in control,'' she said. ''Someone else is.''

Still, he said nothing.

How could she convince him? "Like tonight. Our meeting. Our being here together. Our talking about this on this porch. Do you think this is an accident? Maybe we found each other for a reason. You asked me to marry you, didn't you?"

"I didn't even realize what I was doing."

"Exactly! You asked me because that Big Someone up there put the idea in your head."

"You think so?"

She stared at him in wonder. "I know so."

"Then you'll marry me?"

It was her turn to choose silence. "She'll tell me what to do," she finally said, looking upward.

Little Red took a big breath and said, "You do make me feel new. You give me hope. Damn it, Willa. I feel better, even knowing I'm dying, than I felt be-fore...before the Feds caught me.... Why?"

"Good. I'm glad you do. Because you can be a new person," she concluded. "This terrible diagnosis could bring out the best in you. Maybe the miracle has begun."

"Do you really believe that? In miracles?"

"Absolutely."

"Almost, almost, you make me believe it." He smiled wanly, the momentary flicker of hope leaving him even sadder than before. "I'm not young, though. Nobody that's been to prison is young. People don't ever forget you're a con."

"Bad things happen to everybody. You must forget all the bad things. Think of those events and mistakes as words on a blackboard. Just erase them. It's where you go from here that counts. I'm going to forget Brandon Baines if it's the last thing I do!"

Little Red was studying her again. His gray eyes reminded her so of McKade's. Yet this man, prison convict that he was, didn't judge her the way McKade did. No, he respected her as McKade had not. He listened to her. As McKade had not.

"The past is like chalk dust," she said.

"In decent clothes, why even in those jeans, you look classy," he said. "Real classy. I'd like to have a wife who looked classy."

She didn't have the heart to tell him she wasn't known for the classy way she dressed. In fact, most people thought her style a little weird. What did what she wore matter?

He had McKade's eyes. Only there were shadows under this young man's and a terror that hadn't lurked in McKade's. Yet, his uncanny, if slim resemblance to that oversexed tyrant, whom she detested, made her like this man more.

"This is going to sound crazy, wild, I mean really crazy, girl."

He had no way of knowing that that was just the kind of proposition that would most appeal to Willa.

"Shoot."

"I meant what I said about marriage."

"Oh?"

"But I really mean it now. Will you marry me?"

"You make up your mind in a hurry."

"Maybe because I don't have a lot of time."

"Neither do I. Like I told you, I'm pregnant."

"I need a nurse. A pretty sweet face at the end. A soft, kindly voice to soothe me. You need a home for your baby."

"A marriage of convenience?"

"A marriage that would suit the two of us. It won't be easy. My daddy's the biggest asshole in all of New Mexico. But he's rich and powerful. So rich he thinks he's this big god or something. He makes me feel like I'm nothing. Then there are the sisters. I've got the three most difficult sisters in the universe. They're jealous of me, but they spoil me rotten, too. Especially Hesper."

Sisters. A family. Willa longed for sisters and a family. Babies needed families, respectable families.

"My sisters are prissy and proper and filled with their own narrow-minded self-importance. They stifle every bit of life out of you. We live on a huge ranch in northern New Mexico. Talk about desolation. There's nothing but rattlers and mountains and cacti."

"The ranch sounds wonderful. It all sounds wonderful. Except for the rattlers. I'm sure your daddy and your sisters can't be as terrible as you describe."

"Maybe not. But I can't stand to spend my last days with all of them hovering and fretting over me. Willa, you're easy to look at. You're the nicest person I've maybe ever been around. You give me hope."

He got down on bended knee and took her hand in his. Those sea-gray eyes, McKade's eyes without the devilish dark lights, implored her from his thin face. Maybe he saw her more clearly than McKade because he was dying.

"Marry me," he begged.

She didn't answer. There was a lump in her throat and tears in her eyes that told him her answer.

"I can't last much more than six months."

"Don't say that," she breathed, dabbing at her

cheeks. She placed her damp fingers in his. "I want to be with you," she said.

"I'm impotent," he confessed.

"That doesn't matter."

"You're not me."

They both laughed nervously, and she knew she could never confess how relieved she felt.

"I'll leave you everything I've got. I'll work on Daddy to do well by you, too. I can take care of you, Willa. Or at least my family can. I can take care of the baby."

He had sisters. A real family. "My parents have been dead so long," she confessed wistfully. "I—I was so lonely growing up. Sometimes I feel like I've been alone forever."

"Oh, so do I."

They'd each suffered. That drew them.

"You will have to avoid Hesper. She's the oldest. But our baby will fill the house with laughter. God, how our house needs laughter."

Our baby. His saying that made their life together come alive. Almost she believed, she would have a respectable home.

Willa hadn't told him about her aunt, the notorious Mrs. Brown. She had to tell him.

No. Later, she would confess. Not now. She didn't want to spoil the mood. Maybe deep down, she already knew, she would never tell him.

"Let's go buy a ring," he said.

That evening they went downtown, visited the Alamo. As they walked along the River Walk, he began to plan their wedding.

"What do you say we take a detour by way of Vegas for a few days? You've got McKade's thousand dollars. We could get married in one of those little drive-through chapels. We'll honeymoon there.''

The River Walk was alive with tourists. Bars and restaurants overflowed. After dinner, they walked along the river in the direction of McKade's Porsche. Barges moved over the brown glistening water. Above them, sirens sounded on the downtown streets. But the moon was bright and full. Willa noticed the moon, wondered where McKade was, what he was doing.

''I can't believe we're really going to do this. We're strangers,'' she said, to distract herself.

''It's a long way to Vegas. We'll get acquainted on the road.''

''Yes.'' They would. She would forget all about Brand. All about McKade, too.

Suddenly the preposterous scheme sounded ever so logical. It was the only solution. It solved everything.

''It sounds too good to be true.''

Under a bridge, near the stairs that led up to their car, she began to fumble in her purse for the car keys. Little Red stopped walking and began to laugh.

''I went to Laredo to kill me a lawyer, a drug lord and a bastard brother. And look what I got—a wife. The prettiest wife anybody ever married. How's that for a crazy stunt? And I'm known for crazy stunts.''

''So am I,'' she said absently, fingertips searching hidden pockets in her purse.

''So we have that in common.''

''That and our common enemy,'' she said. *''Him.''*

''Don't forget Baines.''

Her fingertips touched something sharp. ''Ouch!''

''Them.'' They said it together. Then they laughed.

She stared into Little Red's sea-gray eyes. Somehow she knew better than to tell him how nice his eyes were and how much they reminded her of McKade's.

They began to climb the stairs. What would McKade do when he found out they'd run off in his car and married each other?

At the top of the stairs, she pulled her hand out of her purse and stopped.

"Little Red, I have a confession."

"What?"

"The car keys. They're not in my purse."

He smiled gently, fondly. Then he patted his pocket and made the keys jingle.

"Where?"

"You left them on the table back at the restaurant."

He pulled out a set of keys and rattled them noisily in front of her nose. "See what I told you—we're perfect for each other."

Mrs. Willa Longworth.

As a girl she carved *Mrs. Brandon Baines* into her school desk.

Mrs. Willa Longworth. The name sounded so respectable.

When she smiled her fingertips fluttered against her lips.

He took her hand, kissed each finger.

"You know something?" he began softly.

"What?"

"I'm beginning to believe in miracles, too."

9

McKade paced his penthouse offices restlessly. His businesses were booming. He had meetings scheduled all over the world. He was in the middle of a takeover. The government was still determined to sue.

He needed to focus on his IPO.

But he was a mess. He was coming apart at the seams of his custom-made, exquisitely tailored suit that fit his sleek muscular bulk to a tee.

On Monday when he'd canceled his trip to Hong Kong, he'd started to worry. When he canceled his trip to Moscow, too, sending instead his next-in-command, he'd known he was in real trouble. When he canceled all his appointments with his attorneys, he'd been sure he was sinking fast.

He was a man in a fever. A man obsessed. Every day, it got worse.

Where was she? Baines had called and asked the same question. He'd blown Baines off and pretended not to care. But Baines's interest had bothered Luke. Made him jealous.

Why the hell was he so obsessed by that yellow-haired, Porsche stealing, betraying witch? Why couldn't he forget that sexy, sassy, brat woman-child who'd run off with his brother...and his favorite black Stetson?

Where were they? What were they doing?

Why hadn't he sicced the cops on them? Sicced Baines on them?

Because he had first dibs on that delectable brat himself.

If she'd slept with Little Red, he'd kill her.

Right after he made a eunuch out of his brother.

His mood got hotter when he heard Kate's brisk high heels, tap, tap, tap, tapping toward him. When he refused to acknowledge her, a dozen fast-food napkins with scribbled names of important CEOs and vital appointments fluttered onto his gleaming mahogany desk right in front of Marcie's picture. Out of the corner of his eye, he caught Marcie's smile.

He clenched his fist. Pounded his desk so hard he snapped his favorite pen in two.

Kate picked up the spring from his ballpoint pen and tossed it airily toward his garbage can.

"You missed," he said.

"It's a woman," said Kate, smiling from ear to ear. "You've finally fallen for somebody."

"What the hell did you just do to my desk?"

"You look like you hit the sidewalk like a ton of bricks dropped from about a hundred stories. Who is the lucky lady?"

"Show a little respect. Marcie just died, remember?"

Kate lifted Marcie's picture. "Marcie never got within a mile of that iceberg you've got for a heart.

This girl hit a bull's-eye. Cupid's arrow, do you think?''

"Damn!" He seized Marcie's picture from her. Then he picked up a napkin with a dozen scribbled appointments. "Burger-Chicken," he growled in disgust. "You're going to get fat eating there."

"No! I'm not! I've got the metabolism of a shrew. Did you know shrews eat three times their weight every single day—"

"Do they keep the messiest nests in the universe, too?"

"I didn't get that far into the shrew article."

"How many calendars and notepads do I need to buy you, to get you to behave like a proper secretary?" he yelled.

He caught himself. He never yelled. Never tried to intimidate an uppity employee, even his impossible Kate. That was one of his rules.

"Oh, I have plenty of notebooks already," she said sweetly, pearly whites still ear to ear. Her voice took on that keen, sharp, dangerous edge that meant she was getting down to business. "What's *she* like? Not so malleable as poor sweet Marcie, I bet."

"Why the devil don't you use those notebooks?"

"Where'd you meet her?"

"I'm the boss. I asked you a question. You're supposed to act like a professional."

"I will use those notebooks…someday…when I run out of napkins or scrap paper. And you know why I don't. I've told you umpteen times, every time you get into this unreasonable lecture. I hate to waste paper. The girl at Burger-Chicken stuffed all these napkins into my carryout last week." Her brow knitted.

"All those poor trees… Do you know how many trees are being chopped down this very minute? On beautiful tropical islands?"

"I don't. And I don't give a damn."

"What's *she* like? Who is she?" persisted Kate, zooming from her environmental concerns to that passionate interest of hers, his love life, or rather the lack of it. According to Kate, people needed a lover, a kid or a cat. She'd been upset, to no end, when he'd told her Sheila had kept Mr. Tom.

"You're nosier than hell. One of these days I'm really going to fire you."

"Oh, please. You know you wouldn't survive without me," she mocked. Then in a big-sisterly voice she said, "Oh, okay. Go right ahead. I can get a job anywhere. Any time. And find a boss twice as nice as you."

He glared at her.

Her ear-to-ear grin was jaunty.

She'd be snapped up in a second. That's why he paid her more than most CEOs earned. That's why she could afford her bridge-playing, lazy, extravagant hubby.

She damn near ran every single one of his companies. Luke would fall apart without her.

She was a genius. A mother of six, she thrived on chaos. She could do ten things at once. She never ever forgot anything important.

And she was intuitive as hell.

Too damn intuitive and too damn nosy when it came to his love life.

"When you do fire me," Kate said with annoying enthusiasm, "I'm going to work for a woman. Someone who doesn't get all cranky when asked a simple question. Someone who understands all about those trees.''

''Chop-chop,'' he threatened.

She stuck out her tongue. ''You'd have to hire ten people to replace me.''

''At least stack the napkins,'' he said, knuckling under. ''It wouldn't hurt you to show a modicum of respect.''

She popped a wad of gum into her mouth and considered that last statement.

The phone rang.

She grabbed it. ''Stack them yourself,'' she whispered with another ear-to-ear grin. ''It's Albertson from COMCOM. I've been on his case for a week. This is vital. Besides, if I spoil you, I'd have to keep spoiling you. I don't want to ruin you for *her*.''

Like a whirlwind, she grabbed a napkin, along with his gold pen from his designer desk set, and raced to her own desk where she began to give Albertson what for.

Luke almost pitied the man, his rival. Almost.

Luke searched for a pen, but Kate must've stolen them all. He dug in a drawer and grabbed a pencil. Then he pretended to go back to work.

But he was too restless to sit still. He got up, sharpened the pencil. Then he sat back down. Instantly, he was up again, pouring himself a cup of coffee.

The stuff was delicious. Steaming hot.

Kate made the best damn coffee in the universe. He was so mad he swallowed too fast.

''Ouch.''

The stuff scalded his lips, his mouth, his throat.

Strangling, he threw the rest of the coffee in the sink and stuck his mouth under the faucet.

He stood up, his shirt and tie thoroughly drenched.

He remembered his meeting at ten.

Damn. This was *her* fault.

Since Laredo, since *her*, he hadn't been able to get anything right.

Where was the golden-haired witch? And how was she amusing herself with Little Red?

For ten days these questions had drummed in McKade's blood. For ten days the men he'd hired to find her had come up with no answers. McKade was gobbling antacids as if they were sweets and he was a candy addict.

The phone rang. Kate buzzed him.

"It's Will Sanders calling from Taos."

"Willa de Mello is honeymooning in Vegas," Sanders said as soon as Kate got off the phone.

"Vegas? She got married?" Since Kate was watching, Luke fought to shrug indifferently. He made his voice harsh and cold. But Kate's eyes tracked him. "Just a minute," he said.

He got up and went outside to Kate's desk. "Something's come up. I'm going to miss my ten o'clock meeting. You go."

Kate didn't argue. She loved stepping into his shoes, into the seat of real power.

When Sanders finished his tale, Luke was in a complete rage. His hand shook as he poured himself another cup of coffee. The part about her aunt, Mrs. Brown, was interesting. But... But what gripped him, what shredded him was not her scandalous past but what she'd done since he'd seen her.

Vegas—where else would a gold-digging whore with a Porsche and a thousand dollars and a rich sap, fool enough to marry her, go? Lucky for her Little Red had gotten sick and collapsed as soon as he had.

So sick, he'd had his stomach cut out in Vegas. The doctors gave the kid six months, max.

Six months...with her.

Six months in her bed. The mere thought was enough to make every muscle in Luke's taut body tighten, to turn his face to cruel black stone.

He didn't care. He didn't.

He smashed his cup into the sink.

"Whoa there, cowpoke," teased Kate from the doorway. "She must really be something."

"Aren't you late—for that meeting?" he demanded through gritted teeth.

"I was just returning your gold pen."

Dressed elegantly in an English custom-made suit, McKade arrived at the Vegas hospital at 2:00 a.m. He parked his rented car, a dark Buick, beside his own blue Porsche. With grim indifference he noted his car, his blue baby, was caked with desert dust. There were several new dings on his doors and a dent in his fender.

She'd married him.

They were on their honeymoon.

What had the imaginative minx done to thrill Little Red? Had she stripped, hummed? Tied herself to the bedposts and squirmed? What costumes had she chosen to titillate her new bridegroom? She'd better not be wearing a diminutive little number in polka dots tonight. He'd kill her.

No doubt the little gold digger was thrilled her rich groom was dying so soon, thrilled at the prospect of widowhood and wealth.

McKade's livid black gaze jerked up from the dented fender, focusing with laserlike precision on the blaze of lights above the ER entrance. He thought of Marcie, the long hours he'd spent by her hospital bed.

Always before, Luke had associated Vegas with glitter, gambling and women—with fun and flamboyant spectacle—not with cancer. Not with hospitals. Not with his only brother dying.

Little Red was no brother.

But he was.

McKade's mood improved slightly when he stepped inside and saw the nurses and techs at work in their little cubicles at their monitors and decided that at least this hospital was state-of-the-art. Maybe…maybe something could be done for Little Red.

Marcie had died despite the best medical care, despite everything he'd tried to do to save her.

Luke didn't care a fig about the punk. The kid was a con, a con who'd come after him with a gun, kicked him in the groin, and left him to a bad bunch of bikers. He'd been spoiled rotten since birth, and wasn't likely to improve.

He was only twenty-three.

Two floors higher, the smells of antiseptic were thick and overpowering. The long hours he'd spent beside Marcie hit him full force. Maybe he was too late.

He quickened his pace. McKade's open palms rammed doors that said No Admittance and left them swinging behind him. Then he strode down the glistening tiled hallway of the intensive care unit, peering quickly into every room like a doctor in a hurry.

The staff bought his act. Not a single person screamed, "Stop. You can't go in there."

Oh, they looked up, but when he scowled as arrogantly as any doctor, they quickly averted their eyes. Doctors were tyrants. The staff, even the R.N.s, knew better to cross that impossible breed.

Luke figured a man in a three-piece suit with an air of authority could go anywhere, anytime, in any hospital—so long as he acted like he knew where he was going and didn't ask questions.

Luke gazed into the last room at the end of the long hall. They were all there—the Longworth bunch that wouldn't own him, all of them jammed into one tiny room—Little Red, his sisters, *his* father. Not that he claimed kin to them, either. Then there was Willa. *Willa.* She seemed to fit in with that blue-blooded bunch as he never had.

They looked lost and sad, bound by grief—five hushed, slumped figures grouped around that inert, white-sheeted form with spiked red hair on the bed. The white lump, fed by dozens of tubes, hardly seemed human. Little Red's face was bluish, or maybe it was just the blue lights flickering on the monitors that gave him that sickly hue.

Willa. Her golden curls were caught at her nape by a black ribbon. Her brilliant blue eyes were moist with tears as she studied Little Red and the monitors. What was it about her? It was as if he had some sixth sense when he got near her. He absorbed her, connected to her. She looked up, saw him, and knew him in that first soul-jolting second as thoroughly as he knew her.

Those startlingly blue eyes burned him, branded him hers. Then as demurely as any well-bred lady, even Marcie, the brat shyly averted her gaze. In that brief moment there'd been overpowering emotion scrawled across her exquisite, tear-streaked face—joy, desire, regret. He'd sensed her wild, keen pleasure to find him again, to know he was alive, to know he'd come, *to know he was hers.*

Hers? His mind railed.

What a joke.

She was married to Little Red.

He hated her.

He barged inside anyway.

10

One moment Willa was weeping quietly and praying for a miracle as she watched Little Red's thin chest heave in and out, praying as she listened to tubes gurgle. She, who never worried, was worrying, worrying. Then suddenly, when she was done with her prayer, every nerve in her being sparked.

Willa hadn't heard or seen Luke McKade at the window of Little Red's hospital room. Just the same, she'd known he was there. Why then was she so stunned to look up and see his dark features, sharpened by anger, his silver eyes alive with demonic desire and jealousy?

His fierceness mesmerized her. She couldn't look at him, couldn't let herself realize how much she'd missed him, couldn't let her new in-laws, who were suspicious enough of her already, see what was surely written on her face as plain as day for anybody with a whit of sense to see. And Hesper had way more than a whit.

Dear Lord, help me.

It was almost painful to look away from that gorgeous male face and watch Little Red's labored breathing again.

Her husband was fighting for every breath. A minute ago she'd been so proud of him. Now she felt distracted and keenly on edge.

"Don't give up," she whispered, patting Little Red's hand. "Don't you dare give up."

"What's he doing here?" demanded Hesper, her sharp stare drilling Willa.

Only then did Willa glance from Little Red's ashen face to meet those turbulent gray eyes of McKade's once more. Oh, why did those gorgeous eyes of his have to be the exact color of the raging seas that had almost drowned her? For a single second, her gaze clung to that stony, handsome face. Odd, how this man, fiendish temper and all, made her feel soft and female, made her feel wanted in the most visceral and wonderful sense, made her feel she'd come home.

Ever since the boating accident, she'd felt she had nowhere to go, no one to turn to, no one who cared if she came or went. Baines had never seen her for who she really was. Luke McKade cared in every cell of his being. She'd thought about him every day they'd been apart.

Her fingers curled into her palms. She was married to Little Red now, but she felt... Oh, how could she feel this way? She felt...she felt she belonged to McKade. As she'd never belonged to Baines, who she'd slept with; as she could never belong to Little Red, who she'd married.

Her nails dug deeper, made little red moons in her palms. She knew such pleasure, such guilty, secret, unbearable pleasure at the sight of him.

"Oh, God," she whispered as her marriage took on

a disturbing, triangular dimension. McKade had only to look at her, to see deeply inside her, to see secrets and longings she hadn't even known were there until they blossomed for him, secrets and urges that could destroy her new precarious life if she wasn't careful.

Ten days—how she'd missed him.

Ten nights—how she'd dreamed of him—longed for him! Oh, how most shamefully had she dreamed! Always, she was tied to bedposts. Then he was there, to set her free.

"Bad enough to have a new wife on our hands. Now him," Hesper said as McKade shut the door of the hospital room behind him. "Do you two know each other?"

Without answering, without a glance toward Willa, McKade ignored the thick tension and went to Little Red's bed.

"You have no right," Big Red began, "to come here at a time like this."

Willa swallowed as if her throat were constricted.

"He tried to kill me. He stole my car. And this woman, his bride, was the ringleader," said McKade. "She's a thief and a liar...and worse. I could press charges."

Hesper was all ears. "I knew it."

"He's your brother," Willa said, defending Little Red before McKade could say more. "He had to get home."

Hesper's face was very dark now, but McKade was looking at Willa. So, Willa really couldn't think much about the others.

"He's never claimed me before," said McKade. "Maybe I will call the cops."

"Good idea. Get out, or I'll call security," said Big Red.

Little Red stirred, mumbling something incoherent.

Hesper rushed to his side, adjusted a pillow anxiously, hovered in that smothering way that annoyed Little Red so much.

"What did you say, dear? Can I do anything?"

"McKade," came a hoarse little whisper from the lump of white.

"Don't try to talk," Hesper ordered, patting his spiked tresses with her bony fingers. "Especially not to him."

"McKade." Little Red's whisper shuddered louder.

"I can't believe he wants you," spat Hesper, her disappointment acute.

McKade froze. Then his manner gentled as he slowly knelt.

Little Red's eyelids flickered, revealing gray slits of dim light. He was breathing harder. "McKade..." Willa saw her husband smile wanly at the bigger, healthier man. "Don't count on my dying anytime soon. Tell that to your pal, Baines, too."

"You're gonna be fine. Just fine," said McKade, his deep voice strangely soothing.

"Not dying," Little Red breathed defiantly. "Not dying. 'Cause I've got something to live for. 'Cause I've got her. She married me, didn't she? Not you! You still want her, don't you?" He beckoned McKade even closer. "You want to know something else? I've got some really good news." He paused, gasped. It cost him his last ounce of strength to choke out his next breath. "You're going to be an uncle."

McKade's eyes widened in surprise, but that was the only reaction in his face as he turned to stare at

Willa. "So, you're pregnant are you? Why does that surprise me? Who's the lucky father...or don't you know?"

Thunderstruck, Willa went uncharacteristically still.

"Me," lied Little Red. "Dad, you'll be interested in this. Willa's going to have a baby. My baby. "

McKade leaned toward his brother and whispered so low only Willa heard. "I feel sorry for you, kid. You married a whore." Little Red started wheezing and McKade recovered himself. "Congratulations, Mrs. Longworth." His voice was oddly calm, soft and resonant, a little too pleasant to her ear. To anyone else he might have sounded gentlemanly. To her he was insulting and insolent. His dark, mocking eyes stole from her red face, to her breasts, to her belly. "What a splendid accomplishment for a new bride." He paused. "And how many days have you two been married?"

"Get out," she said. "Just get out."

She was crimson with shame. Her breath came as rapidly as Little Red's. She wanted to strangle him, but she couldn't tear her gaze from his swarthy piratical face no matter how hard she tried. It was as if he willed her to gaze into his sea-gray eyes, willed her to lose herself in their turbulence.

Again, she was a little girl drowning in a wild gray sea with no one to save her. But as she struggled not to sink, she saw he was even angrier and more hurt than she was. He had saved her baby. Why couldn't she forget that?

Hesper and her sisters were whispering among themselves. Her husband was struggling to breathe. But Willa was aware only of the tall, dark, infuriating man and his rage over her pregnancy and marriage to his brother. His *legitimate* brother.

For long furious seconds, their eyes clung with the terrible patience of lovers who can't be together.

She didn't feel this way. She didn't. Not about him.

Then security arrived—two bulky men dressed in uniforms.

"Throw the bastard out," ordered Big Red. "He's not one of us. Not part of this family."

"Thank God," Willa said.

At the word *bastard,* McKade's black head jerked backward as if he'd been punched. Then he looked from Willa to Little Red, to the tangle of white linen and tubing.

"Why didn't you tell me you were pregnant?" A muscle in McKade's hard jawline flexed.

Willa felt the wasteland of pain in his silver eyes and shivered. "Would it have mattered?"

He stared at her. And she suddenly knew it would have.

"You don't have to throw me out," he said. Then after what seemed a long while to Willa because his eyes clung to her face, he turned toward the others. "I'll go."

The sound of his hollow footsteps retreating down that long hall echoed in Willa's mind for several minutes after he was gone.

She had to stop thinking of Luke McKade, stop dreaming of him and stop believing he might truly care. He was horrid, cold, unfeeling. She had a sick husband to worry about. A new family to win.

A new life to live.

And there was the baby.

McKade had insulted her. He could mean nothing to her.

Luke didn't leave the hospital. Instead, he talked to Little Red's doctors.

"Your brother? I'm so sorry. Only a miracle can save him."

So, McKade got on the phone to Houston and consulted with the best doctors in the world. Little Red's records were faxed, his X-rays sent. Luke ordered a plane sent to have Little Red flown to M.D. Anderson so he could be entered into an experimental program.

"If his insurance won't pay, I'll pay," Luke said. "Only don't tell them, the Longworths or his wife, that I had anything to do with this. Money is no object. All that matters is saving his life."

"There are no guarantees."

"There never are. Do what you can."

After hours of such phone calls and tiring conversations with doctors and their medical staff, Luke hung out in the basement near the cafeteria, watching Willa with the others as they dined. He saw how the Longworths talked to each other and not to her. Saw how she smiled at them, winningly. How she tried to please. Saw how they hated those sweet smiles that made his own hard heart race with needs he didn't want to have.

Even so, they endured her, as they would not suffer him. Finally, he caught her alone. She was thinner, paler. Was it morning sickness? She was pregnant, like Marcie. And like Marcie she hadn't told him in time for it to make a difference. He noticed that she hadn't touched her tray of food.

Her golden hair was drawn back from her delicately

boned face. She wore a black suit that accentuated her narrow waist and large breasts. His gaze climbed that row of gold buttons that went up her delectable middle that was still narrow. He imagined her naked, smiling, cupping her breasts, offering them to him.

The suit made her look sleek and classy—like she was a true Longworth—and as snotty as the rest of that bunch that disowned him. Would they teach her to despise him even more than she did?

He moved soundlessly toward her, and when he got closer he saw the circles under her eyes. She looked sad and exhausted, both mentally and physically. Her movements were slower, heavier. Vegas was a drive. She'd been on her honeymoon. Long nights. Lots of sex. Maybe that's why she wasn't so light and quick.

Rage.

The sad act had to be a lie. She couldn't care about Little Red. But he could believe she was exhausted. She was pregnant, wasn't she?

By whom? Who the hell was the father? Baines? He felt green with jealousy.

She didn't look up until he loomed over her, till his shadow darkened her pale face.

"Can I sit down—*Mrs.* Longworth?"

Her dazed eyes settled on him. Even though he'd called her by name, it took her a moment to recognize him.

She *was* tired.

Well, so the hell was he.

"I—I was just leaving," she whispered, pushing her chair back.

He seized her wrist, held her down.

"This won't take long."

"I really don't think we have anything to say to each other."

"Wrong again."

"The Longworths warned me about you," she said.

"I'm sure...especially Hesper." He spat the name viciously. "I could tell you a story or two about her. But you didn't need to be warned about me. You know me far better than they do."

"I'm married to—to your brother now."

"Which makes you my sister-in-law. Tell me, does that make our feelings for each other incestuous?"

"I don't have...feelings for you."

"Well, I have this thing for blondes—especially blondes I meet tied to bedposts by their black nylon hose. Especially natural blondes."

She gasped. "Would you quit?"

His hard gaze stripped her. "Only after I get what I paid a thousand dollars for."

"That was a—a joke."

"Not to me. I can't forget how you looked when you took off that robe. You owe me a romp in the hay, *Mrs.* Longworth."

"I'm a married woman now."

"Not for long."

"That's a cruel, hard thing to say."

"It's what you want, too."

"Oh! If—if you think I'd sleep with you or any man when I'm married, you are wrong!"

"We'll see. You're blushing," he whispered. Then he grabbed her and kissed her, hard on the lips, blood pumping fury and desire through him in a lava-hot rush.

She kept still. So still. Not by so much as the flicker of an eyelash did she respond. And yet he felt and connected to the passion inside her she fought so hard to conceal.

"You owe me. You have to pay me back," he said.

"Soon. Give me your address. I'll mail— I—I just don't have the cash on me right now."

"I don't want money, you little fool. I want—I want—" Her lips were so red and moist. "Damn you for making me feel..."

He kissed her again. Harder than before.

Once more she froze.

When he was done, she said tightly, "Is that all?"

"I want—"

"You're not going to get what you want. I'm married to another man."

"To a dying man."

"To your brother."

He stared at her. "Like I said—not for long."

"Don't count him out. Don't you dare count him out. Not yet." She paused. "You're—you're like a vulture. You want him to die, don't you?"

"Have you screwed him?"

She drew back her hand, but let it fall without striking him. He saw that her eyes were as lost and dark as his own soul. "How dare you?" she whispered. "How dare you!"

"Or is he impotent? Have you already had somebody else?"

She bit her lips, and looked so stricken, he knew she hadn't.

"You're so cold, so heartless."

He'd hurt her, and her pain affected him more than he wanted it to. Still, he smiled his coldest, cruelest smile. "A girl like you—"

"A girl like me?" she repeated.

"You're going to get horny married to a dying man." He pulled out a business card and dropped it into her hand. "My address and phone number. Cell phone and pager, too. Don't send money. Call me when you get the urge."

She jerked her hand back. His card fluttered to the ground. Then she closed her eyes. "I'm glad we had this conversation," she whispered in a dull, lost voice. "You see—I was finding it very difficult to forget you."

He saw tears beading her thick, closed lashes. A deep pain stabbed his chest.

He swallowed. Still, he forced himself to reach down and pick up his card. With an air of chilly indifference he stuffed it in a side pocket of her purse. "Like I said, call me...when you get the urge. I'll be waiting."

She waited for him to leave, but he didn't.

"By the way," he whispered, "where's my hat?"

"In your car." Her voice was choked.

"And where the hell are my car keys?"

"I'm k-kinda careless with keys," she whispered.

She got up slowly and began to fumble blindly for them in her purse. As she searched, she picked up her unfinished tray of food. When she found the keys, she flung her trash and his keys into a huge garbage receptacle near her table.

"Dig, McKade!"

She shot him an outrageous smile and ran blindly.

Book Two

*"The trouble with most girls is
they don't put nearly enough
emphasis on whim."*

11

Taos, New Mexico
Four years later

Luke McKade had caught her with her pants down too many times to count. If he discovered her on the cliff tonight, she was done for. So was her young son, Sam.

Desperate moments. Wild impulses. Reckless deeds.

Four years married to a dying husband hadn't changed Willa nearly as much as it should have. Or, maybe it had. She felt near bursting inside—for adventure. For life.

Rash actions were still Willa's special forte. She wasn't nearly so different from the scared woman who'd offered herself to the highest bidder that terrible night in Laredo as she wished she was. Not so different from the woman who'd recklessly married a dying man with a fortune.

Tonight, when any other woman would have known all was lost—she'd taken the money.

So…she was a thief now.

Oh, well…

Willa still believed in beauty, in prayer, in spirits, in gypsy fortune tellers, in gold at the end of rainbows, in signs from above, in wishes that come true, in love at first sight, in witches that ride fireballs, in all sorts of wondrous, New Age concepts. She was still scared of the dark, too.

Despite several regrettable experiences with that dangerous, dashing breed of men Willa fell for, despite a marriage that hadn't been a real marriage in most people's sense of the word, she still believed in true love. But until the plane crashed just north of her ranch house outside Taos during the storm earlier tonight, on this same night she was being driven from her home, until she'd found the ten briefcases stuffed with fifty-dollar bills inside its wreckage, she'd never received such dramatic proof that her beliefs held merit.

There was a god. And *She* loved Willa.

Or was the loot devil-sent—to tempt her? whispered Mrs. Connor.

No matter.

The sisters couldn't drive her and Sam away now. Even if Sam wasn't a real Longworth.

Neither could that nasty, foul-mouthed Luke Mc-Kade who knew about her past and enjoyed threatening to destroy her.

The suitcases were heavy as lead. There was probably a million dollars in them.

So much money. And it was all hers.

Not yet.

Not until she hid these last two briefcases.

Move, girl.

A strange fear paralyzed her. The last two briefcases

seemed heavier, the cliff higher. Maybe it was her guilty conscience weighing her down.

She thought of the twisted fuselage. There hadn't been any bodies. That meant the pilot and his passengers were still alive. What if *they* came back? Tried to take it from her?

If she kept the money, she and Sam could stay. She could tear up Hesper's check, act high and mighty like a real lady and announce primly, "You can't buy me!" She would send that oversexed McKade packing, too.

One thing she'd learned. She had to stand on her own two feet. Nobody, no man, was coming to her rescue.

The narrow shelf high above the desert floor upon which Mrs. Willa Longworth perched would have been tricky in broad daylight. In the cool, wet, midnight dark of that November evening, the ledge sheered off into nothingness. The chill that raced up her spine had nothing to do with the low temperature or her fear of the dark.

Far beneath her the New Mexican desert slumbered as peacefully as a baby. Not a sound, not even a night bird or the slither of scales against stone, did she hear. Nothing. Still, she sensed unseen eyes in the darkness and shivered at the thought of Luke McKade. Fortunately, he'd gone off to sulk for a spell after making another tasteless play for her at Little Red's funeral. Still, McKade had a bad habit of turning up when she least wanted him to.

The stormy evening had begun innocently enough. She'd put Sam to bed and read him *Ali Baba and the Forty Thieves*. Sam's spiky, red lashes had closed just as the clever Morgiana had become suspicious of the chalk cross on Ali's gate. Willa had barely shut the book when she'd heard a plane overhead, followed by that sudden crash of metal against rock.

And then nothing. No explosion.

She'd picked up the phone to call 911.

No dial tone. It had taken her a while and a prayer or two before she'd found enough live batteries for her flashlight and summoned enough courage to venture out into the scary dark to see if anyone was injured.

The rain had stopped by the time she got to the plane. Nobody had been inside the twisted fuselage. Only the ten briefcases jammed with money.

To be a thief. Or not to be. That had never been a question.

She'd acted on wacky impulse—as usual.

Ali Baba had found a fortune in his fairy tale.

And kept it.

Surely a modern lass with a bit of adventure in her spirit was up to more of the same.

She had lost her parents during a storm. She had found the money after a storm. If that wasn't a fortuitous sign, what was?

Moonlight silvered the cliffs and the beautiful valley where she and Sam lived. Where they could have been so happy, if only...if only the sisters, especially the high-and-mighty Hesper Longworth, had accepted them. If only McKade would quit burning a hole through her with his eyes. If only he would quit threatening to expose her. He liked to flirt with her in the most public places. He'd never respected her married state. It pleased him to no end that he had the whole town talking about them.

Willa forced herself to begin climbing again. A few twists and turns had her panting, but soon she reached that spot where the path seemed to end at a sheer, blank wall. Only it didn't. One tricky step, a jump into darkness had her inside the small opening where she'd hidden the other briefcases.

She set the last two briefcases beside the others and then sank to her knees like a nun before an altar. Her stomach tightened as she clicked open each briefcase. Excitedly she ran her flashlight over the clumps of tightly bound fifty-dollar bills. With trembling fingers, she picked one up, ruffling the bills like a Vegas dealer shuffling cards.

She wasn't really a thief. No, this was like Robin Hood. She needed the money badly.

Now, she and Sam could be free. Respectable.

Marriage hadn't given her that. Not with the sisters thinking she was trash just as Brand had. Not with the sisters determined to throw her out.

She grabbed more wads of bills, but just as she began stuffing them into the pocket of her jeans, heavy footsteps crunched dry earth outside the entrance.

Tensing with terror like a little girl up to mischief, she sprang to her feet.

Pebbles spun. Then there he was, huge and dangerous, trapping her inside the shadowy cave as he had beside Little Red's grave.

McKade. He was tall and dark, in jeans and a new black Stetson and, as always too handsome for her own good. There was that overpowering energy about him, that magnetism that both drew her and frightened her, that keen interest he had in her. As always, his glinting gray eyes swept her from head to toe, branding her his possession. She quivered as she had that first, terrible night. She'd worn a tight red dress with big white polka dots and he'd planted ten crisp hundred-dollar bills in her shaking fingers when she'd so foolishly sold herself to him. He'd never stopped saying she still owed him.

He'd offered way more for her at the cemetery two months ago.

"How can you be so disreputable at a time like this?" she'd whispered.

"I know what I want, and I'm willing to pay for it. Besides, you're a girl of action. No doubt, you'll snag another rich man fast. I want to be first on your list."

His eyes blazed in the cave's darkness, bringing her back to the present.

"Finders keepers, *Widow* Longworth," he jeered in that same silken, deadly voice. His cold smile and the gleaming black barrel of the gun in his hand filled her with dread. He wasn't just after the money. But he'd take it and whatever else he could tonight.

"You!"

He laughed, some of his tension easing at her obvious dismay. "Your worst nightmare."

"You wish, you conceited devil. I'm not scared of you."

"Did you miss me?"

"I'm always glad when you disappear."

He laughed as he eased the gun into his waistband. "I don't believe you."

Their gazes locked.

"Do you realize that this is the first time we've been alone in four years? Feels good, doesn't it?"

"Not to me," she retorted.

His silver eyes drifted, devouring her pale face, her breasts. Her blood thundered, and she began to shake.

"Liar."

When she gasped in outrage, his devilish grin broadened.

His unwanted hunger was spiced with her guilt and resentment and fear as well as by his own fury that he still found her so attractive.

"If it's any consolation, I don't like you any better than you like me," he said.

Quickly she averted her eyes to a red wall. Just as rapidly he forced his gaze from her to the money.

But it was difficult not to turn back and stare at that carved face, at the slashing black eyebrows, the high cheekbones, the bluntly angled jaw. She didn't like being so aware of him as a man. Oh, why did his narrow waist and those wide, heavily muscled shoulders still fascinate her?

What had he said all those years ago?

You're going to get horny married to a dying man.... Call me when you get the urge.

That awful remark had haunted her, tormented her. She had gotten horny although she was loath to admit it. She'd thought of him when she'd lain in bed and couldn't sleep. Maybe it was just that Little Red had been so pitifully thin and frail at the end that made his horrid rival seem so healthy and appallingly appealing.

"Get out, you little fool," McKade said. "The money's mine."

The money was everything. Her future. Sam's. She thought back on her four years of marriage. On her four long years as a nurse. She had earned every penny of it.

She put her hands on her hips and stayed put.

"I said get out! Now!" His gaze darkened.

McKade swaggered toward her, no doubt, confident of his superior physical power.

She stared at his black gun, her heartbeats thundering. He thought she'd run. He wouldn't shoot her. A man didn't chase a woman for four years and then do that.

When she didn't obey him, a menacing smile touched his lips.

He swaggered toward her. She backed away from him, aware of something hot and dangerous charging the air as it always did when they were together.

"You'd do anything for money," he mocked.

"I haven't slept with you."

"You will."

The cave was isolated, and she was very much alone with him. He had made it very clear to her, to Little Red, to the Longworths, to the whole town that he wanted her, and that sooner or later he would have her.

"You can't have my money," she replied.

His burning gaze settled in the exposed hollow between her breasts. She shrank against the wall, breathing hard, her stomach churning with that sickening, man-woman excitement.

"Tell me what else I can't have—" He grabbed her blouse, reached inside, knotting hard brown fingers around her bra. Using it like a harness, he hauled her against his chest.

The shock of his hard hand between her breasts

made her gasp, but she thrust her chin up fiercely and
tried to stare down the length of her haughty, well-
shaped nose at him. But he was too tall and too broad.
With a jerk, he jammed her nose against his white
cotton shirt that stretched over muscle.

Her bottom lip trembled. "What are you going to
do—hit me?"

He moved his hand inside her bra and cupped a
breast.

Blood pumped through her body.

"That's not exactly what I had in mind."

Blunt fingers fondled soft flesh, kneaded her nipple.
When she gasped, he yanked her still closer, so that
she could feel his wildly drumming heart and realize
his rock-solid body was fully aroused. "You gonna
get out of here...or are you gonna stay and play?" His
free hand slid down her jeans between her thighs. "I
bet you're wet. You've always wanted it...wanted me
as bad as I want you. Admit it."

He was right. Not that she was about to admit it.

For a second she was too brainless to reply. "O-of
course...not! No!"

"We both know what you are."

Overload. He'd said that one time too many.

The breath left her lungs. Without knowing what
she did, she drew back her arm and slapped him. "I'm
not—"

She'd never hit anybody in her whole life. The red
imprint of her fingers burning his dark skin like a
brand was a shock to them both. He was breathing fast
and hard. She couldn't believe she'd done it. Tears
sprang to her eyes. She was filled with instant regret
and concern—for him.

Much to her surprise, he smiled. As quickly as he'd grabbed her, he released her. She dropped to the dirt with a defeated whimper.

Ignoring her, he knelt over the briefcases and began opening them, one by one.

Her briefcases.

When his large brown hands, those hands that had just mauled her, began greedily fingering the money, something snapped in her brain. He didn't need the money. He was rich. But he was hard. He would take it, to spite her, to make her need him, to make her come to him on bended knee. He knew that if she had money, she would never come to him.

She sprang. He caught her by her slim waist and rolled on top of her. Attempting to claw him, she screamed and wept.

"Stop it!" he said.

She pounded his chest. Patiently, he waited until she exhausted herself with too much flailing and too many tears. "You can't have it.... The sisters will throw me out.... I can't—can't afford to stay here...without the money...."

"I offered you way more money—"

"But you'd own me...."

"A most delightful arrangement, I assure you."

She thought of the big old territorial house she and Little Red had renovated and lived in. She thought of her long-ago home...of her parents before the accident...of the perfection of her early life and her desire to recapture that.

McKade didn't get it. When she thought of his sordid offers, tears flowed instead of words. He wanted her as a sex object, just as Brand had. Nothing more.

"Hush…"

Only when she stilled against him, and the dust motes settled, did he free her hands and wipe away her gritty tears with a calloused fingertip.

His finger lingered on her cheek as it had the first time he'd touched her that other horrible night.

"Damn it," he whispered.

His intense gaze heated her skin. With a scowl, he yanked his hand away, flushing darkly. As always he was mad as hell she turned him on. Yet he couldn't stay away. "Why didn't you run a while ago?"

Her spine straightened. He was the last person she should have confided in, and no matter what he thought to the contrary, she was extremely shy and unsure about sex, even with him. Tonight, as always he'd been rude and horrible. But then he never missed a chance to make her feel cheap and dirty.

But that was only because he wanted her. Only to keep some semblance of an upper hand. Maybe he didn't know what he felt.

His hand was in her hair. He'd never made a secret that he desired her on a deep and primal level. That's why he couldn't leave her alone. He was bigger and armed. But as always, his body had betrayed him when he'd seized her.

Suddenly ancient female intuition took over. Delilah had bested Samson, hadn't she?

What if she let him tonight? Maybe he'd be done with her once and for all? Better, maybe she'd be done with him.

You're going to get horny married to dying man. And she had. How many nights had she lain in bed beside Little Red and longed for this cad?

Unsure, she stared at his lips.

He went still.

Taking a deep breath for courage, she lowered her lashes and batted them, forcing a seductive smile.

He regarded her warily.

With a fingertip she brushed his jaw, trailed it down his throat. His skin was hot. Suddenly she got so scared, it was hard to breathe. Gently she wound her fingers beneath his collar. He went still as her other hand glided across his torso, shaping the muscular contours of his chest. "You keep saying you want me."

"Finally."

"Yes," she murmured, "finally..."

"You and I are too damn much alike," he growled. But his voice had gentled as it never had before. "Outsiders. Loners. Misfits."

"Not me," she whispered, moving closer. "Not Sam."

"Sam, too. Poor lonely little *bastard*."

"Don't call him that!"

"You're a fighter though, and ambitious. I like that." His warm breath stirred the golden hair beside her earlobe.

"I didn't know you liked anything about me other than..." She squeezed her hand inside the waistband of his jeans, bent on doing what he'd accused her of doing that first night.

He sucked in air. Lots of it. "I—I don't."

But he was staring at her lips with hunger and anger again. She couldn't stop staring at his, either. She hated him, and touching him made her feel so strange.

Losing her nerve, she yanked her hands out of his pants.

He smiled in weary defeat. "How long's it been since you danced the dusty fandango with a virile chap such as myself?"

"My sex life is none of your business!"

"You were married to a sick man. A second ago, you were touching me like...like you did that night."

"I—I was always jealous...and furious that you could remember that...and that I couldn't."

"God— Then you admit—" He sighed. "Oh, Willa."

Before she could lose her nerve again, before she quite realized what he intended, McKade kissed her. Not as hungrily as she would've expected, considering he'd made his need for her in this disgusting manner clear for four years, considering what she'd just done to tease him.

No, he kissed her almost gently. So gently and so reverently, he stole her breath away.

She forgot the money. His hands were all over her. Her quickening heartbeats made her realize that for all her lack of experience, she was every bit as low as he thought she was where sex was concerned.

"I don't love you," she said, terrified.

"What does love have to do with us?"

"I don't even like you."

"Better," he whispered, nibbling her ear with an expertise that alarmed her.

"Better?"

"Better than hate. No telling how your mood will improve once we do it...and the money makes me an even richer man. I'm pretty good at sex. A woman...of *your* background will appreciate that."

His words burned her with shame, but they slapped her back to reality.

"Right," she purred. *A woman like me...* Brand's refrain to keep her in the place he'd designed for her.

The money. How could she have forgotten about the money for one single second?

No man, especially not this conceited devil, who had used his sex appeal to taunt her, was going to use her and discard her as if she were nothing.

She thought of Brandon Baines, who had seen her solely as a sex object.

Never again. But strangely, McKade's warm lips were heaven as he trailed them down her throat, beneath her earlobe, over her breasts. What cruel trick made him so damnably exciting?

"What do you know about me?" she whispered as he teased a nipple into a hard little berry.

"I know you're too thin. You worked yourself to the bone taking care of my no-good brother." He caught himself. His voice took on that teasing quality that maddened her. "I know you oughtta be talented at this. You're a pro, and you got started young."

He always, always had to say something to ruin it.

Fear and rage clutched her throat. "You're so sure you're right," she murmured shakily, remembering how she'd hidden in the bathroom during recess to escape the cruel schoolyard taunts in Laredo about her aunt's house on the other side of the border.

No way would she let this reprobate who despised her, bed her, take her money and destroy her hard-won reputation.

But McKade did kiss divinely, and it had been a long, long time since a man had showed her a scrap of affection...and forever since she'd danced the dusty fandango....

McKade kissed her with arrogant mastery and yet with the tender raw hunger of a virgin schoolboy full of lusty hopes. He was both powerful and vulnerable, almost afraid...of her in the same way she was of him. And strangely, it was not his expertise, but his weakness for her, for her alone. that thrilled her.

Maybe, just this once, Willa would use a man, a man she could never care for tenderly but could enjoy immensely, the way her aunt's men had used her girls, the way the dangerous man, who'd left her pregnant and who still terrified her, had used her. Then, she'd best McKade, take the money and run.

Thief. Wanton.

Deceiving him seemed such a small sin compared to all her others tonight. He deserved whatever punishment she dealt him.

She ran a hand through a lock of ebony silk that fell across his dark brow and noticed that he had the most exquisite widow's peak. "Why didn't you tell everybody at the funeral what you knew about me?"

"Because..." He hesitated. "Because then you'd go. Because I began to look forward to our quarrels. Because I wanted you...."

"I wanted you too, McKade." She couldn't believe she'd said that so easily, but she had to play along.

"You had a funny way of showing it."

"Your courtship style has been weird."

"Memorable," he chuckled. "But then...considering the way we met..."

"Will you ever ever forget that?"

"Never. The image of you tied to those bedposts is a favorite."

He was horrible.

But handsome. So handsome. If his thoughts had been on her all these years, hers had been on him, too.

"Then you got married."

Her gaze flicked past his hard, gorgeous face to the briefcases.

Did he really think she was so stupid she'd let him bed her and then let him steal the briefcases? He'd made her strip, offered her money for sex, in short, treated her like some cheap woman of the night. Marriage to Little Red hadn't stopped him from tormenting her with those memories. Just thinking about all McKade had done through the years made her smolder.

She managed a tight little laugh. Then McKade began kissing her, and it wasn't long before her tense body became pliant and she didn't have to pretend.

Both of them went a little crazy. For too long they had wanted each other. As he kissed her, it was as if she couldn't get enough air. He ripped her shirt. Buttons flew. The fire that burned inside him ignited her, too. His hands moved over her shoulders, slipping the bra straps down.

"Don't," she whispered.

"I can't stop."

She exhaled deeply, her voice a thready moan. "This is going to end badly."

"Well, it damn sure started badly."

When she was naked, he tore off his own clothes. She couldn't help but watch his nimble fingers unbutton white cotton. Soon, too soon, he stood before her like a pagan, tan muscle, oozing male virility. He made a bed for them on the ground out of their clothes. Then he crushed her soft shape against his body.

The night was cold, but soon they dripped with perspiration. It was as if their blood boiled. Lips, hands, tongues were feverish, darting, exploring everywhere. He did things to her she'd never dreamed she'd let any man do, she'd *want* any man to do. The odious McKade took her to heights that made her feel luminous, weightless, on fire. Sex was hot, visceral, immediate. And down and deliciously dirty, too. But sweet, so incredibly sweet.

When it was over, somehow it wasn't. She lay in the dark as insensible as someone under the influence of a terrible drug or disease and yet alert to the tiniest sounds. The moon had never seemed so large and golden. She felt sore and shy and yet sweetly tender. Was she out of her mind?

Afterward, instead of losing interest in her, he held her close, whispering words of love and desire, repeating her name again and again as if it and she were infinitely precious. She couldn't believe him any more than she could trust her own feelings.

He cupped her chin, and she shivered. "Willa...I'm not taking the money from you. I'm taking it to protect you. I want to take care of you. Your marriage to Little Red drove me crazy. All these years... You don't know. You'll never know... It was like being in purgatory."

She wanted him to go on talking, telling her these sweet lies.

He was a liar.

She was a fool.

"To protect me?" she asked sweetly even as some part of her ached to believe him. "Protect me from who?" she whispered shakily.

"Whom?" he corrected.

"Whom?" she parroted.

"From the bad guys, sweetheart. I'm going to take care of you...and your kid."

"Sam."

"I'll make you an even better offer than before."

So, he was back to that.

"Marriage?"

"What I have in mind will be much more fun."

He would always see her as a woman for sale. She couldn't bring up Sam around a man who saw her in that light.

She forced herself to think of all the bad things McKade had said about her to Little Red in the beginning of their marriage, all the things he'd said at the funeral. Bottom line—he still thought he could buy her.

Gritting her teeth to rid herself of any lingering tenderness she might feel for him, Willa closed her eyes. How could she have slept with him? But just thinking about what he'd done to her brought a perverse shiver of pleasure.

He was every bit as good a lover as he'd bragged he'd be.

So, don't think about that.

How would she do him in? He was huge. He'd insulted her intelligence, too. But clobbering him with a rock or her flashlight held absolutely no appeal. She thought about Ali Baba's maid pouring boiling oil into the jars. The thought of hurting McKade in any way dismayed her to the extreme.

Something would come to her. Some bright idea. Something always did. That's why her life and Sam's were in such a mess.

She remembered driving off in McKade's Porsche, leaving him in those whorls of dust.

Finders keepers, Luke McKade had taunted.

She eyed the briefcases, the contours of the shadowy cave, the black Beretta on top of his boots and McKade's position on the rumpled clothes on the uneven floor. That's when she got her bright idea.

It was her turn to laugh and hug him close, to pet his hair and lull him to fall asleep in her arms. She knew they would do it again when he cradled her closer, his mouth moving down the delicate flesh along the side of her throat. She felt the tips of his teeth nibbling silken skin.

The heat of his body washed her like a tide. He was made of hard bronzed muscle and dark body hair. Her heart thudded with slow, meaningful excitement.

She couldn't feel these shivers of delight. Not with him. Not when he considered her an object or a possession. Not when he threatened all her dreams.

But she did. He hadn't been the only one in purgatory these past four years.

She let him make love to her, let herself be carried away by longing and desire and passion. When it was over, it took her a while to settle down, to convince herself that the money was the answer to her prayers.

Not once did it occur to her, not even once that this handsome scoundrel might be the real answer. She knew what he wanted.

And the Widow Longworth wasn't for sale.

The *very* rich Widow Longworth had better ideas for her future.

As she edged toward his gun, her heart accelerated.

She was playing a dangerous game with a dangerous man.

She had to win, no matter what the cost.

Because if she didn't, he'd make her pay. Oh, yes, he'd want his pound of flesh.

Her flesh.

12

He felt quick movement somewhere in the dark. "Oh, Lover Boy... Stud..."

The flirty betrayal in Willa's urgent whisper siphoned the air out of Luke's lungs.

His eyes snapped open. She stood over him, legs apart, commando posture, fully dressed in that mannish blouse he'd torn and those awful baggy jeans that had to be pure grunge. And damn her hide, she was wearing his new black Stetson.

The moon, the full moon, the orange kind that belongs to new lovers who are overly conscious of such things, blazed as brightly as a demon's aura behind her. She was pretty, yet scary and fierce, and yet so sexy she made his dry mouth water.

"Lie back down with me and cuddle," he murmured.

"Not on your chinny, chin chin!"

"I'm not Sam. This isn't one of your fairy tales."

"No, you're the big bad wolf in real life. You eat little girls like me."

"From the first second I saw you tied to those bedposts, that's what I wanted to do. Lie back down here where you belong.''

"Never." She dug an overlarge, ugly-as-hell, lace-up boot into the dirt and kicked pebbles at him.

"Ouch!" He rubbed his cheek. "What the hell—"

His stunned gray eyes widened with fury as he stared up the length of a black barrel. *His* Beretta. He remembered his Porsche speeding away with her and his brother in it while he'd coughed until he wretched and been scared as hell "the little gang" would come back.

This wasn't the first time she'd turned the tables on him. Would he never learn? He was sprawled flat on his back under her, naked, vulnerable—*powerless*. And she'd stolen his hat!

"You wouldn't shoot me, not after… Not after all we shared?"

"Especially after *that*."

His hard mouth was still tender from her kisses. The sweet, tart taste of her lingered on his lips and tongue.

"I can still taste you," he whispered. "Sweet as peaches and as hot as jalapeños." He attempted a smile.

"Shut up!"

Beneath tangled curls, her face went bloodless. Her lethal blue stare scared the hell out of him.

"What do you think you're doing, Willa—"

She bit her lip. "G-get up."

When he reached for his jeans, she shook her head. "N-no! J-just walk down there." She waved the gun toward the darkest shadows in the back of the cave.

A girl as unpredictable as Willa might be dangerous with a gun. He didn't think she'd shoot him on purpose. But who would have thought she'd do any of the crazy things she'd done. When she was scared, she got nervous. He knew she was bluffing, but the thing could go off accidentally.

"Be careful...that's loaded, you know."

"I certainly hope so. That's why I'm pointing it straight at your...your heart...or...where a normal man would have such an organ."

"Now that's not very nice."

"Move it."

"At least let me put on my boots. There could be snakes...scorpions...."

"Goody!" She released the Beretta's safety with a violent snap. "You'll have company."

She certainly seemed to know how to use a gun.

"I was a damn sap," he said.

"So was I, *sweetheart*," she whispered. "But the party's over."

"Doesn't have to be. If you put that gun down, I'll pretend this never happened."

"Move."

Luke had never despised himself more. He had wanted her so damn long, had wanted her more than he'd ever desired anyone. And he'd wanted, no, counted the days and the nights until she'd be free. He'd been jealous of Little Red and yet he'd done everything he could to preserve his brother's life.

God, she'd been soft...and hot...and so sweet under him. How could he have forgotten she'd teased him to distraction that first night when he'd thought her too drugged and scared to be devious, stolen his Porsche, taken his money, left him to those thugs, and then...damn her hide, she'd married his brother, moved in with his worst enemies…. The list of their misadventures these past four years was endless.

Rule number one—in any man's survival manual should be—never let your little head do your thinking. The trouble was, Willa had always been able to best him because… Because…

The because was just as irrational as the woman who inspired it. It wasn't like him—to be irrational, to break all his rules.

"What's wrong with you?" he muttered.

"Hands over your head," she whispered roughly, motioning again toward the far end of the cave.

He cupped his "little head" and was pleased when she blushed. Those blushes. Those charming blushes. They were part of what did him in, what kept him coming back to this godforsaken place to torment her. Little Red? Who would have thought he could've lived four years. But then he'd had *her*.

She was staring at the catcher's mitt his brown paws made at his crotch.

"Not…*there*," she shrieked.

When he raised his hands, her hot blue eyes shot to his groin. She wants a peek, he thought, gladdened when her cheeks went as red as beets.

He'd make those cheeks go darker still.

He forced an insolent smile. "Like what you see, huh?" He bounced up and down, showing off his wares.

"Your conceit is disgusting."

"Conceit?" He strutted some more, just to annoy her. "I'm glad you noticed. A girl like you would."

"A girl like…" Her blue eyes sparkled with fury even as her avid gaze followed that strip of gleaming black hair to where it thickened right where his legs met. She leaned down, snatched up his black briefs, and hurled them at him.

Keeping his hands above his head, he caught the black pants with his teeth, letting the underwear dangle at a jaunty angle.

He was proud of his catch. Not many men were so agile. But then he was good with his mouth.

That beet color on either side of that pert little nose was definitely darkening. Oh, most definitely...

"Put them on."

He unclenched his teeth. The briefs fell at his feet. "That's hard to do...with my hands up...."

Still blushing, she nodded furiously for him to lower them.

He bent over and slowly thrust in his right leg and then his left. After he'd tugged them up to his thighs, she ordered him to raise his hands again and start backing up.

"I thought...we were friends," he said.

"We had sex."

"And wasn't it fun?"

"I was faking, I'll have you know!"

His chest twisted on an odd pain. "Were you, now?"

"I was!"

"A girl like you would be good at faking."

"A girl like me..." Her eyes narrowed.

He couldn't resist taunting her. "I don't believe you were, though! Your pulse raced faster than mine. You were more drenched with perspiration when we were through and you shuddered most delightfully. Inside, you were wet and slick and as tasty as spicy hot butter.

Well, at least I got my thousand dollars' worth. You were worth the wait. More than worth it. You were every bit as talented as I knew you'd be.''

She blushed. "The money…from the plane, I mean…inspired me.''

"Money always does inspire a girl like you.''

They were in the deepest shadows now. He took a step backward. His foot found nothingness, and froze.

"Just one more step,'' she purred, real menace in her voice now.

"Not on your life.''

"Do it.''

"I thought you'd never ask.'' He didn't budge. His gaze devoured her body.

"Jump, or I'll shoot.''

"Go ahead. Pull the trigger,'' he bluffed.

Her blue eyes widened like saucers. When she leveled the gun at his bare chest, her trigger finger shook uncontrollably. "I—I will. I—I can….''

Dear God, there was no telling…

He lunged.

That panicked her. As always, her response was too quick.

His gun belched blue-and-yellow flame.

Twice.

She screamed. His hat tumbled off her head.

Bullets whizzed past him, ricocheted, pinged off walls. At the last second, she'd jerked her hand and aimed at the back wall, and her shots had gone wild.

His street reflexes took over. "Kill.''

He dove, but there was a ledge in the way he hadn't seen. His head hit rock. The next thing he knew, he was seeing stars and stumbling backward.

He teetered on the brink of the hole, yelling at her to help him. She leaned forward to do so. He grabbed for her, but missed and plunged into darkness.

Plunk.

"Ouch! Damn you!" he yelped.

"Are you okay?"

"Now you ask."

"Lucky for you the hole isn't that deep. Ten feet max. But deep enough to hold an ornery cuss like you. At least for a little while."

True enough. Solid red walls entombed him. He'd landed wrong, and his right ankle stung a little, but he could walk on it. He was okay. Nevertheless, he faked a limp and let out howls of rage that echoed deafeningly in the claustrophobic chamber.

Big-eyed and pale-faced, she peeped warily over the edge. Now that she had him, her voice softened in breathy concern. "Luke? Are you really hurt?"

Luke. She never called him that.

"As if you give a damn. You tried to shoot me!"

"I did not!" She stiffened. "The dumb gun went off by accident." Her bright head vanished.

"Willa, come back, damn your hide—"

"You do know how to lure a girl with sweet talk."

Jaunty dialogue. But he thought he heard a sniffle. She seemed to be taking deep breaths. Was she scared, crying?

If so, it was about time she showed a woman's heart. Maybe she'd let him out after all.

A moment later she was back, eyes glistening, her nose saucily upturned, cheeks aflame. And she was wearing his black hat. Wiping those cheeks with the back of her hands, she attempted a breezy smile. "If you're mad, you're okay." She tipped his hat back. "How do I look?"

"Stop playing around."

"Good advice." She blew him a farewell kiss, letting her fingers flutter flirtatiously. More color came back onto her cheeks. "It was your fault, you know...."

"What?"

"That your stupid gun went off. You shouldn't have insulted me and then jumped me. You could've been killed. Guns really are such awful things. But...but good thing you had one. It certainly came in handy."

Had they ever been on the same wavelength? "Let me out of here, damn you."

"Oh, dear. Not more sweet talk." Shaking her head, she backed out of sight.

His heart hammered with rage. He'd never hated anyone more than he hated her in that moment. He slammed a fist against a rock wall so hard he nearly broke his hand.

"Ouch! Damn your hide, girl." He let out a stream of curses.

Then he leaned against a high wall while his fist throbbed.

He was powerless, and she was up there, hands on her hips, gloating. A memory, swift and cruel, took him back to the gutters where he'd gotten his start. He'd lain in the dirt, his face bleeding, his heart filled with hate, the neighborhood toughs kicking him in the gut and legs, gloating when he cried out. Every time he'd tried to get up, they knocked him back down. After that, he'd learned to fight.

Another memory, even crueler came back to haunt

him. He remembered a girl's long sallow face aglow with savage dislike as she stood before a wall of flame. Her narrow face wavered. He still wasn't sure she'd been there that night when somebody had tried to kill him and his mother. But he'd hated her all these years just the same.

He hated feeling powerless. Not that he was about to let on to this slip of a girl.

"Damn you, Willa. If those three jerks that wrecked that plane come back for their money, they'll use you worse than even you have ever been used."

"*Even* me?" she whispered on a raw, hurt note. "I'm sick and tired of you saying things like that about me. You're going to have to sing a new tune about me if you ever want me to cooperate with you...."

"I'd pay to watch what they do to you!" He cursed her savagely, and because he felt impotent and enraged, he pounded the wall again, but with his other hand, all the while issuing more lurid threats about what he hoped the bad guys would do to her when they found her.

"I hope they tie you up," he yelled.

"I just bet you do. We both know how that turns you on."

He finished by yelling, "You're stupid as hell to mess with them or to mess with me. I got to that plane before you. I ran them off at gunpoint.... Then I came back for the money. I tracked you here.... And you were damned easy to find. And, Willa, somebody else, somebody far more dangerous than those guys is looking for you. I came to the funeral...to warn you...."

"I don't believe you."

"Don't compound this stupidity...."

"Stupid? Who's calling who, stupid?"

"Whom," he corrected.

"Whom?" She drew a deep breath. "Well, smart guy, I'm not in that hole, now am I? And I've got all my clothes on, too...not to mention your gun...and the money! And...and I...I have a plan."

"A plan? Oh, really? Like your plan to marry Little Red and inherit. You were being booted out of Dodge tonight weren't you? When that little ole plane just—"

"You don't understand anything about me. Little Red asked me to marry him. I was pregnant. I wanted a home...."

"I offered you more—"

"But not a real home." She paused. "It's true, his sisters want me gone."

Luke had reasons of his own to despise Hesper. Not that he was about to let on he could sympathize with Willa on that score. "No wonder," he said, proud of his heavily sarcastic tone.

"They did write me a check...a large one to buy me out. If I cashed it, I could start over...but it would have to be somewhere else."

"I'd think a girl like you would take their money and run."

"That's because you're too much like Brand. You don't know me and you don't listen to me. I'm not what you think."

"Don't you compare me to Baines!" he declared hotly.

She paused. "Don't you see how cruel it would be

to move Sam? This ranch is the only home he's ever known.''

''Well, if you want to stay here, you can't keep these briefcases. This money could be drug money. The guys who left it in the plane *will* be back for it—and soon. And that other guy...''

''Then I'll deal with them in my own way. For years, I've tried so hard...to fit in here. I've had to fight the sisters every step of the way.'' She paused. ''If I keep this money, I can stay.''

''You stupid fool! You call that a plan? They'll kill you.''

''All my life, I've hated people who said I'm stupid because I don't have a logical mind. In school, every time I tried to talk in class, the other kids laughed.''

He spoke through gritted teeth. ''Surely, even you can see why you can't stay.''

''*Even you...* I can and I will.''

He had to keep her talking. ''How will you keep it? The plane crashed on your ranch. Where do you think they'll start looking for their money?''

''Somehow, it'll work out.''

''Those guys aren't going to give up....''

''I don't want to think about them right now.''

''You're not being logical—''

''That does it,'' she snapped. Then she stopped. ''What would Ali Baba do?''

''What?''

''Just in case you're right, and they do come back...''

''Now you're thinking.''

''When the thief put a chalk mark on Ali Baba's house, Morgiana—''

"Who's she?"

"Ali Baba's slave! Quit interrupting! Morgiana marked all the houses on the street with chalk!" She hesitated. "What if?" There was a smile in her voice now. "What if I dropped a few of these along the trail...to throw them off track..."

"A few of what—"

She waved a hand airily as if she were a good fairy sprinkling pixie dust, and fifty-dollar bills began to rain down on him.

Panic knotted his gut when he caught the first fistful and wadded them up.

"Too bad you're not going any place where you can spend them."

"You're not gonna leave me here like bait for that mean bunch...."

"It seems the *logical* step. Only...only I don't have time to waste marking other caves." She paused. "Next time, watch who you call stupid and illogical."

"Whom," he growled. "If they don't kill me, I'll make you real sorry you ever met me!"

"Kill you, McKade? I couldn't get that lucky. I'd put you up against the meanest bastards alive! And as for being sorry I met you... This is revenge for every mean, hateful thing you've said and done to me since I've known you! Revenge for that first night when you made me strip! Revenge for correcting my grammar!"

"Throw me my clothes, you witch. And my hat!"

She eyed his lean brown body with a quirky grin. "You're cuter naked!"

"I'll freeze!" He began to curse her again. He called her *stupid* and *illogical* because those words seemed to get to her.

"Stupid, illogical, flake, airhead... What kind of grown-up operates on plots from fairy tales?"

With every insult, she slammed the briefcases harder, but she didn't reply.

Finally, she came back. "McKade?"

He glared up at her. She tossed his jeans down and then his boots and shirt.

"What are you doing?"

"There's a tunnel that leads out the back of that hole you're in. It'll take you a while, but if you want out...and are resourceful—"

"If..." He growled.

"You'd better listen up."

He pulled on his jeans.

She continued. "Like I was saying...it winds all the way to the other side of the mountain. It's called Devil's Tunnel. Now concentrate 'cause I'm going to drop you your flashlight."

"How kind." He held his hands up.

"Good catch. Good night," she said.

"Willa!"

Then the cave blackened.

She was gone. So was his Stetson. She'd trapped him like a bug in a bottle. The cold and the darkness seeped into his soul.

"Willa!" he screamed, feeling powerless even after he turned on his light and found the opening of Devil's Tunnel. He hated caves.

Black walls squeezed him. When her name echoed again and again in the cavern, he began to shiver.

He was freezing his ass off. He'd better finish dressing. No telling how long it would take him to get to the other side of the mountain. He'd better hurry, too.

She really might be serious about leaving a trail of fifty-dollar bills up to this cave.

"Willa! Dear God, by all that's holy and unholy, I swear, if I ever get out of this dungeon, if I ever get my hands around your slim, pale neck again, it won't be to caress it. I'll wring it."

13

The voluminous, back pockets of Willa's jeans bulged with fifty-dollar bills. Not that she was thinking about the money. No, she was thinking about chocolate chip cookies. More specifically, she was wondering if Sam or Big Red had discovered the bag of cookies she'd hidden on the top shelf of her cupboard.

Sam was always sneaking from Big Red or her, rummaging in her stuff, taking things he was curious about, or eating sweets forbidden to him.

Had he pushed his yellow stool to the counter and done his monkey number? How she craved a cookie and a tall glass of milk.

Even for Willa, it had been a long night. She was shaky and tired and ravenously hungry. Was it any wonder? For someone who was scared of the dark and scared of sex, she'd spent way too much time in a shadowy cave engaged in both those activities. And the money, having so much money on her person, made her nervous. Any minute she kept expecting someone to pounce on her from the dark.

Ever since she'd left Laredo, she'd been afraid her

past would catch up with her, afraid Brand would find
her and demand that she come back to him or worse—
demand Sam. Her aunt, who loved to criticize and ad-
vise, never missed a chance to warn her that Brand
still sent men by to ask about her.

"He got married...to a socialite, to a Martha, but
he wants you, too. A man like him would. So, be
careful, Willa. Some men can't take no for an answer...especially from a girl they believe is socially
beneath them."

Willa's mind raced to that other troublesome man
in her life.

Sex. McKade.

McKade had more bad stuff to tell on her now. He'd
make the most of their little adventure, too.

He'd insulted her, made her furious, more furious
than she'd ever been at him before. He thought she
was low. Why did she care what he thought? She'd
go crazy if she gave in to her feelings about him.

At least he didn't know where she'd hidden the
money. Trouble was, she'd better hide the cash she'd
taken and draw a map fast before she forgot where the
rest of the loot was herself.

The moon had gone down. The sky was inky black.
Despite a tiny glow from Sam's window, the huge
dark shape of her house loomed as dark as a witch's
castle in a fairy tale.

Wild deeds and her guilty conscience had been her
downfall more times than she could count. Willa was
afraid. Of what she'd done with McKade and to him.
Most of all, of what he'd made her feel. Of what he'd
said "the bad guys" might do to her...and to Sam
when they found them.

Of…of what Luke McKade would do to her himself when he made it to her ranch house.

For four long years, the loathsome, if attractive McKade had made a pest of himself, stalking her all over Taos and in the countryside, too, always showing up when and where he could most embarrass her. Lots of people already thought they were having an affair, a fact that had infuriated Little Red and delighted McKade.

She had sworn time and again to Little Red, who'd been sensitive about his impotence, that she would never ever sleep with McKade. Well, she had. No telling what McKade would do now that he really had something on her.

Sex with McKade. He'd never let her live that down. *A girl like you.* How many times had he said that?

Why did he cling to his first impression of her? Never once had she cheated on Little Red. During her waking hours when Little Red's nursing needs had been so acute, she hadn't given much thought to her lack of a sex life. But in her dreams, McKade had haunted her. In the cave, alone with McKade, she'd been overpowered by those longings.

And if sex with McKade wasn't bad enough, there were Hesper and the sisters to worry about. Better not to think about any of it. Besides, she was too tired. And too hungry for cookies and milk.

Tomorrow. She would face Hesper tomorrow, too. Once she got inside her house and reassured herself Sam was safe, everything else would work out.

With trembling fingers, Willa quickly unlatched her front gate. For a second or two she savored the way the inky desert smelled sweetly of sage and juniper. The dry earth was so fragrant; she could almost smell the violets and hyacinths that had blossomed in summer but lay dormant now in the terraced beds Big Red had built for her.

She looked up and admired the lacy pattern of the bare chestnut and cottonwood branches, and thought about copying those designs for her t-shirts. She hadn't painted a tree in quite some time. On hot summer afternoons, the trees near the old well provided an oasis of delightful shade. Tonight, they cloaked the mansion in deep, dark, scary purple.

So soundlessly did Willa glide up her brick path, not a single one of her stray cats or dogs stirred on the porch. At the foot of the stairs, she paused to pick up a little toy car Sam had flung down. She stared up at her home and felt a surge of pride.

Funny, the unpredictable twists and kinks that spiced up one's life and made the impossible seem possible. If it hadn't been for the storm and the briefcases, she and Sam would already be gone. She eyed her house with its grilled windows, her flowerbeds, the grinning pumpkins she and Sam had carved that lined the stairs, Sam having insisted on buying every single pumpkin in the grocery store.

At the thought of how close she'd come to leaving her home forever, a lump formed in her throat.

The house, her home, was nineteenth century Territorial. How eagerly she had planted a garden and lawn even before the restoration had begun. In spring and summer, the house was surrounded by lush gardens of lilac, forsythia and green grass. How she loved to sit on the porch swing or go into her meditation room with its garden view and be still.

"Lawns and flowers are sinful in the desert," Little Red had teased as she'd explained the names of every flower to Sam when he'd been a baby.

"Reformed sinners must sin a little. Let this garden of sweet peas and marigolds, in the middle of our wild plum hedges full with their little white blossoms, be our sin," she'd replied. "Besides, our valley is not all desert."

How different the charming, fortified structure looming above her was tonight from the broken tumble of stones, half-buried by sharp bayonets of yucca, chamiso and cacti she'd chanced upon that long-ago afternoon, when she'd ridden out to sketch.

Today she'd been instantly seduced by the ruin's remote location beside a stream where long grasses grew and willows hung low. The valley with its sweeping vistas of desert and the Sangre de Cristo Mountains had felt magical after the desert. Willa had felt her entire being relax. She'd clambered to the top of its remaining walls, wondering who'd built the huge place and lived in it.

She might have stayed there all night, had not McKade ridden up and scared her off. She'd scampered to her mare, Molly, kicked the gentle old girl into a gallop, but McKade, a better rider on a better horse, had soon caught up to her and seized her reins.

She'd hated Molly's slowness, hated getting caught. But after a brief struggle, he'd pulled her off and grounded Molly. Willa had fought him when he'd tried to kiss her, and he'd reluctantly let her go.

He'd stared at her swollen tummy and frowned.

"Doesn't anyone around here look after you? It's dangerous to ride in your condition."

"Molly is as gentle as a lamb."

"She's a horse."

"Obviously." Despite her protests, his concern brought a rush of something wild and wonderful, of some rich, lush emotion too deep and dangerous to explore. "Why should you care what I do?" she'd demanded sharply.

"You're too far along, Willa," he'd said, his quiet, low proprietary tone sending a shiver through her. "This place is too far from other people. If you don't stop, I'll tell Little Red to make you."

"If you dare tell him we met here...even by accident—"

"I'll dare—"

The intense, worried look he'd given her had made her heart pound in its moorings. "Why? Why won't you leave me alone? Why do you have to come to Taos so often? Why did you take over that ruined cabin in Lost Canyon?"

"So, you've been keeping tabs?"

"Why?"

He drew a quick breath. "Maybe the desert turns me on. Or maybe it's the people." He was staring down at her, and there was such a frightening glow in his eyes and a flush in his dark face that she couldn't look at him. "My interest in...in the...er...desert and its denizens excites you, doesn't it?"

"No. You, everything you do infuriates me."

"Really?" He grinned, very pleased with himself and her suddenly. "I wonder." Before she knew what he was about, his arms were around her, and his lips found hers again. His kiss was soft and cut short by her skirmish. But during that brief contact, before she pushed him away—everything, her marriage, her good intentions to be the best bride in Taos, blurred into hot, foggy nothingness while she endured what had seemed an endless blistering kiss. Even when it was over, tremors lit her nerves.

Maybe the wild land with its moody clouds, mountains and slanting golden-red lights had made her more susceptible to McKade.

Or maybe it had been the dawning reality of the true nature and limitations of her marriage to his brother.

Maybe she'd begun to realize that from the moment McKade had picked up her red shoe, he'd seized hold of her as Brand and Little Red, as no other man, ever could. Still, all that mattered was that she was married to another, that she had a baby to remember.

"See how the desert makes you feel more alive," he taunted.

When she had fought him, and he had let her go, she turned her head away. "You've got the whole town talking about you, about us."

"Maybe I consider you an investment I need to keep track of."

"Would you quit following me?"

"Taos is a small town. People bump into each other."

"We're a long way from town."

"Maybe I was just making sure you were okay. After all, you are my sister-in-law."

"Until me—you never claimed kin."

"Perhaps I had no compelling reason to."

"You're deliberately making a spectacle of me. I'm married."

"To the wrong brother. You chose him because I offered money and he offered you marriage."

"I had my reasons."

He stared at her stomach. "I would have married you."

"You're like my aunt. *Marriage* is just a word to you, a legal contract, a monetary contract. You wanted to own me."

"And what is marriage to you?"

"In this case, it's about two people who need each other, who are determined to help each other. It's about two people who have made mistakes but now want a better life. But you wouldn't understand that, would you?"

"Be honest. You want his money. I have more. Much more. You should have chosen me."

"But I didn't, and we both have to live with that fact."

"We have weak natures. Or at least I do. I can't forget…what you owe me."

"I sent you a check, didn't I?"

"Which I tore up."

"That's your problem."

"No, you're my problem. I paid for something I didn't get, something I still want…and rather badly."

"That's very flattering, but I'm married. Chase some other woman."

"Believe me I've tried. I can't."

"Only because you're like a spoiled child and I'm the only toy you don't own and can't buy."

"Can't I? Willa, this is no real marriage. Leave him."

"No. You leave me alone. I want to make your brother happy."

"That's a little difficult...when he's dying."

"But I want to try."

He did not answer. Something dark and young and wounded flared in his eyes, the emotion both drawing her to him and confusing her. Once she had wanted Brand to look at her that way. McKade seemed so lonely, so lost, and suddenly despite her baby and new husband, she felt equally so.

"You're not happy with him."

"But I want to be. And I really do want to make Little Red happy, too," she whispered. "So, you stay away from me, Luke McKade."

When his eyes went to her lips, when hers went to his, when she felt herself swaying dizzily into him, she pulled back, licked her lips because they felt so dry. She could still taste him. She gave a little moan. Her gaze grew desperate. "Please..."

"All right. Truce. Until he dies—"

But he'd followed her until she was within sight of her home that evening, keeping his distance, watching her go into the big house alone. His doing so had made her feel safe and protected. That night at dinner, Big Red had retold all his grandfather's old war stories about the ruined house that had been the fabled ranch's original headquarters. Willa had listened spellbound and then begged him to let her restore it.

Big Red had gone quiet.

Hesper had glowered. "I've begged you for years, Daddy. You said we couldn't afford—"

"Everything is different now."

Later, even Little Red had protested. "It's twelve miles down a bad dirt road."

"That's why I love it. It would be ours, our magical refuge away from—" Willa had stopped short before blurting Hesper's name along with his other sisters'. And of course, she hadn't been able to say she wanted to be farther from Taos and McKade.

Little Red had smiled conspiratorially. "I told you they'd gang up on you, and they do, don't they...with good old Hesper leading the pack?"

It was one thing for family to run down family, but quite another for an in-law to agree. Willa had shaken her head, unable to admit how uncomfortable his sisters, especially Hesper, made her by constantly spying, criticizing and gossiping about her. "It's just that there are so many women in one house, in one kitchen. They are used to doing everything a certain way...and I never do anything the same way I did it before."

His smile had died. He'd taken her hand and squeezed it. "And we'll be even more crowded when *my* son is born. They'll tell us how to raise him, too."

"There's a natural spring that feeds a creek," Willa had continued, her hope building. "I could plant a garden."

"You prefer trees to desert?"

"No. I like it here. I will always be grateful to you for marrying me," she'd said.

"And I to you."

"The valley isn't like the desert. There's grass, trees."

"How did you find them, the ruins, I mean?"

"I—I rode Molly."

"All that way? Alone?"

She'd nodded, a little too quickly.

He'd looked odd. "All that way, by yourself?" He'd fallen silent and still as he'd watched her. "Don't do that ever again." He'd paused. "This is wild country. It could be dangerous. Anybody could've followed you."

Had he known?

After that, the harder Hesper and her sisters had fought Willa's dream, the more stubbornly Little Red defended it. Soon, he'd been more excited about the project than she. As for Big Red, he'd quickly folded, only too happy to indulge his dying son's whims.

Hesper had felt hurt, furious and left out. Naturally, she'd blamed Willa and made their life together impossible. No sooner than one room and a bathroom were made livable than Little Red and Willa moved in. To avoid the long drive, they said. Soon Big Red had gotten enough of Hesper's bad temper and constant harping and moved in with Willa and Little Red, too. Once there, the older man had grown a ponytail and a beard and developed a passion for building rock retaining walls and weird rock sculptures, which Willa loved and his daughters loathed.

Big Red found he'd liked getting his hands dirty. He'd become both contractor and architect. They'd drawn blueprints, used local labor. They'd remodeled room by room, as Little Red's bouts of ill health and unpredictable remissions had permitted.

Hesper visited them and carped at Willa ceaselessly. "We want to be near Little Red at the end. You're just doing this for yourself. He won't live to see it finished. Don't you think he has more serious things to think about?''

''I want him to live while he's alive,'' Willa had replied. ''He needs distraction. He and his father are enjoying this project and each other at last.''

''I would think a new wife...and a new baby...so soon—'' Hesper had stared so hard at Willa's protruding belly, Willa had blushed ''—would be distraction enough for any new husband...especially one who couldn't possibly be the father, no matter how frequently he makes the pathetic claim that he is.''

''Hesper...''

''One day, one night out of prison—and he marries you! Why? What kind of woman marries a dying man she doesn't even know?''

''If you're so displeased with his choice, I should think you'd be pleased we've moved out here.''

''A dying man with a fortune, I might add? I'll tell you what kind—''

''You can visit us as often as you like, Hesper.''

''But only if she keeps a civil tongue in her head,'' Little Red had said warningly. For he'd come upon them silently. ''Don't come back, until you can be nice to my wife.''

''You don't mean that. And you shouldn't let Daddy haul all those heavy rocks up from the stream.''

''Willa, the baby and I intend to live here as we please, Hesper. In peace.''

When Hesper had realized that he meant what he said, she'd blamed Willa for that, too. Then Sam had burst into the world even earlier than expected. Hesper had counted on her fingers and played the scandal for all it was worth. When McKade sent dozens of tulips to Willa's hospital room, he made the new bride at the Triple L even more notorious. Hesper made the most of every rumor, hinting McKade was Sam's father.

After that, every time Willa had gone into Taos for so little as a bag of groceries, heads had turned and tongues wagged. But somehow, life had gone on. After the baby, McKade had quarreled over Lost Canyon with Big Red. Then he'd gone away for a longer spell than usual. Big Red had had his first stroke, and Little Red had grown steadily weaker. Life got really hard when Willa had two invalids, a new baby and a big house to run. Then miraculously after a second surgery, Little Red had gone into remission.

When Little Red finally died after four years of married life, he left Willa the house along with a thousand acres and a letter advising her to sell and make a new life for herself somewhere else. But no matter how many times Willa read Little Red's letter, she couldn't change the fact that she loved Taos, her house in the center of The Triple L and Big Red.

Why, Big Red was like a big child, especially after his second stroke. He would be lost without her, without Sam. One afternoon as she'd watched him drawing a new rock sculpture he planned to build in the dirt for Sam, she'd decided maybe she could start painting T-shirts again. But no sooner had she installed equipment in a spare bedroom and shown several dozen T-shirts at galleries in town, than Hesper appeared at her door.

Hesper had marched into the low-ceilinged dining room that Willa had tried to paint her favorite shade of red but which had turned out a little too bright. Hesper stared at the red wall and then at the antler chandelier over the table. Cautiously, she spread her checkbook flat on the dusty oak table which had been littered with Sam's books, toys, and teddy bears as well as two of her beloved, orange "flower power" pillows from her bedroom.

"Willa dear, I'm here to buy you out." She'd tracked a thin finger through the dust. Then she'd lifted a pillow and eyed the cluster of deer antlers dangling in front of her. "Where on earth do you shop?"

Willa couldn't very well say, *garage sales*. Aloud, she said, "It's a dusty day. Would you like a cup of tea first? I was just about to—"

"It's not easy watching you drive across my land to get to—to this house...which should be mine." When Hesper's cold voice named a reasonable figure, Willa felt a hot flush of humiliation surge through her. She grabbed Sam's one-eyed teddy and hugged him close.

"This is the only home I've known since—"

"Your unfortunate past is hardly my concern, Willa dear. What kind of woman paints a room red? I'll double my first figure."

"What about Big Red?"

"My daddy is not your concern."

"He has been."

"I wondered when you'd throw that in my face. I know why you let him haul rocks. You were hoping it would kill him, that's what. So that you'd inherit more."

"No—"

"How much more...Willa dear?"

"Big Red loves me and Sam. And I love him. He's like a child. He would be lost if we went away."

"Nonsense. He's my daddy. And this is my house."

With a snort Hesper scrawled an outrageous sum, enough for a house, for a new life. Enough to educate Sam all the way through college, through graduate school, too.

Only a fool could reject such an offer. When Willa had nodded miserably, Hesper had bitten back a tight smile. "I keep Big Red's original furniture, the family stuff...the spool bed you let...you let your..."

"Sam."

"Sam sleep in. I want Mother's homemade quilts, too. You can have all the rest of this way-out stuff you chose. The antler chandelier, that life-size saguaro cactus and that awful beanbag that's coming apart at the seams."

"Sam's beanbag."

Willa turned away, feeling utterly rejected. Hesper sat down, carefully removing a pair of scissors and two broken crayons. She'd arranged herself precisely in the chair, like a new queen settling down in her throne to rule. Slowly, she adjusted her checkbook, her thin hand scribbling with a flourish. Ripping the check out, she'd nudged it toward Willa.

Staring at the blue piece of paper, Willa drew in a sharp breath, then another. Barely did she hear the scrape of Hesper's chair as her sister-in-law pushed the chair back.

"I'll let myself out, Willa dear. When I come back next week, I expect you to be gone. Can you do that?"

"Yes."

Willa had stared at Hesper in that chair. Willa had tried to be strong and brave. Tried and failed. Sam had come into the room just as his mother had flung herself to her knees, almost tripping her sister-in-law. "Big Red has been like a father to me. Oh, Hesper, I don't want your money. I want to stay. We could be friends...you and I...."

How Hesper had stiffened. "Have you no shame—Willa dear?"

"Mommy—"

"Let go of me, Willa dear. I want to go home." Hesper stood up too fast. Having forgotten about the antler chandelier, she slammed her forehead into a pointed tip.

"Oh—this awful thing! Are you trying to kill me?"

"I—I'm so sorry, Hesper. Is it bleeding?"

"Never mind! I want you gone." She eyed the chandelier as if it were malevolent. "So, I can start cleaning up this mess! That's all I want. Do I make myself clear?" Gray eyes had stared down at her, eyes so like...so like McKade's. Not that Willa had let herself make that connection.

Remembering that awful scene, Willa sighed. She had found a fortune.

She had to keep it.

Hesper couldn't stop her now.

Neither could McKade.

14

When Willa came back into herself, she was still standing outside her house in the dark. The bitter memory of her humiliating defeat by Hesper in front of her son had further exhausted her.

Willa put her hands on her hips. Well, Hesper wasn't going to win the next round.

Willa notched her chin higher and put a slim, defiant foot on the first step that led up to *her* porch. She had to get to Sam's room and sleep. Sleep. But halfway up the stairs, her boot struck something ropy that wiggled.

Willa jumped. A fifty-dollar bill fell out of her back pocket and fluttered under the steps. With a wounded howl, Casper bounded to his feet, sending pumpkins rolling down the stairs, knocking Willa into a row of *ristras*. The thick, dried bunches of red chile peppers swung crazily.

Cats flew off hot-pink wicker furniture and yellow cushions in alarm. Only Lucy-fee, her black Persian was self-assured enough to stay put on top the largest pumpkin. Spot, who didn't have a single spot on his

fat pale body, began circling Willa, barking with more
gusto than Casper. More pumpkins rolled.

"Shhh, big fellas…shhh. Sorry about your tail,
Casp."

The big fellas were a matched pair of overly affec-
tionate golden labs. They'd been puppies when she'd
found them on the highway, dumped, probably because they'd both had umbilical hernias in need of
surgical repair.

While she stroked Casper behind the ears until he
quit whining, she pushed against the door. There'd
been no way to lock it ever since Sam had taken all
the house keys two weeks ago. He'd confessed he'd
buried them somewhere. "Tweasure. Near my dead
wabbit." Trouble was, he couldn't remember where.
And after digging up a great many bulbs in her flowerbeds in the search, Willa had given up.

When the door gave, Casper and Spot barreled inside the spacious, rectangular living room with its
large fireplace over which hung Willa's beloved, magnificent, melon-colored weaving of a Cape buffalo
chewing strands of wheat. The room had high, beamed
ceilings and tall windows. Not that Willa was thinking
about architecture or decor, not with her dogs toppling
all the suitcases and duffel bags she'd piled beside the
front door.

Crayons, storybooks, and sketching pads spilled
down four rounded steps onto an immense Turkish
area rug of magentas, navies, pinks and blacks.

When the dogs barked at her indoor cat, Magoo flew
off Willa's massive, Victorian sofa which she had re-
upholstered in her favorite color, hot-pink velvet. Magoo raced past a pair of orange, overstuffed chairs

flame-stitched in purple, flew past Sam's yellow bean-bag, down the hall to Willa's yellow kitchen. The two dogs gamboled after him.

Magoo leapt on top of Willa's orange fridge. There he transformed himself into a flat-eared gargoyle hissing at the canine barbarians circling Willa's trestle table. Ladder back chairs fell. Then cushions upholstered in fabric with bright artichokes, asparagus and eggplants tumbled onto the floor, too. Sam's yellow stool crashed. Water from the leak under the sink puddled on the floor, which meant the bucket under the broken pipe must be full again.

Casper spotted the now empty sack that had held chocolate chip cookies and rooted his nose in the bag, spraying crumbs everywhere. Soon the floor and all her vegetable cushions were a gooey mess.

Willa righted chairs and stool, pitched the cookie bag in the trash, stacked her plump, upholstered vegetable cushions to be washed later, emptied and replaced the blue bucket, and then dashed down her turquoise colored hall to make sure Sam was all right. No sooner had she opened his door and seen him sound asleep beneath homemade quilts and his chenille spread, than his stool crashed in the kitchen again. Since Sam was all right, the commotion drew her. When she got back to the kitchen, the big dogs hovered over Magoo's bowl, lapping tuna.

"Not tonight, fellas! Out!"

To her utter amazement, when she opened the back door, the golden giants whirled outside.

Willa's nerves were taut as she shut the door and listened for her maid, Candelaria. In the cool, shadowy silence of the cluttered room, the scents of sage and something herbal mingled with the more pungent scent of a dirty litter box in the utility room. When no one stirred, Willa began to ache in every bone and muscle...not to mention other tender tissues Luke's lovemaking had rubbed raw.

To distract herself from thinking about McKade, she opened the fridge. What other sweets did she have?

She saw a jar of peach preserves snugged right against a smaller jar of jalapeños.

Sweet as a peach and as hot as jalapeño.

The memory of McKade's husky, teasing voice set a series of little anguished shivers darting through her. She reminded herself he'd insulted her, that he considered her a tramp, not a woman he valued.

No sweets tonight.

She took McKade's hat off, setting her trophy squarely in the center of her trestle table. How long would it take him to make the long walk from the other side of the cliffs?

Quickly, she made herself a ham sandwich and drank a glass of milk. Then she took the money out of her back pockets, pulled out her recipe file, and stuffed the bills inside with her index cards.

Moving the briefcases had been two tense hours of climbing up and down cliffs in the dark, two tense hours of jumping every time an owl hooted or a coyote yapped in the dark, two hours of imagining McKade behind her...or worse—if anything could be worse— the bad guys.

She had to get some sleep. She put her glass in the sink filled with dirty dishes, turned out the kitchen lights, and headed down the hall past Big Red's closed door. She turned a corner and was gladdened by the faint orange glow of Sam's night-light against the turquoise wall.

From his doorway, she breathed a sigh of relief. Except for the milk mustache and a few cookie crumbs on his lips, Sam really did appear just as she'd left him. Dirty red curls peeped from his blue baseball cap. The rest of her wild darling was burrowed deeply beneath a tangle of storybooks, stuffed animals, snowy sheets and threadbare quilts. Taking a bath and going to sleep were the two things Sam dreaded most. He didn't have a routine such as a regular bedtime or bath time. But then neither did she.

The storm had scared him, and she'd lost the bath battle. So, he was still in his red flannel shirt and jeans.

Picking his Ali Baba book off the floor, she set it on his messy nightstand. When she sat down beside him, the mattress dipped. Gently, ever so gently, she removed the baseball cap that reeked of little boy and wet dog. Unable to resist, her light fingers stroked the silky curls glued to his soft, warm forehead.

When he let out a sigh, she curled up next to him. Oh, how she loved him. She'd made so many mistakes, but Sam was the one perfect thing in her life. Maybe she wasn't the most organized mom, but she was determined to protect him. He was everything.

But when she snuggled closer, she couldn't sleep. She kept thinking about McKade, what they'd done in that cave. For years, he'd tempted her.

She remembered Little Red in his hospital bed and felt guiltily torn. The doctors had said, "It's a miracle he's lived four years." "It's you, Willa," Little Red had said. "I have you to live for."

Then she saw Little Red's mahogany casket floating

above a sea of yellow roses. Her face scarlet, Willa had been sitting at her husband's gravesite after Sam had embarrassed her. Luke had stolen up behind her. He'd been dressed as solemnly as a pallbearer in an elegant black suit. When he'd leaned down and brushed a tear from her face, she'd jumped.

"It's okay. Kids show their grief in funny ways."

"Everyone thinks I'm a terrible mother."

During the graveside ceremony, Sam had crawled under the coffin and had tried to dive into the open grave. McKade had seized him by the collar.

"He's curious. I was the same," he said. "Little boys need a firm hand."

"He needs love."

"I'd say he's got plenty of that," McKade said in a soft, warm tone. "He needs discipline, too."

She'd been about to argue, but McKade had been so gentle, had spoken so softly to her and she'd been so desperate for comfort, she'd simply stared at him. When she'd come back to herself, everybody, especially Hesper, had been watching them. They thought she was a terrible mother. They'd thought McKade was already her lover. And because they had, she'd blushed guiltily.

Well, now he was. No doubt, that fact would be plain to see every time he was near and she turned three shades of red.

But he had been sweet that day at the funeral. Sweet, at least until she'd told him to go. Only then had he made that obscene offer to buy her, saying he wanted to catch her between husbands and putting a lofty price tag on her sexual services. Her fury at him had pulled her out of her grief.

"How can you be so disreputable at a time like this?" she'd demanded.

He'd smiled. "Easy."

She thought of him out there...in that cave...all alone. She remembered how he'd pranced, how gloriously cute he'd been. Color flamed in her neck and cheeks. He'd been sweet after sex, too.

Scarcely knowing what she did, her hands traced the fullness of her breasts, trailing them down her abdomen. For a second or two she let herself imagine she was in that cave with the naked McKade, that it was his hands, not hers, on her body.

Warmth spread from her face and neck until her entire body seemed aglow. Then she remembered what he really thought of her, what he'd said. *A girl like you.*

Dear God.

She realized what she was doing. In a rage, she stopped, balling her fingers into fists. The sex had been sweet. But only because she'd gone without for so long.

McKade. He was nothing special. He was exactly as Mrs. Brown said all men were, which was why her aunt thought it was up to women to cut themselves the best possible deal. Willa had always hated thinking of love as a commodity to be bought and sold. Love should be free and easy and wonderful.

Like what you feel for McKade, said Mrs. Connor.

Willa bit her lips. Why was she thinking about McKade? She hated him.

But was he cold and shivering...terrified in that long dark tunnel.

You threw him his jeans, said Mrs. Connor.

You gave him his flashlight.

Which was more than the sexy rascal deserved. He was awful.

And yet…she had gloried in his lovemaking. He was even better than he'd been in her dreams.

Why couldn't she sleep? Why couldn't she forget him?

As if she could. Fury or lust—McKade had a grip on her. Mrs. Brown had always told Willa she was too idealistic. Her aunt would have said, "I told you so." Strange that Mrs. Connor approved of McKade.

Finally, Willa did fall asleep only to have that all too familiar abyss open, and the old terrors of her mother and father being swept away and huge gray seas swallowing her whole.

Her mother's terrified, white face implored her to save her before she sank. Willa screamed and screamed. Then the fishermen were there, saving her.

Only it wasn't the fishermen, it was Brand. He was here in New Mexico, standing by the ruined airplane. And he was saying, "There's not going to be a baby. Why did you run from me? Didn't you know I'd find you, find the baby? Why did you have to make this harder? He's mine. Mine. Mine…and so are you!"

McKade's voice broke into her dream. "Somebody else, somebody more dangerous than those guys is looking for you. I came back…to warn you."

Willa's mind worked sleepily, making connections it might not have made in a fully lucid state.

Brand? But McKade hadn't said Brand's name. Yet they knew each other. Little Red had said they'd gone to law school together, that maybe they'd worked together to frame him.

Willa grew hysterical, choking back cries as a hand on her shoulder gently shook her.

"There can't be a baby... Mine..."

"Mommy, wake up...."

Her voice and Sam's. *Not Brand's. Not Brand's.*

Not McKade's, either. She rolled away from her son, but Sam wouldn't quit shaking her. And slowly her nightmare dissipated into the blurry outlines of his pale, worried face.

Brand. How could he still frighten her after all these years? But some instinct made her feel that way. The dreams about him had begun even before Sam's birth. They'd gotten worse when Little Red had taken her skiing, and she'd seen a skier from a distance at Angel Fire. The skier had been a golden giant of a man, who'd looked a lot like Brand.

She hadn't told Little Red, and she'd never let herself dwell on Brand during the day even though she constantly looked over her shoulder, but her recurring dreams had made her know the depth of her fear. She couldn't forget what Brand had intended to do to her.

Even before she'd known she was pregnant, she'd left Brand because he'd refused to see her as a real person. To him she'd been a sexual playmate. When she'd found out about Sam, she'd come back to tell him about the baby, hoping everything would be different. But he hadn't listened. Instead, he'd said he still wanted her...but like before. He hadn't been able to accept her pregnancy or understand how she could want a baby.

And ever since that day on the ski slope, she'd been sure Brand would come after Sam.

Pulling Sam closer, she sobbed helplessly against his thin chest.

"You crying 'cause you don't wanna weave?" Sam messed up *r*'s and *l*'s. Usually, Willa found his mistakes delightful.

She held him tightly. It had only been a dream. Brand didn't know where she was. McKade had been lying when he'd warned her.

But some part of Willa believed in dreams and instinct, and because she did, she couldn't shake the fear that someday Brand would find her and Sam...and be as terrible as he'd been that last night in Laredo.

"A bad dream. Just a bad dream," she lied, forcing slow, deep breaths. "Go back to sleep."

Someday she'd tell him about her mother and father. Maybe she'd even tell him a little about Brand. But now wasn't the time. All that mattered was that her parents had adored her, that they'd been proud of her, that she'd never forgotten them. More than anything in the world she wished she could give that secure kind of childhood to Sam. Although Brand hadn't wanted him, she had. Which meant she had to be both father and mother.

But could any mother be a father, too? Little Red had tried so hard. On his good days, he'd been wonderful. For no reason at all, she wondered what kind of father Luke McKade would make.

McKade, the sex maniac? Forget him.

Willa dried her face with the edge of a sheet. Being a single mother was going to be so difficult. But maybe not so difficult as she'd thought it would be this morning. How she'd dreaded leaving this place, leaving Big Red. Providing for Sam without even these flimsy roots had seemed too hard.

She thought of the money she'd hidden in the desert. The briefcases would give her independence. With the money, she could stay and make all her dreams come true.

"Everything is going to be all right now," she whispered, "now that we don't have to go away."

He smiled.

She closed her eyes.

The treasure map, said Mrs. Connor.

She'd forgotten to draw her treasure map.

Blindly, still half-asleep, Willa stumbled from the bed and dashed down the hall, into her living room where she nearly tripped on Sam's crayons. She knelt down, picked up her sketching pad.

For a long time she sat in the dark and tried to visualize the cave, the cliffs. It all seemed so vague, so unreal now.

Nevertheless, with an uncertain hand, she began to scribble.

Before she finished, the phone rang. It was her aunt, calling as she sometimes did when she was away from Laredo.

"It's thoughtless of you to stay out all hours when an old woman is trying to call."

As if she'd known. "I'm sorry, Aunt."

"Knowing you, you don't give my poor health a thought."

Mrs. Brown always began in a negative vein. As a precaution, they never called each other from their own homes. As usual, Mrs. Brown complained that Willa hadn't called, that she'd lost interest in her.

"I'm sorry, Aunt."

"Brand came by himself the other day and asked where you were. He seemed different...even more determined. You be careful, Willa."

"He scares me," Willa admitted.

Willa knew that underneath her aunt's criticism and complaints there was love and profound concern.

Still shaking after she hung up, she forced herself to finish the map.

When she was done, she stood up. Where to hide it? She had a bad habit of hiding valuables and not remembering where they were. For instance, she still hadn't found all those nude sketches of herself she'd let her friend, Cathy, draw of her while she'd painted her master bath that wild shade of tangerine. Cathy had been artistically blocked. She'd said she couldn't afford to hire a nude model.

"If you help me paint—I'll pose."

"You'll take off all your clothes?"

"Even my pasties and G-string, but you have to paint *all* my bedroom. And you have to promise nobody else will ever see those sketches."

"Pasties?"

"I was kidding!" Willa paused. "You didn't promise you'd help paint!"

"I swear on my mother's grave...."

It was only later when Willa had forgotten where she'd hidden those sketches that she remembered Cathy's mother was still very much alive.

Willa folded the map and headed toward Little Red's room. Since his death, nobody went in there.

Inside the room, her gaze fell on the framed pictures

on the bedside table. The tallest, an eight-by-ten, was of Sam at two hanging on to Casper's tail.

She picked it up, slid the back off and inserted the map between the photograph and the back of the frame. When she saw how black with tarnish the frame was, she remembered Little Red's polishing cloth in the drawer. Quickly, she polished the frame. Then she set it back with the others and went to bed.

A beefy fist sent the Mexican bullwhip snaking out of the darkness. Leather thongs hit the dirt beside Luke's face with a resounding crack, spraying his black head with tiny rocks and plumes of dust. Coughing, Luke jumped back.

"Ain't you somethin'...stripped and trussed hand and foot like a pig for slaughter...."

The man was gaunt, tall, mean-looking. Beneath a grimy black Stetson, he had stringy, unwashed hair and black eyes that were too close together. His Texas accent was even slower than Willa's. "You better talk, asshole."

Gooseflesh covered Luke's lacerated arms and back as he curled himself into a fetal position to ward off more blows.

"Talk...or die...I don't much care which."

The hard voice coupled with his friends' laughter made Luke wince. His throat went dry.

"Lemme do it, *gringo*," said a heavily-accented voice from the cave's opening.

"You had your turn, *amigo*." The whip slashed into the small of Luke's back like a saber. When he writhed, the goons laughed.

"He'll be blubbering like a baby soon enough—"

The two Mexicans made scuffling sounds as they jostled to get a better view.

Luke squinted. Through his lashes, the rude wall of the cave swam in a red haze of pain. One of the petroglyphs brightened into thousands of swirling spirals.

It was a new day. Maybe his last. He'd made it back to the plane. That's where they'd found him. They'd overpowered him and carried him back to the cave.

Luke lay in the dirt, limp, helpless, powerless, his body draining.

The whip whizzed again.

And again.

With every stroke, the leather cut him deeper until the torture began to tear him apart.

Then somebody started screaming.

"Where's the money?"

Somebody said something in Spanish. He heard the word *ghost*.

Luke's lips moved soundlessly. "Willa..."

The short guy with the slicked-back hair leaned closer. "Wheeela?" he mimicked, eyeing him, then nodding to the others. "Who eez theez Wheela?"

Luke shuddered. The coppery scent of death filled his nostrils. He was past pain. Past everything of this earth.

Past everything but her.

Wheela. He'd told them her name.

The last thing he saw before the cave went black was Willa's pale beautiful face laughing up at him in the moonlight after he'd made love to her.

For four years he'd felt bound to her by some invisible thread. He'd watched her work so hard to save his dying brother, watched her grow thin and pale, watched the circles deepen and darken under her blue eyes. He'd wanted to take care of her and her little boy, wanted to keep them safe.

How wonderful and warm and right she'd felt under him in the cave. How happy he'd been during those brief moments. How happy she'd seemed, too. He wanted more happiness with her.

Now that he was dying, he felt an insane need, the savage need to stay alive—for her.

For himself.

Little Red was dead.

It was his turn with her.

Willa. Willa.

Don't let me die.

Book Three

"The very worst things that happen to us, frequently turn out to be the best."

15

Hesper Longworth braked her big Lincoln in red, whirling storm clouds of powdery dust. Hardly had the car stopped and the dust settled, than she burst out of it, surveying the house snootily, and leaving her confused sisters in the back seat. Neither of them had understood the necessity of driving out on such a cold, windy day.

Chilled, coughing a little from the dry air and dust, Hesper screwed the knot of hair on the top of her head a little tighter. Then she plunged her hands deeply into the pockets of her lambskin coat and turned her cold, implacable face toward the mess Willa had made of the ranch headquarters.

Her house now.

Where to start? How?

Hesper was one of those energetic, orderly people who believed she could compel life. She had controlled and bested everyone until she'd sailed her iron-willed vessel full steam ahead into Willa and been bested by that misguided slip of a girl. Willa, who'd spoiled Little Red, who'd spoiled her brat, was far cleverer and more devious than Hesper had given her credit for.

The girl had stopped all logging of spruce and fir, saying, "Birds and animals live in forests."

Willa seemed to be a drifter who floated along, someone who let life happen to her. In truth, this cutesy little conniver who could neither dress nor decorate had seized and held on to the reins of power in this legendary family for four long years.

Well, no more. Little Red was dead and buried. Big Red had had a second stroke after the funeral. Was it any wonder? That brat of hers had given everybody a scare when he'd almost dived headfirst into Little Red's grave and Big Red had quarreled with McKade afterward.

Willa's reign was over. The girl didn't grasp the need to husband the ranch's natural resources for the family. She was too willing to share, too fond of animals, whether they were endangered or not. She wouldn't allow hunters. Hesper strode toward the house, the heavy silver necklace of little handmade bears jingling at her throat like a Mexican *bandida*'s cartridge belt heavy with bullets.

Hesper was in charge again.

Still, Hesper's thoughts, usually so orderly, were jumbled as she marched toward the house. Did the house in this beautiful valley by the stream do that to her? Or was it her fury at Willa that did that?

She couldn't forget that Daddy had promised her this house and this enchanting valley when she'd still been a girl, long before she'd married...so disastrously. He'd adored her then when she'd been young and innocent and naive…the same way he adored Willa now.

Hesper cut off that thought. No matter what she herself had done, she couldn't forget that he'd let Willa have this house, let Willa rebuild and decorate the ranch's headquarters, let Willa put the stamp of her abominable taste on everything that by right was Hesper's.

And Daddy had done it to punish. He reveled in punishing her, because she'd broken his heart long before Willa had turned up to feed his fantasies. Willa had told him lies, led him to believe she was pregnant with Little Red's son. Giving her the house had been her father's final revenge, against his good daughter, his best child, Hesper. She'd been his favorite until she'd told Mama about the Pueblo woman he'd kept in the cabin…about their son…that vile Luke Mc-Kade. Been the favorite until the night their cabin had burned.

Mama had stood by her man, in public. But at home, Big Red's bed had been cold. He'd blamed Hesper.

Longworths didn't talk about what really bothered them. They were better at revenge.

It was Hesper's turn to get hers.

Even if Sam had red hair, he wasn't their kin, wasn't the longed-for grandson. Why, any fool with eyes could see that.

Only Daddy was too addled, too far gone to see what he didn't want to see. All he'd known was that for once he'd had the son he'd dreamed of having. For once, Little Red had stayed home and out of trouble.

Cancer had brought out the best in Little Red. He'd fought the illness with a stoic nobility that had made all of them proud of him. The terrible injustice was that Daddy had given Willa credit for the profound changes in Little Red...when all she'd done was marry him for his name and money to give her unborn brat a home.

She wasn't why he'd changed. It was Little Red's good Longworth blood, finally coming out.

The bright sun flashing off the grilled windows on that chilly, too clear November morning was so painful Hesper Longworth had to hold a bony hand up to shield her eyes. Even so, she still had to squint.

The first sign that things weren't as Willa dear had promised was the fifty-dollar bill lying on the ground square in her path in the middle of a tumble of pumpkins. Not that the usual litter of toys wasn't everywhere. But a fifty-dollar bill and all those pumpkins that looked like they'd been hacked by a madman! How much talent did it take to carve proper jack-o'-lantern faces? How much housekeeping skill was required to remove pumpkins after Halloween was over?

Hesper picked the green bill up, flipped it over, and wondered where it had come from. Had Willa cashed her check? With a grim smile, Hesper pocketed the fifty and stepped over a pumpkin.

The second sign was that those nasty dogs and cats of Willa's milled everywhere.

If their willy-nilly mistress was gone, why were those animals still here?

Hesper frowned and that made her long pale face seem even longer. Her mouth pursed even tighter as she studied the two immense golden dogs lazing on the front steps. Then she looked up. Mongrel cats of all colors, shapes and sizes perched on the railings and regarded her through slitted eyes as if they thought they owned the place and she was the interloper.

People had a bad habit of letting animals they didn't want loose on the highway. Starving dogs and cats wandered up to Willa's chaotically run house.

Willa, herself a stray, liked strays. She took them in, fed them, neutered them and added them to the growing menagerie.

You should have taken them with you, Willa dear. If you don't come back for them, I'll put every single one of your fleabags to sleep.

Car doors slammed behind her. Her sisters were racing to catch her.

The closer Hesper got to the house, the faster her heart beat in her skinny, proud bosom. *My* house now, she reminded herself, her excitement building at the thought of battle with her enemy.

Rushing ahead of Claudia, who was thirty-eight and the youngest of her sisters, Hesper ascended the stairs, kicking toys and Willa's two overfed dogs out of her way. Hesper felt full of herself as the dogs dashed off whining. Yes, she was full enough of grandiose, egotistical determination to best an entire army of scatterbrained Willas. Not that her sisters, even today, were much support. When she'd kicked the dogs, Gracie had broken rank and waddled off toward the garage, shaking her red head in disapproval.

If only her sisters were more like her. Still, at least they agreed their mother had been a long-suffering

saint and their famous father a tyrant. At least they
agreed Willa was a gold digger who had to be sent
packing.

Hesper, the eldest, and the brain of the bunch, was
their leader. Claudia, the beauty, was the youngest, the
most selfish and the sulkiest in Hesper's opinion. But
at least Claudia looked like her sister, the two of them
having inherited their adored mother's dark hair and
alabaster complexion. Unfortunately, the long horsy
face they shared, looked much better on the undeserv-
ing Claudia. As did the dark hair that curled at the tips
on Claudia while Hesper's hung straight and limp.

Maybe it was having red hair that made Gracie so
much wilder and so much more undisciplined. Her
claim to fame was her abundant talent in all the arts
and her keen enthusiasm for them. She bragged constantly about projects that she felt inspired to do. Unfortunately, she was lazy and never followed through.
Finally, she'd given up her painting and sculpting for
photography because it was easier to lug a camera
about than an easel or heavy rocks and chisels. Thus,
Gracie had developed the maddening habit of catching
everybody off guard with that camera of hers. She
egotistically titled her hideous pictures, had them hung
in Cathy's bookstore on the Taos square, and considered herself quite an artist.

Before Willa, the sisters had been so furious with
one another over a show of Gracie's featuring unflattering family pictures at the Book Nook, they hadn't
been speaking to each other or to their father. He'd
made the mistake of laughing at the photographs, especially the unflattering ones of Hesper.

But when Little Red had turned up sick in Vegas, married to the blond usurper, Hesper had instantly sized Willa up as a gold digger. To rid themselves of this outlaw in-law, the sisters had forgiven each other and formed an uneasy alliance.

Mustard-yellow? Hesper hesitated before knocking briskly at the door. Who on earth would paint her front door such a revolting color? And if Willa was going to put those awful yellow cushions on that hot-pink furniture, why hadn't she made them match her yellow door?

And who would leave the childish scribbling all over their front door without touching it up?

Who else but—Willa dear.

When nobody answered, Hesper charged to a front grilled window. Lifting her long, aristocratic nose, she seized the bars and peered through a four-year-old's smudged handprints.

With the bright sunshine behind her, it was difficult to see through the glare of the glass. Still, she made out the suitcases and duffel bags littering the wooden planks and pegs of the floor and that awful yellow beanbag Willa had bought her brat at the flea market. Willa had furnished the living room with an absurd mixture of bad choices. First, there was that awful hot-pink Victorian couch, then the Turkish carpet and those orange chairs. Who in their right mind would put a woven Cape buffalo above their fireplace? Or a life-size, stuffed saguaro cactus near the window? Worst of all was that rotund fertility goddess with the big belly that Willa had been so thrilled to find when she was nine months pregnant.

For a second or two Hesper was so horrified by Willa's furnishings that she didn't quite realize what the suitcases meant. She had envied Willa this house, envied Willa her father's easy affection and Little Red's, too. Envied her for being so happy restoring the house.

It was Hesper's turn now to have Daddy, the house and this beautiful valley. How she would love entertaining once she had the place cleaned up and orderly.

For all her faults and mistakes, the artistic Willa had a comedic flair when it came to color and design. Not that Hesper could appreciate the madcap, illicit blend of everything under the sun even after Gracie had pointed out that only a highly creative person with a free spirit could do the things to a house Willa had done.

Indeed, the disaster was brash, but oh, so dreadfully, dreadfully wrong. Every room was so…so Willa…. Who but Willa would have chosen that loud shade of tangerine for the master bath and then put in a hot-pink tub?

Not that the fireplace at the west end of the room wasn't exactly right. Hesper couldn't have done better herself.

What am I thinking? She stared at the Cape buffalo. Unexpectedly self-conscious and a little annoyed for admiring anything Willa had done, she stood up stiffly and backed quickly away from the window.

Then she remembered the suitcases. Like the cats and dogs and the fifty-dollar bill, they spelled trouble.

Willa and her brat were still here.

The fifty means she intends to keep my money and

stay! Why should anything that trashy little adven-
turess does or doesn't do still surprise me? Maybe
she's somewhere with Luke McKade…carrying on.

Hesper didn't allow herself to dwell on Luke
McKade. She thought of the Pueblo, the tall, dark
woman with the sturdy frame and dauntless spirit, the
woman Big Red had given that cabin in Lost Canyon
to when he'd realized she was with child. Hesper knew
too well who Luke McKade was, what he was to this
family. He had the look of his mother; but the stamp
of their father, too. Hesper had resented his fame and
fortune; resented his new, more familiar relationship
with Little Red since he'd come home from prison,
resented his refurbishing his mother's burned cabin in
Lost Canyon. If Luke McKade had a decent bone in
his body, he'd know why he wasn't wanted here; he
would have stayed away as he had for so long.

But he'd changed. He was bold and brash now, the
same as Willa was. He didn't seem to care if everybody in Taos knew who he was and what he was. And
he'd made his interest in Willa damningly clear, too.

They were a pair. It wouldn't surprise Hesper one
bit to learn he was in on Willa's marriage to Little
Red, that he intended to worm his way into the family
through some new back door. Hesper couldn't let
Willa stay, take up with her lover, especially him.

Why was he always prowling about town? Why had
he gone to see Lou, their lawyer?

McKade hated them. He was dangerous.

"Are you going in?" Claudia demanded sullenly
from behind her.

Turning from the window, Hesper wrinkled her

nose and breathed in the dry, chilly air and a whiff of cat smell.

"Where's Gracie?" she demanded when Claudia joined her at the door.

"Around back, taking pictures of Daddy's weird statues. Says the shadows are good today on that one by the fence, that it looks like a stupendous phallus."

"She would admire that one!"

"Says Willa's car's gone. Daddy's not here, either. Gone off with her somewhere, no doubt."

"No sign of Candelaria, either."

"She went to the Pueblo to see about her mother."

Hesper began to pace the creaky porch floor. Not knowing what to do with herself, she plumped a yellow cushion on the pink wicker sofa so vigorously a black Persian with slitted yellow eyes and three toy trucks went flying.

She wrinkled her nose and sniffed the sofa. She'd have to burn the wicker and scour the porch. Finally, she sat down, her proprietary gaze wandering over the fortified adobe walls surrounding the compound, studied the unfinished sections of the house. Her gaze ran along the woody fringe of tall, leafless cottonwoods shading the creek. She admired the orchards, stables, and other outbuildings. Except for jet trails streaking the blue sky, all was as it had been a hundred years ago or even two hundred years ago.

Hers. At last.

The ancestral house was of great historic significance. All her life, Hesper had dreamed of restoring it, begged Daddy to let her. But after...after her one miscalculation...he'd been so autocratic. And lately, every time she'd mentioned the will or the ranch, he'd been equally evasive. He was too fond of Willa.

Where was Daddy, anyway? Maddened, as she thought of him being with Willa, Hesper thumped her foot on the painted planking. Even when he'd been himself, he'd driven Mother crazy like this, too.

Claudia sat down beside her. She gazed at a bizarre rock table their father had built near the well and said, "Willa had no business encouraging the old fool to build all those strange rock formations."

"She probably does it to call attention to his demented state."

Claudia nodded.

"Not being a real Longworth, she doesn't care about his reputation the way we do," said Hesper.

"She doesn't care about anything the way we do."

"How could she?" agreed Hesper. "She never knew Daddy in his prime...when he was governor...when he was so difficult only the most saintly of women could have endured him."

"Poor mother."

Hesper stared up at the blue sky and sighed. "May she rest in peace."

"Willa's wrapped Daddy around her little finger," said Claudia.

"With her lies," replied Hesper.

"She acts nice. She told the old simpleton she thought that leaning thing behind the garage was glorious."

"I asked her what in tarnation she thought it was," Hesper said. "Do you know what she said? 'Why does it have to be anything? It simply *is*.' Then she dazzled the old fool with the same smile that must have besotted Little Red...and Luke McKade. Willa turned to Daddy and begged, 'Big Red, please...please build Sam a table next. I saw the most wonderful flat rock under the bridge.'''

"Was that the rock he was carrying when he had his stroke?"

"I accused her of that. But she won't admit it. Says he started acting funny as soon as they got home from the cemetery."

"He did get red when he got to talking to Luke McKade," Claudia said. "Remember how he argued with McKade right before his first stroke, too?"

Hesper hadn't liked Big Red, Taos's most famous citizen, choosing to move out here with the newlyweds. But it had been worse when he'd insisted on staying on after he'd had his stroke. That he preferred Willa even after Little Red's death made Hesper and her sisters look bad.

Hesper had sent her maid, Candelaria, over to help, so the gossips couldn't say the sisters had done nothing. But behind Willa's back, Hesper told everyone that Willa just kept the doddering old man around so the town wouldn't see through her.

Claudia pressed a scarlet fingertip to a strand of her dark hair. "You should've called her first."

"If we'd called, do you think she would have answered? Does she ever? Does she even listen to her phone messages till days later?"

Claudia stared gloomily at the dirt garden. "Maybe she's gone. Maybe she's coming back for those suitcases later. She said she was leaving last night."

"She never does what she says."

"Maybe the storm scared her. The lightning was simply awful. I was out driving—"

"This isn't about you! Willa's not scared of hell itself!"

Silver camera dangling from her neck and bouncing against her breasts, Gracie's plump figure trotted heavily toward the house. Breathlessly, she mounted the stairs. When she saw her sisters, she lifted her camera and snapped.

"Warn me next time—before you shoot, so I can smile," Hesper said.

"That would look false." Gracie swept past her seated sisters and boldly rattled the doorknob. "Knob's loose," she said as she jiggled and pushed. The door stuck at first, and then gave. She almost fell inside.

"Just like her...careless. The door's in awful shape and to leave it unlocked... Why anybody could just walk in," Hesper grumbled as floorboards groaned under Gracie's ample weight as she stepped cautiously inside.

"You can't just go in her house," said Claudia.

"Why not?" laughed Gracie.

Hesper gave Claudia a withering look as she got up. "*Our* house...now. Besides, what if she or that child of hers is sick or something?"

"His name is Sam," whispered Gracie softly from inside.

"Don't defend that little bastard."

"Little Red loved him and gave him the Longworth name. I think we should honor his feelings."

"As if Little Red had a lick of sense. He went to prison, in case you've forgotten. Federal prison. Then he married *her*, the first day he got out. What sort of marriage was that?"

"A very good one. Marriage and that precious little redheaded boy brought out the best in Little Red," said Gracie who was very partial to redheaded children. "So did she."

"For all we know *she* led him into a life of crime," Claudia replied.

"Hesper just said they didn't meet until after he got out."

"Exactly," said Hesper. "How can you two believe every single word she says. Like that orphan story. Her parents dying in that sailboat wreck. I hired somebody to check on all that. There is no trace of what happened to her after that accident. No trace. Where did she go? Why won't she say? She could have read that story in the newspaper—"

Gracie gasped. "I can't believe you actually hired an investigator."

"Somebody's got to have brains in this family. All Willa ever wanted was this house, Little Red's money...and to tack our name on her little bastard."

"What about Daddy? She took Daddy off our hands," Claudia said. "And he's a full-time job."

"To get his money. It's elder abuse, plain as day."

"If she's so bad," began Gracie, "if she led Little Red into crime, how come Daddy and Little Red were always so impossible till she came? How come they loved her and became such lambs after she was here?

And we do owe her for nursing our brother so tire-lessly. She never hired anyone...even at the end.''

"To make us look bad," said Hesper.

"What I want to know," said Claudia, who of the sisters, had the keenest interest in men, "is why Luke McKade won't leave her alone? He wouldn't come near us, wouldn't claim kin till she—''

"His presence in our community is another strike against her," declared Hesper. "He's always snooping about, bothering Daddy, seeing our lawyers, looking through files down at the courthouse in regard to our ranch. Willa and he are in this together."

"In what?"

"He wants the ranch."

"But why?"

"Just to take it."

"What have we ever done to him?"

Hesper remembered a mad night lit by flame. Her heart darkened with a bitter answer, but she made no reply.

Silence.

Outside a car door slammed.

A little boy cried, "Aunt Gracie's here!"

Gracie's face lit up. She started toward the door.

From behind the stuffed saguaro near the window, Hesper saw Willa alighting from that brand-new SUV Little Red had bought her. She was carrying bundles of shopping bags. Big Red looked like an awkward heron in a new red flannel shirt and new khaki trousers that didn't quite fit. It irked Hesper that he wouldn't ever let her take him shopping, that he wouldn't wear new clothes for her, but that he'd do anything for Willa.

"Sit down! Be quiet! Both of you! Willa's here! Act like…act like we're having a normal conversation while we wait for her. After all, we have every right to be here."

They stared at her.

"Sit!"

Like children playing musical chairs, the sisters rushed around the hot-pink sofa and orange chairs, knocking the fertility goddess to the floor, bumping into one another as they scrambled for the same chairs until finally they each found something to sit on.

"I'll do the talking," said Hesper, who had landed in Sam's yellow beanbag and sunk deeply to the floor beside the lopsided goddess and stuffed saguaro. Still, Hesper was trying to make the best of this awkward piece of mushy furniture and the fallen goddess. She adjusted her bony frame and plumped up her skirts. Then she picked up the goddess and cradled it in her lap and pretended to examine it with great interest. The last thing she did was screw her topknot tighter.

"Smile, Hesper," warned Gracie a second before her flash went off and she snapped.

"Gotcha!" On a throaty chortle, she added, "I'm going to call this one, *My Big Sister, the Goddess, the Saguaro and the Beanbag.*"

In no way did Hesper's grim, toothy expression resemble a smile.

But others would smile at that snapshot in the weeks to come.

Indeed, *My Big Sister, the Goddess, the Saguaro,*

and the Beanbag would start the next sisterly feud. When Cathy, who owned the Book Nook, proudly announced that Gracie's photograph was the centerpiece of her bookstore show along with a series of loud tangerine nudes Cathy had recently painted herself, Hesper nearly had a heart attack.

"Cathy's nudes? That picture you took of me as well as the one of Daddy's weird rock sculptures along with Cathy's flashy orange nudes?"

"Yes," Cathy and Gracie said proudly.

Hesper attacked them both. "You can't show that unflattering pose that makes me look like I just gave birth to a deformed monster and am wondering what to do with it! I won't let you flaunt those obscene shots of Daddy's stupid rocks, either!"

"We are artists."

"This family still stands for something! Do you want to make me and Daddy the laughingstock of all of Taos?"

Gracie planted her hands on her wide hips. "Daddy is an artist, too."

"Well, then...if you are set on this—"

"I am."

"Well, then—" Hesper drew a deep, self-important breath "—then you are my historical sister."

"So be it."

"I will see you at Daddy's funeral."

16

Willa halfway expected McKade to be waiting for her when she got home from her shopping trip in Taos. But there was no sign of him as she got out of her SUV.

She caught her breath. Wide-winged eagles soared like giant kites against the cobalt blue. Never had her valley seemed more beautiful. It must have snowed last night in the mountains. She could see gleaming white caps clearly in the magical Taos air although the peaks were eighteen miles away.

Not that it had snowed on her lush, emerald-green valley. No, her land was an oasis, a verdant island on the edge of sagebrush stretching toward those faraway mountains. Never in Laredo had she felt so alive as she did out here. Indeed, Willa felt exuberant as she watched Sam race up the porch, past all his pumpkins, in his new jeans and a new flannel shirt.

Maybe it was just coming home, seeing the green grass along the sand-edged river, knowing for sure she could stay that made her feel more relaxed. Oh, how she loved the smell of piñon wood that lingered from

Big Red's fire last night. Oh, how much fun it had been, spending money on those she loved.

"Jeans jus' like Big Red's," Sam had demanded. Indeed, they'd had to search five stores before they'd found this particular outfit that was two sizes too large and almost a duplicate to Big Red's and his own old clothes. Thus, her wild little darling's jeans were rolled up at the ankles, as were the cuffs of his sleeves.

His thin arms were filled with sacks and torn-apart boxes brimming with new toys. Pride in his new possessions had him joyously clomping wooden steps, oblivious to the trailing brown tatters of the cardboard boxes he left in his wake.

Cathy had talked Willa into a black stretch mini, black heels and a fake leopard jacket. Everything including her red earrings had been twenty-five dollars in an offbeat import shop.

"Oh, Willa, now that's eye-popping. You do look like a merry widow. Do you know that your posing inspired me to paint?"

To paint what? Remembering her wild poses on her ladder and what she'd done with her paint brush, Willa was afraid to ask. "I feel anything but merry."

"You've suffered enough. Oh, you do look sexy. If I had your figure, I'd wear it. Nobody ever looks at plump girls in big T-shirts. Wear it for all the plump girls who'd give anything to look like you did on that ladder in your tangerine bathroom."

"How you do run on." But Willa had done a little dance in front of the mirror, and her wanton gyrations in the tight black dress had made them giggle like silly teenagers. Suddenly the outfit had seemed fun instead of trashy.

"You'll wear it home?"

Since nobody was home, except just maybe Mc-Kade, who thought the worst of her anyway, Willa had nodded.

"Cathy, er, do you remember where I said I was going to hide those drawings you made of me?"

"Have you lost them?"

"Y-yes."

"No. You wouldn't tell me where you were going to put them."

"Oh, dear."

Following in Sam's wake, Willa picked up bits of cardboard. Not that she minded. It had been so much fun thrilling him with the purchases. She had taken several fifties from her secret stash. In that same festive mood, she rounded the side of the house.

When she saw Hesper's big, dust-coated, black Lincoln, Willa came to a dead standstill. Oh, dear. How could she deal with Hesper in a tarty dress two sizes too small?

Maybe she could sneak in the back way.

No. She wasn't a sneak.

"Darling," she called snappily to Sam, but he was talking to the animals, not listening to her.

Oh, well.

She mounted the stairs with her own heavy bags and heard the voices of her sisters-in-law. Her anxiety level increased, but so did her air of bravado. Theirs was an exclusive sisterhood, and as such, closed to new members, especially dumb blondes in tarty stretch minis.

She tried to pull her short dress down. But that made her breasts stick out. She'd just have to show them that it was a mistake to judge a book or a woman by a hip-hugging, breast-revealing cover.

For a moment she listened almost wistfully to the relaxed chatter of their voices, and she felt as excluded as she had growing up Mrs. Brown's niece, when the "nice" girls at school had snubbed her.

"You'll never guess who Chance Penn is marrying," Claudia was saying.

Her haughty tone made Willa's stomach tighten. They sounded so cozy in her living room. Were they so sure they were rid of her, that this was their house now?

"Jayne Michael," said Gracie easily.

"Oh, no." This from Hesper. "She's nothing. A schoolteacher."

Nothing. The starch denouncement echoed painfully in Willa's mind. What did they think of her...a penniless T-shirt painter?

"What's wrong with a—"

"It's her family...or rather lack of family," said the high-and-mighty Hesper.

Sam got up from the porch floor where he'd been talking to the two dogs and burst into his living room, flying toward his beanbag as he always did with both dogs gamboling behind him.

Through the window, Willa caught a glimpse of the chaos. Willa's scream mingled with Hesper's.

Magoo took a flying leap. Casper barked. Sam

picked up the pieces of his new GameBoy from the
floor and started crying. This toy, which he'd wanted
but was beyond his age level, had frustrated him
mightily in the car when it had been intact and working properly. Now he was beside himself.

Willa rushed inside and found Hesper on the floor
under the beanbag in a scramble with the two dogs
and Sam and his broken toy. Tail switching, Magoo
was hissing from a high bookshelf.

"You little monster!" spat Hesper.

"S-sorry, Aunt Hespy," blubbered Sam, who
looked more scared than repentant. "But you sat on
my GameBoy and bwoke it."

"I'm not your aunt, young man."

When Hesper glared at him, Sam cried harder,
threw his other toys down and dashed into his
mother's outstretched arms.

"How can you be so cruel?" Willa whispered.

She dropped her shopping bags onto her hot-pink
couch. Picking up his electronic game, she replaced
the batteries and the cover and showed Sam it still
worked.

"Do you have no control over your child?" Hesper
demanded.

"In the boy's defense, you were sitting on his beanbag," said Gracie from her orange chair.

"And an awful experience that was—"

Sam was happily punching electronic buttons.

"You could at least apologize," said Willa, stroking
Sam's curls.

"I—I said s-s-sorry, Aunt Hespy," repeated the
trembling Sam, who stopped jabbing buttons for a sec-

ond and looked up. His thin face was white, his blue eyes brilliant. Freckles stood out. He looked scared. Indeed, his entire body shuddered on his next agonized breath.

"And what a nice apology that was, darling," Willa said, eyeing Hesper.

Hesper bristled while everyone waited for her to apologize. Sam started playing with his new toy again.

Willa stared Hesper down.

Silence.

Hesper shrugged. Her lips thinned. "You, both of you, were supposed to be long gone," said Hesper. "You promised, remember—Willa, dear?"

Willa drew a long breath. "Yes—Hesper, dear. I remember. But unfortunately…or rather fortunately—" She sighed. Oh, she couldn't be mean. Not even to Hesper, whose love she still wanted, for some insane reason. But she couldn't tell them her good news in her present state of fury, either.

Willa closed her eyes, hugged Sam, and prayed for patience.

Sam, who was too lively to hold still long, wiggled loose. When Willa opened her eyes, Hesper frowned at her with immense distaste.

"Good Lord!"

"Oh, so you noticed my new outfit! Cathy picked it out!" Willa lifted her own nose and tried to stare down at her sister-in-law. But it was hard because, like her father, Hesper, who had stood up, was quite tall. "Well," she began, still waiting for Hesper's apology…which didn't come, "I'm thirsty."

"Me, too, Mommy," sniffled Sam.

To gather her courage, she scooped the tearful Sam into her arms and headed into her cheerful, yellow kitchen. "Would anybody like some herbal tea?" she called jauntily.

Oh, why had all three of them come? Willa felt outnumbered—three to one. It was an old feeling she remembered from school in Laredo.

Pretend you're brave. Pretend they love you.

Then she remembered those twelve briefcases and her map, and she didn't have to pretend. It was easy, very easy to blush with pleasure and smile. The magic storm had changed everything. She had money now. She was independent. She could do as she pleased, decorate as she pleased.

She would never have to sell out or sell herself again. She wanted to concentrate on art and on wonder and on literature. Most of all she would have more time for her precious son now. She'd let him run free during Little Red's long illness, rationalizing to herself that most modern children spent way too much time in nurseries being socialized with other children or in front of computer and television screens for their own imaginations to form.

"Tea? I would," thundered Big Red and most merrily from the porch. Then he stepped inside. He was tall and thin, even taller than Hesper, but growing thinner with age. His wispy hair blew untidily across his brow. "Hello, girls." His voice was cold.

"Daddy!" They chimed in unison, sounding like frightened little girls, for, although he was mild-tempered now and patient with Sam, he'd brought them up with a sterner hand.

"Tea," Hesper rasped, trying to ignore her father, who, Willa knew from Hesper's stories about him, could still frighten her as he could never frighten Willa who'd known the gentler, milder man. "You can't be serious. This is our house now. You're not the hostess anymore. You can't just offer us tea."

Willa was slamming yellow cabinet doors. She could and she would offer them tea. Defiantly Willa splashed water into her teakettle.

Frowning, Hesper glided into the kitchen. "I said this is our house now."

"Oh, dear." Willa's back stiffened, but she didn't turn around. She remembered tucking the last brief-case into that second cave. "So, you did." Pretending to ignore her sister-in-law, Willa busied herself looking for tea bags.

"Would you stop that! This isn't a tea party. We struck a deal...you and I."

"Oh, that?" Willa paused, reflected on that dreary time when she'd been so desperate. "I think you'd better sit down," she said coolly, remembering the briefcases. "I have good news."

"Good news? The only good thing you could say to me is goodbye."

"Which I won't be saying anytime soon. So, you see, you'd really better sit down."

"Now you see here! I won't be sitting down!" Hesper pulled a fifty-dollar bill out of her pocket and slapped it faceup on the counter. "Don't tell me you haven't cashed my check. Don't think you can keep my money and stay here, too."

Willa picked the fifty up. "Why, thank you, Hesper.'' She slipped the crisp bill into the pocket of her fake leopard jacket and patted it. ''I must've dropped that. Careless of me, wasn't it? Sam, honey, you remind me where Mommy put this!''

Before Hesper could protest, the teakettle began to sing. Willa took it off the fire, poured the hot water into several cups, dropped in sugar and tea bags. Then she began to search for her own favorite Wedgwood cup, which she'd hidden for safekeeping so Sam wouldn't take it.

''For the last time, I don't want tea. I want you to go.''

Big Red shuffled into the yellow kitchen and Willa smiled sweetly at the tall, lumbering giant and handed him his teacup.

''You always make it just the way I like it,'' he said warmly.

Willa gave up looking for her precious cup and pulled out a chipped white mug. Then, aware of Hesper's tension on the other side of the kitchen, Willa smiled at Big Red who grabbed the eggplant cushion, put it in a chair, and sat down. His answering smile was so brilliant, she blushed.

''Can I have a Coke, Mommy?''

''In a minute, darling,'' sang Willa as she headed toward the pantry.

''Don't you know a boy his age should be drinking milk?'' Hesper said. ''He's supposed to be growing bones.''

''Don't wike milk as good as Coke, Aunt Hespy.'' Sam's big eyes peeped imploringly up through his curly red bangs at the tall scowling woman.

"Young man, life isn't about getting what you want." Hesper flung herself at a cabinet, seized a glass, opened the refrigerator and poured him a glass of foamy white milk. "It's milk or nothing," she said.

Sam eyed the glass, eyed his aunt. When his mother put the cola back in the pantry, he clumsily stuck a dirty hand toward the fat glass.

"Both hands," Hesper ordered. "And why doesn't your mother ever cut that impossible mop of yours?"

"I wikes it wong." Sam slurped greedily. Willa smiled, watching them as she sipped from her teacup.

Hesper caught herself. "You were saying, Willa dear," she began anew, her voice harsher than before. "And don't make such awful noises when you drink, young man."

"I'd so hoped we could be civil to each other," Willa said. "After all, we're practically sisters...."

"We are not anything remotely approaching sisters."

"But if I stay..."

"What? You can't change your mind about that."

"Like I said, I have the most wonderful news."

Sam swigged down the last of his milk, slammed the empty milk glass on the edge of the table, and then companionably pushed his yellow stool nearer the older man. While Sam climbed, Hesper rushed over and pushed the glass to the middle of the table where it couldn't be knocked off and broken.

While the man and boy relaxed with one another, Gracie and Claudia entered the kitchen and added to the tight little sisterly knot of tension coiling around Hesper.

"News?" Hesper demanded.

Willa began fumbling in her purse. Oh, how she wished these women in this room could be her friends, could be a real family—could love her precious Sam.

But when she found Hesper's check stuck in a side pocket with her chewing gum and handed it to her along with a stick of gum, the tightening of the sisters' faces told her they were anything but family.

The piece of paper she handed Hesper was smudged and crumpled, but the scrawl at the bottom and the enormous sum had not been altered. Nor had the check been cashed.

Hesper gasped.

"You didn't cash it," Claudia said, taking the stick of gum from her sister and placing the check on the trestle table.

The three women stared at it, and then at her with equal horror.

"No...and I'm not going to."

Sam snatched McKade's cowboy hat off the table. Then he grabbed the piece of gum and noisily unwrapped it.

"But you obviously went shopping.... All those bags... Daddy's new shirt..."

"Oh, yes, indeed I did. And we had a great time."

Sam was smacking his chewing gum under the Stetson as he played his new game.

"Whose hat is that?" Hesper demanded. Then to Willa she added, "What are you saying?"

"You're not getting rid of me," Willa said. Alarmed, she lifted McKade's hat off Sam's red curls.

With a flip of her wrist, she sent it sailing into the utility room.

"But you promised."

"I fell in love with Taos. Freedom and wonder are in the air out here. So is art. The mountains, my valley...they make me feel alive. This is my home."

"This is our home, yellow kitchen, vegetable cushions and all. You took it!"

"I want to be part of this family."

"You?" cried Hesper. "You're a mess."

"I know, but..."

Before Willa could adequately defend herself, a shot rang out in the distance.

"What was that?" demanded Hesper.

"That sounded like gunfire," said Gracie.

"From the canyon." Big Red sprang to his feet and grabbed Sam.

Another shot. Two more.

Willa screamed. "Call the sheriff!"

"Willa!" cried Hesper.

As always, Willa, who seemed so willy-nilly and free-spirited when life was ordinary, became a gutsy woman, a seize-the-bull-by-the-horns phenomenon when her life was suddenly spiced by danger. "Now! Call him now!"

"What is going on?"

"Take care of Sam!" Willa called to Big Red.

Then Willa ran.

First to her dusky pink bedroom to get McKade's gun. Then she darkened her voluptuous mouth with glistening red lipstick and her brows and eyes with black pencil.

War paint. Sometimes there was no better weapon in a woman's arsenal.

Then she ran outside, racing past pumpkins, cats and dogs, toward the desert and the canyon beyond.

McKade.

The bad guys had McKade.

If they did have him, it was all her fault. Willa felt crazy, crazy desperate to save him.

Maybe they didn't have him.... Maybe...

But if they did...

Willa had never been more terrified.

17

Where's the money?

The bad guys chanted this question like a mantra. Oh, occasionally they got creative. Once the short one got more specific and asked, "Where's our two million dollars?"

Three bad guys, one Anglo and two with darker hotter blood, had McKade, his hands tied behind his back. Their semiconscious prisoner was clad in nothing but his tantalizing black briefs, and the three bullies kept pushing him under in that steaming pool in front of the old rock-walled house at Jeffrey's Springs.

"Where's our two million?"

The amount finally registered in Willa's subconscious.

Two million!

It was hers! All hers—if she had the guts to hold on to it.

McKade didn't reply.

Wide-eyed, the determined millionairess in her fake leopard jacket watched them dunk him again. Only after an unendurable length of time, did they pull his

head up by his long black hair and holler the same
question at him.

Whatever he muttered infuriated them because they
pushed him under again and held him down even
longer. When that big fist just stayed on that black
head beneath the dark-brown water, Willa's blue eyes
dilated and her heart began to flutter in panic.

She glanced around wildly. The house and the
springs were but a short distance below the cliffs and
the caves where Willa had left McKade in that dark
hole for her own safekeeping. Not so far from her new
hiding place, either.

It was her fault they'd found him.

Her fault, they were drowning him.

Let him up. Please let him up, said Mrs. Connor
while Willa chewed the glossy, red lipstick off her
mouth anxiously.

When, at last, they pulled him out, McKade's lean
face was bloodless, his body limp as curls of steam
drifted around him. They shook him, got no response.
"¿Dónde está el dinero?" Same mantra. Different
language.

"Callate."

They talked among themselves. Willa tasted blood
as they hauled him to shore. Her jaw ached.

McKade's shoulders were bloody. So was his back.
When at last water dribbled from his lips, his handsome face was ashen and pain-tormented.

Willa's heart continued to beat too fast, but her fear
had nothing to do with the fact that the men were
grouped alarmingly near the second cave where she'd
rehidden the money, her two million, and everything
to do with McKade's precarious predicament.

They were killing him.

Kill you, McKade? I couldn't get that lucky. Had God heard her taunt the big lug?

Crouching behind a boulder, Willa studied the house with its small window high in its rough stone walls with guilt-stricken remorse. She studied the ladder made of natural rocks, heaped one on top of the other. Then she stared at the fire the men had built, at the thick logs that were snapping and crackling. She almost gasped aloud when two of the men flung McKade down too near the fire just as the third man laid the tip of a branding iron upon the flames.

There were no animals in need of branding.

Only the stripped and bound McKade who lay mere inches from the black length of iron. Only the man who'd made such intense, wild love to her a few short hours ago. *Don't think about that.*

McKade was spitting water into the sand, coughing, gagging. In an agony of suspense, she watched him vomit while they toyed with the branding iron and laughed at him.

They'd beaten him, nearly drowned him. Much more torture, and the brutes would kill him.

And all the while, around this diabolical group and their trussed-up victim, the spring water bubbled and steamed in the cool, crisp air. Willa knew the water to be hotter than body heat but not hot enough to scald one. It was salty, too, so salty you couldn't force yourself below the surface. Sometimes she came down here and skinny-dipped. Once McKade had caught her there, stolen her clothes and made her stand up before he'd handed them to her.

"Where's the money?"

She was used to that question. But her head snapped around when one of them said, "Wheela?"

McKade, the same ruthless rat who'd stolen her clothes, had told them about her.

So what? said Mrs. Connor. *He was probably out of his mind when he did.*

"Where's thees Wheela?"

That voice. It echoed in some dark chamber of her mind. She stared at the small dark man with the slicked-back hair and remembered being tied in that shack. She'd heard that man's voice *that* night. He'd laughed at her, said lewd things about her long legs. Said what he'd wanted to do to her until Brand had told him to shut up. Or was she only imagining this man was the same man?

This man was the same height. But he was heavier, his shoulders more stooped. But it had been four years since that night. People changed, and mostly they got heavier, as this man now was.

Brand had pestered her aunt. Was this Brand's man—here? Willa shivered.

The tall man who held the branding iron prodded McKade's limp body with the toe of his boot. "You aren't going to be pretty when we finish."

Willa could see the structure of McKade's bones and the pattern of his sinewy muscles beneath the slashes and bruises across his wide back. He'd been her lover. Maybe that was why she was struck with the profound meaning of that hard male body, weak and broken as it was.

He was McKade. He was her McKade. For four years she'd lain beside his sick brother and dreamed of this rogue. He'd saved her that first night. She owed him.

They would kill him...and soon.

If she didn't stop them.

Which was the last thing a sensible woman would do.

She said a quick prayer.

Wheela. McKade had ratted on her.

But he'd been a divine lover.

The big man lifted the branding iron and shuffled toward the fallen McKade. "Where's the money?"

"And Wheela?" said the small guy with the combed black hair. "Ees pretty? Where ees theese pretty Wheela?"

The branding iron glowed devil-orange as it neared McKade's dark cheek. Suddenly, as if he felt the heat, the nearly unconscious McKade jerked away from the poker. His silver eyes were wide-awake, alert, round with fear. His bullying assailants savored his shuddering response with laughter.

"So, you're not dead...not yet," the tall one said.

Maybe she gasped or made some other sound because very slowly McKade looked past the branding iron, past the men—straight at her.

His pale eyes burned hotter than any brand. She felt his fury, his searing hatred...and more, much more in his avid, dark gaze.

Why had she left him? Because he was so strong. Because she'd been unable to imagine him helpless, at anyone's mercy.

She could save him. She wondered if he knew that.

He could betray her to them.

"Wheela? Where ees theese Wheela?"

Those hot gray eyes that never left her face glittered cruelly. But he didn't plead with his tormentor.

His were the eyes of an animal trapped in a cage facing certain doom. His lips moved. She wondered what his last words and last thoughts were. Was he telling them where she was? Then even as that burning-hot branding iron neared his exposed cheek at that inexorable pace, he squeezed his eyes shut and pressed his lips together. And waited for them to burn him.

Dear God...he thought she'd betrayed him.

And she had.

Yet he was protecting her.

He was going to let them maim him.

For her sake.

That didn't matter. It couldn't.

Without thinking, she screamed. "Here's Willa! Here I am!" She got up, fluffed her yellow curls, threw the leopard jacket halfway off her shoulders so they could see her body in Cathy's tight black dress.

As their tongues lolled, she smiled invitingly.

"Wheela?" they cried in exultation.

She licked her red lips, raised her gun and took aim. "She's right here. Come and get me." Then in Spanish, she yelled, *"¡Cobardes!"*

Cowards.

When they sprang to their haunches, she pulled the trigger.

18

Luke had to be alive or else in hot-pink hell. He was alive. Nobody hurt this bad if they were dead. His shoulders burned. Every muscle in his huge body ached. When he tried to lift his hand, he was too weak to do more than wiggle his pinky finger.

Was he dying? Like Marcie? Like Little Red? They'd been weak like this right before the end. What was with these pulsating hot-pink walls? Surely, nobody sane painted walls this color.

Watching Marcie and Little Red die young, knowing death as a gut-level reality had made Luke afraid of dying. No. Not afraid. He just wasn't ready.

Still, his bowels felt cold with bottomless fear. Ever since he'd set eyes on Willa, he'd known he'd never really lived. Computers, software innovations, mergers, stock options, IPOs—none of his business triumphs were enough. Which was ridiculous. What else was there for a man like him? Why this insane urge not to die—until he'd had his chance with her?

Willa. He had trusted her after that bawdy romp they'd shared in that cave. Sex. Odd, how her defection had befuddled him with baffling, sappy heart-break. Him? He had no heart.

Where the hell was he? Where was she?

Here's Willa, you bastards.... Come and get me!

She'd been hell on wheels in that black mini with his gun—magnificent.

He remembered what she'd said after she'd run off the bad guys.

It was my turn to save you.

He owed his life to her.

Hell, she was the one who'd gotten him into that jam in the first place.

He could hear wind rustling dry leaves across a wooden floor outside. A bush scratched his window-pane. Dogs were yapping in great excitement some-where nearby. Then a cat hissed, and one of the dogs yelped as if a cat's claw had snagged a canine nose.

Animals. The vivid pink room smelled earthy...of cats and dogs...of musty yellow sheets with hot-pink cats all over them that needed washing.

Willa kept strays. He was a stray. Maybe she'd keep him.

Fool. Baines had asked about Willa every time they'd had occasion to bump into one another, usually on opposite sides of business deals or legal battles gone wrong. Baines was always after him to know where she was and yet pretending he didn't really care even while he seemed to seethe underneath his suave facade.

Luke hadn't told him. Baines never missed a chance to tell him just how trashy Willa was. Which was somehow suspicious. According to Baines, she'd put out for him, for all his friends on both sides of the border. Yet when Luke had offered her a thousand dollars, she'd acted so shy and scared he'd backed down.

"She even said she was pregnant," Baines had said. "Said she wanted to be a mother. What a joke. A girl like her? Said her brat was mine."

"And was he?" Luke had demanded.

"He?"

"It..."

Baines hadn't seemed to notice his slip. "Oh, that was good. She was after my money. Not that she wasn't a talent in the sack. A real talent. They broke the mold in the whorehouse when they made her. It runs in her genes. Her aunt, you know..."

Fury had bubbled in Luke's blood, but he'd kept his voice low and indifferent. "What do you mean—her aunt?"

"Good old Mrs. Brown." Baines had told him about Mrs. Brown's business.

Baines had married. So, why was Baines still looking for Willa?

Another strange thing. The notorious Mrs. Brown had refused to talk to Luke about Willa when he'd gone to see her. Her demeanor had been brusque and protective.

The notorious madam had been holed up in front of her computer in her library with a cigarette and a shot of whiskey. He didn't know much about fine literature, and was surprised she did. The leather-bound volumes of the great classics lined her shelves.

"So you read Homer?" he'd asked.

"Dozens of translations. Even the original...in Greek." She hadn't looked up from her computer;

rather, she'd continued to type. "You work for Baines?"

"No."

She took a drag, exhaled. Then she pushed her bifocals up her nose and squinted at the screen. "I didn't want a child. Didn't want *her*. She was difficult in her own way. Too artistic and idealistic. But now she's grown, and I don't want the wrong sort bothering her, either."

"The wrong sort?"

She'd looked up at him and frowned. "She's a respectable, married woman and as such should be of no interest to a man like you."

"A man like me?"

"You. You're all for you. A money type. No heart and soul."

She damn sure had him figured. "I would think you'd go for a money type."

"I do. But not for Willa." She had paused for effect. "Besides, you wouldn't know what to do with a wife if you had one. She's a good girl, my Willa, maybe a little thoughtless toward me sometimes...forgets to call.... And when she does, she won't listen to a word of my advice. But that's no concern of yours."

She'd ordered Luke out. When he'd lingered she'd called her bouncer.

For some reason, he'd liked the no-nonsense, hard-bitten Mrs. Brown, the intellectual madam, a great deal more than he liked the slippery Baines. At least she was trying to protect Willa from Baines and men like Baines. Men like himself.

Mrs. Brown believed in Willa. If Luke hadn't

known Willa and what she was capable of, maybe he would have respected the older woman's voice of experience.

Willa had been deceitful from beginning to end. She'd acted like a brainless floozy that first night to best him. Then, in the cave, she'd put out for him in order to keep the money. The sex that shouldn't have meant anything to him, had damn sure meant nothing to her.

Voices floated toward him from some other room. His thoughts grew muddled. He recognized Willa's Texas drawl, and strangely, despite all that had happened, her deep slurred tones relaxed his torn muscles and soothed his mind.

A door creaked. A child's voice said, "Zoom, zoom, w-h-hoom!" Something metallic on wheels crashed into a wall. "Oops." Small feet scampering, sliding on a bright-yellow throw rug with tangerine fringe. "Didn't know anybody wuz in Daddy's woom."

Luke opened his eyes and experienced an odd pang of grief. Little Red had died in this room, in this same rumpled bed piled high with homemade quilts and yellow sheets in which he lay. He'd come here that last day.... He'd been so upset about Little Red he hadn't even noticed the hot-pink walls.

Next to the bedside table cluttered with dusty, tarnished frames, a messy stack of curling photographs, a telephone and a tall lamp, a thin, red-haired little boy gripped a toy car with avid delight. In his other hand, the child held a huge, rumpled Stetson.

His hat. She'd given the kid his hat. Had the brat sat on it? Probably.

The kid, tiny though he was, had been a regular Dennis the Menace at Little Red's funeral. Sam's bright blue gaze fastened on Luke's face in worry and wonder. Feeling disconcerted, Luke stared past him at two trees outside the window that had wound round and round one another until they'd grown together. Their entwined branches were bare. From the topmost branch, a pair of owls hooted. He'd stood out there under that tree the day Little Red had died.

"Whoo...whoo," mimicked the kid, following Luke's gaze. Then he leaned closer and set the toy car, a red Porsche which was a lot like Luke's own car, an inch from Luke's nose. "Are you going to die?"

"No."

The boy began to roll the car back in front of Luke's nose, which pulled the sheets and was unendurably nerve-racking.

"Good," said the boy. "How come your skin's so brown? Like Candy's...."

"Candy?"

"F-wom the Pueblo. She talks funny, too."

"You mean Candelaria...."

The kid nodded.

The Native American maid.

Luke's gaze narrowed. Instead of the brat, he saw adobe walls, dirt streets, flies. He smelled liquor on old men's breath, dirty linens. He saw garbage, rusted cars and dirty children. He saw littered yards. The Pueblo, or at least other places where he'd lived with his mother after the fire, belonged to worlds he wanted to forget.

But the memories wouldn't stop. Nor would the songs quit. "Hie! Hy-a! Hy-a! Hie!" He remembered that time when they'd been accepted by neither the white nor the Native American world.

He saw strange dark faces wrinkled from the sun. He heard wild shouts and drums. Then he saw the dancers with their aspen twigs, and remembered that his mother had held him while they'd watched. As always, they'd stood apart from the others, and he'd felt sad and unwanted.

The Longworths had come that day, Hesper too— rich white tourists. His mother had looked at his father with such yearning, but Big Red had stared through her. Luke had run up to him, held out his hands, but the tall man had turned away. Only Hesper had stood her ground, met his gaze. He'd never forget her proud, defiant smile.

Since Luke didn't speak, the kid hopped up onto the bed. Jarred, Luke groaned aloud. "Slow down, kid."

"Sam."

"I know who you are."

"Only call me Harry." As usual he messed up the *r*'s.

"Harry?"

"'Cause he's magic. He's in a story 'bout...'bout..."

"About grave divers?"

"'bout magic." Sam set the black Stetson down on the yellow rug and fiddled with the front tires of his car.

"So, it's to be Harry?" said Luke, amazed at the kid's self-confidence. Sam felt he belonged here...in the Longworth headquarters.

The kid beamed. "Yep." Then he leaned over and

yanked the light chain, flooding the loud room with harsh yellow light.

"My daddy's in heaven." Sam grabbed a picture off the table, but in doing so, knocked half a dozen more over. One, the only untarnished one, the largest, a picture of Sam pulling a big white dog's tail, fell facedown to the floor.

Sam shoved the picture of Little Red toward Luke's face. "See! This is him. 'Tween me and Mom. In 'ospital. He was sick. Like you."

"Hold the picture back a little farther, kid."

"Harry," the child corrected, staring at him.

"Right. Harry."

Sure enough, the picture was of Little Red with his arm around Willa.

Suddenly, Luke remembered another picture, one that had fallen out of Brand's jacket a few months ago. It must have been taken shortly before Little Red's death. It had been of Willa and the kid and Little Red laughing together as they'd lunched outside.

Luke had been both stunned and alarmed. Brand had been deadly serious about finding Willa, and he'd found her. On another level, the photograph had made Luke jealous of the way Willa had smiled at Little Red. He'd kept the picture. He'd rushed back to Taos to keep an eye on Willa, to keep an eye out for Baines.

Again, his brother's thin, happy face brought pain. Little Red had had a life with Willa, four long years.

"He's not coming back. My wabbit died, too. He's in a hole by the fence. Is my wabbit in heaven with Daddy?"

"Sam!" Willa called.

Sam kept spinning the little tires. "Why did my daddy die?"

"Everybody dies."

"Why?"

Why? So, the kid was already philosophical.

"Some things just are, kid."

"Mommy has bad dreams."

"Cookies!" Willa yelled.

Sam flew off the bed and down the hall.

Luke didn't think he'd ever seen any kid move that fast, but he was glad he was gone. The brief exchange had exhausted him. Luke's gaze drifted to the floor, to the fallen picture frame.

Willa was one lousy housekeeper, one lousy decorator. He could tell by this weird pink room alone, by the messy grouping of pictures in those dusty, blackened frames. But the kid seemed to feel secure and happy in this house where Luke could never belong.

He closed his eyes and fell asleep instantly. When he opened them again, the curtains had been drawn and the lamp beside him was still lit. Willa was hovering near, her hand gently stroking his damp black hair. For once, her outfit was both tasteful and flattering. Indeed, she was gorgeous in that voluminous, soft, white cashmere dress. Her long legs were bare except for moccasins. A chunk of turquoise dangled from her throat on a silver chain. In her right hand, she held a tall plastic cup of water with a straw in it.

"Are you thirsty? I think you're a little feverish."

He tried to focus, but her pretty face above the turquoise rock wavered. His mouth did feel parched, his throat swollen and dry. His skin burned. What he wanted most was a taste of her. That desire infuriated him. She was the enemy—this hateful, destroying, flaky woman-child.

"Your fault," he accused.

"Yours, too," she whispered in a voice that sounded chastened.

How long had he been in the desert? In this bed? Under her power?

Behind her, he was aware of the photographs he'd seen before on the table, photographs of her with Little Red and the other Longworths. All were there except the one that had fallen. Then someone spoke from the doorway in a harsh, low tone.

"It's about time he came around," said Hesper.

"I don't understand what happened to him," Gracie said.

His sisters didn't want their bastard Indian brother here.

"He's hurt. That's all that matters," whispered Willa.

The air fairly crackled with a mixture of curiosity and hostility. With a start Luke realized Claudia, Gracie, his grim-faced father and that dark woman from the Pueblo stood in the shadow near the door.

"Surely, even you can see why you can't keep him here," goaded Hesper.

"Just for a little while," Willa pleaded.

"You always do the outrageous thing, don't you?" Hesper accused.

How right his disagreeable and dangerous half sister was. And yet, because of Willa, he had a foothold in the Longworth household.

"What will the town think?" Hesper persisted.

"Nothing...if you say nothing."

"As if I'm a common gossip—"

Everyone was silent.

"You do like to tell tales on me," Willa replied after a charged interval.

"There are no shortage of tales to tell."

Luke could have told them a tale or two. While they argued, his woozy mind wandered.

Why hadn't he carried through with his threats to do just that? Usually, he destroyed his enemies. Why was he all bluff and bluster when it came to Willa? She'd called him a pussycat once, right to his face, in the town square. After that insult, she'd elaborated. "I knew you were soft on me, McKade, that first night...when you didn't force me."

"Soft?"

She'd laughed. "No man likes that word."

"I should have forced you. You'd be out of my system by now."

"You sure?" She'd laughed again and then disappeared into that little bookshop after Little Red, leaving him to stew in his own jealousies. For long moments he'd stared into that shop window and watched them together with Cathy Wilkes, the shop owner, Willa's friend. They'd bought Sam the book Cathy had started reading to him. Then the four of them had had tea in a nearby restaurant with Gracie. Once Cathy had caught his eye and winked, almost slyly.

It seemed to Luke that the Longworths, who had rejected him, had embraced Willa, as if she were real family. Not that he cared. Not that his increased feelings of alienation had anything to do with the constant tightness in his chest every time he saw Willa with them. His feelings toward Willa hadn't intensified. They hadn't.

For four long years he'd damn sure stewed about something, though. Sometimes he'd gone into the Book Nook and talked to Cathy, who was an aspiring painter turned bookseller. Cathy was always hanging strange artwork on her walls. Unlike Willa, Cathy had always been gratifyingly eager for his attention. From her he'd learned more details about Willa and the Longworths. Even though he'd gathered from the plump, overfriendly Cathy, who couldn't help gabbing about the most prominent family in the valley, that Hesper hadn't fully accepted Willa, Willa had rebuilt the Longworth headquarters and tried to make herself a real Longworth.

"Not that she'll succeed," Cathy said. "Not with them so set against her."

"Who?"

"Hesper. And because she's so awesome, all of the sisters. After Little Red died, do you know what they did?"

He'd shaken his head as if he hadn't much cared.

"First thing—they went to their lawyer to see if Little Red's will could be broken."

"And you know that, how?"

"Lou is a customer of mine, too."

"Lou is the Longworth lawyer, too?"

"And a good one. Had him draw up the papers for my shop."

"Does everybody in Taos know everybody's business?"

Cathy had flashed him a wide grin. "It's a small

town." She had paused. "Do you want to see my work in progress?"

When he had said that he had, she'd pulled a drape off a loud orange canvas. A graceful nude woman with a head full of golden curls lounged in a hot-pink tub. He couldn't help noticing that she was a natural blonde. But the painting was impressionistic and could have been of any pretty young girl. And yet... For no reason, he'd been riveted. Why was she holding that eggplant pillow?

"Very nice," he'd said in a general way because he liked paintings, especially nudes. "Personally, I prefer more realistic detail."

"I thought you'd think it's awesome," Cathy had said slyly. "I expected more of a reaction."

"Maybe when you finish the face and I can tell who it is... What inspired this painting?"

"A friend posed for some sketches." Cathy unscrewed a tube of bright paint. "See, the sisters don't like Willa laying claim to the headquarters and the thousand acres surrounding the house. Her acreage is smack-dab in the middle of their ranch. She can't get to it, without driving across their property. They see her go in and out every time she takes a notion."

"These sisters own the ranch then?"

"Not yet. Not till their father dies."

"Sounds like they're counting on these eggs hatching mighty hard."

"Who else would he leave it to?" She'd stared at him slyly again, but Luke had merely waited for her to continue.

"See, that awesome house and the surrounding acreage was what Little Red left her. But the sisters are hopping mad. They think it should be theirs. It's not right, though. Willa's good nursing is what kept their brother alive so long.''

"I thought he had experimental treatments.''

"Oh, that. Everybody knows Willa was absolutely awesome.''

"Really.''

"Did you know she and he helped high school boys in trouble? She inspired Little Red to be a better man. She said he did the same for her.''

From Cathy he'd learned that Willa had fought for her place in the family like a tiger, fought for all the things he'd told himself didn't matter to him even though they were more rightfully his than hers. Bold as brass, Willa had come along, married Little Red, and stolen his birthright out from under him. Not that Luke cared.

Luke had started coming to New Mexico, telling himself all the time he was indifferent to all of them. Indifferent even to the woman who'd stood against that wall of flame. Most of all he'd told himself he was indifferent to Willa.

Still, he'd kept coming and every visit had increased his need to do something.

Then Willa had slept with him, and like a sap, he'd almost believed in her soft kisses, warm body and dazzling smiles, almost regretted some of the steps he'd taken in Taos to make things right. He stopped himself. Better not to let his mind travel down those dark avenues.

Better to concentrate on the fact that she'd taken the money and sicced the bad guys on him. Better not to admit that the sex, instead of assuaging his needs, had had him aching for more.

Not that he had meant anything to her. All she'd cared about was the money. She'd left him in that cave. Because of her, he'd damn near died. If he still wanted her, he'd have to make her tell him where the money was. Then he'd work out some kind of financial arrangement that would satisfy them both. She wanted money. He wanted sex. He was sure they would soon come to an arrangement.

He was through with bluff and bluster.

He saw her in that tight black mini, her gun raised. His lips curved.

Hesper's sharp voice cut through his thoughts. "He needs a real doctor—Willa."

"After nursing Little Red, I know enough to take care of Mr. McKade. He's just worn-out. His wounds are superficial. I cleaned them and dressed them. I gave him antibiotics that I had left over."

Superficial? What did she know? *Antibiotics?* Poison, more likely.

"You should call a doctor."

"That is your opinion." To him Willa said, "You've got to sit up."

When he couldn't and was gasping in humiliation that he was so weak, Willa consoled him. "You'll be all right. Soon."

He grumbled darkly.

"I promise."

"As if you care," he growled.

It took three of them to turn him.

Then Willa held a cup of water beneath his chin

with infinite patience and gentleness. She smiled when he was done.

That smile. It lit her face as well as every black corner in his icy heart.

He felt lost, unsure—powerless.

In her power.

But that was only because he was so weak and susceptible. Tomorrow he would be stronger. And the next day…and the next… Soon, he would find the money. She would be in *his* power then. And he'd get his revenge on the Longworths and force Willa to cut a mutually beneficial deal.

"That Stetson was in the kitchen," said Hesper. "What was he doing on Longworth land in the first place—to get himself hurt? Who were those men?"

Willa blushed.

Luke was aware of Big Red glaring at him. The old man looked almost afraid. He didn't want to share a roof with Luke any more than Luke wanted to share one with him.

"You want him here because he's your lover," Hesper persisted on the same tack.

Everyone gasped; Willa's blush deepened against her white cashmere neckline until she was almost as pink as the wall. Big Red stalked out of the room.

Maybe McKade wouldn't have to wait until he was stronger. "Come here, Hesper," he rasped. When she did, when she bent her narrow, sour face closer and began to twist her hair tighter, he said roughly, "Yes, this is my hat, and she's my woman. I've had her. And I'll have her again…and again…so get used to it. And another thing—I'm here to stay in this house.

I have as much right, maybe more to be here—than you!''

"Mommy!" shrieked Sam. "A scorpy! Under my picture."

Willa, who was purple with shame, bent down to help Sam. "I'll see about the scorpion. Go to your room, darling."

The kid was poking his toy Porsche at the scorpion's curled tail. "Is he mean?"

The scorpion jumped. So did Sam.

"Yes. He's very mean." Willa stared at Luke as she picked up the picture. Despite the drama of the moment, Luke noted that she started to put it back with the others and then blushed guiltily when she saw he was watching her and got so flustered she did not replace it.

"Go!" Luke growled to the boy.

The kid ran and the scorpion vanished under his bed.

"Where was I?" Luke's gaze locked angrily on Willa's frightened blue eyes. "Oh, yes. I'm here to stay...because of her." He paused for effect. "She's a blonde," he snarled, letting his insolent gaze drift lower than Willa's face. "And I have a thing for natural blondes. Especially wild ones."

"No," Willa whispered, but her face had gone hotter and darker. Guilt-stricken tears made her soft voice raw and her blue eyes luminous with pain and regret.

Hesper drew back. "He *is* your lover! That's why you were so vague when you talked to the sheriff! You barely answered his questions! And you wouldn't let him near McKade. I knew then that you and McKade are up to some low-down scheme. I mean to find out what it is before the two of you destroy this ranch and the Longworth name!''

"I—I couldn't leave him out there to die.''

"If he isn't your lover, I say call an ambulance. Get rid of him. I want him off our property.''

Suddenly, Willa seemed aware of her gaping audience, and the need to end this argument before it escalated even further. "No! You go!'' She turned. "All of you! I'm tired of being judged your inferior. This is my house now. Sam's home, too. I have the money to stay, and I'll do as I please. If I decide to call an ambulance, I'll do it. But only—if I decide.''

"Let's go,'' said Gracie.

Everybody left. Even Big Red, who'd been in the hall, shuffled gloomily down that turquoise tunnel out to the barn, saying he didn't want to sleep in the house with the likes of McKade, that he'd rather sleep with Molly in her stall.

Except for a big black Persian that leapt onto the bed, Luke was alone with Willa.

"I will get rid of you,'' Willa whispered, her soft drawl filled with regret. "I wish they had killed you!'' But her thin face held no enthusiasm for his murder. Indeed, he sensed that tender vulnerability in her that always drew him.

"Why? Why did you save me?'' he demanded.

"On impulse,'' she lashed. "If I'd given it even one microsecond of...of logical thought, if I'd known how ungrateful and hateful you'd be, I would have aimed my gun at you! At...at...''

He laughed bitterly. "I wonder... Would you have shot the part you most admire and desire?''

"Desire? Ha! I'll show you!'' She lifted the phone, punched in three numbers. "I need an ambu—''

"You lying, conniving, betraying witch! One minute you almost had me believing…"

She stared at him. "You're a conceited fool, McKade."

His gaze narrowed. "No more!"

"Ambulance," she repeated into the phone.

Fury exploded inside him. From somewhere outside himself power fueled this driving rage. With his last ounce of strength, he seized her slim wrist and flung the phone to the floor.

"You are my lover, Willa Longworth! You fucked me in that cave! Then you left me to die! You're not getting rid of me! Not tonight. Not ever. Not till I decide. You're going to pay for what you've done."

He drew her closer, intending to ravage her with his hands and mouth.

"I—I had to do what I did."

"Did you now?"

"And—and you just humiliated me in front of Hesper, my sister-in-law," Willa said.

"So what? I could tell you stories…." He stopped himself. "Anyway, she already despises you."

"You think I'm so cheap and low," she protested, "that what we did in the cave…"

"I don't think…. I *know*…."

They glared at one another.

"Baines told me about you. Told me that kid you spoil rotten could have been anybody's in Laredo. Told me you went after him before you snagged Little Red."

"You're still in touch with Brandon Baines?" Her eyes grew huge.

"He told me you were raised by a Mrs. Brown, who ran a whorehouse on the other side of the border."

Willa was white, save for two livid splotches of color that stained her cheeks. "My life is complicated. Mrs. Brown isn't what you think. She's a hard woman in a way, but she did the best she could by me."

"Don't give me that bull. I met her, talked to her. Your Mrs. Brown is a madam. The best. Baines told me she trained you to be the best little whore in all of Texas. He said I should sample your wares, first chance I get." He paused. "Which I did."

"You…and he… Oh… Y-you—you *bastard!*"

He sucked in a hard breath. As always that particular insult stabbed him like the keenest blade. "Just like your son!"

She fought him. He held her fast.

"Baines told me to give him your phone number when I'm done—so he can enjoy a repeat sample himself."

Her eyes widened…with what emotion?

Luke didn't add that what Baines had said had driven Luke mad with fury and jealousy. "Baines was right. The Widow Longworth always goes for the money. Well, I've got money, Willa. You don't need the money you stole. I've got lots and lots of money. I'll cut you the best deal a man in my position ever cut a girl like you."

Her thin face whitened. Never had her huge, pain-filled blue eyes seemed more brutally beautiful as they did when she struggled to push free.

"Did you tell Baines about me?" she whispered. "Did you tell him where…where I live?"

His grip tightened. "Not yet! Because I'm here, in your house, in your bed, because I'm not done with you." Suddenly, Luke's mouth was on hers. God, even when he was livid, she tasted sweet. Even when he felt profound pain and wounded pride and jealousy, the male animal in him was wild for her again.

She'd called him a bastard. Nobody, nobody got away with that.

God, how he wanted her.

For a second her moist lips were warm, responsive, tender almost. Her sad, eager, terrified gentleness in that brief instant inflamed him even more. Then she began to flail wildly, and it took the last of his strength to try to subdue her.

Just as suddenly, she stopped struggling and wound her arms around his neck and went sweet and still. As always when he was in her clutches, he was too far gone with desire to be suspicious.

When he deepened their kiss, thrusting his tongue inside her lips, she retaliated, digging her fingernails deeply into the open wounds of his upper back.

Pain. Ten thousand white-hot knives flayed his shredded nerves and torn muscles.

He screamed and fell back onto the tumble of yellow sheets with those pink cats.

The last thing he remembered before he fainted in her arms was Willa's strangled, heartbroken cry.

He held on to her even when he was past consciousness. And in that silent dark, cradled in her arms, as she rocked and crooned to him, he knew a peace he had never known before.

When he woke up the next morning, he was still in her arms. How strange and sweet it was to find her there, sleeping beside him, her face relaxed, her body boneless.

His fury toward her was gone. She had saved his life. She had brought him home to care for him. She'd fought his sisters for him. Had she been so worried about him, she'd stayed with him all night? Or was it the money he'd offered her?

More than anything he wished that she loved him and trusted him, that she would wake up and be glad to find him there.

He wanted her soft lips on his in love, not hate. He wanted to wake up beside her every morning. To make love to her.

Gently, careful not to wake her, he brushed his lips into her hair.

When she stirred a few minutes later, he pretended to be asleep. Through his shuttered lashes, he was aware of her easing her tangled limbs free of his.

She got out of bed and stared down at him for a long time. Then she went to the window where a blaze of pink light lit her face. "Dear God," she muttered as she sank to her knees and pressed her fingertips together. "Dear God...tell me what to do."

For the first time since he could remember, he prayed, too.

19

Even out here, in the desert under the big bright dome of cloudless blue, Willa felt trapped by blue sky, red desert—and McKade. In the week McKade had been with her, he'd taken over her house, her life, her kid—her.

He didn't like the way she dressed, the way she decorated, the way she kept house, where she shopped or how she raised Sam. And he had plenty of "helpful" or "constructive" advice, as he put it, on all those subjects.

Indeed, as she scanned the cliffs, she felt small, hopelessly lost.

Where was her cave? Her briefcases? Her security? Her future? Her means to escape McKade?

She'd been confused about the cave's location even when she'd drawn her map, which she'd failed to bring on this trip, and so much more had happened to confuse her since then.

By morning, the soaring, red limestone walls of the canyon seemed high, long and totally unfamiliar. Every cliff and every sage bush seemed the same.

"Where?" Willa cried in desperation. Wildly, she clambered down a narrow ledge, causing a diminutive avalanche to flow in front of her.

Oblivious to Willa's panic and the rocks trickling down that sheer edge, Molly snorted and continued nibbling at the sparse tufts of greenery that sprouted through red earth.

Suddenly the natural stillness and silence of the solid, red cliffs was broken by a sonorous stream of long drawn-out echoes.

"Where? Where? Where?"

Willa sank to her knees on the path, black hopelessness gripping her as she listened to those repeated cries. Under the best of circumstances, the early morning hour was too cold for an enjoyable ride. Having McKade on her case was hardly the best of circumstances.

Willa had felt too sick to her stomach to eat breakfast. Thus, she was both shivering and queasily hungry. Now she had more to be frightened of than the mercenary McKade. The cave, all trace of it, had vanished.

She got up, dusted her jeans off and went to Molly. There was nothing she could do but go on to McKade's cabin. As impatient as he was, if she didn't return, he'd soon come galloping after her. She put a slim foot into the stirrup and swung herself into the saddle.

Perhaps there's no better way to rethink one's life than a solitary ride in the desert. With the highly energetic McKade at home to distract her, she needed to think. As she rode, scenes from the past week replayed themselves in her mind.

Willa hated losing things, but McKade had her so flustered, she did so constantly. Several times a day she was turning cushions upside down, rifling through drawers for lost papers, jewelry or lists. McKade teased her, telling her that everything should have its own place.

With bleeding fingers she clung to the reins and worried about where the money was, worried about McKade finding her map while she was gone and then sneaking out and finding the money first.

This latest disaster was McKade's fault. Because of their fight this morning she'd forgotten her map. No doubt at this very moment he was home, sifting through her possessions. The more she thought about him, the more she worried. By the time she and Molly reached the high basalt boulders that formed the entrance to Lost Canyon, Willa's pretty face was strained. She'd wasted an hour climbing those plum-colored rocks in search of the money. McKade would ask what had taken her so long. What if she couldn't find the money again?

She could. Her map was back at the house, behind Sam's picture that she'd buried under her nightgowns in her bureau. But—but had she been confused that night when she'd drawn it?

Better to think about McKade than the map and lost briefcases. Their squabble this morning had broken out because he'd had all of them up at daybreak, so he could send Pablo, the ranch manager, to get the registration numbers off the plane. Then McKade had made a noisy game of Sam cleaning his toys out of her hot-pink bathtub. While Sam had bathed—even happily scrubbing behind his ears for McKade,

McKade had made calls to his staff, demanding they get him his Blackberry pager and that a T1 line for his fast-speed modem be installed so he could work. He started talking about money, deals. The man lived, breathed, thought money.

"You can't just move in," she'd said when he hung up.

"You don't get it, do you? I already have."

If the big, restless lug, who was used to running companies, was going mad with nothing to do and nobody to run but her and Sam…well, so was she. She'd grabbed the phone when he was done issuing orders to his staff, remembering too late when she bumped up against his big tanned body and heard the dryer banging, his habit of stomping around the house every morning clad only in a towel while he did his laundry.

"Just what do you think you're doing?" she'd demanded, glaring at his brown torso, at that thick mat of black hair at his chest, and then at his dark, carved face and yet, all the time, wondering if he was completely naked under that towel. Feeling her keen interest, he'd met her eyes with his most wicked, beguiling smile.

"Want a peek under my kilt?"

She'd reddened.

"Did you steal a peek that first night you slept with me?"

"Would you forget about that night?"

For a moment he stood without moving, watching her in the sunlight in that heated manner that made her so sexually aware of him. His gaze had darkened as it drifted over every curve. "What? And give up one of my most cherished memories? Willa, I'd take very good care of you...."

He'd meant he'd pay a lot to have sex with her any time he felt like it. And, she...she'd felt turned on, furious, confused. The conflicting emotions had struggled within her. "You had no right to send Pablo—"

"Those guys aren't going to forget about that money," he'd whispered huskily. "I want to know who they are, so we can be ready when they come back."

"We? There is no we! I want you gone! I won't have you taking over my house—"

"It's time someone did. Admit it. What really scares you is how much better your life is with me around."

"I think you're a greedy, grabby, mercenary beast."

"Or...maybe I'm just a competent, rich and successful businessman who knows how to make order and sense out of chaos."

She wasn't about to admit that she did feel safer...that she didn't worry about Brand nearly so much as she always had before. Which was ridiculous. How could she feel safer when McKade himself was so dangerous to her? When McKade was a link to Brand? Little Red had believed McKade and Brand had set him up.

"Sam is happier, too," McKade continued. "I mean Harry."

What McKade said was annoyingly true.

"What about Big Red? He won't come anywhere near the house because he dislikes you."

McKade's face had darkened, but he'd ignored that reference to his father. "Your routine has benefited enormously by my determination to get you organized, neater and more consistent in your approach to Harry.''

"Don't call him that!''

"You should follow me around and take notes... maybe adopt a few of my methods. Until I came, you lost everything. I am an expert on efficiency.''

"You are too conceited for words!''

"You're just jealous.''

"Am not!''

"Then why didn't you thank me for fixing the front door...not to mention that pipe gushing water under your kitchen sink.''

"Big Red liked emptying the bucket.''

Again, McKade had ignored her reference to the older man. "Well, be rude. Don't say thank you.''

"I won't define myself by your insults!''

"Well, neither will I! I'm proud of my accomplishments...and believe me...there was plenty to do around here. I could hire you a decorator—''

"Don't you dare insult me! And I don't believe for one minute you do anything helpful out of altruistic reasons.''

"Harry—''

"Sam is none of your business.''

"Children—who live in the same house with me—need limits. Just as disorganized women, albeit very pretty ones with a penchant for loud colors and baggy jeans, could do with a few guidelines.''

"You don't live here! And as for children, they—my son—needs love, which is something a man like you knows nothing about.''

"He was a four-year-old tyrant till I showed up. In short, my love—he's cute like his mother, but a brat."

"I am not your love!"

"Ah, but you will be! I would pay you way more than what was in those briefcases."

The mention of money got her mad, but the warm glint in his eyes got her flustered. "S-Sam was a free spirit...till you started bossing him around. How dare—"

"I heard what that teacher of his said when she called."

"Miss Goodwin is an anal-retentive drill sergeant and has no more business in the classroom bullying sensitive, creative children than you do."

"You spoil him. At his age he has no business sleeping with you. You need me in your flower-power bed...not a four-year-old."

"Would you—"

"Harry needs to bathe in that hot-pink tub of yours, to eat properly, to get places on time, to keep his things where he can find them."

"Much as I hate you offering to buy me, I dislike you pretending an interest in my son, Sam, even more. I want you gone."

"And I can't forget how wonderful it was to wake up in your arms."

Even before he'd grabbed her, she'd seen the brilliant fire of his silver gaze intent on her mouth. She'd known then that she had to get away. Maybe he had, too, because that's when they'd really fought.

"Why don't you wear something besides that towel?" she'd squeaked.

"You know Big Red only loaned me one pair of jeans and they're in the dryer."

"That's no excuse to parade around my house with nothing on."

"Willa dear, if you want nothing, and my God, I believe you do—here's nothing."

He let her go. Even before he ripped the towel aside, she'd scampered to her bedroom for safety. When she'd slammed her door, she'd heard him laughing.

"You peeked."

And she had. Oh, she had. She had watched him strut around exactly as he had in the cave when she'd refused to give him his clothes. "I did not!"

He'd laughed. "You couldn't resist. That's what I like about you. You're a wanton. You don't fool me in those baggy clothes and no makeup, Willa. You can't repress your true inclinations any more than you could resist the temptation to ogle. Every time we're in the same room, I feel the electricity."

"Maybe it's just the wild paint colors getting to you."

"I don't think so, do you?"

Every time he touched her, she sizzled.

Dear God, with him around, the atmosphere in the house just got hotter and hotter. So hot she almost longed for pale-beige walls.

"Too bad the electricity doesn't shock the life out of you—McKade *dear!*"

"You don't hate me...you just wish you did."

"Indeed I do."

"I know who Heathcliff is now," he whispered proudly one day. "How the hell did that spoiled Cathy get such a grip on him?''

"I don't remember giving you permission to read my books.''

"I didn't think you'd mind. You kept saying you wished I'd do something besides pester you or offer to pay—" She'd glared. "I don't like *Wuthering Heights* too much.''

"It happens to be my favorite book.''

"If you ask me, it's a wordy melodrama.''

"Well, I didn't ask…any more than I asked for your decorating help, now did I?''

McKade was staying, invading her world, every part of it. The temperature between them was rising, and no matter how much she wanted him out of her house, he wasn't about to budge. When he was on the phone he spoke in terms of millions, even billions. He was very rich. He could take lavish care of her. And of Harry. *Sam!*

Don't even think about it.

Think about how sick and tired you are of him parading around your house with a quilt or a towel tied around his slim, brown waist.

Mainly because she was tired of the shivers that virile strutting of his caused—and because she'd wanted to check on her briefcases—she'd ridden over to find him something to wear.

It had been a hellish week for both parties, a true battle of wills and senses and yet a funny week in that peculiar way that makes horrible things amusing. McKade did tempt her both financially and sexually.

Which was why she had wanted her own money in the first place. The briefcases were supposed to give her command of her own destiny. Instead, they had brought McKade into her life, who like most men, had control issues as well as sexual issues. She was being bossed around and hit on by an impossible, oversexed control freak who'd obsessed about her for four years. Whom she'd obsessed about, too.

He was handsome and rich. He said he'd set her up in a mansion, give her everything money could buy, give Sam every opportunity. And all she had to do was sleep with him in her flower-power bed...which was something she wanted to do, anyway.

Not good enough.

And why was McKade so deliberately cruel to Big Red?

Molly snorted.

Ahead, Willa saw McKade's ramshackle cabin nestled beneath raggedy cottonwood trees and more basalt boulders in the dark canyon. There had been a fire over many acres at some point. The trees were still blackened and stunted, the land barren. It took the desert a long time to recover. The house itself had been a charred ruin when Little Red had first shown it to her. McKade had caused quite a furor when he'd sued the Longworths three years ago and taken possession.

"He has no right on Longworth property," Big Red had ranted, for he'd been stronger then, a completely different man before his first stroke.

But McKade had ended their dispute when he'd produced title and deed.

Willa knew Big Red had given the house and the land to McKade's mother, that the lovers used to meet there, a fact that had scandalized all of Taos, especially after their child was born. Then one night the house had burned.

Willa had only been to the canyon that one time before. Alone, this morning, she gasped in awe at its stark, tortured beauty. She noted the deer tracks, the piñon trees, the crystal blue of the sky, the distant purple of the mountains. The ancient canyon was as disconcertingly haunting as her green valley.

It was as if something lived on here. Did she feel the presence of those who had gone before, of the Native Americans, who had passed here through the centuries on their mysterious errands?

As she dismounted she remembered Hesper flinging herself at Little Red three years ago. "McKade's back. Says he's staying. Says he wants Lost Canyon. He intends to restore the cabin. You must stop him. At all costs, you must stop him."

For some reason, as soon as Willa had married a Longworth, McKade had had to have that canyon.

Willa had been excited, terrified, curious to see the place after that. Big Red had paid McKade a visit in his hotel room and offered to buy him out. Later that night the older man had suffered his first stroke.

Not that his father's stroke or Hesper's strenuous objections had deterred McKade. He went after what he wanted, and he got it. Willa realized that Big Red had begun to fade slowly after McKade took possession.

But always, during those four years, Willa had known the exact moment when McKade had come to his cabin. Just as she'd know the exact moment when he'd left.

For years she'd wanted to see his restored cabin, to

know what he did here, to know why he came, why he went. *To make sure it was because of her.*

Willa was trembling as she pushed the door open. The interior was drably colored and as neat and orderly as hers was loud, messy and chaotic. One foot over his too tidy and too dull threshold had her as tense and uneasy as if McKade stood behind her, barking orders and advice. ''See how much easier it is to live when everything has a place and you put things back? You wouldn't lose everything all the time, Willa.''

As she had lost Cathy's nude drawings of herself on that ladder above her hot-pink tub dipping her brush into loud orange paint.

Computer equipment, phones and a fax machine lined one wall. Books and technical journals lined bookshelves. There were copies of magazines with McKade's handsome picture on the cover.

Her eyes drifted to McKade's bed. How many nights had she lain awake feverishly imagining McKade lying in this cabin?

She drew a quick, embarrassed breath. Wasting no time, she collected his clothes. His jeans were old, but she even noticed they had knife edges pressed into them. All of his cotton shirts were exactly alike—long-sleeved, starched and snowy white. *Boring.*

The nerve of him—to criticize her colorful wardrobe! He'd offered to take her shopping in the best shops in Santa Fe.

''I love my clothes,'' she'd said.

One day she could wear grunge, and the next day she felt free to dress up in a skintight mini and fake leopard jacket with earrings. She felt adventurous with her clothes—flexible.

''What do you know?''

In his top drawer, she found three photographs. One was of a beautiful woman with golden hair.

Marcie. His wife. His dead wife. *She did look elegantly attired.* He must still love her, respect her. Willa had seen pictures of them together in the stories about him she hadn't been able to resist reading because he'd gotten so much press ever since the government had gone after him on that restriction of trade issue. Marcie was highborn, a real lady. If she'd grown up in Laredo, Marcie would have been a deb, a Martha. Men like Brand would have married her if they'd accidentally gotten her pregnant.

The second, much tattered photograph was of a dark-haired Indian woman who reminded Willa a little of Candelaria. The woman held a small boy in her arms as she stood near this very cabin. Was that solemn black-haired, brown boy, McKade? Willa blinked back a tear. Then she smiled.

Her expression tightened when she saw the third picture. It was of her and Sam and Little Red, taken with a telephoto lens when they'd lunched on burritos outside just off the town square not long before Little Red's death.

The three of them were laughing. They'd been so happy that day. For all his faults, and maybe even because of his mistakes, Little Red had valued the real Willa, the best Willa. He'd brought out the Willa she had always wanted to be. With him she'd been loving and courageous and good—someone of vital importance. His partner, for better or worse. He'd said she'd brought out the best in him too, and she had.

They'd known so many dark times, but always they'd leaned on each other. That particular sparkling moment had been one of Little Red's last good days.

But it had been a deeply personal, precious, private time, meant for them alone. Tears blurred the frozen images. How could McKade have invaded their privacy by taking this picture? The picture wasn't his. It was hers. Before she thought, she seized it and stuffed it into her pocket.

She slammed the drawer and opened another. Quickly, she gathered up brown leather belts, boots and crammed them into a duffel bag. Then she stuffed his jeans and shirts inside, too.

She was over her tantrum by the time she and Molly got home. From a distance, her huge ranch house seemed to ride on a smooth green sea just beyond pink desert. Nor did her anger return when she saw McKade, who'd sworn he detested all dogs and cats, lounging on her hot-pink wicker sofa on her porch with her book and her cat. How could Lucy-fee nap in such a peaceful proprietary coil on the cushion behind the scoundrel's black head? Casper's nose lay on the rogue's polished black boot as he, too, dozed contentedly.

McKade was loathsomely handsome. The mere sight of him, relaxing with her pets in the deep quiet of her valley, made her breath catch. Somebody, McKade probably, had lined all her pumpkins up in two neat rows.

When she started up the stairs, McKade sprang toward her. Eagerly, he peeled her duffel bag from her shoulder and opened it.

Not that he thanked her. No, when he pulled out his wrinkled jeans and shirts, he said, "You're a slob, Willa Longworth." But his quick, white grin made her heart race.

She remembered the picture he'd stolen of her and Little Red and tried to recapture her anger. Then he smiled and she could feel nothing except... She forced herself to stiffen. "I rode over there and got them, didn't I...while you lazed...."

His broad grin made her feel reckless with longing.

"Probably 'cause you wanted to raid your stash of loot," he teased.

She blushed and tried not to look worried as she innocently scanned the mauve desert and Taos Mountain, which was deep purple with huge white clouds boiling above it.

As always, when he sensed a raw nerve, he pursued the subject. "So, how come your low-slung jeans aren't bulging with more fifties? Or weren't you able to find the cave?"

The last thing she needed was for him to figure out she wasn't sure where the second cave was.

"Where's Sam?" she snapped.

"Sifting through the house probably...seeing what else he can swipe of mine."

"How dare you insult my child?"

"Where's your ironing board?" Still grinning, McKade opened the front door for her.

"I don't have one."

He saluted. "Cute."

When she rushed to her bedroom and dug in her nightgowns for the picture of Sam, it was gone.

Her heart pounding, she emptied the drawer onto the plush green carpeting and stared in horror at her nightgowns. She shook out a drawer-load of filmy panties.

No Sam and Caspy! No map!

"Looking for something sexy to entice me into your flower-power bed?" purred McKade from the door. Then he leaned down and picked up a pair of see-through, lavender panties with her initials on them.

She glared at him through them.

"These'll do," he said.

She lunged.

"Finders keepers," he whispered, pocketing the panties. "I'll keep them till you're in a better mood."

"What else did you take?"

"You know, it's kind of amazing you've got such good taste in underwear...."

She threw a bra at him.

He pocketed that, too. "What are *you* looking for?" His wolfish grin was very white. "Maybe if you'd put things back...if you weren't such a slob..."

"Don't blame me!"

For once he shut up.

McKade. Did he have her map? Was that why he'd looked so smug and contented on her porch?

She felt desperate. If he did have it, he might find the briefcases first. Which meant—she had to keep him here where she could watch his every move. When he went out into the desert, she would have to follow him.

Then she thought about Sam and his...er...habit of

taking things that weren't his. After replacing her underwear in the proper drawer, she went to his room and asked him about the picture.

"You won't get in trouble if you tell me where it is."

Sam stared guiltily out his window at Big Red who was building a rock sculpture.

"Sam?"

"You mean the picture of Caspy?"

"Yes."

He spun the front tires of his toy car. "The picture on top of the scorpy?"

"Exactly, darling."

Sam shook his red head and bit his lips which either meant he hadn't taken it or he couldn't remember where he'd put it. In the past, she hadn't worried about him taking things. McKade had accused her of spoiling him, of not instilling discipline.... Was she a bad mother?

"Darling, if you do know..."

He stuck out his bottom lip.

It was no use.

A smiling McKade stood in her turquoise hall when she came out of Sam's room. "Something wrong?" he asked solicitously.

He was like a big black spider ready to move in for the kill. "You wish!"

So, McKade watched her.

And she watched him. It was like a game. They followed each other everywhere. And every hour she spent in the house with him made her jumpier, but made her feel sexier, too. He was so damned handsome. Just the way he looked at her got her hot. And when she listened to him do deals on the phone, even that turned her on. There was something about a powerful man...

By no means were McKade's being the sexiest man she'd ever known, and the richest, not to mention a probable thief, and a better housekeeper than she, all of his irritating faults. He was also a hypochondriac who enjoyed malingering.

"And why shouldn't I stay in bed?" he'd growled, plumping her eggplant pillow that he'd stolen from her kitchen as he complained his shoulders ached after so much ironing. "I've waited four years to share the same house, the same bed...."

"You seem to forget I'm not sharing the bed."

He'd grinned charmingly, beguiling. "But soon..."

Were all men so hopeful? Or just large, brown conceited ones that ran computer empires? Were other women that easy for a man like him to get? The thought made her green. Aloud, she said, "Don't make this more difficult."

"Me...difficult—Willa dear?"

You move in my house, woo my kid, steal my map... But had he? Was she just messy? Had Sam... She sighed.

Willa dear. He had a rare talent for getting under her skin. Somehow he'd gleaned how she hated that endearment.

When she didn't take the bait, he persisted in the same teasing vein that didn't quite mask his deadly seriousness. "Tell me where the money is so we can give it to whomever it belongs and get the hell out of here."

She glared at him.

"I want us to start our life together." His silver eyes sparkled. "Where did you hide it?"

How could she tell him?

He was maddeningly handsome and arrogant. "You're not the only one who's been in this situation for four years, McKade. I found that money, and it is mine. I married into a family that won't have me. Little Red meant this house to be mine. My sisters-in-law would throw me out of it in a heartbeat."

"Only Hesper." His eyes darkened.

"She's the leader. With the money in those briefcases, I don't have to worry about my future. Nobody like you or Hesper can push me around ever again."

"Willa, it's not *your* money."

"It is now."

"Finders keepers?"

"Don't you dare say—" She broke off.

He smiled in that superior, mocking way that made her long to strangle him. "There we go again, round and round," he said.

"You started it."

He'd taken her hand in his larger, brown one and stroked the inside of her silky palm. "And I'll finish it, too. Give up, Willa. Admit I've won."

"Am I... Is this just a game to you?"

He smiled. "A game that's fun. You're fun. Did you know that? Everything about you is fun. I haven't had much fun in my life before you."

His saying that made her heart lift.

He brought her fingers to his lips and she felt on fire. "Willa, this isn't just about the money. Harry's a doll. So are you. I never knew it could feel so good…living in a wild, grossly decorated house with a rambunctious kid…with you.''

He'd said it wasn't just about money. He was right about that constant electricity between them. He had only to touch her in that almost impersonal way and her breasts tautened. The mere sight of his broad shoulders, his huge but surprisingly lithe body, stirred all the earthy longings that had made her easy pickings in the cave and left her all the more vulnerable to him now.

He'd held on to her hand as if to kiss it again.

"I—I'd just be another of your conquests," she'd said. "One of many… Not much more important than my friend Cathy.''

"Cathy?'' He'd laughed, pleased that she'd noticed. "Why, you sound almost jealous.''

"Don't be ridiculous. I'd give anything if you'd run off with some other woman.''

"I wonder…. What if I called your friend, Cathy?'' He paused. "You know she's interested in painting nudes. Maybe I could pose…in your tangerine bathroom. Maybe she's got a yen to peek under kilts.''

"What?'' Alarmed on some primal level, Willa had yanked her hand free and avoided him the rest of the day. She'd searched frantically for, and not found, those nude sketches of herself on that ladder, too. Why had he suggested posing in her tangerine bathroom? Did he know…?

"Looking for something?'' McKade had taunted when he'd found her rummaging behind her bed. "Tell me what you're looking for and I'll help.''

"You've done enough.''

"Finders keepers?''

She'd kill Cathy if she'd told him about those drawings. Kill him if he had them.

But Willa knew that her own growing attraction to him, her constant awareness of him, was what really terrified her. She thought of that photograph he'd taken of her. Did he have those embarrassing sketches, or didn't he? And where, oh, where, was her precious map?

If only Sam wasn't as avidly interested in their new houseguest as she. Sam popped in and out of Mc-Kade's room at all hours. If she told Sam to leave McKade alone that would have only made such adventures more appealing to the curious little boy.

Not that troubles at home were her only worries. Cathy called from the Book Nook and mentioned slyly that the whole town was counting the months since Little Red's death and talking about her and her handsome houseguest. She made McKade sound so illicit.

"But how on earth does everybody know?"

"Hesper. The whole town can talk of nothing but the plane crash, gun shots, you running off some men who were holding Mr. McKade.... Why didn't you call and tell me?"

"Exaggerations."

"But even the sheriff said..."

"It wasn't like that."

"Then how was it?"

"Why are you, and all of Taos for that matter, so obsessed with McKade?"

"Why are you?"

They were both silent.

"Willa, McKade was in that cabin the night it

burned. Somebody tried to kill him. He's a powerful man. He has a lot of enemies. Do you think…''

''That fire was a long time ago. This has nothing to do with that!''

''Are you going to tell me what happened or not?''

''Look, Cathy…'' Willa stalled. Her thoughts and emotions were too jumbled. The truth was too terrible, too strange and bewildering. She'd taken money… robbers' money she was sure…. And on that same stormy, magical night when she hadn't been so aware of life's little rules, she'd had sex with McKade in that cave, and then left him there, and he'd fallen victim to those villains.

But I saved his life. And I risked Sam, everything, to do that…. And…and…I'm not sorry I saved him….

Willa didn't know what to say or how to defend herself. The past was over and done with. All she knew was that if she wanted people in Taos to respect her, she had to send McKade packing.

The sooner, the better.

But how?

''I've gotta go, Cathy. Bye.''

20

"Not so fast, Willa!"

Cathy was bursting with way too much excitement to take the hint and hang up.

"Was McKade really naked when the sheriff brought him home for you?"

Willa blushed. Did Cathy have to be so fascinated by nudity, especially McKade's?

Her voice was cool. "McKade? Next thing, you'll say you're blocked again. I hope you don't suggest sketching him nude in my hot-pink tub."

"Awesome! Do you think he would?"

Willa wasn't about to mention that idea was McKade's. She made her voice even chillier. "How you do run on."

"You know those drawings you posed for?"

"If only I could forget them."

"I—I can't thank you enough. I'm painting again...for a show...with Gracie."

"Why, Cathy, that's wonderful."

"You know it really would be awesome if McKade would pose. I'm doing a series...."

"Of nudes?"

"Gotta go."

"Cathy!"

The line went dead.

Dear God.

Unbidden came the image of McKade's muscular brown body stretched full length in her tub. Willa remembered how cute he'd been strutting in the cave, and her heart began to pound. An unsettling little dart of pleasure fluttered inside her stomach.

The next phone call upset her even more. The news about the plane crash had reached the press, and a local reporter said he wanted to come take pictures.

Willa told him no, explaining that she had an injured houseguest to tend to.

"Can you tell me more about this Luke McKade, Mrs. Longworth?"

Of course, said Mrs. Connor.

"No," said Willa aloud.

"What exactly is the nature of your relationship with this man? How did he get hurt on your land?"

What would you say if I told you the truth? Oh, it all got started when McKade found me tied to bedposts.

Bedposts?

Yes, you see, Mr. McKade was looking for his little brother—my recently deceased husband, not deceased then, of course—for Little Red was very much alive and very much wanted to kill his lawyer, a Mr. Brandon Baines, who just happened to be the father of my unborn child. Mr. Baines, by the way, was the one who had tied me to the bedposts in the first place so a so-called doctor could perform... As always Willa skipped that most horrible part.

That said, sir, well, er, years later Mr. McKade saw the need to resume his relationship with me when he discovered me in a cave trying to hide briefcases that contained two million dollars that I just happened to find in that crashed airplane you're so interested in and just happened to take. So, to distract him from that purpose, well, I—I had sex with him, you see....

Just the memory of her wild behavior in that dark cave under the virile McKade, sexually charged Willa. And the sting of remembered desire made her heart rush in tight little beats. Suddenly it was hard to breathe.

Good sex, too, if I do brag myself.

Willa felt hot and flushed from her mental rehash. Not that she was about to let on. "T-that is none of your business," she said primly.

"Did you really fire at trespassers?"

"I don't even remember pulling the trigger." All she recalled was McKade lying there, barely conscious when she'd taken him in her arms after the bad guys had fled.

"Don't you understand what *no* means?" Willa said. "Maybe when Mr. McKade leaves, you can come out. Maybe then, we'll talk."

"News has to be timely. Everyone will have lost interest...."

"Then I'm sorry. Mr. McKade is a handful. That's the long and the short of it. Like I said, until he moves out—"

"When I move out?" McKade had shouted to her

from down the hall. "Let me talk to whomever the hell that is right now."

"I've gotta go." She slammed the phone down and whirled. "You are even nosier than Hesper."

"Must be a family talent," he bragged.

"I wouldn't be so proud of it if I were you."

"It's called staying on top of things. It's the trait that's made me rich." He paused, doubtless to let that last buzzword buzz. "I'd like to get on top of you."

Suddenly the room was too small and too stifling, or maybe McKade was just too large. "You have the ears of a lynx and you use them, too. You eavesdrop every chance you get."

"Maybe you'll tell somebody where you hid the money." His eyes were sparkling as they wistfully drank in her beauty and anger.

"Fat chance."

Still, every time the phone rang, McKade appeared out of nowhere. When she took her walks in the desert, he carried binoculars out onto her porch, his eyes tracking her across the pink desert every time he looked up from *Gone with the Wind*, which he'd begun to read and make irritating comments about.

"Do you know who Harry's father is?" he demanded one evening after supper when she'd gone out to the porch with a cup of tea for some peace and quiet.

"Go back to your reading," she said grumpily.

"You're more fun than Scarlett, who is mean and manipulative." He hesitated. "I want to know about Harry."

Willa remembered how McKade always thought the

worst of her. "Why don't you ask your friend Brand for an update?"

"But did he lie?"

"Interesting you should ask."

"Did you tell Little Red who Sam's father is?"

She thought of the picture he'd surreptitiously taken of them on the square. "Our marriage, what we shared, is none of your business."

"Why him…and not me?"

McKade's voice sounded odd, almost hurt that she might have shared confidences with Little Red.

"He was my husband."

His expression darkened. "You were his nurse, not a real wife."

"How would you know?"

He stared at her for a long moment, and she wondered if he would be pleased to know that Little Red had felt caught between his successful father and successful bastard brother, that he'd been as avidly jealous of McKade as McKade was of him. She'd grown tired of Little Red's jealousies, especially of McKade, and she didn't want to hear more of the same from McKade.

"You were after his money," McKade persisted.

"You always believe the worst of me."

"When I met you, you *were* tied up."

"Not by choice."

"Then you took my money, did that dance, stole my car, married my half brother…."

"If you'd been nice to me and helped me like a gentleman, I wouldn't have had to be so resourceful, now would I?"

"Resourceful. Is that what you call it?" He began to laugh. "You do have a curious attitude."

"I was desperate. I had to get creative. I knew you'd be okay." It's called survival, she thought. She stared into her tea mug. "You wouldn't understand," she said softly. "So there's no use talking to you. You're far too literal. Go back to your reading!"

"Maybe it's time we resorted to a more basic form of communication—the only kind that's ever worked between you and me." The deep timbre of sexual desire in his low tone made her shiver. But she didn't stop him when, carefully, he removed her cup from her fingers.

"What are you doing?"

"Me, Tarzan," he whispered, sizzling undercurrents even in that resonant fragment of sound. "You, Jane." His rough voice had softened. So had his eyes. "Or...er...Me, Rhett, you Scarlett."

She held her breath.

"And," he murmured thickly, "frankly, my dear, I do give a damn...."

She licked her lips, stared straight ahead, past him.

His pale eyes raked her. "I'm tired of you ignoring me."

Before she knew what he intended, he hauled her against his chest. His big capable hand was in her yellow curls. Yanking her head back, he crushed his mouth to hers. For an instant she strained to free herself. But needs too long suppressed overpowered her, too.

Maybe she should've fought him harder, but the explosion that rocked him caught her on fire, too. Every day and every night she'd thought of that night in the cave when he'd made love to her.

Burning, aching, she clung to him, every muscle in her body going slack. Her arms wound around his neck.

"You're not going to hurt me again, now are you, Willa?" he whispered.

"I—I'm sorry about that. So, so sorry."

Her lips parted and let his tongue inside. His kiss was thorough and sensual, an all-body kiss, inflaming every part of her.

"Let's go to that flower-power bed of yours," he muttered.

"You don't get it, do you, big guy?"

"Do you? We started something in Mexico. Something more powerful than I believed possible. You married my brother, for God's sakes. But I can't forget you. God knows I tried. Then you made love to me in the cave. I can't forget that, either."

"We had sex, McKade."

"Why can't I forget about it then?"

A small muscle twitched at the corner of her mouth. "Because you're a sex maniac."

"I don't think you can forget me, either."

"At least I'm trying."

He snugged his hips to hers, so that she knew exactly how much he wanted her. "I want to do it again...and again."

"That's not a very romantic way of putting it."

"Is this romantic enough for you?" He ran a finger lightly across her eyebrow, feathered it down the side of her face, across her delicate cheekbone. Then he touched her lips with his in a tender kiss. Afterward, he said, "Maybe I should carry you up the stairs the way Rhett carried Scarlett."

Willa held her breath. Her lips still puckered, she willed him to kiss her again.

"Willa," he whispered, instead, his voice low and husky, pleading. "Willa, I want you so much."

All week on a deep level she hadn't wanted to dwell on, she'd found his constant attentiveness most thrilling. There was a protective, heroic quality at the bottom of it, too. She said, "You mean you want to have an affair…till you tire of me…."

He let out his breath in a long, exasperated sigh. "If you're so anxious to get rid of me, maybe that's a way for both of us to be happy." He slid both hands on either side of her face. Smoothing her golden hair back, he gazed into her eyes. His were raw, aglow with a passion that was deep and dark. For a second, foolish woman that she was, Willa felt he'd let her gaze straight into his heart. Then she remembered—McKade didn't have a heart.

"Willa…"

Oh, God. He was so handsome. And in that moment, he seemed as completely vulnerable as she felt herself. But he wasn't. He couldn't be. He bought things, cars, companies, people—women. He was like Brand.

No, he wasn't.

She swallowed.

"Please, let me," he said.

"But where would we go from there?"

"Maybe it's too early to know. Maybe we should just play this by ear."

"Or not play at all."

"I can't live here with you and not..."

"Then you can always leave."

His grip tightened. "Is that really what you want?"

"What if you didn't tire of me? What if you were like that awful woman in *Fatal Attraction?*"

"You mean the hot blonde who boiled the kid's bunny?"

Willa nodded.

"For God's sakes, I have no desire to cook one of your pets, even your bad-tempered Lucy-fee."

"If we had sex again, you could become so obsessed I might be stuck with you for good."

Again, for a split second, she felt his humanity beneath his tough-guy facade.

"Would that be so bad?" he demanded roughly. "My head on your pillow every morning?" He paused. "Willa, sometimes I feel like I've been alone my whole damn life."

"Because you're a handful. And you're bossy, McKade. See how you run this house...and my child...like one of your companies. You give unasked for advice. It gets old. And you haven't been here that long."

"Okay. Okay. Normally, I don't have time to play housemaid. I have a very demanding bunch of businesses to run. I'd go off to work and come home tired. What if I promised never to retire?"

"I'm not even tempted, McKade."

He laughed. "I'm very rich."

"So, you've told me—umpteen times. But it's *your* money, McKade. Not mine. You'd think you owned me."

"You're attaching way too much importance to whose money is whose."

"Because I've been struggling without it...till I found those briefcases. Because nobody has ever respected—"

"Respect? So, that's what you want—"

"Now, that I have them..."

His eyes sparkled, and as always she imagined him in possession of her map. "Yes? And where are those precious suitcases?"

"Now, that I have them," she persisted with stubborn resolve to pretend she was in control of the situation, "people like you can't come along and try to push me around. You're forced to respect me."

"Respect—" He started laughing again.

"What's so funny?"

"You want me to respect you...and I want..." He smiled. "We are at cross purposes." He hesitated. "So, I can't tempt you into my bed with my money?"

"No."

"Then...taking a lesson from Rhett Butler—" With a low growl, his arms came around her.

"McKade, McKade, what are you doing?"

His voice was dangerous silk. "Tempting you, my love."

As he drew her into his arms, sensual terrors coiled inside her stomach.

"Cool it, McKade."

"Impossible around you."

The heat from his body burned into her breasts, her belly and her thighs. "Do you still think I'm a whore?"

"Right now I almost wish you were."

"Will you never forget you found me tied to bed-posts?"

He touched her face with a gentle fingertip. "It's a cherished memory."

"Driving off in your Porsche is a favorite of mine."

He smiled.

"And stealing your hat," she whispered, burying her lips against his shirt collar only to be stirred all the more by his thudding pulse. "I kinda like that one, too."

The desert was beginning to darken; the moon was coming up over the mountains. She clutched him closer.

"Willa, Willa..." His fingertip traced the shape of her jawline and then moved down her throat. "I don't want to fight. I want to make love." When he pulled her even tighter, she bit her lower lip. She shut her eyes, but the enveloping darkness heightened her awareness of every other sense. He felt so hard and warm. He smelled clean and masculine. The way he touched her was so lovely. Already he knew her body, knew how to please her, so that even his lightest and most casual gesture became the deepest and most intimate and cherished of caresses. It was as if God had fashioned him only for her.

She couldn't let him know this. She couldn't.

To her surprise, she whispered huskily, wantonly, "The scary thing is...I do, too."

"Oh, Willa...I thought you'd never, ever admit..."

He grasped her by the waist, lifted her and held her high. Casper and Spot began to bark.

With the dogs circling them so excitedly, pumpkins began to roll. McKade carried her inside and said, "Just like Rhett Butler..."

"Better," said Willa.

21

Luke stood outside Willa's bedroom door. Impatiently, his brown hand flipped through the nude sketches he'd found when she'd left the house to go to his cabin.

Finders keepers.

Who the hell had she posed for?

Every one of her smiles, every expression, every lift of her eyebrows, every wink was cuter and more provocative than the last. In one picture, she tilted her head back so that all that iridescent yellow hair flowed down her back. God, those breasts, those ultralong legs...those thighs.

In one picture she hung from the ladder with the paintbrush in her mouth. She'd given birth to Sam, nursed a dying man, but she still didn't look a day over twenty. She was as innocent as a girl-child yet seemed as willing to do whatever a man might want as a courtesan. Whenever she got in trouble, she turned into Rambo in high heels. Each pose was more alluring than the one before.

She was devastating.

There was no other word.

Priceless.

What had she said that first night?

"I'll do anything...."

For days, every time he'd looked at her, he'd thought of that promise and stripped her in his mind. He'd had to ball his hands into fists every time he got near her so as not to touch her.

Anything.

Because he'd thought she was a whore, he'd let her get to him sexually. He'd thought his heart was safe. He'd given free rein to his sexual imagination where she was concerned, and those feelings were powerful and intimate. Because nothing was what he'd thought, because she wasn't a cheap woman of the night, sexual desire had gotten a grip on long buried, unwanted emotions.

Instead of the wanton he'd thought her, he'd discovered she was a wholesome young woman raising a child. Strangely, her reticence, her courage, her joy in living, her love of books, even her sloppiness made her a far more enticing woman than what he'd believed her to be. He'd never have been satisfied with a mere sex object. She was far more than he'd ever imagined she could be. She'd been so damned good to his brother.

When they'd come inside a little while ago, she'd purred in a playful tone, "Give me five minutes...to set the stage...and then...my darling...I'll do anything...."

Anything. God, how that word, the way she'd said it, had lit him.

"My darling." How sweet that endearment was.

She thought he dreamed of the whore who'd submit.

He wanted this particular woman who was warm and complex and utterly adorable, who believed in fairy tales and read romantic literature. She was braver in a pinch than most combat soldiers. She wanted to be independent and respected.

And he was beginning to hope she wanted him, too…every bit as much as he wanted her. And it was odd, damned odd, he was glad she'd refused his money.

Thus, he was standing outside her door, as excited as a kid waiting for Christmas. He, a jaded man, who hadn't believed in love, was on fire to experience a repeat of what the minx had given him in the cave. Only he wanted more than that. Much more. And he thought she did, too. He thought of Heathcliff, of Brontë's concept of undying love. Willa had said that was her favorite book. What would it take for a man like him to win Willa's love?

Love? He didn't want love. He wasn't that sort.

"Ready," she whispered, laughing softly from the other side of the door.

Luke stepped inside the velvet darkness to the scent of gardenias. Behind the distant mountains, lightning flashed—faraway flickers of fire as white-hot as his own blood. The faint roar of thunder echoed the far louder poundings of his own heart.

Usually her bedroom was alive with color; the bed an atrocious mix of blossoms, checks and polka dot designs was cheery on the darkest winter day. Tonight the room was dark except for silver moonlight sifting through the high windows and the low fire that burned in her corner fireplace. Outside her window, he saw stars through the branches of the cottonwood trees. Inside, he saw her big lavender bed with its flower-shaped pillows and a yellow-haired woman tied by her wrists and ankles with remnants of her own nylons.

Only she wasn't a stranger. She was Willa.

A floorboard creaked under his weight as he stole across plush green carpet toward her. All those flowers, all that color. Usually he felt like he was stepping into a vat of femininity when he put a foot over her threshold.

"What do you think you're doing?" he whispered.

"Remember, you're supposed to be my Prince Charming," she quipped, her light tone somehow profoundly emotional and sexual.

Moonlight rippled over her long shapely legs that were spread widely apart. Luke felt a fiery twinge race up his spine.

Her slanting eyes were open, wide-open, and yet her gaze was trancelike, as if she'd already abandoned herself to the pleasure he was about to give her. "You wanted me that night. You thought I was bad."

"I don't now. I will never think of you like that again."

She laughed throatily as if she wasn't afraid, yet he knew she was. "You can have what you wanted then…. I'll pretend to be that woman for you. I'm serving myself to you on a silver platter."

Again that distant fire lit up those craggy peaks. Nearer, Luke felt like he'd been consumed by an inferno. Heat lit every male nerve. A more profound emotion lit his soul.

He really didn't want a whore anymore. He

wanted... What he wanted was too terrifying to dwell upon.

The room with its triple-doored armoire and the doors with beveled mirrors seemed to shrink. He drew a sharp, savage, frightened breath.

Masses of reckless, yellow hair framed her exquisite oval face. "Untie me," she said breathlessly. "Love me."

Her slanting eyes flashed like deep, dark sapphires in the moonlight. Her lips were full and red. "Let me love you," she continued.

He wondered if she was blushing as he began to unbutton his shirt. Not that he took his eyes off her as he tore at his buttons.

"I've dreamed of this," she said, straining at the bonds, her long legs and hips undulating on that bed full of flowers.

Sexy. Sexy as hell.

He said, "Willa..."

"Untie me, so I can make love to you...."

She wore a wisp of a red silk—a see-through nightie. The tidbit of silk was even more revealing than the polka-dot dress had been.

How many nights had he dreamed hot, lascivious fantasies of her, willingly opening herself completely to him?

Too damn many to count.

But this was different. Completely different. Because tonight, when he crawled on top of her, she would be real. Her feelings for him were real, as were his for her. Maybe it was the intoxicating scent of those gardenias, making him think and feel so crazy. But, as he hurriedly shed boots and jeans and everything else, the sexual charge that coursed through him was a thousand times more disorienting than that first night.

Then he was on top of her, shoving her flower pillows out of the way. She was warm and eager and trembling as he fused her slim, warm body to his. He untied a wrist, and she wound her soft fingers through his hair. He untied the other, and that hand came down and inexplicably touched him exactly where he wanted her to. She began to stroke him—there.

He gasped.

He felt her hunger, and it was as fierce and terrible and avid and all-consuming as his own.

"All that time when you were married to my brother…" he began.

Her fingers drifted over his bare shoulders down his arm. "But I'm not…anymore."

"I felt so alone in that cabin…knowing you weren't alone, knowing you were with him."

"I thought of you, too…." She hesitated. "I felt so guilty, being married to him and wanting you. But I don't want to think about that time. I'm all yours. All yours…tonight."

The best thing about her was the worst thing about her—she was a creature of the moment. Which meant that in this magic moment, if in no other, she belonged to him.

He kissed her, his mouth hard against hers. His tongue piercing her lips, invading their sweet-swollen softness, conquering and tasting their depths. He untied her ankles, and she wrapped her long legs around his lean waist.

"You feel so good," he whispered.

Her legs tightened around him.

He held her. But not long. He had to have her. He couldn't wait.

"Willa—"

She was breathing and shaking at the same time, sobbing a little as he slid himself against her wetness, positioning himself against her sex. For an instant they stared at one another. Her eyes seemed carbon black, and so hot they burned him all the way to his soul. Her feral look mirrored his. He felt alive...to his core, as he hadn't ever felt before. *Alive.* God, how it hurt. Willa was so damned beautiful. So damned sweet. He still couldn't believe it.

Then he thrust inside her burning silkiness. And felt pleasure that was incomparable. She rocked against him urgently. They were breathing hard and fast. It was over too soon for both of them, and yet she had exploded at the exact moment he had. It was as if she had sensed on some instinctive level, as if her body had seized her pleasure, the better to share and savor his.

The moment had been exquisite.

The little death, the French called it. It meant so much, that they'd shared the little death at the exact same moment.

"I couldn't wait," he said, brushing a lock of golden hair from her brow.

"Suddenly I couldn't, either. It was perfect. Too perfect. We both waited so long for this."

They were compatible on a profound level. "Did you love him?" he demanded.

"Who?" But she knew. "Don't be jealous," she said.

"Little Red?" He ground out his brother's name. "Sam's father? Anybody else? Any damn guy you've ever been with?"

"You don't have any reason to ever be jealous."

"But who—"

Her fingers found his lips. Gently she traced them with the back of her hand. "I've never felt like this about anyone else. And...and as for sex...there was only Sam's father.... I was young, inexperienced, foolish. Mrs. Brown tried to tell me he didn't care deeply for me...that he used her girls...that he'd be too prejudiced to ever believe I was special. But I was blinded by who he was, too. In fact—" Her voice broke as she remembered.

"I—I thought I loved him...but not for long. It was all surface between us. I believed what I saw and so did he. I thought he was high-class. He thought I was one of my aunt's... W-we weren't ever real people to each other. Toward the end, it started to get scary."

She was quiet. "I—I don't like to think about him now. He scares me. So, don't ever think about anybody else...any other man and me...especially him...ever again."

But she went on. "You have become precious to me. You saved me in Mexico. You saved Sam. Even when I was married, I couldn't ever forget that." She paused. "You were awful, too, of course. You made me feel cheap...the same as Brand did. And I didn't want that ever again. But since you've been here...since the cave..." Her voice died. "I wish you weren't so dear...because...because...you and I are too different, you know."

"What do you mean?" He held her gaze for a long

moment, jealousy still gripping him in its evil black power.

"I know you couldn't ever care about me. You're so into money. It's everything to you. To you, everything has a price. I listen to you on the phone. That's all you talk about. All you think about. With me, money would be a tool…. I want to live my life. To love. To be happy. You need someone with your same values. That's why you and I won't last."

How did one change one's whole approach to life, he wondered?

"Just don't ruin it tonight," she whispered. "Don't mention money. Wait till morning."

He nodded and closed his eyes. How would he woo her, if he didn't use his fortune? In her own way, she was just as scared of commitment on a profound level as he was.

She'd had one man, a man who'd been a mistake according to her. From the first, Luke had been quick to doubt her. Maybe it was time he took a chance. He'd formed the wrong notion about her and then clung to it stubbornly. He'd wanted to cling to the notion that she was a cheat and greedy, because it was too scary to admit she was even half as wonderful as he was beginning to believe she was. He'd been afraid he'd care too deeply. Hell, if he'd been scared then, he should be terrified now.

But she was, too.

They slept. When they awoke, hard, violent raindrops were spattering against the glass outside.

"I've always wanted to make love in the rain," she said.

"It's too cold."

"But I want you wet," she whispered.

"Ever done it in the shower?"

She giggled and hugged him closer.

Once there, he pushed her against that loud tiled wall and licked droplets of hot, oozing water that tasted like gardenias off her skin. Dizziness washed him, when she sank to her knees and buried her face in the dark hair below his navel and worked her lips lower. Then she drank warm water off his bare brown skin, off the shaft that was thickening and pulsing in her talented mouth. He cried out, pushed to free himself, but she clung, refusing to let him go until he was done. When it was over, he sagged back against the tangerine wall and could barely stand.

Violent thunder shook the house. He said they might get electrocuted if they didn't get out of the shower. She laughed when he limped toward the bed, accused him of being a sexual hypochondriac.

"There's no such thing," he grumbled in his own defense.

"There is. You are one! I should know."

"It's a damn fine thing to be then, I'll have you know."

Then she was beside him, nestled deeply in white sheets, pillows and quilts, her head on top of his arm, and he was asleep, holding her close, knowing that paradise on this earth was in that bed with her, knowing that he could never let her or her darling little boy go. Wondering how the hell he'd ever talk her into moving to Texas with him.

Would she insist on taking her hot-pink couch and her orange, flame-stitched chairs?

He didn't care.

He slept long and soundly. He would need his strength for the coming battle.

The sun was bright after the storm last night. Too bright. Every time the extraordinarily energetic McKade strode restlessly across the yellow kitchen or just looked across that trestle table at her, Willa was too aware of him, too aware of what they'd done the night before.

How to seize victory when McKade had mastered her so completely in the bedroom? Not to mention her orange shower stall.

Had he really stopped thinking of her as a whore? Even after she'd debased herself like that in her very own shower?

Her cheeks reddened. She hadn't been thinking. She'd gone with the moment. What she'd done had seemed like a good idea at the time.

Wild impulses. Reckless deeds. Would she never learn?

She toyed with her paper napkin, dabbed it daintily at the corner of her mouth. "This...er...I mean last night... That—that can't mean anything," she said throatily between more embarrassed bites of toast.

He sloshed coffee into a chipped mug. "Why the hell not?"

"What are you saying?"

"It means you're mine," he said, his tone all male and full of authority.

"Oh? You think so?"

He looked up, his pale eyes scorching her like lasers. He let his insolent gaze drift over her breasts.

She felt her nipples peak and her stomach go light as air when she gasped.

"I won't be some man's possession," she stated tartly.

"Not *some* man's! Mine!" He sipped his coffee way too casually after such a passionate remark. "Me! You belong to me."

"I belong to me."

"That's okay, too. We'll both own you. We'll be partners."

"Why do men always have to be into control?"

"I don't like the word *men,* in the plural, connected to you. We're talking about me."

"I'm not some sex object."

"You are that." He stared through her knit shirt, grinning fiendishly, sensually, as if he could actually see the sheer black material confining each breast. She flushed. "Yes, you are that and more, Willa my darling. Much more."

"I won't be owned."

"I can't let you go."

"Then where do we go from here?"

"After last night...I'm sure it will be most interesting."

"I won't sleep with you again."

"Then we'll do it in your loud shower."

"You are a sex maniac."

He flashed her another wicked grin. "Thanks."

"It wasn't a compliment."

"If I'm a sex maniac, it's your fault. And what does that make you?" He got up, and moved toward her.

Thinking he meant to try something crazy, she tried

to scoot her chair back and escape. He placed a boot behind the leg of her chair, preventing her departure.

He was close enough to touch her, to pull her into his arms. But he didn't. Nevertheless, his nearness charged her. Her pulse went wild.

"Willa...Willa... I'm only this wired about *you*. Think about it." He moved away, put his plate in the sink. "If you said I was yours, I wouldn't argue." Then he left her.

He'd said he belonged to her. That made her too dizzy to eat, to drink, to think. What was happening to her? To them? Where did Mr. Moneybags, Mr. Sex Maniac see this going?

She had a child. He had businesses to run. He couldn't stay here indefinitely. Could he?

He was on the phone for an hour. She snuck up behind him in time to hear him giving his men that list of electronic equipment he needed installed in her house at once. "What do you mean you can't get a T1 in here?"

Without thinking, she grabbed the phone and hung it up.

"Thanks. I was almost done," he said, circling her waist with his large brown hands.

"You can't stay. This won't work. We're too different."

"If I'm the Mr. Dot.Com King, deal maker of the century and you're the highly creative Rambo-ella who needs to stay away from hot-pink paint samples, we'll just put our heads and talents together and make it work."

A strange heat suffused her. Could they? "Where's Sam?" she whispered, to change the subject.

"Outside...with Big Red," he said. "My computer guys won't be here for an hour or two. I've got time for a quickie...or two."

She drew in a sharp little breath. "McKade, you are a sex maniac."

"Luke." His silver eyes were incandescent. "Think of this as our honeymoon," he whispered huskily.

His voice, what he'd hinted at trembled inside her. "Nobody said anything about marriage."

"What would you say if I did say something about it?"

"You presume a lot...."

"Yeah, when a girl comes on to me like you did in that loud shower of yours...I do."

"Would you forget about that?"

"Not in this lifetime."

"I regret last night."

"Then I'll have to get my act together. What do you say to another rehearsal? Maybe on your hot-pink sofa? It's big enough."

She knew she should be objecting to everything he said, to more sex now, to where their relationship seemed to be going in general. But when he folded her into his arms, she melted.

"You are beautiful, Willa."

He kissed her. Then he lifted her and swirled her round and round before he carried her down the turquoise hall to the wild pandemonium of her flowery bedroom.

"I wish you had stairs. Then I'd play Rhett Butler for you."

She laughed as he kicked the bedroom door shut.

They did it against the green wall, half-dressed. If

he was fast, so was she. He entered her, and instantly she was at the brink of an A plus orgasm. Like before, he thrust inside her and she was trembling, clinging, sighing. Again, she exploded when he did.

Afterward, they sank to the plush carpet. He was so apologetic, so sweet. Sweeter than he'd ever been before.

He held her in his lap. "If I hurt you—"

"No..." His tenderness, his deep concerned voice filled her with unbearable joy. "It was wonderful," she said. And it had been.

His hands were in her hair. "So you admit it." He pressed his lips into her hair.

"What's happening to us?"

"Just enjoy it." He was kissing her hairline, her brow, her eyebrows, the tip of her nose. "Haven't we both suffered enough? The past four years... My whole damned life, until I found you..."

"If you offer me money...I think I'll die."

"Oh, Willa. I never realized all the things money can't buy. Or maybe I did. Maybe that's why I was so damned bent on buying the world. Maybe the whole damn time I was looking for this, for you."

She thought of Little Red, how sick he'd been all those long months. She remembered the operations, his acute pain, his towering heroism in the face of such dark despair. Then she remembered Brand, who'd had to have a rich girl, a deb, a Martha, for a wife, Brand, who hadn't wanted Sam or her.

Willa hadn't let herself think too much about what Brand would have done to her in Mexico if McKade hadn't come. Suddenly, she forced herself to do so.

Not going to be a baby. I know a doctor here in Mexico.

No. No.

He's good.

No.

Brand had encouraged her to drink. As his face had begun to blur, his words had run together.

Not going to be a baby. I know a doctor here in Mexico.

He had called the doctor from his car, told him she was a whore, that she would use the baby to blackmail him, that she'd be a terrible mother. The doctor had refused. Then Brand had offered him an immense sum of money.

She'd been too woozy to defend herself, to grab the phone and tell the reluctant man that she would love her child. In the shack Brand had named a sum of money that no poor Mexican could easily refuse. And yet, as Brand had tied her up, the man had hesitated again. Hesitated long enough for Little Red to burst in with his gun. The doctor had vanished out the back way.

Was it fair to dwell only on what McKade had done wrong? What if that doctor and Brand had killed Sam? Her?

She began to weep.

McKade held her head against his shoulder. His own face was hard and set when she told him about Brand, about the doctor. McKade seemed to share her pain, to even reexperience his own.

"I know what Baines is capable of...with women. A long time ago he got a friend of mine in trouble. I'm glad I was there for you that night. I had a lot to atone for that particular night." McKade didn't elaborate. Instead, he told her about growing up alone, about hating his Indian blood after the fire. He told her about his father coming to the Pueblo and turning away from him, about hating himself after that, about needing to be powerful just to feel halfway human.

"I went to the Longworth house once. It was beautiful. There were flowers. White children. His other children. I picked a flower." His voice broke. "Their mother…" He couldn't go on.

But she understood. When he didn't continue, she told him how difficult it was to feel different from other children, not to think like other people, not to have a family like other children.

"When I was in school, I never got the right answers," Willa said. "My mind didn't work like everybody else's. The kids laughed at me in class. Outside of class, they whispered about my aunt…about what I would do sexually. And I—I never did anything. I never even dated. I was too afraid. I didn't go to proms…or participate in school plays."

She told him about her dreams for Sam. "I wanted him to have a normal life. A mother and a father. Brothers and sisters. I wanted him to feel loved and accepted the way I never was after my parents died."

They listened, and held each other.

He was right, she decided. They had both suffered. And after a while, their pain and their sharing gave way to hope and consolation and to all the other emotions they'd both been too afraid to feel.

"Maybe we could help each other forget, help each other make our real dreams come true," he said.

A tender smile curved his mouth. His eyes were still

infused with pain and yet she felt his hope for the future, for their future.

For a second or two, she let herself dream, too.

Not that she could entirely trust him.

Any more than he could trust her.

"You make me feel happy," she whispered, her eyes caressing him.

"I feel the same way about you."

"But for how long?" she wondered.

"Feelings like ours don't come with guarantees."

"I don't ever want to hurt you again," she said.

He raked his hands through the tumble of her yellow curls. "Nor I you."

22

Willa knew it was dangerous to be so happy.

Yet when Sam shot out of the ice-cream parlor, waving his ice-cream cone over his head like a tomahawk, she laughed. Reveling in his childish exuberance, feeling almost as young and giddy as he did, Willa chased him onto the Taos square.

The glorious fall air was crisp and far too cool for her lively wild child to be licking his strawberry ice-cream cone with such gusto.

"Why don't you buy a cookie instead," she'd pleaded, "or a hot brownie?"

"Strawbewy!" he cried, pointing.

"It's too cold for ice cream."

"No!" He'd jumped up and down. "P-weeze."

One minute he was a tyrant. The next, he could be so sweet, so darling. And she was such a sucker.

"All right. All right."

So, here they were, waiting for McKade, who'd had errands of his own to run while they'd shopped for groceries. She sat on a bench just outside the Book Nook and was, thus, half-hidden in the purple shade.

Near a statue, Sam ate his cone in brilliant sunshine and stalked a pigeon on tiptoes.

They were supposed to meet McKade at Cathy's Book Nook in fifteen minutes. For once Willa was determined to give McKade the surprise of his life by being early.

Until Sam had demanded ice cream, she'd thought she'd have time to browse and find something new to read, both for herself and for Sam. But even Cathy, who was a woman who lived by fewer rules than Willa, didn't allow four-year-olds near her precious books when they clutched dripping strawberry ice-cream cones.

Not that Willa minded waiting in the square as she watched Sam. After living with a dying man for so long, time suddenly seemed her friend again. She could think of the future without dread. Life felt magic today, as if nothing could ever go wrong.

Was she in love? Did it matter? Was she being wild and reckless and impulsive to enjoy McKade and what he did to her and what she did to him in bed and out of it so completely? All she knew was that she couldn't stop herself from flinging every part of herself into what she felt for McKade. Even now, when he wasn't with her, she thought of him, looked forward to seeing that craggy brown face, that white grin, those gleaming silver eyes.

She was young and healthy. The whole time she'd been married to a sick man, she'd had to stifle so many impulses, especially her longing for McKade. When she'd awakened after dreaming of him at night, she'd had to tell herself how awful he was. During those dark years, laughter had left her life. Now, she could savor the good things about McKade. He was gloriously handsome and very sexual. He made her feel young again and feminine...and beautiful...and wild.

Ever since he'd lifted her into his arms on her porch, she'd lived in a wonderland of carnal and emotional delights. He'd brought laughter back into her life. More and more, she lived for the nights when Sam and Big Red went off to bed and she and McKade could be alone together. She loved the feel of him, the clean male scent of his black hair and skin. It was harder and harder to refrain from hugging and kissing him even in front of Sam and Big Red. She wanted to make love to him on her hot-pink couch, on one of her orange chairs, on top of her trestle table and vegetable cushions.

McKade had said, "I've never done it on a stuffed eggplant."

"Does everything turn you on?"

"Just the loud, wild things in this house that scream Willa."

Did all women feel about their lovers as she felt about hers? Was she blinded? Was what she felt real? Would McKade ever respect her as a person?

She didn't know. For the moment, she was having too much fun to care. All she knew was that life felt very wonderful again, as wonderful as that magical time when her parents had been alive to adore her.

McKade was good with Sam, too. He said he could identify with him because the Longworths hadn't wanted to claim him, either.

"But do you respect me?" she'd asked him once, as he'd nibbled sardines straight from the can in bed after they'd had sex.

"I crave you. Does that count?"

Oh, it did. Yes, it did. And the way he said it, as if his heart and soul were in his silver eyes, counted even more.

Last night when they'd made love, he'd demanded things of her she'd never conceived of doing. With him, such shameless, wanton activities had brought ecstasy. His body was lean and hard, and yet when she lay under him, she became part of him, part of his wild, frenzied, quiet imaginative passion. And she feared that even if he left her, she would never utterly belong to herself again. Maybe she should have been mortified at the things they did together, but the feelings she had for him made everything right and gloriously wonderful.

Be careful, Willa, said Mrs. Connor. *It is dangerous to be so happy.*

It is dangerous to give yourself so completely...to such a man.

But an easier man, a tamer man would have bored Willa.

And in that moment while she hugged herself as Sam chased pigeons, Willa was perfectly happy to wait for her tall, dark, dangerous lover.

Then suddenly she heard a familiar voice from her dangerous past, and her glorious dream shattered into nightmarish shards.

"This is good."

Willa's heart ceased to beat.

Brandon Baines, as tall and golden and elegant as he'd been on that tennis court when he'd touched his nose to hers was kneeling before her precious Sam.

The handsome monster held Sam's shiny toy Porsche in his big tanned hand.

When Sam reached for the toy with pink, sticky fingers, Brand grabbed the little boy's sleeve and pulled him closer. "Where's your mother—son?"

"Over there," Sam said carelessly pointing toward the ice-cream shop as he spun the front tires of the little car. "Ice cweam."

Suddenly Sam's eyes widened with alarm when he didn't see Willa.

"Mommy!" he shrieked. She shrunk out of sight. When she didn't answer or come running, he set up a howl. "Mommy!"

"Shut up, kid!" Brand whispered.

Wild panic exploded inside Willa.

Brand had Sam. Brand wanted her. Sam, her baby, was screaming.

Fear paralyzed her. *Dear God, help....*

Brand was here. She'd always known this would happen. Sounds came to her, hollow, muted sounds, as if from a deep well. Each syllable was soft and seemed to echo afterward. Brand was talking softly to Sam now, trying to soothe him. Cars roared on the highway that wound through town. A woman, Lupita Joyce, a rancher's wife came up to Sam and demanded to know who Brand was and what he wanted with little Sam Longworth.

"Where's Willa?" Lupita wanted to know.

"Longworth?" Brand's raised voice seemed to come through a thick fog.

"Willa Longworth. That's what I said."

Lupita was scanning the square. Willa stayed hidden. Her mind raced. She had to save Sam and herself…but for the first time in her life, in a moment of crisis, instead of doing something wild, she froze.

Which, as it turned out, was exactly the right thing to do.

Suddenly McKade was there, talking to Brand and Lupita in easy, reassuring tones, distracting them so Sam could break loose and run to her. As Willa grabbed Sam and hurried him inside the Book Nook, McKade got between Brand and herself, so Brand, who was straining to look back over his shoulder, couldn't see her. Lupita came inside the shop, too, and Willa embraced her. Together they watched Luke and Brand wander off down a side street together. The two men laughed and talked as if they were the best of friends.

Were they?

Why had Brand come?

Lupita said goodbye.

After she left, it seemed an eternity before the bells jingled on the door, and McKade strode inside Cathy's store. Sam was on the floor, legs crossed, his Porsche on the chair beside him. He was totally absorbed in a pop-up book which was a reproduction of children's books made in the nineteenth century.

McKade came to Willa and folded her into his arms. Even so, she couldn't stop shaking. "Tell me it's just a coincidence Brand's here."

McKade stared past her out the window. "He's staying at Angel Fire…to ski."

"But there's not enough snow."

McKade's mouth thinned. "I know."

"What's he doing here?" She bit her lip, sighed. "Dear God…"

The door jingled again. "Careful," he whispered tightly against her ear. "Hesper just came in. She's been following me all day."

"Tell me Brand's really here to ski. Tell me he misjudged the snow."

"Everything's going to be okay," he said, which wasn't the same at all.

He pulled her closer.

"I want to go home—"

"Play like nothing is wrong."

"Hello, Cathy," Hesper said crisply. "Well! Now that's loud! Another one of your art shows?" Hesper screwed her topknot tighter as she studied the new paintings.

For the first time Willa noticed the splash of neon orange on the walls behind the bookshelves.

"The color grabs you," said Cathy.

"It certainly does," muttered McKade.

"See something you like?" Cathy asked Hesper.

Again, the little silver bells jingled. Gracie said, "Hi."

"Oh, my God—" Hesper shrieked from the back wall. "Something I like? Are you out of your mind?" Glaring at Gracie, she turned on Cathy. "*You!* You two actually hung it?"

"May I help you?" Cathy asked in her most helpful, saleslady voice.

Hesper erupted like a volcano. "*My Big Sister, the Goddess, the Saguaro and the Bean Bag!*"

"I didn't expect to see you here, Hesper," said Gracie.

"I know you're proud to be the subject of your sister's wonderful piece," said Cathy to the oldest

Longworth sister. "I've made it the centerpiece of my show."

Hesper began a rant, which put Gracie on the defensive.

"Taos is an art colony."

"How could you hang this photograph of me...with these loud, pornographic— What is that woman, whoever she is, doing to herself with that paintbrush?"

Willa caught the phrase *flashy orange nudes* again and her own name.

"Actually, your sister-in-law inspired my wonderful series."

"Willa! I don't doubt it for a minute!"

McKade let go of Willa so fast she nearly fell. To her horror his black glare devoured the bold enormous nudes that lined every wall of the bookstore.

Willa forgot all about Brand.

"Willa," he growled. "Shouldn't you be using your paintbrush to paint...the wall...not your..."

"Oh, no," Willa gasped, recognizing her own body in vibrant brush strokes of flaming orange. And why had Cathy painted her pubic hair that bright shade of turquoise?

Hesper attacked Gracie. "Until you and your camera, our family stood for something!" Hesper turned from her sister to Cathy. "And you—you encourage her with these lewd, salacious shows."

"They're all of you," McKade accused Willa. "I'd know that tangerine shower and hot-pink tub anywhere!"

Willa's face went an even brighter shade than the canvases. But she notched her chin up. "I—I haven't done anything wrong."

McKade quelled her with a look. Then he stalked up to Cathy who stood guard at her cash register. "How much for those paintings?" he demanded.

"This isn't about money, McKade. This is art," Willa whispered. "Don't you dare think you can buy—"

"I bet your cute ass, correction—your orange ass—they're for sale."

"Don't you dare sell them to him, Cathy," Willa said, stepping between them.

"What title are you interested in, sir?"

"I don't want a book, woman! I want to buy all your paintings. Those big orange nudes! And fast! Before any more customers come in!"

"All? You couldn't possibly afford them," Cathy said slyly.

"Try me."

"You said you didn't much like impressionistic art."

Lethal, hot glances passed between Willa, Cathy, and Luke. "Your...er...series...blows me away."

Beaming, Cathy dreamed up the most exorbitant figure she could imagine and then quadrupled it.

"Don't you dare—either of you—do this deal!" Willa exclaimed indignantly when she heard the outrageous price.

McKade whipped his credit card out of his wallet and slapped it onto the counter. Cathy began writing out a cash receipt with equal speed and passion.

"I've never sold a painting before," Cathy said brightly, quickly tapping out the price and his credit card number and zipping his card through her machine. "Willa, for me this sale is the thrill of a life-time."

The transaction went through.

"It's a thrill of a lifetime for all of us," said McKade in a grim, low tone that zinged Willa to the core. "That's an incredible shower stall."

The door jingled. A man let out a wolf whistle when he saw the pose of Willa dangling from the ladder with the paintbrush in her mouth that dripped turquoise. "I'd like to meet the wicked lady in loud orange with the turquoise.... I can think of a few things I'd let her do to me with that brush.... Is she anyone local?"

"Those paintings are mine! Get out of here before I deck you," thundered McKade.

One look at McKade's dark face, and the man said something about somebody's medicine needing to be changed. Then silver bells jingled, and the door slammed.

The customer with artistic inclinations and medical knowledge was history.

"That was a very good customer," Cathy said.

"That was a major asshole," said McKade.

Hesper and Gracie stared a little too knowingly at him, at the paintings and then at Willa.

A few minutes later, when McKade ushered Willa and Sam outside, Willa heard Hesper say, "How much for *My Big Sister, the Goddess, the Saguaro and the Beanbag?*"

On the drive home Sam fell asleep in the back seat. Up front, it was hard to tell who was angrier, Willa or McKade.

"Like I said, I let Cathy make a few sketches. She swore she wouldn't show anybody...."

McKade focused grimly on the road. "Don't defend what you did."

"You had no right to buy them. They're of me. They're personal."

"Oh, so you prefer them hanging on the town square so everybody can have a look?"

"I didn't say that! I said they're personal."

"Which is why I bought them. Your body is for my personal pleasure. Mine only."

"This isn't about you and your money."

"Tell that to your greedy friend with the paintbrush and cash register. She charged thousands."

"And you, Mr. Moneybags, Mr. Control Freak, Mr. Sucker of the Year, played right into her hands."

"What was I supposed to do, let every Tom, Dick and Harry who walks in her shop ogle you? Willa, show me a man who sleeps with a woman, who gives half a shit about her, and then tell me he wants to share her with other men too. Tell me you really want me to be like that."

"I—I—" Somehow the words stuck in her throat.

"Drop it. You've lost this one."

"I don't like the way you always think you can buy—"

"Think about it. Would such a man *respect* you?"

"Respect… You're using my buzzword just to confuse me."

"Or maybe I'm using it to get through your illogical mind! Admit it! Am I right? Or am I right?"

"What you are is impossible."

"What kind of flake lets somebody like Cathy sketch her nude?" McKade grumbled under his breath.

"I heard that! You called me a flake. You're arrogant."

"You're illogical!"

"You use your money to get what you want even when I ask you not to. You don't respect me or you wouldn't—"

"You had your say. I've had mine. We're not getting anywhere fast, so why don't we drop it?"

"Because you bought those paintings and I don't want you to have them!"

"They were for sale, damn it!"

"Not till you flashed that credit card!"

"We wouldn't have this problem if you hadn't flashed your body in the first place!"

She was too enraged to speak.

"A word of advice, Willa *dear*. Don't take your clothes off for other people again…for any reason…anywhere. Cathy or whomever she sold her paintings to could have beamed them off satellites onto every computer screen in America."

"She wouldn't do that. I trust her."

"After what she did?" He turned, stared at her so long the car weaved dangerously. "And you don't trust me?"

"Watch the road!" For once he obeyed her. "How could I…after what you did?"

He exhaled heavily. "Oh, that's rich. I'm always the villain."

Equally furious, they both lapsed into silence until they got to the house. There, they flung open their own doors as noisily as possible. Sam got up sleepily and followed them as they stomped up to the porch, banging the gate, causing the dogs to swarm and bark. The cats, realizing something was up, flew off the porch in choreographed pandemonium. *Ristras* swung crazily. Pumpkins rolled.

Then the phone started ringing.

Willa stopped. "Brand? Oh, God. I got so mad at you, I forgot all about Brand."

McKade took her hand, steadied her. "If you could do that, then at least the furor over those damned paintings served some positive purpose," he muttered almost gently. "Willa, I swear I won't let him hurt you...or Sam."

"Answer the phone," she whispered in a shaking voice.

"It'll be okay. I swear. It'll be okay. Stay out here with Sam."

"Harry," corrected Sam sleepily as he yawned.

McKade raced inside. By the time she and Sam got to the yellow kitchen, McKade was already off the phone. But his face was darker than before.

"What?" she whispered, terrified.

"Not Brand. At least...not directly..." He hesitated. "Harry, why don't you go outside and find Big Red?"

"'Cause I thirsty."

As always, McKade was patient with her son. "Okay, Harry."

A hard tight lump formed in her throat as McKade got a glass and poured Sam cold water into it. No sooner did Sam grab the glass than he set his glass down after a sip or two and was out the yellow door. He took off running.

"The plane is registered to a man in Nuevo Laredo," said McKade.

"Oh, my God. Brand?"

Even before McKade took her in his arms and led her to a chair, she was trembling again.

He poured her a glass of water. "To one Emilio Rodriguez."

"Little Red's old boss," she said in a dull voice.

"Brand's biggest client," McKade said.

"Little Red always thought Emilio…and you framed him," Willa said.

"Unlike Little Red, I don't do business with scum like Spook."

"Why was Spook flying over my land?"

"I doubt if he was. Probably his men, those same creeps that would've killed me, messed up big time."

"So why is Brand here?"

"I'm not sure."

"Tell me it doesn't have anything to do with me. Tell me Brand doesn't know I'm here, that he doesn't know about Sam. Tell me…tell me Brand isn't here to take Sam away. I've always been so afraid he'd do that."

McKade stared at her. Then he put his arms around her.

Finally, she said, "So, you think the money belonged to Emilio? You think Brand is here to collect?"

"I'm not sure, but drug lords don't like to lose money."

"Two million can't be much to Emilio Rodriguez."

"It's the principle of the thing."

"Do men like him *have* principles?"

"It's about power, machismo, winning. About holding on to what is yours. You don't let anybody stomp on you 'cause the next time they'll stomp harder and take more." McKade spoke with convincing passion. Was that how he felt about his own enterprises? She thought of Brand who'd believed she was his, always.

"So, Brand... Maybe he's here...because I... because I took... Maybe this wasn't about Sam or me. But now...because of what I did...it will be. Oh, McKade. Sam... What have I done?"

"You've got to give me those briefcases. And fast. If they belong to Emilio, this is very serious business. As soon as I have them, I'll contact Baines.... We'll give them back. Maybe I can cut a deal and they'll let us off."

"You mean pay them more?"

"Whatever it takes," he said in a cold, ruthless tone. "I intend to make sure Brand never bothers you or Sam again. No more bad dreams."

Money. He would use his money to buy her out of trouble.

Would he think he'd bought her?

The briefcases? The cave? Her head had begun to throb. Turning away from him, she rubbed her forehead. "It's not that simple."

"What do you mean?"

Her mind raced. "I can't find the cave or the money."

McKade was staring at her, his face dark and hard.

"I've looked. I can't find the cave. I had a map.... I drew it the night I left you in the cave, but I—I lost it. I can't find the money."

He was silent for a long time. "So, you did search that day you went to my cabin?"

She nodded miserably.

. To her surprise, he smiled. "I wondered what it would take for you to confess all to the big bad wolf."

She jerked her head toward him in sudden understanding.

McKade flashed white teeth. "Yes! I've got your map. And some sketches that match those loud paintings I just bought, too."

"You took my map!"

"Not exactly."

"All this time, you had it. You courted me, made love to me!"

He smiled his big bad wolf smile.

"You snake!"

His smile broadened even as she hurled herself at him with a vengeance.

The desert was cold and so bright that every tree and cloud and rock stood out, their shapes etched and vivid that crystal morning. McKade stood some fifty feet higher on the ledge than she.

"Nothing up here!" he called down to her.

Willa turned the crayon drawing upside down, smoothed it flat against her denim-clad knee. She had drawn a twisted tree in front of the cave. Looking up at McKade, whose lean, handsome face seemed darker than ever against the brilliant, cloudless blue, she scanned the sandstone and limestone cliffs behind him. Turning, her gaze wandered over the red hills of sand and gypsum and sage toward the purple mountains in the distance.

She'd spent her fury on McKade last night in her flower-power bed as he called it. Now she felt lost and all alone—and in terrible trouble. The desert was immense. Nothing in this chaotic tumble of rocks was familiar. There had been some sort of avalanche since she'd been here that night.

The storm the other night... What difference did it make how or why? Everything *was* different. Her cave could be anywhere. Buried anywhere.

McKade looked as exhausted as she felt when he skidded down to her. She had railed at him the night before. Then he'd made very energetic love to her. All morning he'd clambered up and down the cliffs like a crazy man, sure the cave had to be somewhere just beyond the next boulder or over the next hill. Now, even his vast energy seemed diminished.

She twisted the smudged map around again. "My map! My sketches! I should have known! I did know! You're a devil."

"That again." At her fierce expression, he glowered back at her. But just for a second. "You stole, too— money that wasn't yours!" Then he grinned. "Do you want to fight and make up all over again?"

"No!"

"Then concentrate! The cave! Where the hell is it?"

"You just want my two million! That's all you've ever cared about!"

"I liked the nude sketches...and the paintings, too...not to mention—all the sex in your tangerine shower stall."

"Don't even—"

"Get a grip!" he whispered tenderly. "If it'll make you feel better, I found the map and your nude sketches in Harry's Ali Baba storybook."

"Now don't you dare accuse Sam—"

"See—you drew the same conclusion I did. Your kid's got sticky fingers."

"All four-year-olds are curious."

"Willa, we've been searching for hours...I'm damn near done for. Think."

"The cave is gone," she said, sinking to her knees. "What am I going to do now?"

He knelt beside her. "We'll think of something."

"We?"

Staring beyond him, she saw a black vulture with white-tipped wings rise from behind the cliff.

McKade met her eyes. He took her hand in his, wound his fingers through hers. "Haven't you figured it out yet?"

She stared at him blankly and then beyond him at the soaring black bird.

"We're in this together," McKade said.

The black bird circled, round and round McKade.

"Are we?"

"You showed up the same night I found the money," she whispered.

"To save your ass."

"You came and you stayed. Why? Why that night? There's no such thing as coincidence."

His long-fingered brown hand was on her shoulder now. "Just a damn minute. Those guys damn near killed me."

Her heart jumped at his touch. Defensively, she jerked away from him even though his nearness filled her with painful longing and reminders of all they'd shared last night, shared all the other nights, too.

She rushed on. "You admitted you found the plane first."

"What are you saying?" he demanded quietly, his tense hand falling to his side.

"I'm saying what I'm saying."

"Yeah. That you are." He swallowed harshly.

Strong, dark feelings chased across his face as he stood up. She got to her feet, too. Not that his anger and obvious hurt changed the course of her wild thinking.

Maybe, just maybe he'd been in the plane that night, too. Maybe he'd run off with the others and then circled back intending to protect the money...or maybe steal it for himself. Maybe he knew a lot more than he was telling her.

"Little Red always said that you and Baines and Emilio set him up."

"So, that's how it is." McKade's handsome face was suddenly cold with bitterness.

"I'm asking you, McKade. Tell me the truth."

McKade's features twisted.

"Did you tell Baines where I am?"

"You tell me. You seem to have me and this whole damn business figured out."

"I want you gone, McKade."

"That was easy."

"Easy?"

As McKade stepped back from her, the light that had shone for her alone died in his eyes. "A long time ago, not too far from where we are right now, my father looked at me just like you did a while ago. He didn't want me any more. Something died in me then. Damn you, Willa, for making me feel small and alone like that again."

Something shattered inside her, too. Even before he

headed back to the house without her, tears burned behind her eyelids.

He'd saved her life. Sam's, too. Because of her, those horrible men had nearly killed him. Even now the livid red wounds on his back weren't entirely healed.

He'd been good to Sam. So good. He'd been good to her, too. Unlike Brand, he wanted a real relationship with her and her son. Every day they'd been together, their feelings had deepened on every level, not just the sexual.

"McKade..."

He kept on walking.

Tears raced down her cheeks. "McKade...I'm sorry...."

Finally, he stopped, drew a short breath. "Do you remember Rhett's parting shot to Scarlett?" His unendurably cold voice was light and soft.

He didn't have to say it out loud for the famous literary line to resonate in Willa's imagination.

When he turned, the strides that carried him away from her were long and deliberate.

23

All the way back, Willa chased McKade. But her struggles were in vain. His strides were lengthier, the fury driving him greater.

Just keep on his tail, she told her panicky feet. *You'll think of something to say to make him forget how angry and hurt he is.*

But in the end, she didn't have to say anything.

The minute she got halfway up the drive and saw McKade leaning down to catch every word Big Red was saying, she knew something was dreadfully wrong. Usually, the two men avoided each other.

When she reached the stairs, they fell silent and stared at her. Then she saw the toy Porsche in Big Red's gnarled fingers.

"Where's Sam?"

They didn't answer.

"Tell me everything is all right," she pleaded.

Never had McKade, who was tall, lean and dark seemed so terrifyingly stern. Big Red seemed older and more shrunken. He reminded her of a lost child. And yet, never before had she realized how much they resembled one another. Both were tall and lean. And their gray eyes were they same. Their frozen gray eyes.

Why were they looking at her that way?

"Tell me Sam's okay," she begged.

"Willa," McKade began at last, his tone infinitely gentle, "we'll find him...I swear...if it's the last thing I do...."

"Where's Sam?" she murmured. She was running past them, pushing at McKade when he reached for her. Dimly she heard the front door bang behind her. "Sam, Mommy's home!"

"They took him," Big Red said in a dull idiot voice from behind her.

She turned and stared at the gaunt figure with the wispy white hair from the length of the dark hall that led to Sam's bedroom. "They?"

"A man in a black ski mask. He pushed me into the closet in Sam's bedroom. He said stay there or he'd hurt Sam.... So, I did what he said."

Willa gasped.

McKade moved toward her wordlessly. His face was gray, his eyes icy cold with fear.

How could she have doubted him?

"It's gonna be okay," he repeated. "I'll find him. I'll bring him back."

She wanted him to take her in his arms. She wanted to tell him how sorry she was and for him to forgive her. But the vastness of the surrounding desert and the immense silence of the house bound them. The shared terror in their hearts made such words trite and unnecessary.

When he reached her, he touched her face with the

back of his hand. She pushed her wet cheek against his warm fingers.

"Stay by the phone," he said.

Then he turned and was gone.

She chased him and caught him on the porch.

"Where are you going?"

"To town. To find Baines."

"How?"

He was holding his cell phone. "I want to check out the hotels…make some calls…. Trust me," he said. "Call me if anything breaks. You know my number."

She nodded, and even when she saw he didn't believe she trusted him or would confide in him, she didn't reassure him.

McKade didn't come home, and she was nearly mad with grief and terror and yet half-asleep when Brand called late that night.

"Willa. This is good, so good to hear your voice."

She clutched the phone, wound her fingers in the cord. "Brand."

"I always knew I'd find you." His voice sounded disembodied, unreal, dead and terrible. "This is good."

She got up, went to the window, and stared out into the terrifying dark. He could be anywhere. "What do you want?" she whispered, her words sounding vague and slurred.

"What I've always wanted…and more. You're the kind of girl that makes a man want things he shouldn't want. My last memory of you is…"

The cold, black windowpanes seemed to press in on her. "Don't...."

"All right. After all, you are the mother of my son."

"What have you done with Sam?"

"Where's my money?"

"Your money?"

"Emilio pays me in cash."

"Then it's not Emilio's money?"

"Those briefcases on his plane were mine, Willa. I want them back. I know about your little shopping spree with fifty-dollar bills. I know you found my briefcases."

How could she have been so unlucky for the plane with Brand's money to crash on her land?

As if he read her mind, he began to speak.

"This probably seems like a big coincidence. But maybe it's not. I've known where you were for a while. It wasn't so hard to figure out really...Little Red and McKade turning up in Mexico at that shack...your aunt, the overly suspicious, pretentiously virtuous Mrs. Brown refusing to tell me where you were."

"Why would she?"

"Who needed her? You disappeared that same night. How? Who helped you? It occurred to me that McKade always acted odd when I asked him about you. Then I found out McKade had begun to make regular trips to Taos, and I followed him here last year. I bought a timeshare at Angel Fire. I've flown over your ranch many times. I even took a picture of you and my son on the square one day right before Little Red died. It disappeared after McKade paid me a surprise visit. So, you see, I intended to get in touch with you and my son even before the plane crashed. But when you took my money…when you scared my men off…I knew I had to come after you myself.'' He laughed. ''I would have come weeks ago, but I was in trial. Besides, I told McKade to enjoy you, that I'd wait. I figured you were having too much fun with him for me to worry you'd disappear. He had quite a reputation with the ladies back in law school.''

''Shut up.''

''If you want your kid, bring me the briefcases.''

''Where?''

''Go to the first cave where my guys tracked you and McKade to. You'll find a note that tells you where to go from there. And Willa, come alone.''

He hung up.

Willa opened the window and let the cold dark envelop her.

She began to shake when she dialed McKade and he didn't answer.

24

From the bedroom Brand watched Willa open the door to McKade's cabin. He almost heard her quick intake of breath. She was as white as a sheet; scared to death, the way he liked her.

This is good. Scaring her had been one of their old games, one of his favorites. God, he'd missed that, missed the delicious thrill of moments like this, knowing he had Mrs. Brown's top girl, a girl he'd trained to please him, a girl who would do anything he wanted, any way he wanted.

Ah, the things he'd do to her tonight...the irony of doing them right here in McKade's cabin...on his bed...before he took her away to Mexico. Not that Brand would have chosen Lost Canyon or this rustic, sinkhole of a shack as a love nest under ordinary circumstances.

The canyon was burned-out, treeless. The primitive shack lacked sunken tubs, mirrors and all the other luxurious amenities Brand was used to for nights like this. But the idea of doing her in McKade's bed, staking his claim, so to speak, nearly got him off.

Brand didn't like thinking about McKade, but whores weren't wives. They didn't have to be faithful. After he was finished with her, McKade wouldn't want her back.

She looked sexier than ever with her hair up in that Tinkerbell knot, and her body crammed into that low-cut, tight blue mini. She was all breasts, hips, and legs—all woman, as always, the perfect whore.

"This is good! I see you wore an uplift bra just like I told you to when I called you back."

She jumped a little. "W-where's Sam?" Her whispery voice sounded low and strangled...sexy.

A wave of something warm and tickly-sweet swept him. "He's safe. What we're about to do together in McKade's bed is X-rated. Inappropriate viewing for a little boy his age. For my son," he reminded her with a paternal smile. "Come here, hot stuff."

She blanched.

This felt so right: he and Willa, finally alone together, her scared; him excited. She was back with him, where she belonged.

He popped a cork. "I brought champagne. Want some?"

"Sam?" She was moving frantically about the cabin, looking for their son.

He watched her breasts jiggle beneath the blue knit fabric. Quiet pleasure expanded inside him, warmed him, got him so hot, his blood pulsed.

Not that she got it yet. She hadn't brought the money, either. He'd have to punish her for that...and for the rest, too.

First things first. He had to make her understand that what they had was special and permanent. After all, he'd picked her out when she'd been a raw kid, waited for her to grow up and trained her. Then she'd let herself get pregnant.

Whores weren't supposed to be mothers.

He'd do her. Then he'd make her show him where the money was.

She'd opened every closet door, peered under the bed and behind the chairs. Finally realizing he'd lied in his note about Sam being here, she whirled on him, her eyes wild and defiant.

"Where is he?"

He'd hold her down, tie her up, the way he used to.

When he moved toward her, she ran for the door. Laughing, he stepped in front of it, blocking her with his larger body, trapping her.

Her eyes got bigger.

She was so beautiful. So goddamn beautiful.

"It's just me and you, sweetheart. We're all alone in the middle of nowhere. I didn't think McKade would ever consider that I'd choose his place for our reunion."

When he reached for her, she put her hands against his chest. He liked her to fight him, but when her fingers curled hard, and he felt her fingernails, he got mad.

"You've been a bad girl," he said, yanking her closer. "A very bad girl. You got pregnant. You ran away. You had the baby. You married a man who tried to kill me. You didn't bring my money tonight, did you? You deserve to be punished. I brought ropes. We won't have to use your hose this time."

"No, Brand... No!"

She tried to twist free, but he held on tight. He knew

he was bruising her wrists. But he didn't care. He crushed harder, liking it when she whimpered. She had to learn. "You're going to remember me every time you hurt."

"I'm not what you think. I never was. Let go of me. Please..."

He unzipped his slacks. "Get down on your knees."

She jerked free. "Never!"

When she ran, he dove for her. The full force of his body slammed into her. She lost her balance and fell with a thud. He landed on top of her slighter frame, and they went sliding.

Now he had her underneath him, right where he wanted her.

He was about to kiss her, but something wasn't right. Her eyes were closed, and she was too still.

In a panic, Brandon felt for her pulse and couldn't find one.

"No, no, please don't die!"

He couldn't lose her, not after watching her grow up, not after training her, not after waiting...waiting; not after these last four long years of waiting.

She was his. His.

He picked her up, carried her to the bed. Then he sat down beside her, pulled her golden head into his lap and crooned to her. "Wake up. You have to wake up."

Outside the hangar, McKade crouched behind a tumble of boulders along with Will Sanders and two of his men. The chilly air was crisp with the scent of sage. Wired by rage, caffeine and fear, McKade put on the safety of his automatic. Two men had Harry in the squalid hangar beside a desolate landing strip in the middle of nowhere.

Make your move, assholes. What are you waiting for? Where the hell are you, Baines?

Luke had to get Sam. He'd promised Willa. Then he had to get back to Willa—fast.

"We've been here for hours, Sanders."

Sanders was squinting through binoculars, his gaze glued on the hangar.

Luke punched Willa's number into his cell phone for the fiftieth time.

No service.

"*No damn service.* Four hours I've been trapped here unable to call her. What if she's tried to call? What if Brand... She'll think I've abandoned her. If she gets scared, there's no telling what she'll do."

"She's okay," said Sanders. "I've got my best two men at the Triple L—"

"So why haven't they checked in? This is it... I'm leaving. I've gotta make sure she's—"

Just as Luke got to his feet, the door of the hangar opened. Sanders shoved him to the ground.

They watched two dark figures emerge, the taller holding a wiggly bundle in his arms. When they bent double and dashed for the plane, all hell broke loose.

McKade was everywhere at once. First, he was on top of the bearded man, the two of them rolling over and over in the dirt. One of Sanders's men took the other man. Sanders got the kid.

The fight was over in seconds.

Then McKade had Sam in his arms. He peeled the heavy quilt off his flushed face. "You hiding somewhere in there, Harry?"

Sam blinked drowsily, as if drugged. "Tha's not my name," he whispered. "I'm Sam today."

McKade ruffled his hair, hugged him close.

"Where's Mommy?"

Sanders was inside the hangar on the telephone. "Willa doesn't answer," he said to Luke. "Neither do my men at the Triple L. But we got a trace on her phone. Do you have guests at your cabin—"

"Baines! T-take care of Sam. I—I've got to get there before—" Luke stared at Sanders in horror, realizing he was losing his cool, cerebral competence, that he was beginning to stutter badly.

Marcie. He felt raw and horrible. This was even worse than the day when Marcie had called to tell him about their baby and he'd told her she'd just called because she wanted more money.

Willa. If he lost her, he lost everything.

Luke McKade, the ice man, was melting.

He should never have left Willa. She was too unpredictable. If anything happened to her, if Baines raped her, worse if he killed her, it would be his fault.

Sanders was watching him worriedly. He handed Sam to his men and told them to take him to the Triple L.

Luke had to get a grip. He took two quick, calming breaths.

Then he broke into a dead run. Sanders was right behind him.

The windows of his cabin glowed like the wicked eyes of an orange jack-o'-lantern among the charred, ruined trees.

Brand had Willa inside. Luke had to get her out.

Sanders edged forward. "McKade, we'll take it from—"

But Luke was already striding toward the back door. As he moved through the shadows, he remembered that long-ago night when he'd been a child, when he'd awakened to orange sparks shooting through the inky night, and been afraid he'd die.

He'd been so scared, he'd called out for his daddy. Only his daddy hadn't come. Hesper had been there instead, her eyes filled with hate.

Luke smashed in the back door with a heavy black boot. Two strides had him inside his bedroom.

All three of the people in that room froze. At first Luke didn't recognize the cheap-looking, yellow-haired girl in the blue mini-dress tied to his bed as Willa.

Brand smiled. "This is good."

Then Brand's handsome, smiling face went wrong.

Willa shrieked, "He's got a gun."

"She's right," agreed Baines in a low, pleasant tone. "And it's pointed straight at your heart. Tell me you brought me my money." Baines's mouth twisted.

"Yeah, I brought your money."

"Where?"

"Outside." Luke directed his attention to Willa. "Did you hurt her?"

"When I do, you can watch." His voice got silkier. "Where's my money?"

McKade nodded toward the door. "Go and get it."

Willa began to moan and McKade moved cautiously across the room, hands above his head, avoiding Baines, but keeping his eye on his gun. McKade sank down beside Willa, stroked her hair, kissed her brow. Then because she was wearing so little and, thus, lay exposed and shivering in the icy cabin, he unzipped his jacket and threw it over her long legs.

"Let her go." Luke's quiet voice was deadly.

"Not till I'm done with her."

Old terrors from being bullied, from being powerless, made Luke's stomach writhe. He'd been powerless to save Marcie. No matter what tonight cost him, he had to save Willa.

"She's mine," Brand said.

That's when it happened: that's when Luke went a little crazy.

In the next second, Luke tipped his black head to the right, silently signaling Sanders who was on the alert right outside the window. Then Luke dove just as Sanders's bullet shattered glass and went into Baines's hand.

With a yelp, Baines dropped the gun. Blood spurted everywhere. Luke sprang for the gun. Then he was on top of Baines, straddling him, his dark fists pounding the golden man's prettier, preppier face until both men were slippery with sweat and Baines's blood.

"Stop it, Luke," Willa called in a thready, terrified voice.

Then Sanders was inside pulling Luke off.

"She's right, McKade. He's not worth it."

Luke got up dazedly, blood throbbing in his temples, wiping his forehead with his arm. Panting hard, he stumbled toward the bed, toward Willa. When he cut her loose, she flung her arms around him, heedless of the blood staining his white shirt and cheek. Gently, wearily she laid her head upon his wide shoulder.

"Sam? Where's Sam?" she whispered.

"We've got him."

Watching them, Baines began to laugh. "Look at her. She's a whore. My whore."

Luke stared at her bulging breasts, at the tight blue mini, and went green. Why had she come all the way out here, dressed like that, to meet Brand, her former lover, alone?

"Why?" Luke whispered, his expression hard and implacable. "Why did you come to him?"

"If you have to ask...you don't have to."

The pleading hurt in her luminous eyes scared the hell out of him, but the dark fury and the insanity of his jealousy locked such gentler feelings inside him. The aftermath of physical violence always left him filled with blood-lust and a little crazy.

The thought of her coming here alone, luring Baines in an attempt to save Sam...

Suddenly Luke felt himself pulsing, about to explode.

Who the hell was she? What was she? How could he have thought such a woman was worth everything?

Wrapped in McKade's jacket, Willa sat slumped dejectedly in a ladder-back chair of his kitchen. Her eyes were dazed and unfocused as she listened to McKade bargain with the devil in the next room.

Sam was safe. McKade had sworn to that. Willa was so jittery she had to struggle to hold on to that thought. No matter what else had gone wrong tonight, that was what was all important. Somehow McKade had saved Sam.

But now McKade was buying her.

Sanders sipped coffee from a mug, but she ignored

hers. She was so nervous, every word McKade said as he negotiated with Brandon Baines in the next room made her scalp tingle and her skin itch and burn until she felt she was a bundle of jangling nerves.

He was buying her, like one of his companies or a car or maybe even a boat. Her future, her heart and soul, were no more than credits or debits in the sordid deal McKade was cutting. To him, what they had shared, all the memories that were so precious to her, was just money.

Bottom line—what would she cost him?

He was sitting on his couch with the golden devil, buying her.

"If you ever come near Willa or Sam or me again after tonight, I'll kill you," McKade said calmly.

"You're out of your mind! If I sign these outrageous documents, I give up all rights to Sam—my son."

"Sign."

"No way."

"My certified check—says you will."

McKade must have handed him the check because Brand whistled. "Willa doesn't know where she hid your money. I'm doubling what she owes you."

"That's a lot to pay for a whore."

"It'll be cheap—to get rid of you."

McKade didn't hit Brand or say a single word in her defense. Suddenly, Willa felt numb and shaken. She remembered McKade's cold face when he'd cut her loose and then stared at her, believing her a whore again because he'd found her tied up and at Brand's mercy.

How she'd fought Brand—she'd kicked and

screamed. She had a lump the size of a hen's egg on the back of her head.

Brand laughed. "You'll regret this, McKade. She'll leave you someday, too."

"I already regret it. I wish I'd never met you—or her."

Willa felt hot tears pricking behind her raw eyelids.

"I need a doctor…I'm bleeding like a stuck pig."

"Sign. Or bleed to death. Either way I win."

Willa's hand began to shake so hard she spilled her coffee.

Willa had to get back to Sam. Sanders was driving the washboard road too fast. The bumps jarred Willa, but she was too numb and heartbroken to care. All she wanted was to get across the endless black desert, to go home, to be safe. She couldn't wait for Sanders and his men to drop McKade and her off at her house. McKade had told her Sam was already home, that Big Red and two of Sanders's men were watching him.

And yet devastated as she was, somehow, before this horrible night was over, Willa had to talk to McKade—alone. She had to explain.

But when they got home, Hesper's car blocked her drive.

"Damn," whispered McKade from the porch when he saw his three sisters and Big Red in the living room.

"I knew you were in this together," Hesper gloated when Willa stepped into the room with McKade.

"I can't deal with anything else tonight, not till I see Sam."

Willa rushed past Hesper, down the hall to Sam's

room. Her heart lurched when she found her bright-haired darling whimpering in his sleep. Quickly, she sat down and circled her precious child within her arms, rocking him gently until he quieted. With a fingertip she traced the new bruise on his forehead and discovered the lump beneath his ear that was almost as big as hers.

"Oh, my precious, precious darling." She hugged him close and began to weep.

What had they done to him? She'd nearly gone out of her mind with worry. What if they'd gotten him onto that plane? Flown him to Mexico?

She stroked his fiery curls and then kissed them. He was all right now. McKade had sworn he was all right. She had to hold on to that.

"Sam's very brave...like his mother," McKade had said in a grim, dead tone.

"Sam? You're calling him Sam. Not Harry?"

"He said he's Sam now, that he's not Harry anymore."

In spite of everything she smiled. McKade's mouth had curved, too.

"You're good with him. He likes you," she said.

"He's a good kid."

Sam stirred, and she smiled down at him.

"Mommy...I wooked for you everywhere. I called and called. The bandits shoved Grandpa in the closet."

"I know, my darling. The important thing is that the bandits are gone and you're safe now."

"Uncle Luke had a big gun."

"Sleep, my darling."

Sam didn't hear her. His spiky red lashes were closed. He was already sound asleep again.

When she returned to the living room, the sisters had McKade cornered against the giant sculpted head of the Cape buffalo above the fireplace.

Hesper turned on Willa. "It's all his. But I'm sure you know that. I'm sure you helped him. He owns the ranch. Lock, stock and barrel. Every acre. Every cow."

Willa's brain felt fuzzy. "What—what are you saying?"

"This is your fault. He left us alone till you came, till you married Little Red and made him so jealous."

"Maybe he shouldn't have…left you alone," Willa said, defending McKade before she thought. "After all, he's your brother. And you're his sisters. Even if you didn't have the same mother, you shared…"

McKade didn't look at her. His full attention seemed to be focused on the strand of wheat the Cape buffalo was chewing.

"We share nothing with him! All those experimental treatments Little Red had to have that you were so in favor of? Now I know why you wanted Little Red to live. You wanted to bankrupt us."

"What?"

"You knew McKade loaned Daddy the money and then forced him to pay it back at exorbitant interest that ruined him."

"Is that true?" Willa whispered, turning to McKade, who was leaning against the wall beside her Cape buffalo, his lean face, sharp and angled, his pale eyes glittering.

Then he shrugged and turned his back as if he found the buffalo better company than anybody in the room.

But she saw he was shaking with nerves and tension as she was from the long night's work.

"The bastard took our ranch. One of his companies, TKZ, holds title. When Daddy realized what he'd helped McKade do, he went crazy. That's why he had those strokes. And you, Willa, you, were in on it all the time. You pretended to be so sweet to Little Red and our father. You took care of Daddy. You fooled the whole town. But all the time, you both wanted our ranch."

"That's not true," Willa said, her voice choppy, her heart wildly distraught. "Tell them I didn't have anything to do with this awful, low-down, vengeful scheme of yours, McKade."

"Awful? Low-down?" He arched a cynical brow. His mouth twisted bitterly. "Naturally you believe them."

"That's why you stayed here, Willa, after Little Red died," Hesper said. "He gave you money, so you didn't have to cash our check." The grandfather clock ticked like a death knell. Everybody waited. "McKade was your lover the whole time you were married to Little Red, wasn't he? McKade was behind you all the time, wasn't he? Wasn't he?"

"No!"

"I, for one, believe her," said Gracie.

"Thank you," Willa said.

"Well, I don't," said Hesper.

"Neither do I," added Claudia.

Willa crossed the room to McKade. She couldn't believed they thought she'd married Little Red to steal his ranch, that she'd used his illness to bankrupt them. How could they know her and think... Dear God, to be accused of such treachery… Willa clutched herself, shivering. Suddenly she felt like she was flying to pieces inside.

"Tell them the truth, McKade—or else!"

"Or else?" He sneered, turning on her. "You dare threaten me with an ultimatum…after what you did tonight?" His face was gray and old; his voice savage.

"All right—the truth." Again his eyes glittered hotly, but he laughed as he faced Hesper. "Your precious ranch is mine. And so is Willa."

Everybody stared at them. Even Big Red and Gracie now believed she'd used Little Red's illness to steal the ranch for her lover, their bastard brother.

Seething, Willa lunged at McKade. His arms came around her like a vise. Half dragging her, half carrying her, he made his way to the door.

"You let me go—you—you bastard."

McKade ignored Willa. "I don't know about the rest of you," he said in a low, almost pleasant tone, "but I've had a helluva night. And so has my sexy partner in crime. Willa's overwrought, aren't you darling? We're anxious to get to bed."

"Together?" queried Gracie.

"Of course," rasped Hesper.

"I'll kill you, McKade," Willa whispered.

He smiled at her. "So, Hesper…dear…Claudia… Gracie…my esteemed…er…sisters…and Big Red, will you leave, so I can put your sister-in-law to bed, or do I have to throw you out? Out of *my* house?"

Hesper swished past the struggling Willa and the stony-faced McKade in a dignified rage. So did Big Red and the rest of them.

Then Willa was alone with McKade and frantic to

get away from him. When he slung her over his shoulder, she began pounding his back. McKade strode down the hall, kicked her bedroom door shut behind him, and locked it. Then he let her go and whirled on her.

She backed away from him, letting out desperate little breaths, growing increasingly terrified when he stalked her.

Her back hit the wall. His face contorted. He seemed to struggle to regain control.

Then he seized her again. Pushing her backward, he used his huge body to pin her against the wall.

She had to make him stop. "You took your sisters' house, my house? You think you've bought me?"

"You always make me the villain." His huge body rubbed up against hers. He was hot and hard and fully aroused. Very slowly he ran his hand over her breasts, down her belly. Last of all, he put it between her legs, every broad finger sending melting heat into the very marrow of her bones.

"You think you've bought me?" she whispered.

He lifted his black head and stared into her eyes. "Guilty on both counts. Maybe it's time to find out if you're worth it."

"Is it really always only money with you?"

"Usually. But right now it's sex. It's been a long night. I'm still wired."

The wall was cool against her shoulder blades. His wild, dark face leaned closer. Then his angry mouth was on hers, his tongue ravaging.

She shook her head, twisting it on the slender stem of her neck to get away from him. "You were jealous of Little Red the whole time I was married to him."

"I was even more jealous of Brand. Because I was sure you'd done it with him."

"You bastard!"

"Tell me something, did you do it with him tonight before I got there?"

She shuddered. His face began to whirl in a sea of stars. "This whole thing is about revenge then?" she whispered weakly.

"You know what they say...." His warm, expert hand curved inside her blouse and lewdly stroked her breast. He popped the cup of her bra down and kissed her taut pink nipple through her blouse. Then he turned his attention to the other nipple. "Revenge is sweet."

"You're a vulture. You wanted Little Red to die so you could get his ranch. You used—"

"Miracle cures don't come cheap. You owe me, Willa."

"Four million dollars," she whispered.

"You're forgetting about all those miracle cures. They cost a bundle, too. I don't usually spend so much to acquire a desired property."

"No woman is worth that much."

"We'll see. I expect a lifetime of good loving out of you."

"Sex," she corrected.

"I'm glad you get it."

He pushed her dress to her waist, unhooked her black satin bra. Feeling exposed, she shivered, but her breath came faster.

He was right. She owed him. Most of all, she owed him for Sam's life.

How could she ever repay him?

It wasn't long before he showed her.

"Get down on the floor, Willa."

When she just stood there, his hands closed on her shoulders, and he pushed her to the ground. Then he pulled her closer, until her face was against his thighs.

"Unzip me," he whispered.

She felt his heat, caught his hot male smell.

"No…"

But he tightened his hold, crushing her even tighter against his groin where his jeans bulged. "I've paid a lot for this sexual favor, wouldn't you say?"

With his other hand, he unbuckled his belt. Beneath her lips, she felt him pulsing and hard, straining against blue denim.

Dear God…

"Don't," she pleaded.

"You owe me," he begged through clenched teeth, his voice raw and choked, inaudible. His entire body was shaking as he ripped his shorts down and gripped her by the shoulders.

She went still.

He wanted her to be his whore.

"*Willa…*"

His anger was gone. All she heard was passion and desperate need, and that made her respond to him. Slowly, she did what he wanted, sliding her lips back and forth, flicking her tongue, pleasuring him, and in doing so pleasuring herself. When she went wild and got really inspired, he sighed with relief.

"Slower…" he begged, leaning back, his hands still pressing the back of her neck.

Wanting to please him, to thrill him, as his mad dark passion thrilled her, she found a rhythm that made her heart race, too. Soon he was gasping and shuddering his completion inside her soft, swollen lips.

"Willa...Willa..."

He came to his senses first. "My God." He stared down at her. "What have I done? What the hell have I done?"

She hardly knew what happened next.

She was still on the floor when he yanked his jeans up, raked his shaking fingers through his tangled black hair.

Dully, she heard her front door bang behind him. An engine started somewhere outside.

Had somebody gone?

Slowly she realized that she was alone in her bedroom, that McKade had left her, that he was never coming back.

Cones of light arced outside against the bare limbs of her trees, struck her flower-power bedding and the brown spider monkey dangling from her bamboo chandelier.

She turned away from her bright window, fighting to pretend she didn't care.

But in reality her reason for not watching the brightness of his headlights dim was far different. McKade had treated her like a woman he'd bought. And yet...she'd reveled in his wild, dark passion. Beneath her despair, he'd made her feel thrillingly alive, completely his—his alone.

She couldn't bear to watch those vanishing lights. She couldn't bear to think of him gone forever.

He'd come. She was still wet, hungrier than ever for him. She wanted him in her bed, ached for his warmth beside her while she slept. More than she wanted anything, she wanted to wake up every morning for the rest of her life and find him beside her.

But instead she'd lost him forever.

The room went totally black.

Never had she loved him so completely.

Whatever his reasons, he'd saved Sam. He'd saved her—twice.

He was right; she owed him.

If only he knew, she'd given him everything she had to give—even her heart.

Book Four

*"Finding true love is the rarest and best
treasure of all."*

25

"You're pacing again, McKade," said Kate.

Why had he been cursed with the most maddening secretary on earth? Did she have eyes in the back of her head?

"You're late," she persisted. "Everybody's in the boardroom. There's a reporter from the—"

"I'm not going."

"They're here to congratulate you. The Feds have decided to compromise on still another point."

"Thank everybody. Tell them..." Luke paused. "Oh, just make whatever excuses seem best."

"It's *her*...isn't it?"

"You have the meeting to go to."

"You look worse than when Marcie died."

He glared from his wristwatch to her impatiently. "Like I said, you're late." When she planted her hands on her hips and stayed put, he knew he had to say more. "If I need advice-to-the-lovelorn from a coffee-cup psychologist, I'll ask for it."

"Oh, no, you won't," she quipped tartly, but her eyes were kind.

"Why don't you take a hint for once in your bossy life and butt out?"

She laughed.

"Your good humor and zest for life is damned irritating this morning!"

"Redheads don't do hints," she said.

"Then get to the meeting and do what redheads do best—bully the hell out of those other men. God help them...."

"Go after her," Kate prodded gently. "If you do, I might consider turning over a new leaf and becoming a tidy secretary."

"You wouldn't know where to start."

She laughed again. He began to pace the gray carpet in his penthouse office even more restlessly than before.

"For a smart guy you're pretty stupid...I mean when it comes to women. You've got everything in the world. But you're not getting any younger. When I go home, I have a husband—"

"Who's lazy as sin..."

"Laziness isn't all bad. He likes to spend a lot of time in bed."

Luke imagined Willa at home in his bed at the end of a long day and felt a wave of jealousy. "Spare me the details."

"You're the loneliest person I have ever known."

"And you're ten minutes late, right.... If you don't get your long nose out of my personal life and your ass into that meeting, I really will fire you."

"No, you won't. And if you're here when I get back, I'll really give you what for. And—and sit down...before you wear a path...."

Luke sank into the leather chair behind his desk and

wearily raked his fingers through his hair. "You—you don't know what I did to her."

Why had he admitted that...to Kate of all people?

"Whatever it was, go back. Tell her you're sorry. And, McKade..."

"*She* calls me that. You're supposed to call me Mr. McKade."

"And McKade...if you want her—grovel."

Tell her you're sorry. The words rang in his mind, in his soul. He hadn't had the guts to tell Marcie he was sorry. Which was why... Which was why she'd slammed head-on into that limestone cliff.

"She's probably just as miserable as you are," Kate said.

Luke stared at his desk without looking up. She sighed. Then her heels clicked. The door shut softly.

After she was gone, he edged closer to his computer and stared at the blinking cursor on his screen.

Suddenly, his office felt hot and airless. What the hell was the matter with him? He needed to be on top of things—to put in seventeen-hour days. His businesses were booming. His net worth had climbed to staggering levels. Yet, when he'd walked out of the courtroom victorious last week, all he'd felt was depression that he was going home to an empty house, that he would never see Willa or Sam again. He even missed her no-good fleabags.

When he stared at his perfectly decorated house, he longed for wild, vibrant hot-pink walls, for plush green carpeting and flower-power bedding, for gross, flower-shaped pillows, even for that awful couch....

He was alone in his perfect house that had one of the best views in Texas. Even Lucinda was gone. Her daughter in Mexico had had a baby. His maid, Lucinda had taken the month off to be with them.

"I hate to leave you up here on your mountain, all alone," she'd said smiling at him gently before she'd gone. "You need a family, Mr. McKade. A pretty wife. Children. This big house is too quiet. I miss Mrs. McKade. But she's gone.... Life goes on. A handsome man like you should marry...." She'd broken off, suddenly as embarrassed as he was.

So, he had his flawless palace on the lake. His face and name were in all the papers ever since he'd defeated the Feds. He was on top of the world.

What the hell was wrong with him?

He had everything he'd ever wanted, and he didn't give a damn. Instead, he ached for a woman who was all wrong for him.

Then it hit him. Long ago he'd told Marcie he could never love her. He hadn't thought he could love anybody, ever. Marcie had accused him of being a dead man. But her death and their unborn son's death had brought him back to life.

He loved Willa. Maybe he'd loved Marcie, too, and just hadn't known it. Maybe that was why her death and their child's had hit him so hard.

Suddenly he knew what he felt for Willa. He loved her with every cell in his being. But instead of joy, the realization filled him with despair.

He loved her, but he'd lost her. After that final heartless stunt he'd pulled on her in her bedroom, she'd never forgive him. He'd been mad with jealousy when he'd found her with Brand. Then he'd gotten even more furious when she'd sided with the sisters against him.

Not that he'd told her how he'd come to acquire the

ranch. He'd let her go on believing he'd deliberately bought the ranch.

Hell, he'd had no intention of taking the Triple L away from his sisters. Big Red had forced him to buy it out of a sense of false pride after the old man had found out all that Luke had done for Little Red.

As soon as he cooled off, Luke intended to deed the ranch back to them. He would have done so already, except for Hesper and the things she'd said.

No matter what they'd done, his father, Gracie, Claudia and even Hesper, were his only living family.

On a generous impulse that he was highly suspicious of because he was still livid at Hesper, Luke picked up the phone and dialed Lou in Taos.

Big Red was in the hospital. It had snowed the night before, but the sun was shining, and water dripped down the windows outside.

There's nothing like a crisis or two, happy or sad, to bring a family back together. McKade had deeded the Triple L back to his sisters and the house with its surrounding acreage back to Willa exactly as Big Red and Little Red would have wanted him to.

When Big Red had found he had to live with Hesper, he refused to eat. Then he'd gotten sicker.

"You'll be well and home by Christmas," Willa whispered encouragingly to Big Red, who was thin and pale as he lay in the hospital bed, with his daughters and daughter-in-law amicably grouped around him. The old man's third stroke and their return of the ranch had brought them together as four years of being sisters-in-law had not.

"We have a lot to celebrate," said Gracie. "Getting

the ranch back, having Willa here with us today, Willa who is so unique and special in her very own way.''

The melting snow sounded like rain to a woman from south Texas.

Suddenly, for no reason at all, every nerve in Willa's being sparked.

"McKade only deeded it to us to make us look greedy," said Hesper. "Are you hungry, Daddy?" she asked, hovering nearer, lifting a cup of soup.

They were talking about Luke. Maybe that was why Willa felt so edgy and tingly all of a sudden. Or maybe...

Big Red twisted stubbornly away from the cup of soup. "I'm not hungry enough to eat that," he growled.

"Claudia and I invited Luke home for Christmas," said Gracie.

"What?" Willa whispered, hoping she didn't betray her shock.

"He is our brother."

"He won't come," said Hesper. "At least, I hope he won't."

Hope died in Willa.

"You're wrong," said Claudia, her voice filled with self-importance. "You've been wrong about quite a few things of late, Hesper dear. Willa wasn't in on taking our ranch, for instance!" She dug in her purse. "Luke wrote me the sweetest note. I have it right here in my purse if any of you care to read it."

He'd written Claudia. And not her.

Willa got up abruptly and went to the window. The glass was as cold as ice when she touched it, as cold as she was without Luke to hold her and kiss her on snowy winter nights, without him near to warm her with his gaze.

"I don't care to read it, thank you very much," snapped Hesper.

"Could I?" whispered Willa, hating the weakness that made her long for every scrap of news about him.

Claudia handed her a crisp blue note. Cautiously Willa unfolded it. His handwriting was black and bold, but his tone was friendly.

Willa refolded the note. Luke hadn't written her. He hadn't called, either. Not a single time.

Not that she'd expected him to. Still, for the first week after he'd gone, she'd run to the phone every time it had rung. Finally, she'd realized, he was never going to call. After all, he'd shown her what he'd thought of her.

Nevertheless, she longed for him every single day, and the pain in her heart wasn't getting better. She ached for him.

He's coming home for Christmas. That's something to hold on to, said Mrs. Connor.

"I hope you didn't tell him about Daddy's latest stroke," said Hesper. "Not that he'd care, coldhearted bastard that he is."

"Don't you ever call our brother that again," said Gracie. "I'll have you know, I spoke to Kate, his secretary, this morning. What a delightful woman, she is! She promised he'd call as soon as he could. So far he hasn't."

"That certainly doesn't surprise me," Hesper said.

Out of the corner of her eye, Willa caught a glimpse of a door at the end of the hall swinging open. Even before she saw black hair and broad shoulders, a telltale spark of excitement shot through her again.

The voices of her sisters-in-law droned into nothingness. Then Willa no longer heard them at all. Her eyes, every nerve in her being, were focused on the tall, dark man in the gray suit who was striding purposefully toward their room. Toward her.

McKade had been gone a month.

This man was lean of build, his hair jet-black. He was cruelly handsome in an unfair way.

Her heart raced. She began to tremble.

McKade.

She would have known him anywhere.

Wordlessly, she got up and walked toward the door. Her eyes met his; their gazes locked.

He flinched.

Her heart stopped.

"Are you all right?" he whispered when he finally reached her. "You're very pale. Maybe you should sit down."

"Hello, McKade," she said, fighting to make her voice sound normal, fighting tears, too, as well as a curious breathlessness.

"You look good." His deep voice was strange, awkwardly clipped. He glanced around as if he preferred looking at anything more than her.

"So do you. Gray becomes you."

She wanted him to look at her again, to take her in his arms. But he didn't.

Then he brushed a light finger against her cheek.

She gasped and caught her breath.

"Willa…" His husky voice was deep and tender and way too dear.

In the next instant he saw Hesper and went cold. Then he swept past Willa into the hospital room. And this time, nobody, not even Hesper, was rude to him.

A smile on her face, Gracie went slowly to him and put her arms around him.

He let her hold him. When she was done, Claudia smiled, too, and came forward to clasp his brown hand which she held for a long time.

"Thank you," they said together.

Then Gracie continued alone. "Thank you for everything. Thank you especially for what you did for Little Red. We had four extra years because of you."

"Because of Willa, too," McKade said, turning to Willa. "Where's Sam?"

"With Cathy," Willa whispered.

"I'm glad you came—son," Big Red said in a gruff, low tone that belied the depth of his emotion.

McKade went to his father's bedside. "You look good."

"I—I never said thank you...for all you did for Little Red."

"He was my...brother."

"Yes, he was. He admired you, in his way."

"Concentrate on getting better. Then you'll be home in no time."

"With Willa?" the old man asked Hesper. "Can I live with Willa again?"

"You can be with whomever you want to be, Daddy," said Claudia and Gracie.

"Willa," the old man repeated. "I want Willa."

"Of course, you can live with me," Willa said soothingly.

"Well, then that's settled," Gracie said. "And since visiting hours are nearly over, we need to go so you can rest." She turned to Willa and McKade. "There's a new gallery...a new show...I think you'd both enjoy."

Hesper eyed Gracie suspiciously. "Not more of your photographs..."

Gracie ignored Hesper and concentrated on McKade and Willa. "I highly recommend this show."

McKade turned abruptly from Gracie to Hesper. "You were there the night my mother's cabin burned. Did you set that fire?"

Hesper was silent for a long time. "I used to think so. I think I wanted to have done it. But I saw the flames from a long way off."

"And you just stood there?"

"I don't remember much about that night. I was so afraid. Suddenly you were outside. You hated me and I hated you. It seemed simpler to keep it that way."

Everyone was silent.

"But you're my sister."

"Yes," Hesper hesitated. "Yes. And I'm glad."

"I'm glad, too," he said.

"The gallery I was telling you about," Gracie said, "is on the way to the Book Nook."

McKade was silent again, seemingly indifferent.

"Well, why not?" Willa said almost flippantly. If McKade no longer cared about her, if he'd only come back to see his father and sisters, if he didn't want to talk to her, she might as well do something to distract herself.

"What sort of show?" she asked.

"It's a surprise," said Gracie.

"Oh, no!" exclaimed Hesper.

If Willa was surprised when McKade tagged along with Gracie and her along those wet sidewalks, she was even more surprised when they got to the gallery and Gracie had to pull out a key to unlock the door.

Then Gracie pushed Willa inside first and let McKade follow.

The room was so bright and warm Willa barely noticed when Gracie waved goodbye. One foot across the threshold had Willa gasping and McKade laughing.

Flaming orange nudes surrounded them. Or rather dozens of loud naked ladies, no, dozens of naked Willas lined tall white walls.

He shut the door and locked it.

In one painting Willa stood beside her tiny brown spider monkey and shared his banana. In another she lay on her flowered bedspread clutching her chartreuse orchid pillow.

"I think they're wonderful, Willa," McKade said behind her.

Her eyes were startled when she turned, her tentative gaze clashing with his. His face was so hard and set against her, a tremor went through her.

No… She was misreading him. His dark features were ravaged, his pale eyes haunted. There were shadows beneath his eyes. Had he suffered, too? Missed her, as she had missed him?

Her voice fell softly. "I don't understand. Why did you do this?"

"To say I'm sorry," McKade whispered.

Her mouth was suddenly too dry to speak. "But why…" She stared from him to the pictures. "If you don't like these paintings, why did you display them like this and bring me here?"

"They're yours now. Like you said, they're personal. I want you to have them. They can't belong to me."

"But why not?"

"Not unless...unless you want me to have them. Not unless...you'll forgive me...and...not unless you want me....'' He couldn't seem to find the words to go on.

Was he saying he still wanted her?

She continued to look at him.

"I know that after what I did, I don't deserve you,'' he whispered in a low, agonized tone.

He was saying he wanted her. He was! Suddenly, she knew he was.

"Oh, Luke. My darling...'' Relief flowed through her. Joy, too. "I've missed you so much.''

She stared at him, at the paintings. "They're yours,'' she said softly, inspired.

"What?''

"All of them! I give them all back to you. They're a gift. My love is a gift to you, as well.''

"You didn't even give me a chance to really say how sorry I am...or grovel for what I did to you before I left. My secretary was most emphatic that I had to grovel.''

"Later. You can do that later.'' Willa laughed. "I'll make you crawl across my bedroom and kiss my feet.''

"God, I'm sorry.'' He moved toward her, touched her face with the back of his hand as if she were infinitely precious to him.

"I missed you,'' he said.

Cautiously she reached out and touched his gray sleeve. She felt the man beneath, warm...hot... vital...*hers*...

He stood very still, his muscles tightening beneath her fingertips. She moved her hands up his arms, over his shoulders. Then she leaned into him and put her arms around him as she laid her head upon his chest. He crushed her closer, holding her so tightly she could barely breathe.

He sighed. She felt the tension drain from him.

"Sam missed you, too," she whispered a long time later.

"What's he calling himself these days?" Luke murmured thickly, his low voice muffled because his warm lips were moving through her hair.

"He seems content with Sam."

"I'm sorry, Willa. Will you ever forgive me for what I did?"

"What do you think?" Her voice held tears. "I love you."

"Then will you...will you and Sam and Big Red and all your fleabags and weird furniture move in with me?"

"What took you so long, McKade?"

"Guilt."

"You must've had a lot of it."

"Oh, yeah. I've made a lot of mistakes. I hate myself sometimes. I'm damn sure no bargain, believe me. You deserve a prince and to be treated like a queen."

"The ruthless Dot.Com King will have to do as my very own Prince Charming."

"What about those briefcases? Did you ever find them?"

"I haven't even looked. I think they served their purpose. I was always so afraid...of Brand. I don't think anything happens by coincidence. Those briefcases were my destiny. I found them and that made Brand more determined than ever to come back into my life. That had to happen, don't you see? We had to confront our past, to end forever my connection to

Brand, so that you and I could begin anew…fresh. You were right. I was so foolish the night I took those briefcases. I thought that having my own money meant I could do as I pleased, take care of Sam as he deserved to be raised.''

"We'll do that together. I want more children.''

"So do I.''

She was staring at him, dreaming of those children in their happily-ever-after future, wondering if their hair would be black or yellow, their eyes gray or blue.

"Will you marry me?'' he asked.

"You're supposed to get down on bended knees and tell me how much you love me.''

"I love you. I hurt so bad in Austin I finally figured that out.''

She smiled at him. "For an efficiency expert, you're slow McKade. You gotta speed up if you're gonna keep up with me and Sam.''

Then she kissed him, and they didn't talk for a very long time.

Finally, he let her go. "Let's go tell Harry he's got a new daddy….''

"Sam.''

"Right. Till you read him some new book and he identifies with the hero.'' Luke laughed and took her hand. Then he bent his head and kissed each fingertip. Next, before she realized what he was about, he knelt and slipped off her shoe.

"What are you doing?''

"Groveling. Kissing your feet.''

She chuckled. "Not here. At home. In my bedroom where you can get carried away.''

"I can't wait.'' He stood up, kissed the tip of her nose.

Willa closed her eyes and nestled close against him. He was so hard and warm, so strong. He'd saved her and her son twice from terrible evil. He'd won her heart somewhere along the way.

For now it was enough to know he was hers and that she was his, to know he loved her as she loved him, to know that they would marry. To know that what had begun four years ago would end happily ever after just like one of Sam's fairy tales.

"Let's elope," he whispered. "The sooner, the better."

"Oh, no! I had that kind of wedding the first time, remember? I want ours to be special, to be unforgettable, so I'll treasure the memory forever."

"What exactly do you have in mind?"

"It's a surprise. It's sort of wild. You'll have to trust me."

"You're not going to wear hot pink. Swear you won't!"

She grinned at him. "You'll have to wait and see."

"All right." Love flared in his eyes. "Have your wild wedding."

Even before he kissed her, she felt as untamed and gloriously alive as the vivid orange paintings Cathy had painted of her.

Then his mouth seared hers, and she wasn't at all sure she could wait until they got home.

Savage DESIRE

New York Times
bestselling author

ROSEMARY ROGERS

reunites her beloved couple, Steve Morgan and
Virginia Brandon, in this brand-new adventure
of an epic love that spans time, distance
and the cruel whims of fate.

"Her name brings smiles to all who love love."
—*Ocala Star-Banner*

On sale December 2000
wherever paperbacks are sold!

Visit us at www.mirabooks.com

MRR621

He gave her his name...but would he give her his heart?

LINDA HOWARD

A tragic accident took everything that mattered to Rome Matthews—his wife, and their two little boys. And it robbed Sarah Harper of her best friend. In the years that followed, Sarah wanted nothing more than to reach out to Rome, but a tightly guarded secret kept her away: she had been in love with her best friend's husband for years.

But now Rome needs her, desperate to lose himself in the passion he feels for Sarah. Knowing that his heart belongs to another woman, Sarah agrees to be his wife. Then an unexpected fate rekindles her hidden hope that a marriage of convenience could become a marriage of love....

SARAH'S CHILD

"You can't read just one Linda Howard." —Catherine Coulter

Available December 2000 wherever hardcovers are sold!

ANN MAJOR

66548 INSEPARABLE   ___ $5.99 U.S. ___ $6.99 CAN.

(limited quantities available)

TOTAL AMOUNT $_____
POSTAGE & HANDLING $_____
($1.00 for one book; 50¢ for each additional)
APPLICABLE TAXES* $_____
<u>TOTAL PAYABLE</u> $_____
(check or money order—please do not send cash)

To order, complete this form and send it, along with a check
or money order for the total above, payable to MIRA Books®,
to: **In the U.S.:** 3010 Walden Avenue, P.O. Box 9077, Buffalo,
NY 14269-9077; **In Canada:** P.O. Box 636, Fort Erie, Ontario,
L2A 5X3.

Name:_____
Address:_____ City:_____
State/Prov.:_____ Zip/Postal Code:_____
Account Number (if applicable):_____
075 CSAS

*New York residents remit applicable sales taxes.
 Canadian residents remit applicable GST and provincial taxes.

MIRA®